VANILLA BLOOD

Dear Sybil & Ed,

The future may be filled with wonder, innovation, and intrigue — but let it always be filled with friends ....

Love,

Nancy

VANILLA BLOOD

■ ■ ■

Nancy Martin

TECOLOTE PUBLICATIONS
SAN DIEGO

TECOLOTE PUBLICATIONS
4918 Del Monte Avenue, San Diego, California 92107

First printing 1996
Printed in the United States of America

Cover design and illustration by Jolee Martin
Author photograph © Alexandra of La Jolla

Library of Congress Catalog Card Number: 96-60282

ISBN 0-938711-36-9

To Uncle Joe,
who made all the difference

ACKNOWLEDGMENTS

When it comes to creation, finally you must believe in yourself, your work, your vision. But frequently that dream dissipates. Without the encouragement from my husband, the inspiration through my children, and the availability of my friends, this endeavor might have nestled forever half-in the womb, half-out. They helped deliver this story. Thank you all.

Any book concerning chimpanzees must pay tribute to Jane Goodall. She has pioneered the universe where people and chimps connect, and I thank her for sharing her wisdom with the rest of the world.

I'd also like to acknowledge Dr. Jared Diamond, professor of physiology at UCLA Medical School. His research into humankind's biological and social development as presented in *The Third Chimpanzee* (HarperCollins Publishers, 1992) added to my understanding of the genetic similarities between human and chimpanzee. And I support his contention wholeheartedly: we are just another species of ape.

ACKNOWLEDGMENTS

One

Somewhere in the nineties, along with face-lifts, fat-free ice cream, and the finish of the twentieth century, people started changing their last names. It was a statement. A protest. A trend. A sign that the paltry human being could become more and wear his coat of arms in his signature.

It was a *his* thing, for very few women followed the transmutation. Who knows why. Perhaps, between working for their families, their bosses, and themselves, they chose not to follow one more *ought*. But the majority of females held onto their birth name. A few rebels, those among them who craved defiance, appropriated their married name while others acquired a professional name, but future anthropologists would have to discover why women emerging into the political voice of a country chose not to follow the leader. And so far, nobody bothered to ask why women did what they did.

Yet the men, caught up with the opportunity to preen themselves in public, clasped the chance to become more than a mere number in a long line of lineage. They could begin again. So the telephone books changed to headings like "WarWarrior," "MuscleHead," "GlamorGuy," "TallTower," "BraveHeart," and became a repository for all the unborn yearnings alive and well in the male imagination. What he couldn't be in life, he could prevail on paper, and a feeble attempt at crushing depersonalization, the fear of not being noticed, quietly took place.

Although he usually paid no attention to the shooting star fads that manifested themselves in the must-make-money marketplace, Scott Futura favored this recent revolution. It felt right to him. It felt real. He had been a private investigator for seven years, and he wanted more than a P.I. after his name. It wasn't that he wanted people to think he was famous, only that they know he was better. He was better because he was smarter, and he did whatever it took to get the job accomplished.

If he could get across this notion of commitment, of efficiency, of know-how to his potential clients in one word, his name would become the Cadillac in a world of Chevys. No slick advertising, no catchy motto, no fancy business cards. Just a single utterance that could express his expertise. A marker that would remain on the lips of people long after the crime was solved. And one morning, thirteen long years ago, he opened his eyes and knew who he would be, what he would be forever: FutureDick. His brain had found its niche, his body had found its challenge, and he had found his imprint, the designation that would sling his prowess before the public eye: FutureDick. His was no hint at competence, but a sonorous fanfare blaring his proficiency. FutureDick, the name that would drive the commonplace into the shadows as he became tomorrow's type of investigator, who found facts, who found answers, who found murderers today.

But neither FutureDick nor the world was prepared for the next modern killer to enter their lives. Certainly, killing is killing. One moment, breath. The next moment, nothing: no air, no sight, no self. Yet killing in a new way, a methodical way, where you remain miles from the crime, now that is genius. That is truly the wave of the future, and AceArrow had the massacre completely mapped out. His mobile men would storm the seven service center cities, the main concentrations of his enemies—the DoRights.

Planning mass murder is somewhat like marketing a new product. You select your city, you pinpoint your potential consumers, and you offer them the opportunity to purchase your matchless merchandise. In AceArrow's case, he was liquidating life, and death was going for bargain-basement prices.

"Okay, Tully, are you clear on the details? Timing? Locations? Have you familiarized yourself with the area?"

"No problem, boss." Who did the guy think he was talking to? Some dumb ass who couldn't plan a campaign? Was he kidding? Tully knew more in his little finger about waging war than this guy could get in any kind of scientific research. "I've planned for the unexpected. Got everything covered. As long as my men operate according to your specifications, we're solid. In and out. A matter of minutes."

"Look, Tully, no foul-ups. No clues. I want nothing left behind but bodies. We've gone over the targets, the time, the evacuation, and I want those men back in the van, hidden, in split-second timing. Speed is everything. It's absolutely crucial to the attack. Have I got your word on that?"

Tully bit his lip before he answered. There was too much money involved for him to tell AceArrow to fucking do it himself. Talking to him like he was some kind of novice. What the hell! When he replied, Tully exhaled slowly, "It's all taken care of, sir. I put my men through a practice exercise using stuffed animals. What a blast! Of course, the stuffing flew out all over the damn place, and I had a hell of a time cleaning it up, but they were beautiful, just beautiful. Toughest army in the world, I'm sure of that. Quick, clean, precise. I swear to God, boss. Micro-managed massacres—a dream come true!"

"Only if it works, Tully. Only if it works."

As Tully and AceArrow scoffed their way through a conversation considering the most expedient way to murder, no one in the small, featureless city of SeaBank predicted the onslaught about to take place. They were busy with the daily regularity promised them by the diurnal cycle: the sun pledged them light and prosperity, the moon offered them rest and regeneration. Yet, no one guaranteed them immunity, and AceArrow chuckled as he imagined the shock, the absolute horror, that the seven selected families would walk into after his unexpected extermination occurred. Seven households, from the SoulShines to the Franks, unaware, unsuspecting, and each so worthy of his reprisal.

Francie Franks lived alone in a life full of people. She had her children, her clients, her friends, the many demands on her attention, her time, her love. But she also had a separate world, the world of her mind. It was there she escaped when everyone else was put to rest, and she could contemplate the larger meaning of what brought her to this juncture of her life. She sometimes hummed the tune to an old-fashioned song, "What's It All About, Alfie?" And she tried to answer the enigmatic question, "What's it all about, Francie?"

On her blithe days, she'd respond quickly with, "It's about love and family, friendship and felicity, work and play." But on her sunless days, she wasn't as assured. Might there be more? Was there some way to rise above the recurring loneliness that crept uninvited into her bedroom when the rest of the household slept through their own dreams of anxiety? Was there a method whereby she could escape the tears of the human heart, her children's hearts, her clients' hearts, and glide to a safety zone that nuzzled her under its protective quilt and promised her eternal security? Or was that safety zone only inside her soul, and she had to figure out the way to get there?

Sometimes, she was certain she could march through life, unimpeded, self-contained, unequivocal, "on target, Mr. Spock." But those other times, those times of doubt, of fear, she hid from her family; of skepticism, she hid from herself. Those were the times when she crouched in the corner of her brain, crying tearless sobs for the sun to rise once more and the demonic shadows to disappear. Those were the moments she called her dreaded intimacy with aloneness, and after countless years, Alfie, she still hadn't discovered what it was all about.

But Emma had. Unlike Francie, she knew who she was and why she was. It had always been that way: simple. She ate, she slept, she loved. Life was not complex; it was complete. And she comforted herself in her blanket of well-being, wrapped in the warmth of her chimpanzee-human connection.

Sighing ever so slightly, Emma dreamed her playful ape dreams, content in the protection of her people-home, oblivious to fear or suffering or sadness, for she feasted on the fullness that comes with motherhood. Her infant, Edmund, lay beside her, suckling, one small thin arm splayed across her simian chest. Feeling the softness of his hair gently touch her breast, she allowed the warmth of his tiny body to penetrate its way to her heart. She was whole. She was mother.

Her baby grunted faintly, unaware that the safety he enjoyed was an exception in this civilized world of turmoil. For Edmund, that's all he ever knew: the sheltered confines of his mother's delicious body. As for Emma, her capacity for affection, for love of her fragile child, knew no bounds. He was the only reason she knew for her existence. And as her arms surrounded him, she felt at peace with nature. In her chimpanzee world of unpredictable events, this moment was the most reliable, for this moment was her lasting link with genetic survival, and she would preserve her child with her life—if she had to.

Yet AceArrow didn't know Emma, he never met Francie, and he couldn't give a rat's ass about any of those misguided families who chose the DoRights. Whatever happened, they had it coming. He needed to build his empire, and empathy wasn't part of the foundation. First murder, then money. Easy! And that's what life was supposed to be. Easy. Remain emotionally calm, like machines, and the world comes to you.

When was the last time he cried? Six years old? Maybe seven? He remembered the angry eyes flashing across his father's face and the even angrier squeal that roared from those brittle lips, "Look what you did, Michael! Sloppy, very sloppy. Now get down from your chair and clean up that milk!"

"I didn't mean it, Daddy. Really. It was an accident."

"There are no accidents, Michael. Only inattention to order. You don't care about order, do you Michael? Because if you did, you wouldn't have spilt your milk."

"But I was trying to be careful, Daddy. My hand just moved too fast!"

"That's not good enough, Michael. You've got to learn how to control your hands, your feet, your head. You are certainly a sorry excuse for a boy if you can't be more careful. Now get off that chair and clean that mess immediately! With your mouth shut!"

As the tears slid down his fallen face, the young AceArrow, racing to the kitchen and grabbing paper towels, doubled back to erase the evidence of his mortification, unable to wipe away his tears, his spilt milk, and his humiliation at the same time. Though his father's fury remained forever etched in his mind, those were the last tears he remembered as he shoved his emotions into a corner, where the dust of disuse would eventually settle.

The boy grew into adult, emerging as a bright, cold-blooded iceman, unsusceptible to feeling, to anguish, to pain. That was how he operated. And his failure to feel served him well. It got him laid without the allegiance of love. It earned him profit without paying attention to his employees' personal lives. And it supplied him time to get the job done, any job, any project, any accomplishment, without the hindrance of affection. His sole attachment was to attainment and accumulation—not love. Provide the product and reap the reward.

AceArrow had it all, and he had it under control, for evil was in the eye of the beholder. How could he be judged by the mediocrity of the little guy when he knew better than others what needed to be done? And if killing was the most expedient way to win his market, so be it. *Good* or *bad* were concepts used by the Church, not him. If he had spent his time considering ethics, he'd still be programming computers, and he was above that. Let the poor slob worry about morality. The schmuck had nothing to lose anyway. So he could afford the wasted time.

AceArrow never worried about whose toes he crushed when he came down hard because people were disposable. They religiously reproduced, and like particles of soot, they were irrelevant. Use them when you have to and discard them.

But then again, AceArrow might have learned a valuable lesson about sensitivity had he been privy to FutureDick's thoughts. For at that very moment, the private investigator knew the world, his world, was about to be shattered.

FutureDick always knew. Like that time on the mountain, when he and Tendra were nearing the peak, crossing the last switchback, and suddenly, he pushed her up against the granite.

"Scott, are you crazy? That hurt!"

"Just hold tight, Tendra. Get your body as close to the mountain as possible. Try to melt into the rock as if you're making love. Now!"

"What's the matter, honey? I don't see anything, and we're so close to the top."

"Something's wrong. Trust me. Something's just wrong, I know it."

Tendra knew not to question her husband's instincts. His uncanny sensitivity to disaster stifled any objection that raced from her lips. She fused her body into the wall of granite and waited—but not for long. Because in seconds, stones, than rocks, pelted their way past them, flying down the 2500 feet they had just ascended. Before she could ease herself from the unbending escarpment, a roar crushed her ears as she and Scott watched a huge boulder tumble in front of them, grazing their bodies as it plunged fiercely down the mountainside.

Wide-eyed, Tendra looked at FutureDick and spoke quite deliberately, "Honey, I trust you. Hell, Scott, I thank God your antennae are in my life. Makes me feel like I have an eternal electric security blanket constantly plugged into red alert!"

As she kissed him, snuggling her head under his chin for a hug before they continued to the top, FutureDick swallowed the acid that had jumped to his throat when, for a split-second, he thought he might lose her.

That was long ago. Another lifetime, another world, unaccounted-for happiness, when he and his heart existed as one. A time primeval, but now obsolete, when he had loved. He closed his eyes to blot out the memories of moments passed and concentrated on the moment now: the sounds, the wind, the smell. The invisible smell. The sweet, murky, close-to-death odor that hovered inside his consciousness, sending tremors of terror into his soul with each step he took.

Tonight smelled evil. It hung in the air malodorously, penetrating his opened mouth so he could taste it. Isn't it funny when you know something's wrong, how the sensation seeps into your pores, your hair, your nose and mouth, till it invades your totality? You literally taste tension. But he didn't know where the threat was coming from, and he had no idea how to find it, stop it, or even what it was. Yet his acute senses told him, as they had in the past, that something terribly wrong was about to happen.

FutureDick walked back to his office. He had gone for a jog on the beach, watching the sunset as his powerful legs sprang along the shore. He listened to the waves, but their roar wasn't harsh enough to smother his sixth sense. Every once in a while, over the course of the last twenty years, he would be hit by a premonition so strong, so horrible, that all he could do was take deep breaths and finish whatever it was he was doing. This was one of those moments. "Finish the run. Finish the run." He composed a song in his head so he could continue, and his strides kept up with the beat of his melodic words.

He really wanted to halt abruptly in his tracks and hide—hide till the evil passed. But he couldn't hide anywhere, for he knew whatever was out there would find him. And he knew this apprehension was good because it made him careful, more watchful, suspicious of any approaching atrocity, so he wouldn't be attacked unawares. Besides, he never fled. He fought. He spent his life fighting crime. How could he run away now?

Two

"Finish the run. Finish the run." FutureDick eagerly allowed himself the luxury of his athletics. When he ran, it was his personal moment. The outside world couldn't touch him as he loped along the edge of water meeting sand. He sometimes felt he was running near the rim of the earth, and if he inadvertently veered a little to the right, he'd swiftly be sucked into the void.

He played with the waves, courting risk, but invariably showing them he could outwit their intrusion and, just at the last moment, run away from the wetness. Still, when his mind wandered and he forgot where he was running, the waves ambushed him and enveloped his feet. Consequently, he always kept extra running shoes at home as he routinely seemed to have a pair of shoes drying on the porch.

If he had to pinpoint some of his happiest, or at least more satisfying, moments, he'd admit they came when he was running, when his body was continually moving. FutureDick wasn't sure if his gratification came because his muscles enjoyed the exercise or because he was running away, away from the old painful memories, away from the requirements of civilized survival, the necessities our physiology imposes on us like eating, sleeping, thinking—leaving behind him a trail of invisible obligations that constantly impinge on the human being.

When he ran, he ran away from all of it. And he relished the glory of the physical motion, for in those sixty minutes, he tapped into his biological center. The human body was born to move. That's why man has a frame composed of muscles, strong, flexible, growing bands of tissue that provide power to the puny skeleton.

FutureDick would wager any amount of money that nature didn't plan for its elite animal to spend the rest of its life pushing TV buttons or placing food orders through a microphone, microwave, or micro-robot. You don't give that sort of strength or potential for strength to any organism if it's only designed to sit in its bed, its chair, its car, or its hammock. Those muscles were planned for a body that worked, that moved, that foraged for food in a competitive environment where wit and brawn outsmarted bulk and instinct.

Granted, our intellect beautifully engineered our constant and secure supply of food, but did that mean we must forget we still have the anatomy of a creature born millions of years ago, born with the capability to hike the entire globe if he wanted to? FutureDick was certain the human body had to exercise as much as it had to eat, sleep and defecate, and he gloried in his ability to run through the seasons, the three southern California seasons he had grown to cherish.

From January through April, he jogged in the Empty season, the best season of all, the time of the year when he owned the beach. He'd imagine he was running during the dawn of the earth, and he had happened upon this terrestrial treasure chest of sand, and rock, and waves, abundant ten foot grey-blue mountains of water that would crash against the shore, greeting him with the spontaneity of nature's roar. Alone, he cantered alongside the rushing water, staring at the horizon, basking in what it felt to be fully human. No people, occasional birds, just the vast Pacific Ocean and him.

By the time April arrived, a few people started their daily trek to the shore. When the warmer days of May attacked the colder temperatures of the sea, more people claimed their square yard of territorial prerogative and set up blankets, umbrellas, and beach chairs, silently announcing, "This is my space. Stay clear. I requisition this little plot of land for eight hours of sun, of seclusion, of sanity." FutureDick flew by them, welcoming the People season and pleasantly ready to divert the isolation of his runs to the company of others.

He could now people-watch as his strong legs pounded the earth, and since the air was heavy with heat, he never minded his attention being drawn away by the continually changing human dynamics. At least, it soothed the mild discomfort that warm weather introduces upon its runners.

But FutureDick especially enjoyed the July and August of the season when the beach was littered with children. They ran, they dug, they challenged the water, and he never tired of confronting each child's pure joy as they reveled in nature's bounty. To watch a youngster focus on the seriousness of building a sand castle clearly put into perspective why we must always hold on to our ability to play. FutureDick knew of no better way to relieve stress but to somehow slither into the mind of a child and understand what's actually important. It's only the moment. That's all he had. That's all anyone has.

By September, after FutureDick had hip-hopped around the ambling children, carefully watching for holes in the sand leading to China, he welcomed change. He wanted his poseidonian solitude back, and he was quite ready for the Bird season. FutureDick didn't mind sharing his coastline with the hundreds of birds wending their way to Mexico. They were entitled. It was their earth as much as it was his, and they gracefully moved out of his way as he cut through their feathered carpet of squawks and flaps. We inevitably need interruptions from routine, and this was the supreme avian coffee break, when those faultless aeronauts rested their titanic wings.

FutureDick ran through the Bird season, a hermit among his winged collaborators and celebrated his moving body. He soared, not in the air, but in his mind, confident that he'd be running at ninety years old if the evil didn't catch up with him at the finish line first.

The notion of intuition never entered AceArrow's mind. In fact, if anyone would have mentioned the study of paranormal phenomena or extrasensory perception, AceArrow would have sniggered at the concept. His was a world grounded in machines, robotic machines. You could touch the metal, you could feel its crisp hardened alloy against your cheek, and you could see it revealingly respond by using mathematics to control its mechanisms. Machines were real, not some far-flung wisp of a sensation that invaded your brain and took over. Fairy tales, he would have called any accounts of clairvoyance. Pure imagination! All we know is what we see, here and now. Prediction must be predicated on fact, not fantasy.

Who could argue with him, a prosperous CEO who built his reputation on well-engineered robots. His machines worked! Nobody jeered at financial success, even if the champion lived a solitary life. Nobody peeked through AceArrow's blinds and saw that he said hello to a robot when he returned home, not a wife, not a lover, not a soul. Nobody saw the man behind the office who had left few family, fewer friends, and fathered no children, in order to create his electromechanical dynasty. AceArrow epitomized the human component of corporate strength. He needed no one.

Perhaps a would-be Peeping Tom might have been moved when he saw AceArrow lie in his crib, screaming, not for warmth, not for food, but for touch, a brush, a graze, a brief something. Those screams lingered, unheeded by a mother too busy to be bothered. So AceArrow learned early that wailing was worthless. Best to keep your mouth shut.

Possibly the same would-be eavesdropper would have wept when he heard AceArrow's father reprimand him at six years old because his toys were not placed in alphabetical order. The repeated rebukes that started at two continued to eighteen, endlessly, for the sake of order, regularity, precision. The little boy learned well that a mother supplied only food, money and a bed. And a father demanded orderliness. No love, no emotion, no warmth spilled into AceArrow's cemetery of a childhood, and the toddler grew into a teenager who shrouded himself in a cloak of non-tenderness. Feelings were for fools and interfered with his plans to be somebody—and bring order into a disorderly world.

Yet the delight of disorder, or at least what resembled an at-ends existence, is what kept Francie going. Too much to do and too little time to get it done. At the moment, Francie and Reba were preparing to take the children out for dinner, their kind of dinner: pizza for nourishment and a movie for dessert.

"Okay, Micky, hurry and change. No, Lanie, you can't have just one Oreo. We're going out for dinner in five minutes. April, did you call Rachel back? She called while you were at gymnastics. Reba, are we all agreed it's a comedy tonight, not suspense? Lanie's still having nightmares since *Aliens Inherit the Earth.* Tell Marc we'll pick an adventure next time. I promise."

"Francie, I'm up for laughs this evening. It's been a triple Advil day. Besides, I think the kids see too much brutality anyway. In the movies, on TV, in the newspaper, on their video games—it swallows them whole. Jesus, I don't how they stay somewhat normal! I need the humor, and I'm damn sure my kids could afford a good guffaw once in a while."

"Thanks Reba. Your knack for turning anxiety into acknowledgement ought to be bottled and sold like lemonade. Let's check the DoRights and split. We've got the pizza choice obstacle ahead of us before we even get to the theater options."

And that's a comedy in itself, Francie thought. Trying to accommodate nine different mouths made political negotiation a way of life in their household. Between the two women, there were seven children to manage, ranging in age from kindergarten through high school. Getting each of their time tables to mesh sometimes metamorphosed into a cerebral feat, yet, the two mothers made sure that these family excursions took place regularly.

They wanted the kids to remember growing up as a time when they played together, all together. And the two adults figured whatever shared memories they could carve in their children's brains would give them sustenance for later on. That *later on* was a vague term, but for Francie and Reba, it meant the inevitable rough times that plagued the human condition, the times every adult is forced to experience more than once in a life span.

With enough of the playing in their history, perhaps their children might know how to get through the obligatory stress with some of the necessary fun. It was insurance, a hedge against loneliness, against sadness, against boredom. But it was also a way to develop playmates, lifelong playmates for the children as well as the mothers. You remember your parents, but you play with your friends, and both women wanted their children to become their future friends.

They were getting a late start because of Micky's swim meet, but who cared? Tomorrow was Saturday. Without any alarm to set, no one seemed particularly concerned about how late they returned home. In the outer room, the DoRights were bedded down for the night, and everything appeared quiet enough.

Francie smiled. What would she have done without the DoRights? Modern man's response to the velocity of the computer age, the DoRights helped keep the hectic scheduling manageable. With seven children to take care of, the house, the cleaning, the cooking, the shopping, the repairs, she could spend 24 hours at home and still never finish. And what about her job? If she didn't work, they wouldn't eat.

Sometimes Francie wondered what possessed her to opt for divorce. But those moments passed quickly. She knew why she left the marriage. It didn't work anymore. She and Alan were traveling along different roads, getting miles and miles away from the starting point. They held hands in the beginning, but let go nine years later and tramped alone on diverging paths. While Francie wanted to stop and smell each rose along her way, Alan was hell bent on amassing as much money as he could in as short an amount of time possible, no matter what cost to his wife, his children, and his long forsaken love of life. Somehow, their destinations got messed up.

And their marriage got messed up too. "Were they really that different?" Francie mused. "Couldn't Alan see that the riches were in each other and the children? Wasn't that fortune enough? Didn't he realize there's no replay button on life? Once gone, these moments couldn't be retrieved. If he didn't pause to play now, his aching joints would prohibit the fun later."

Besides, there was no later. Francie knew that. Their family was young now. This was the building time. This was when you made a difference. Couldn't Alan understand what parenting was all about? He had to be there for the children now—not ten years from now. Otherwise, he'd never make the real connection, the bond that's created when child and father grow together.

But whatever Francie inherently understood in her gut became lost in the translation to her ambitious young husband. He wouldn't listen. The more she pleaded for him to hear, the thicker his armor became, till her words bounced off like pebbles hurled at an impervious target. They hung in the air, briefly, then clattered to the floor, unacknowledged.

"Listen to me, Alan. I'm begging you. We've got to spend more time together. You've got to make room in your schedule for the family."

"Let it go, Francie. I'm way too busy right now."

"But Alan, the children are growing now. Later's too late.

They won't need you then!"

"Francie, cut it out! You're here to take care of the kids. I see them when I can. Besides, it's not quantity of time, but quality."

"There is no quality, Alan, when you budget every minute. It's like you're doing them a favor by being with them. Just like you make it seem a big deal to be with me. Where's our quality time, Alan?"

"Don't start that tape with me again, Francie. I've got work to do. I'd think with four kids you'd have enough to do. Get a job if you've got time on your hands, but leave me alone!"

Clearly Alan's disregard confirmed Francie's decision to purge whatever shrunken emotions lay gasping for the once-upon-a-time man she used to love. When Alan denied her thoughts, he negated her womanhood. She was her words, and her brain broadcast her femininity, not her breasts. Sure, her body could produce babies, but her mind produced music, the music of logic, of ideas, of sound psychological sense. Couldn't Alan figure that out? Hear my mind, Alan. Listen. Please listen. This is the real me. But Alan never heard, for the marketplace was calling.

Francie knew what he wanted. She tried to understand his desire to succeed, but when he came home later and later every evening, her empathy failed her. She wanted a man now—not tomorrow. Tomorrows were too unpredictable. Sometimes, they were suddenly swiped from under your pillow. She had married for companionship, not for the loneliness of empty nights. She knew from the fairy tales that young men must go out and find their fortune in the world, but did that mean abandonment of love, of family, of *together?*

She found herself thinking more about the future, and the vision was usually singular. Alan never stayed around too long in her dreams. When she decided to go back to school and study psychology, she convinced herself she was doing it for their marriage. With her degree in hand, she could work part time, the children would all be in school by then, and she'd be able to contribute to the financial demands of the household. She'd be able to help Alan. Perhaps if she became a worldlier woman, she and Alan could bond again in a more mature way, not the college freshmen they were at eighteen, thrilling to romance and sex, but ignorant of future or finances or family.

What Francie hadn't counted on was her own awakening. Somewhere between Child Psychology 101 and Brains, Drugs, and Behavior 342, she realized she had gone back to school for herself, not for her lost marriage. She didn't love Alan anymore. He was a boy. He would always be a boy. He never had the capacity to do more than one thing at a time, and since his business was his present thing, his woman and children would have to be sacrificed. Knowing she had outgrown her child-lover, Francie confronted the greatest decision of her life: should she go it alone with her children?

She well-remembered those sleepless nights laced with tears of regret as she watched the digital clock inch closer to dawn. Worrying about the rightness of her decision, Francie became prosecutor, defendant, and judge in her own trial. "We have a life here, Your Honor. And we must decide how it is going to be lived!" When the verdict came in, deliberated by a one person jury, herself, Francie surrendered her security in exchange for promise: a possibility of happiness, of love, of connectedness was better than a present of detachment. Their marriage was over, and her never-ending nights ferried her through the ordeal of acceptance.

But finality doesn't necessarily translate to happily-ever-after. And Francie shifted from anguish to antagonism in one ever so slight sidestep. How could she have possibly thought that she and her four children would march into life saying, "Here world, here we are. Let's get on with the process of living." How naive could she have been not to see that Alan would fight, and he'd fight hard.

"Come on, Alan. You know we can't get along on so little child support. You can afford more than that."

"That's all I'm legally obligated to pay, and that's all you're going to get!"

"But it's not fair to the kids. You're taking your anger out on them when you're really angry with me. You're their father. You should want to see them taken care of in the best way possible. They're part of you!"

"Too bad, baby. You see what it's like to earn a living. If you can't take care of the kids, I'd be happy to have custody."

Francie saw red for a moment, and she pushed down the tears trying to drown her eyes into blindness. Caught between her fury for Alan's even posing the suggestion she relinquish her children and her instinct not to anger him into doing less than he was already doing, softly she pleaded, "Please Alan, please. Look at what you're doing."

"Oh Francie, I know perfectly well what I'm doing. And you'd better be damn sure that you're not getting more child support than I've just agreed to. Consider yourself lucky that I pay it at all!"

So Francie ran out of words to beg with. They didn't work anymore. Two years after the divorce, she was poor, in debt, using child support to pay the rent, and worrying about buying enough food to feed four and a half mouths. She figured she wouldn't count as a full stomach because she'd eat less and lose weight. Turning a minus into an advantage was a talent born out of necessity, her need to survive with a touch of grace and a whole lot of humor. She could joke to herself, but she surely couldn't laugh. It wasn't very funny to contemplate the fate of a family barely holding on, dependent on child support to keep a roof over their heads and their bellies barely full.

Fortunately, Alan's financial intransigence motivated her. She used the energy of her anger to get through the 25 hour days. No matter how hard life became, she'd never go back to what was. This may have been Alan's victory, but it wasn't going to be her defeat. She'd show Alan that she could make it in spite of him. He would have loved to see her drop out of school.

Then he could say, "I told you so!"

Francie entered her finest hour. She thrived on challenge, and Alan sparked her belligerency. She became stubborn. She stuck with school even when it took student loans to finish, and she became determined to prove Alan wrong. He would relish her giving up, taking whatever job she could find, and plodding her way through an eight hour day, unstimulated, unchallenged, and, most definitely, unhappy. Let him eat his money. She'd have the last laugh, the bastard.

Every profane name she had learned from her youth, her peers, her children, and her books passed through her lips when she thought about Alan and his revenge—to pay the least he could in child support, even if he could afford more. No extras. Nothing for braces, for clothes, for the recreational perks children dream about. "Take it out on me, you son of a bitch, but why the children? The four beautiful, young children. Don't they deserve a chance?"

When Francie spoke with Reba, she called him "the asshole." With her children, he became "your father." She tried hard to keep the disgust out of her voice because the emotional barometers of the young are more acute than radar. And she explicitly didn't want her children to see how angry she was. But pretense was not Francie's best quality, and she knew, invariably, when her frustration reached its usual breaking point, they heard the derision in her tone. She never uttered the words, yet the kids understood what was behind her silence.

No matter how hard Francie tried, she was out of her league in the legal zone. She had been a wife, a mother, a student, and didn't know how to mobilize the confidence to fight Alan in the business battlefield. He had been a financial consultant since he left Data International nine years ago, and he knew how to disguise money. He also knew a host of lawyers. She was outflanked from the rear before she ever commenced her campaign.

But his greed inspired her. It breathed fury into her desolation and made her work doubly hard to prove him wrong. She'd not only be the best of mothers, she'd also be the best of students. When she felt frustration had reached its pressure point, that the rage would eat her alive, cell by cell, she went to the community center, reserved a court and hit the racquetball as hard as she could. That ball became her nemesis, her foe, a rubberized receptacle that sustained the ferocity of her anger. And, ultimately, that ball became her savior since it tolerated her assault game after game.

Somehow as time passed, frustration passed. She had won something: a piece of sanity or, perhaps, an emptying of her bitterness. But the intensity passed. Even though the hurt, the anger, the sadness continued, their force diminished, becoming mere embers, slowly, slowly fading. The fire was finally dying, and she remained unbroken, scarred, but intact, and certainly stronger than before. She still couldn't measure what type of mother she was, but she did graduate with honors, and she did play A level racquetball.

"Hey Mom, April can't find her left tennie. I think she left it at gymnastics."

"Wait, Lanie, I'll help you look."

Francie charged upstairs to fend off anxiety from reaching her baby daughter. Her mind, now light years away from the divorce, the asshole, and the struggle, concentrated on the immediacy of the situation. Whenever she heard a whimper from one of her children, she shifted into protector mode and zoomed ahead to intervene, believing she could prevent the pain from pouncing on their innocent souls.

THREE

Francie had never met AceArrow. And she had no inkling of his scheme to turn her family's harmony into havoc. If she could have peered into a reliable crystal ball, she'd have seen AceArrow, the engineer of destruction, aiming his sights toward the Franks' household. His glory time had arrived, the target date for implementing his ultimate business plan: the creative elimination of competition. By the completion of his well-designed "eradication program," consumers would turn once again to his robots, his beauties. And AceArrow would regain his dominion over the domestic service industry.

His patience pushed to the breaking point, AceArrow suppressed his ambition with reveries of a total mechanical world. In such a realm, he would be king, for he would be the reigning expert of robotics service. The world would need him the way humans need air, and he could easily manipulate trans-global business highways.

Ignoring social amenities, AceArrow, the adult, used his upbringing to his advantage. He had matured into the kind of merchant who would crush his competitors to gain an unequivocal stronghold in the marketplace. Empowered by a belief in himself, unencumbered by any sort of sympathy, he thoroughly enjoyed snuffing out the other fellow. Only he never called it treachery. Rather, he preferred to think of his efforts as increasing earnings.

But in the past, he accomplished his victories by undercutting price, industrial espionage, and corporate raiding. Now he would take it one step further: torment his rival till the company bled, till the consumers dried up, till the inventory rotted on the shelves, till the final showdown—insolvency. And AceArrow smiled as he wallowed in anticipation of more money, more power, and more customers.

"Ya know, sir, we can reevaluate the numbers. Will seven households be enough?"

"It's a strong beginning, Tully. I'd advise sticking to the schedule."

"But those headlines would be eight inches high if we scared the shit out of people. We can double the inventory, eliminate 112 instead of 56. Christ, we'd get over a hundred in a single evening!"

"Tully, keep your targets in a minimal range. At least, in the beginning. Let's check efficiency first. We can always grow, but I want fear to seep into each heart, slowly, gradually, like a cancer. Start small and increase to big. In this case, one household would easily warrant front page—seven households will be a media blitz."

"I hear ya, sir. I hear ya. But Christ, a few more dead dumb shits wouldn't hurt my feelings one bit, believe me. The more the merrier! I just thought since we got the arsenal, we should annihilate the enemy on a more impressive scale. Kinda like showing people the strength they're dealing with."

AceArrow answered patiently, as if talking to a child cut loose in a chocolate factory storeroom, "Tully, do it my way. I know it'll work!"

While AceArrow lived in his hungry dreams of more, six hundred miles to the south, FutureDick erred on the side of simplicity. He was never what you'd call a conspicuous consumer, but he indulged a single extravagance: his sports. When he played racquetball, sometimes six days a week, he used the state of the art racquet, the best he could buy.

In fact, whenever there were any innovations in the world of racquet sports, he was the first to find out about them, and he studied the improvements with a careful eye. Even his squash racquet was the newest model on the market. Although he had the greatest respect for that gentleman's game, he only managed to play once a week. Still, he used the finest racquet available.

If he was going to invest his energy in an athletic activity, he wanted to be certain his sports equipment served him well. And his closest guarantee to excellence was paying for premium. So he continued to purchase top of the line running shoes, believing the sporting aids rather than his coordination gave him the upper hand. Let his clothes fray to loosened threads—he didn't care—as long as his athletic gear remained top-notch.

FutureDick paid no attention to religion, any religion, yet his devotion to his athletics rivaled the most devout worshiper. And every once in a while—depending on the day, the case he was working on, his memories—when he laced up his running shoes or strapped on his racquet glove, he knew he was donning his sacred vestments, preparing to enter another spiritual plain. For there were moments on the court and during his run when he left the ordinary and entered the divine. Yet, more importantly, he was the architect of his own tabernacle, and the hymns he sang were praises to physical prowess. In FutureDick's faith, inspired intervention was the deity in each of us and our ability to become our best through athletic redemption. He truly believed we could continually grow better.

So he splurged on his sports. They were the one outlet that allowed him to walk away from the real world, the world of pain, of death, of hostility, and walk into his uncluttered space where he could play uninterrupted for sixty minutes, his hour—he owned it—and no one could get to him there.

He could care less about clothes, or cars, or fancy sound equipment. His TV was fifteen years old, but it still worked. His Volvo was fifteen years old with 261,000 miles, but, hell, it still worked. In fact, it didn't just work, it purred. That car had been there for him, always! He sometimes felt he could put it on automatic, and the automobile would know exactly where to go. Even his dog, Cleopatra, made it to fifteen years of age, but then she died, three years ago. He hoped that he could push his fifteen year senescence to twenty because he hated to take the time away from play or work and use it for purchasing.

There was some kind of integrity in owning and operating a piece of equipment for a long time. The mechanical little beast became quasi-human, and as long as you cared for it, it would remain loyal. It would run every time you turned the switch, for it delighted in serving you because it knew you wouldn't discard it the moment a new model appeared. And FutureDick's covenant with his few belongings became an endurance contest. Who or what would outlive each other? The TV was as good as ever, the Volvo had yet to be vanquished, and he was still remarkably strong, even though middle age had managed to mark him.

His mom tried to encourage him to pay more attention to fashions when he was a teenager. She called it the "necessary style with how you present yourself." She'd sneak new sweaters into his dresser drawer. Or a pair of chic slacks would suddenly materialize when he opened his closet door, late for first period. No matter how much she cajoled or tried to subvert his mundane tastes, she rarely succeeded. He'd put on his Levis, sweatshirt, and high tops to face the world of teenage trauma.

Even his wife attempted enhancing his wardrobe, and every once in a while, she triumphed in getting him to wear the latest in shirt and tie combinations. But that was rare, very rare. FutureDick wanted his clothes comfortable, and he couldn't be bothered with the trappings of either trends or conformity. He wanted to put on his garments quickly, so he could get on with the business of living. And extra time spent on matching fabrics, or patterns, or particular pairs of pants was one more minute taken away from the essential: the need to get up and go and do and think. "I don't care about clothes," he'd nastily repeat to his mom.

But to his wife, he said the same words, only a little sweeter, "Gee, honey, it really doesn't make any difference to me. I like what I've got on." And it really didn't make any difference, for FutureDick was most concerned with making wrong things right, and today, that something wrong was taking over his life.

Once the sense of danger invaded his running, all he could do after his shower and light dinner was go back to the office and wait. He never had to worry about being overlooked. If evil was out there, it would find him, for FutureDick had made a name for himself in the last twenty years.

When he graduated from the University of California, he was going to be a teacher. Four years into the profession showed him that colleges didn't want good teachers. They wanted publishing machines. They wanted workhorses. Each quarter, he was loaded with four courses; that meant 120 or more students, that meant 120 or more papers to grade every other week, that meant three or four class preparations, five days a week, and that meant getting to know and understand the lives of 120 vulnerable, emotional, believing freshmen.

"Here in this paragraph, Todd, you write about how weak you felt stepping in front of your mom to protect her from your dad. You go on to say you should have done more. That's good. Your willingness to express your feelings makes for an intimacy in writing that touches your reader. But," and FutureDick paused briefly before he uttered the rest of the sentence, wanting carefully, but significantly, to penetrate the crystallized consciousness that had protected the young man's awareness for the past twelve years, "have you ever stopped to consider that it may not have been the six year old's responsibility to take care of his parents? Perhaps the parents should have assumed more responsibility for their own children?"

FutureDick observed the boy's brow crease for an instant, a quick shudder that might have gone unnoticed by a less attentive teacher. Yet if he taught Todd anything, he would at least get him to look at issues from another vantage point, particularly when those concerns collided with the young man's sense of self-worth.

"Holly, when you write about your mom's drinking problem, have you thought about expressing your feelings, fears, thoughts during one of her binges? Where's the *you* in this paper?"

Feel! Feel! That's what writing's all about. The paper won't betray you. You can tell it whatever you want with no fear of reprisal.

"Sarah, this is an especially powerful paper, and I admire your courage in writing it. It takes a clear writer as well as a strong person to discuss child abuse. I applaud you."

At moments like this, FutureDick wondered who was the teacher and who was the student. Would he have been able to express himself so eloquently or so honestly at eighteen years old? He rather doubted it. It took the Sarahs of the world to once again remind him how profound the human mind could be.

"Thanks, Steve, for writing this paper on your gang. It allows you to get a new take on your own history. Once you distance yourself from the event, you see it differently. And I know it becomes easier to gain emotional acceptance of the whole thing. Writing about the experience changes you forever. Good work!"

And on and on and on. The stories never ended, for every student walked into his life with their private drama, their own narrative, their singular pain. Each paper shared with them became a step on their personal journey toward wholeness. All

FutureDick could do was help point the way. Shouldn't that have been sufficient? Wasn't that the essence of teaching—quality teaching—real teaching? Wasn't that the reason he taught more courses than he should have? Wasn't the student-teacher connection impetus enough to rationalize the stress, the responsibility, and the low, very low pay? Because he made a difference? Because he helped a human being veer toward understanding instead of remaining stuck in the isolation of unknowing?

Till one night at 4:33 a.m., when FutureDick eased out of a dream, opened his eyes, and knew his romance with teaching was over. He could ignore the pressure to publish the babble read only by other harnessed instructors trying to publish. He could ignore the department power politics, tacitly rampant in a state college. But the budget-cut dismissal of ten instructors in his department, which meant he, along with the remaining teachers, would have to add extra courses to his hefty schedule, left him too angry to continue another year in a system so insensitive to its educators as well as its scholars.

Loyalty to the faculty had been replaced by the bottom line: use less teachers to do more work. So what if students get the short end of the deal. So what if teachers develop burnout. There's more where they came from. There might be more, thought FutureDick, but there's not more of him. And he turned in his resignation. He just walked away from the whole thing.

He walked away from the grind and felt twenty pounds lighter, but he frequently missed the interaction with his students. Those eighteen and nineteen year old's were the best. Somewhat jaded, they still believed in fairy tales, and the exclusive ingredient necessary to give them hope—along with a sense of self-worth—was a small bit of encouragement on his part. He could affect their lives, for he helped them believe in who they were and what they could do.

All these young people needed was an advocate, someone on their side. He taught because he constantly believed in them.

He knew the young could make a difference. And sometimes, it only took one brave voice to change the direction of the world. Who knows if that voice would be one of the students who frequented his office during his brief four years of teaching?

But he walked away. His instincts upstaged his magnanimity, and he wanted something for himself—he wanted action. He wanted to be on the front line where he could fight in his own way. He wanted to be on the streets where he could effect immediate change. So he rented an office, put an ad in the Yellow Pages, in the newspaper, in his own neighborhood weekly and waited for clients. The sign on his door read **Scott Futura, Search and ReSearch.**

Business was slow in the beginning, but he was patient. He sat by the phone and read the many books he had put on hold during his four year tenure of five hour nights. Now he owned a bottomless pit of time, and he could get through his Faulkner and devour his Michener. He even started the Durant series, but in the middle of *The Age of Faith*, he landed his first case.

Twenty years ago, and it seemed like yesterday when Mrs. Bradshaw came in soliciting his help with her lost child. The daughter had been whisked away by a rejected boyfriend, and the case brought FutureDick some notoriety because he solved the problem by posing as a high school senior who recently moved into the neighborhood.

Perhaps his genetic inheritance allowed him his youthful appearance. No one could ever guess his mother's age either. But his believable pretense and his penetrating experience with his former students brought him inclusion in the high school's inner circle. From there, it was one short step to sharing confidences and one gigantic leap to rescuing the frightened teenager from the camouflaged cave in the foothills.

Still, twenty years has its way of wrecking havoc with a human society where jobs grew scarcer, and crimes grew scarier. He thought he had seen it all: drug wars, serial murders, crimes of passion, of greed, of lunacy. Now as he waited, he wondered how man's betrayal of goodness could get any worse than it already was. But he knew he'd find out soon—very, very soon.

While FutureDick used youthful years to weatherproof his world against crime, AceArrow washed through three marriages, tossing away his wives like paper clips. They got in his way. After the thrill of the hunt and the gluttony of the infatuation, day to day routine became a drag. He objected to expectations, to being home for dinner, to conversation at night, to sharing his dreams with a counterpart. They were *his* visions, nobody else's. And he wanted the exclusivity on their fleeting patent.

His wives became intrusions in his race to run his company to the top of the charts. AceArrow spent days with his work, nights with his strategy, and resented any connubial claims that distracted him from his unyielding intentions. He had robots to build, robots to sell, and in some vacuumed corner of his mind sprouted a supposition he shared with no one: What if? What if his robots could be developed into a private army? That's the essence of pure power, real power, his power.

But during his wife-years, he was just starting to build his metal men, and these women became gnats, little annoyances he flicked off one by one. Inevitably, each mate eventually requested children like you request a reservation to the Bahamas. But AceArrow remained adamant. Never! No babies. No mess. No added obligation to his life. No crying. No damn disorder. For that's what babies did. They induced disorder into your life. Children disheveled your game plan, messing your home, ruffling your nights, and generally tampered with the blueprints of your glory. None of that irregularity for AceArrow. Not on his life.

So at 22, he had a vasectomy and signed a covenant with his gods never to beget a child. But his oath remained private as he shared his snippet of an operation with no one. Renouncing his fractured family, disregarding his discontinued wives, and shrugging off any loyalty to friends, colleagues, acquaintances,

AceArrow lived with the private knowledge that his seed stopped with him. And he had all the time in the world to substantiate his shadows, to construct gleaming, glorious mechanical men in his mind, on the drawing board, at the factory, primed to invade the chaos of people's lives and bring about order. Ready to meet the household of Francie Franks.

Finally, everyone was ready to walk out of the house, when the phone rang.

"I'll get it," shouted Francie. "Go. Go wait for me in the van. I'll be right there."

As she ran for the blaring instrument, Francie ignored the childish sulks she heard in the distance. *Wait* was not a word accepted graciously by the teenagers in the group when it applied to others. But when it came to them, time ceased to have any relevance.

She knew she could let the answering machine pick up the call, but Francie hated that. Somehow a ringing phone demanded attention, and she had never learned how to walk away from its promise of prosperity. Who knows? Her name might have been selected in a lottery. She realized her fantasy derived from the many movies she watched as a kid, but one day, one call might make them millionaires. Maybe she really liked the momentary anticipation before she said hello, wondering how her life might be transformed by picking up the receiver, but Francie could never bring herself to ignore the insistent peal of the interruption.

"Hello."

"Hi, Francie, it's Dave EverSharp here. I've got some bad news. I pulled my hamstring today, and I'm out of commission for awhile. Sorry, kiddo, can't play racquetball tomorrow."

"God, Dave, that sounds like it hurts, mucho. What are you doing for it?"

"Just icing it now, but it's tight as hell."

"Listen, get yourself to a good masseuse. Works every time, Dave. I swear by it. The sooner you get the muscle to relax, the less you develop inflammation."

"Francie, I'll do anything at this moment. Cancelling a racquetball match is worse than missing Christmas!"

"Aw Dave, you'll just be tougher at our next game. All that pent up energy. I'm in big trouble. But seriously, get the muscle worked on so we can play next week. Take care."

As she replaced the receiver, Francie debated with herself whether to take the time and try to find another partner now or call later. Seven anxious kids were waiting hungrily, and their patience was measurable in nanoseconds when they were squished together in Reba's van. She knew who she'd call for a game since she had been thinking about it for the past two weeks. FutureDick. Even though he was a stronger player than her, she'd be able to give him competition. Who cares if he won? She was quick, exceptionally accurate: she'd make him sweat. And that was half of the game, anyway—getting out there and making your body work overtime.

For months now, she had condensed conversations with FD every time they saw each other at the courts. Their terse talk started when she kicked him off the court because his hour was up. He introduced himself and told her to watch the walls. The rain had made them slick. Of course, she already knew who he was. Who didn't? SeaBank was a small town, and he was a big name: FutureDick, Tomorrow's Detective Today.

She couldn't clearly remember when she started calling him FD, but every time they met at the gym, she'd wave and ask, "Hey, FD, how's it going?" And he'd wave back, with a wonderful half smile matched by an embarrassed inquisitiveness in his eyes. He never said much, but he looked at her so directly, using his gaze to penetrate her athletic facade, that she inevitably lowered her eyes like an adolescent. "Oh God, don't let me blush" passed through her thoughts, intermingling with the game strategy she was arranging for her oncoming match.

Francie smiled, since now she was ready to take him on. She had perfected her reverse corner shot, and Francie knew she could score a few points off of him. The shot surprised everyone she played because they never expected it. But her competitive tryst with FD would have to wait. There were seven starving stomachs clamoring for pizza, and they were invincible rivals to racquetball.

When Francie climbed in the van, she put the day to rest. Work was over, and there was no way she'd let her clients intrude on this part of her life, this precious playtime with her children. Three years ago, she opened her own counseling practice and finally had enough clients to make what she called a mild living, not enough to go on a vacation or buy a new car. But this increased income allowed her to pay the monthly bills that incrementally grew larger the older her children became.

That was solely what she wanted right now—to support her family. She considered herself one of the lucky ones to be living her dream come true. She was able to have a profession and a family. But she knew her success as well as her sanity depended on two factors: Reba and the DoRights.

Reba was her best friend. And when Francie and Alan were about to sign the divorce papers, Reba's husband, Sammy, picked up and left. Just like that. One day he's home, the next day he's gone. No word. No hints. Just vanished. A year later, Sammy filed for divorce. Francie thought that was terrific because she never liked Sammy anyway. He was a loud, gruff man, funny sometimes, but pitifully inadequate in a masculine sort of way. He always thought the more unpleasant he became, the more macho he'd look. Somehow, it backfired, and he'd look woefully insecure—like someone pretending to be a man but isn't exactly sure what it's about.

So there was Reba with three children, a big house, and ready, in fact eager, to find work, since Sammy would never let her get a real job. He'd only let her teach Sunday School or an art class at the community center. By the time Sammy filed for divorce, Reba had sold her house, found a job as director of an art school and enjoyed two lovers in her spare time. Apparently,

Sammy's absence was the spark Reba needed to get her back on course. She jumped into life feetfirst and has been running ever since.

In fact, Reba's tales of two hour lunchtime liaisons with her tireless, but virile men made Francie laugh during some of her desolate times. For a brief moment, the tears were shoved aside by the vitality of Reba's humor.

"I've got to hand it to him, Francie. I met Larry during lunch, and he put a picnic banquet on the bedspread, replete with champagne, sour dough, and Brie. Only," and Reba softly chuckled, "there was very little time to eat lunch."

"Reba, filling your nutritional, your sexual, and your athletic needs during a work break makes a hell of a lot sense to me. And you're not even infringing on the kids' schedules! I call that expert management, my brilliant friend."

"Francie, you're not kidding about a workout! Larry was a wrestler in college, and I think he's studied moves I didn't know the human body could perform. And talk about endurance! He must come from a family of marathon runners."

"I hate to tell you, Reba, but you don't sound like you're out of breath yourself. I wouldn't be surprised to find wings on your running shoes!"

"Well Francie, it's not hard work when it's this much fun. I'm just sorry I waited so long. It's too bad Sammy didn't know these things. Look what he missed!"

Francie could never understand Reba's compassion. When Sammy's name was mentioned, Reba would smile and somehow feel sorry for him. All Francie could feel was anger at his irresponsibility. But then she wasn't in Reba's shoes. Reba, who couldn't hurt a soul, much less Sammy, probably blessed the day he set her free. Who wouldn't feel some sympathy toward your liberator? However, she failed to realize that he had once been her jailer also.

Yet Reba didn't experience the same financial instability that Francie fought each month. Although Francie and the children still lived in the house she and Alan bought five years ago, the monthly payments were pushing her to look for something less expensive. When a huge house with a view of the water came up for sale, Francie grabbed for it and approached Reba with the latest of her risks.

"I've got a great idea, Reba. I found a house, but it's too much money for me. Wait till you see it, six bedrooms with a view. A gorgeous view of the water!"

"Francie, that sounds terrific, but where are you going to get the money?"

"Reba, I've been thinking about this all night. Let's buy it together. We can double up the kids in the bedrooms, and sharing would allow us to keep expenses down. Just think of it, Reba. We can put two families together and do something we've wanted to do for a long time. There's a large enclosed porch, big enough for that clan of DoRights we've talked about. Picture us with DoRights, Reba. Doesn't it make everything look promising?"

Reba's eyes lit up at the suggestion, and without hesitation, she replied, "Sold, kiddo! You've got yourself a housemate. Hell, you've got yourself four more additions to your family." And she grinned at Francie, locking eyes in affirmation of their agreement, "To *our* family!"

"That's what I love about you, Reba. The exorbitant amount of time you take to make up your mind."

As the two women hugged each other, they gave birth to a new experiment in living, an experiment Francie and Reba toasted often. The proud owners not only purchased a plot of land that gave them aesthetic gratification, but they also bought themselves a piece of personal life—a piece of private time they thought they'd never retrieve again, given the demands of their children, their jobs, their home. Francie and Reba bought themselves a clan of DoRights.

Four

The DoRights were a piece of genetic engineering mastery, introduced to the world on January 2, 2000 by TriCubed Scientifics. While people were still nursing hangovers or celebrating 24 hours of kept resolutions, TriCubed hoped to start the next century with a new concept: the alliance of ape and human. Destined to prove that man and his closest ancestor, the chimpanzee, could mutually benefit each other, the company began its work in the mid seventies, experimenting with female apes. For nearly two decades, TriCubed attempted to breed out aggression and breed in domesticity, loyalty, and gentleness—in effect, create an ape-dog who would willingly do household chores.

The scientist-dreamer responsible for the domesticated chimp was Adam BrickWell, a true visionary. He loved animals, he hated machines, at least, robotic machines, and he was well aware of the chimpanzee's vulnerability in a human-centered world: the ape was on the verge of extinction. Man's ethics rarely rose to the occasion when humans were involved and, most certainly, never extended to animals, who had agelessly been looked upon as disposable. BrickWell remained determined to change that callous view. His mission was to bring animal and man together, create a union whereby the ape could be saved.

Although he was accused of tampering with nature, BrickWell dismissed the criticism. Tampering doesn't always mean folly. It could very well mean improvement, growth, evolution, and that's how he looked at his Grand Experiment. He was keeping the chimp alive and ushering into the 21st century a new kind of partnership, the marriage of simian and human.

For BrickWell, it was undeniably rational since this was what nature had originally intended. Man was cousin to the chimpanzee. His genetic distance from the animal was infinitesimal, as was discovered when science refined its methods for measuring changes in DNA structure. By doing experiments in mixing DNA from two species, researchers were able to determine the percentage of difference between the species. Unexpectedly, it turned out that man shared 98.4 percent of his DNA with chimpanzees and was more closely related to this particular primate than to gorillas, orangutans, gibbons and monkeys.

This finding indisputably meant the genetic difference between human and ape was less than 1.6 percent. What made this discovery remarkable was that this difference was even less than that between two species of gibbons, which was 2.2 percent, or less than two closely related North American bird species, the red-eyed vireos and white-eyed vireos, which was 2.9 percent. We were unquestionably closer to chimps than many animals from the same species were to each other, and for all our grandiosity, 98.4 percent of our DNA was just normal chimp DNA.

Scientifically, we're almost twins. An example of our simian similarity shows up in our principal hemoglobin, the oxygen-carrying component that gives blood its red color and is identical in each one of its 287 units with chimp hemoglobin. In this respect as in several others, BrickWell noted, we are just a third species of chimpanzee.

Consequently, the scientist, more curious than ever, had to ask himself, "What closer relative did the human have in the entire animal kingdom?" Instinctively, BrickWell felt a link to the chimp. And when he studied their social strategies, they, over and above any other anthropoid, proved more human-like. With the discovery of shared DNA, BrickWell knew that the rest of Science confirmed what he had understood all along. Wasn't he bringing about the proper conclusion to a design that started around seven million years ago when both man and chimpanzee split apart from their common ancestor? Wasn't he resurrecting the bond that was certainly there primordially?

BrickWell, who worked with primates his entire life, could never understand why people had such a difficult time accepting the similarity. It was blatantly obvious how much human behavior resembled the behavior of apes. Part of his DoRight marketing campaign had been to educate consumers with public information messages on TV and in magazines. He produced little vignettes showing chimp maternal behavior, the affiliation between females, and their sexual preferences.

Chimps, like humans, enjoy a wide variety of positions during copulation, including the face to face position, which had generally been touted as man's singular contribution to romance. Additionally, copulation could be initiated by either sex, nullifying male exclusivity, a fact that brought wide smiles to the Feminists for the Preservation of Chimps Society. They applauded the female chimp's ability to copulate with several males at a time. She never knows and never really cares who actually fathers her child. And much to the chagrin of the creationists, these same chimps, like their human sisters, were sexually receptive for most of the month, not just during the few days of periodic sexual heat that other mammals exhibit.

Take away the hair, dress them with fashionable clothes, turn off the lights, and a few drunken sailors probably wouldn't be able to tell the difference. In fact, BrickWell sometimes wondered what it would be like if you constructed a zoo that caged a few unfortunate people who couldn't speak and placed their prison next door to the chimps. Let them romp naked, and the passersby would either see a hairless chimp or a hairy human, depending on their perspective. But could the audience feel what it must be like to be locked up your whole life when you haven't done anything wrong? The only crime you're guilty of is being born in the first place.

Capturing chimpanzees for zoos had been one of the major threats to their survival, and BrickWell viewed it as genocide, the slow but determined destruction of a species. Even in the process of capturing a chimp alive, ethical considerations flew out the window because several other chimps were killed in the chase, particularly the babies carried by the mothers.

Zoos were not the only bounty hunters in the business. Medical researchers jumped in years ago to use the chimps for deadly experiments, but now they rationalized the animal's decimation as necessity, since three new viruses were dangerously cascading upon American shores from Europe and South America. BrickWell remembered the early years of habitat destruction when the chimps' rain forest dwellings in Africa and Asia were silently demolished. Since the US refrained from putting its money where its speeches were and helping Uganda, Zaire, and Indonesia build national parks, BrickWell looked upon himself as a savior rather than destroyer when he began his ape experiments. If not for him, the species would have quietly disappeared. He was sure of it. As much as he was sure that the DoRights were destined to take their place, not behind, but alongside their next of kin—the human being.

"Human beings? Absolutely not! They don't belong in the equation," hissed Tully into the phone.

"Okay, Tully, cool down. I'll try it your way for awhile," stabbed back AceArrow. "But I've got a hunch a few humans eliminated along the way would scare the hell out of our potential buyers."

"No sir. Chimps are just as effective. Smart buyers don't want any trouble, and we'll cause enough of a disturbance to attract all your consumers. There's no need to go after humans." Tully mentally calculated the correlation: police, FBI, National Guard. Too soon—way too soon. "We're not ready, yet!"

But AceArrow remained adamant, "Don't you remember the Burger Bash food poisoning years back? A couple of contaminated restaurants and they had to close down stores across the entire US. That's what I'm aiming for. Just a few dead examples."

"I don't buy that. The chimps will do the same job. We'll frighten just as many people by the time we finish. Now if ya want to kill more chimps, let's go at it. That's what I've been saying all along! We can eliminate a shit-load of apes in a single evening."

"No, Tully. Goddamn it, no! Stick with our original estimate. I'll put the people idea on hold for now." And AceArrow snickered as he hung up the phone, knowing he'd get the little scumbag to do exactly what he wanted—sooner or later.

FIVE

As FutureDick looked around his office, he tried to second-guess what the next eruption to strain the provisional peace would be. It could be drug-related, but he didn't think so. A new wave of community commitment had spread through the city of SeaBank, and more informants were coming forth. Consequently, law enforcement was enjoying a heyday in drug-busts. They were determined to wipe the small metropolis clean of drug-related crimes.

Still, there were other antagonistic forces gaining momentum, not only in SeaBank, but across the country. Too many people had been out of work too long, and they were organizing. Desperate, they needed relief. Fuming, they needed an outlet. If money and jobs weren't reaching their lives, then they'd stampede toward support, toward any palliative that would offer them solace for a brief time. Some cessation to the raging frustration, the feeling of nowhere, of not counting for anything, that occupied every spot of their brain.

Even temporary salvation, if only a night's worth, eased

their personal image of uselessness. So they sought some way, some group that sponsored their individual reclamation. And when that association, who promised them concern, action, results, ordered up anger, the displaced happily obliged and quickly delivered. Give them a reason, a person, a something upon which to vent their fury, and the chief-craftsman carefully chiseled an instant powder keg ready to explode.

A few looked for a higher good. Most looked for scapegoats. What they didn't have within had to be found without, in a leader, in a fellowship, in a purpose. Their self-worth had seeped out through their toes, and they were ready to follow. Perhaps a false prophet was better than no prophet. At least, the promise of family, of favor, of future was offered. To those who are empty, beans become bullion.

Overnight, organizations appeared, opening their arms to potential protestors: The Society for Sane Driving, Association for American-born Grandparents, The Foundation for Free Travel, Women Surfers for Sanitary Sand, The Alliance against Pollution, Poverty, and Population, The Alliance for Adolescent Anguish. Women protested against wimps and parents protested for privacy.

Lately, the noisiest groups centered around animals. It wouldn't be long before the advocates for animal rights would clash with the demonstrators against animal laborers. In the middle, trying to protect themselves would be the members of HEART: Help Each Animal Remain True. They supported the rights of animals, which meant they also supported their freedom to work. But they vociferously opposed genetic tampering of any species. And at the top of their hit list were the DoRights.

Loud and clear, their chants hit the streets every Sunday. "The DoRights do wrong! The DoRights do wrong!" FutureDick wondered if the police were being too lax in their attention to these splinter organizations gaining in popularity. Maybe he ought to have a heart to heart with Detective TigerTail, his closest friend in the Department.

Over the years, FutureDick aided the police in many criminal apprehensions, and he and the Department had a nice way of working together. They accepted his unobtrusive way, and he accepted their need for belonging and loyalty. They knew he worked better alone, and he knew their allegiance would always be to the force, but they also appreciated his expertise. FutureDick had a way of tracking down hunches and never letting go. A human hound dog, the officers called him when they were joking. But when they were serious, he took on the semblance of genius. He'd analyze a crime and zero in on some off-the-wall notion, then single-mindedly pursue his supposition.

Most recently, his undercover stint as a TrailWays passenger helped cut short the series of rape-murders occurring across the country. Like clockwork, a woman's ravished, beaten body would turn up near a convenience store located on a major US car route. There seemed to be no criminal pattern, and the cases were easily dismissed as a random local homicide.

When FutureDick stepped in, he recognized that the murderer traveled from point *A* to point *B*, and then to *C*, via buses, TrailWays buses. And all the slayings occurred at the rest stops when passengers hopped off to replenish their paper bags with Snickers, potato chips, Cokes, and cigarettes. FutureDick had to ride a lot of buses, but so did other undercover cops, and one of them from Wichita nailed the sorry psychopath just before he committed his sixteenth homicide. Yet, it was FutureDick's theory that proved correct.

He joked with the men at SeaBank's downtown station, saying they almost lost a good man.

"How's that?" GoodGuy asked.

"The smoke, man. The smoke," FutureDick replied. "It nearly killed me. Every time they stopped, a mob of passengers jumped off and lit up. I would stand outside the bus, talking, watching, and breathing. Goddamn, if that secondary inhalation didn't go right into my lungs, man. I thought for sure I was a goner."

With a respect that glistened in his eyes, GoodGuy responded jokingly, "No way, FutureDick. It's going to take more than tobacco to put you under. You're a god damn piece of human velcro. There's no prying you away from your criminal scent."

But tonight, there was no case to track down, so FutureDick sat at his desk and waited, hoping the events about to unfold would not be as horrible as his nose suggested. Yet his uneasiness spoke otherwise, and he knew that nothing good was going to come out of the next 24 hours.

A few miles from FutureDick, in a simple, secure, window-filled condo, lived BrickWell, the world-famous scientist. He owned his apartment, half of his company, two Oldsmobiles, and a perpetual passion for inquiry.

BrickWell was a man of few pleasures: his work came first, then his family. This was not a problem. His wife understood long ago that she would share him with another mistress whom he loved just as passionately—his devotion to science. In fact, she claimed that's why she cared for him so deeply. His concerns went beyond the ordinary, and if minds like his weren't kept comfortable, a world advanced as ours would not have originated. Their marriage was a testament to her support and belief in her husband and his allegiance and ardor to his calling.

"You make me proud, Adam, really proud," she would whisper when she had him alone.

And he would smile, answering, "Bette, you're my kind of woman."

For Bette, Adam was her kind of man, the best kind, born to make the world different. He was no quitter. When he believed in something, he gave it his all, and every ounce of his brain blasted ahead to bring his theories to fruition. "My scientific soldier," she called her husband, as she watched him campaign for the creatures he created: his DoRights.

But the DoRights were the critical culmination of BrickWell's scientific understanding. Countless hours, endless diligence, numberless setbacks accompanied his search for a new approach to apes. BrickWell fought hard to raise human consciousness concerning its simian relative. He believed in an alternative school of taxonomy called cladistics, which argued that classification should be objective and uniform, based on genetic distance.

Since birds, classified in the same genus, and gibbons, classified in the same genus, were genetically more distant from each other than humans were from chimpanzees, he argued that humans don't constitute a distinct family or even a distinct genus. As far as BrickWell was concerned, humans belong in the same classification as common and pygmy chimps. Couldn't his colleagues understand this? We share the same DNA with these apes.

He knew that our genus name *Homo* was proposed first, since man has usually been rather pompous when it comes to his place in the universe and, therefore, took priority over the genus name *Pan,* used for the "other" chimps. But this was wrong. Chimps weren't the other. They were like us. If knowledge was to be advanced, then the words of science must ring true. They must describe accurately.

For BrickWell, this improper classification was like teaching 2 + 2 = 5, and he spent a lifetime advocating a terminology change. Before he died, he hoped to see scientific texts teaching a new way of classifying information that would read, "There are three species of genus *Homo* on earth today: the common chimpanzee, *Homo troglodytes*; the pygmy chimpanzee, *Homo paniscus*; and the human chimpanzee, *Homo sapiens*." This change was crucial for the next step in scientific exploration. Otherwise, we were training our potential pioneers entirely wrong.

And with the change in terminology, BrickWell prayed for a change in attitudes and ethics. Why is it acceptable to subject apes, without their consent, to lethal experiments for purposes of medical research? Certainly, human criminals, caged in prisons under worse conditions than zoo apes, would provide medical scientists with more valuable insight into human anatomy than deadly experiments with chimps.

If we condemn the use of human subjects, shouldn't we, then, condemn the use of our closest cousin, the chimpanzee? BrickWell wasn't sure if human beings should be used in lethal experiments, although he knew that medical science would advance faster if they were. All he wanted was for chimps and man to be treated equally. Don't do to a chimpanzee what you wouldn't do to a human being. Respect its sanctity. After all, humans have had only a short history as a species distinct from the ape, a mere six to eight million years. The venerable chimps had been around a lot longer than that.

"I don't care how many chimps are in the compound, Tully. I'm against it!" AceArrow almost lost his composure as his words sizzled into the mouthpiece.

"But sir, just think of the number of bodies we could take with one hit!" Tully wouldn't give up.

"That's not the mission here. I want a few at a time. I want to gradually instill fear. Let it build up, let it escalate." This guy's not listening. I'm speaking words, and they're not getting through.

"But a harsh assault on the main installation would wipe them out." Tully couldn't understand why non-soldiers remained blind.

And AceArrow couldn't understand why the military mentality spoke such nonsense. "Listen to me carefully, Tully. That's not what I'm after. I don't want one massive attack. I want little ones, bitter ones, even human ones, so we engrave the element of mistrust on everyone's minds. I want their dreams filled with alarm. Suspicion, Tully. Even hesitation, but not panic."

Panic was the feeling most remote in Francie's mind as she drove her family home, the few hours of fun nearly finished. Pleasure fades quickly when reality ruptures its timeless quality to remind you of what you're supposed to do tomorrow: take Lanie to the orthodontist, buy April ballet shoes, drive the carpool to gymnastics, make a grocery list, get Miller's new book on child abuse, and—oh shit—I need a racquetball partner. Call FD first thing. Saturday's list always seemed endless, and yet, Saturdays always got done. But Friday wasn't over, and at the edge of her memory lingered a must do, a something she was supposed to satisfy.

"Wait, Reba, I almost forgot. Stop at FoodFair. We're out of bananas."

The minute she said that, the inside of the van echoed with laughter as she knew it would. "Out of bananas" had become such a repeated phrase in their family, that the kids made up a limerick they enthusiastically shouted whenever they could:

A young lady from southern Havanas,
Went by the name of Fat Annas.
To the store she would skate,
But get there too late,
Cuz all the shelves were out of bananas.

Then Francie and Reba, right on cue, added their verse to the tradition of humor that had grown quite naturally within the blended family. The two women beamed with pleasure at the smiles on their children's faces when they comically recited their stanza:

She thought she'd be rather clever,
And whispered to Whomsoever,
"I'll go shopping at four,"
But found a sign on the door:
We're out of bananas forever!

The staple of their household: bananas. She ate them, the kids ate them, and the DoRights devoured them. If she could grow bananas in her backyard, Francie would have started a plantation. Next to water and toilet paper, bananas were a necessity.

She could see Edmund right now, scampering up to her for

a hug, stroking her shoulder, and then stretching his soft hairy hands out for the yellow fruit. The two year old had the most winsome ape smile she'd ever seen. She could say no to her own children at that age, but not to Edmund. He won her adoration completely.

And his mother, Emma. What a beauty! She went about the household accomplishing her work quietly, efficiently, clearly knowing where Edmund was. Sometimes she'd stop in the middle of a chore and go over to hug her baby, just for a moment. So free to respond to the music of her heart. When would humans ever learn to not think but simply act, automatically, when the inclination toward tenderness crossed their consciousness? No matter how often Francie watched the DoRight mother with her son, the look of serenity on Emma's face still made her catch her breath. The maternal love was surely as it should be. But Francie's intimate acquaintance with the sad side of human emotions didn't provide this scene too readily. Any one of her clients would have traded places with Edmund in a second.

Shirley was less active than Edmund, and she stayed close to her mother, Rose. Although the little male chimp tried to engage Shirley, she'd only play a short time, then realize her mother was in the yard pulling weeds or watering. She'd scuttle out there quickly, making sure Rose existed, safe, sound, and certainly within reach.

Francie was more familiar with these four chimps because they worked around the house. Lila and Henry worked next door during the day, and Tulip and Terrie worked down the street. At seven, the clan came together, and Francie relished watching the reunion when she was home. Even though the DoRights had been apart scarcely twelve hours, you'd think it was twelve years. They hugged and groomed and chattered, their joy contagiously spreading through the household till it infected the humans as well.

When Francie and Reba originally bought the chimps, they

only expected domestic help. The two women had a large house, a large family, and a large workload. Little did they realize that they were purchasing a paradigm for affiliation. These uninhibited chimps showed their human children the spontaneity of affection. They hugged because they loved. And no lesson on earth was more important to Francie than the freedom to touch. She wanted her own children to be able to hug, to be able to express their fondness with the same gusto as the DoRights. In a world where people were frightened of contact and covered up their feelings, let her children dare to imitate the newest members of their family.

Little Edmund, you lucky soul. If only my mother would have hugged me half as much, I don't think the aloneness would be so intimidating. But the dismal thought faded as Francie jumped out of the van to buy bananas, ensuring her DoRights the delectable breakfast they absolutely deserved.

"Just get the designated DoRights! Do you hear me, Tully? Do not go to the company," commanded AceArrow.

"Yes sir," Tully replied sullenly, his voice trailing off in anger, doubt, frustration unheard by the condescending CEO. The mercenary would save his day in the sun for later, even if it meant defying an order.

"Just so we understand each other. This has to be spotless. No mistakes. I mean it. Just follow the plan. Agreed?" AceArrow remained adamant.

"You got it, sir. We'll prove you proud." Tully was a patient man. He'd pick the right time.

"Okay, Tully. Good luck and safe mission." AceArrow's voice had softened for a moment.

"Thank you, sir. Thank you." Tully's excitement almost escaped through his expression of gratitude, but soldier that he was, he quickly checked his voice so the tone came out neutral, strong, courteous, and forever guarded. He would obey orders now, but future decisions definitely belonged to him.

For all his knowledge, his ability to postulate premises, to synthesize complex information and see the logic of his connections, BrickWell could never have understood the conversation between AceArrow and Tully. The scientist dealt with life, not death. And no amount of explanation would clarify for him how man can come into this world mad. With its widespread beauty, its wonder, its wealth of improvable resources, you fell into a treasure waiting to be polished.

When BrickWell began his genetic research, he had trouble achieving the correct emotional balance in his new breed of primates. His earlier apes were inattentive. They wouldn't sit still or concentrate during any of the training sessions. Although BrickWell created a somewhat docile animal, he also affected their intellectual competency. There appeared to be a connection between changing aggression patterns and ability to learn. The more volatile the chimp, the more capable the primate became at paying attention.

But BrickWell kept at it. Determinedly, he'd walk into the lab every morning, thinking this is the day we'll have a breakthrough. This is the day we splice our gene properly and grow the kind of ape who will cooperate fully with man. This is the day we'd do it right.

And when that day arrived, when the first genetically engineered baby chimps grew old enough to learn household tasks and smile their unabashed, toothy chimp smiles at their achievements, BrickWell knew exactly what to call them. These were DoRights. The beautiful, gentle, accomplished apes did it right, and they were quite pleased with themselves. But so was BrickWell. He proved that his dream could become reality. He had created the perfect home-helper.

From then on, it was a matter of breeding and training. You could walk into the lab kitchen any day of the week and see primates loading and unloading dishwashers, folding laundry, vacuuming, dusting, and cooking. They performed these chores with loving care, grateful to be of service to their human teachers.

Every once in a while, a lesson would go awry, but it was usually correctable. It took months to stop the DoRights from drinking the window washing detergent. Something in the cleaner appealed to the simian taste. Each time they washed windows, half of the liquid soap ended up in their stomachs and would make them ill. But the trusting trainees never correlated their all-night vomiting to the caustic solution they drank that afternoon.

No amount of behavioral training could keep the animals from downing the blue liquid till the researchers mixed the fluid with anise seed. That did it. The soap never neared the DoRights' lips again. They seemed to have an aversion to the smell of licorice. So when a DoRight clan was sold, they came equipped with their own organic window cleanser and explicit directions to not substitute any other soaps.

What BrickWell considered his crowning achievement was the DoRight's gentleness. He modified their genetic inheritance until he came up with a species altered enough to cuddle a human child. That was a breathtaking sight to see: the tiny hairless infant in the arms of its brawny, mammalian ancestor! The hairy beast cradled the baby and rocked it lightly, emitting low guttural noises that somehow soothed the human child while offering protection at the same time.

"Was there any better place to be than snuggled in the ape's breast?" thought BrickWell. That baby instinctively knew it was solidly sheltered from harm. It was safe. "Wouldn't we all like a ready-made refuge to crawl into whenever we felt threatened?" he mused. And he smiled at his new invention: the perfect therapist. It protected while it comforted. He could wreck havoc with the healing community if he slightly changed the name of his creation and called his chimps PsychRights, the only living pillows around.

But when BrickWell wasn't being facetious and took some precious time off, away from the lab, where he could contemplate his genetic triumph, he felt a warmth invade his chest, an almost physical reflection of his fulfillment. He had no doubts that ape and man could work in synchronization—they belonged together. When he saw the chimpanzee mother hugging the human child, he knew his theory was sound, and he had penetrated a biological barrier that would forever change man's perception of his status on the evolutionary ladder.

As a scientist, he tried to ignore the growing fervor tarnishing his triumph. There would always be *anti's* for every breakthrough in our understanding of the universe. How many of the fearful insisted the world was flat?

It was too scary for people to invade the unknown. They preferred the sameness, the security of the unchanged rather than risk a voyage into the uncharted. Most men enjoyed the comfort of predictability. Then they could count on routine, on habit, on what BrickWell called the living death: to not venture is to not learn. And to not learn is a stifling monotony inflicted upon the human brain. BrickWell knew that throughout history, the world-changers never had carte blanche. Instead, they fiercely fought for implementation of new ideas and theories.

Generally, BrickWell's practical nature rewarded him by permitting his intellect to ignore the resistance kicked up by his colleagues, his critics, and the crying voices of frightened do-gooders.

"What do they know, Bette? They're blind. They can't see what I can."

"I know, dear. I know. But you've got to give people more time. We're a timid, superstitious species, and you're trampling on some of the gods."

"But all they have to do is open their eyes and take a good look at the DoRights. That's progress in the most personal of terms. Goddamn it, Bette. When you see the chimp embracing a real flesh and blood baby, holding it as gently as you would a feather, and nuzzling the child like it were her own, you know we've entered a new age. Why fight the future?"

"Adam, I wish I had answers. Sometimes, I think the past

was so painful for these people that they consider themselves lucky to be alive and well in the present, and they're going to hold on to that security blanket—the *familiar.* All they have is what they know—now. And you're trying to take it away from them by marching them into a new world where they haven't been taught the rules."

"Jesus, Bette, it's remarkably easy, if they'd pull up the shade of dread covering their eyes. All I'm asking them to do is look without using preconceived vision. See what I see."

"Adam, if more people could see what you see, our world wouldn't be shivering so much."

Six

As he pushed the touch-tone luminescent buttons, FutureDick knew before the call was answered what Captain BlackArm would say. Since he hadn't heard any sirens slice through the long, sluggish night, he suspected the world, or at least their seaside township, was calm. BlackArm confirmed it by saying, "Take a rest, FutureDick. There's nothing happening here. Go home, man. It's bedtime!"

Despite BlackArm's advice, FutureDick couldn't go home. He couldn't read or watch TV. He couldn't concentrate on anything when his instincts were simmering, ready to boil over at the imminent peal of his phone. This heightened sensitivity didn't happen often, but when it did, he zombied out, remaining in a tense state of readiness, prepared to jump on short notice.

Scores of sordid scenarios played through his brain, yet he had no idea where to go to thwart the terror before it began. Sometimes in these altered moods, his mind replayed history, his story, his past. That's what he hated most. By now, he was used to it, but in the beginning, the pain was too much, and he'd end up weeping till early morning.

He'd weep for what would have been: 22 years of marriage, a grown daughter, perhaps two or three other children, perhaps a life of birthdays, of Mother's Days and Father's Days and photographs and anniversaries and *first's*. The *first's* that every family experiences when they have children, buy houses, and relive their childhood through the next generation. But he had no *first's* because his newly formed family, his sole companion Tendra and their one year old daughter, Bounty, had been killed. In a blink of an eye, erased—wiped off the earth by a mere decision to get ice cream instead of popcorn.

The tears didn't come as easily now, but for years after that fateful night, all he had to do was say her name or smell her smell, and his eyes welled up with the regrets of sunsets unlived together.

Finished with his thirteenth month of private investigation, FutureDick was trying to figure out how to file his taxes. It was easier when he taught. As an employee of a school, he filed a single form and sign his name. Now the complexity of discretionary deductions for a sole entrepreneur took his attention, and he was determined to understand tax procedure before putting his books in the hands of an accountant.

The family finished dinner, and FutureDick wanted to spend some time reading the tax manual. So Tendra gave him a kiss and said she was taking Bounty out for a walk. She'd surprise him and bring back ice cream or popcorn. Then they could pig out while watching their 9 o'clock sitcom.

FutureDick became engrossed in the section on authentic allowances and didn't hear the bell the first time it rang. On the second ring, his consciousness caught wind of that familiar sound, and he slowly walked to the door, still concentrating on deductions. The minute he opened the door and recognized the blue uniform, his gut cramped together as if a vise grabbed hold of his muscles and forcibly squeezed the blood out of them. For a moment, he wanted to crawl back in time, crawl back to

Tendra's kiss and say, "Don't go, sweetheart. I'll do the taxes tomorrow. Don't go, honey. Please don't go!"

But reality barged into his void with the words of the police officer, "Does a Tendra Futura live here?" Frozen, all he could do is nod, no sound, no words. "Please come with me. There's been a terrible accident." And with those two barely audible sentences detonating in his ears, FutureDick took the initial step into his relentless nightmare, a nightmare that would haunt him for nineteen years of what-could-have-been's.

Tendra and Bounty were on the curb waiting for the light to change, just two blocks from home, when a silver Mercedes going around ninety miles per hour side-swiped a pickup. The truck veered to the right, hitting the stroller, the child, the woman head on and continued across the street into the lamp post. Tendra and Bounty, smashed by 2000 pounds of steel and rubber, were killed instantly. The driver of the pickup had his brain crushed by a flying toolbox, and the Mercedes kept on going. To this day, FutureDick followed any silver Mercedes that crossed his line of vision. And to this day, he wondered if the driver ever received some sort of fateful retribution, some sort of hell on earth existence that slightly approximated FutureDick's pain.

He had to identify the pieces of life laid out in the morgue, the remnants of his love lying cold, defunct, over. No one, no living being should ever have to validate the bloody human shape who used to hold him in her arms or hug his cheeks and smile when he lifted her in the air. No one deserves to have their life's reason obliterated because of mere coincidence—the wrong place at the right time.

FutureDick never knew how he pulled himself together. Perhaps it was his work, aided by his athletics. So many nights, so many tears, the never-ending sorrow of pity, but somehow the time passed and he survived. A heart mangled forever, but he survived. Every once in a while, he puzzled over his ability to love again and considered the depth of his emptiness. Was there any resemblance to the human he once was tears ago? Would he be able to resurrect some kind of feeling for a woman? Some type of passion? Something? Anything? Or had all affection withered away, replaced by insistent remorse intentionally pain-proofing his existence into watertight numbness.

When he changed his name six years later, he hoped he would collect a new lease on life, a chance to start over, subdue the grief that still grabbed hold of his chest in the middle of the night. Except changing your outside doesn't always guarantee an inner renewal. Becoming FutureDick, Tomorrow's Detective Today, brought him new clients, new celebrity, but his bereft soul remained the same.

Sometimes the quiet tears inadvertently slipped from his eyes as a sweet memory swished across his mind. That's when he grappled with his lost yesterdays. And FutureDick realized a renovated name might bring him more adventure, but there was no exchange policy for a broken heart.

At the moment, broken bodies rather than broken hearts were foremost in Tully's thoughts. Just think of the amount of enemy he could wipe out at main headquarters. Goddamn AceArrow! Why was the guy being so chicken-shit? Tully saw it quite clearly, and yet, he couldn't get his impression past the boss's thick skull.

Well, he'd obey this time. But he'd be fucking certain to scope out the site and check their security. Then he'd bide his opportunities for a next time. He'd make sure of it. Even if it meant doubling back during the march. This was just too ripe to pass up. Besides, he was the one with the troops. He could do whatever he damn well wanted, whenever he damn well pleased. Okay AceArrow, I'll lie low, now. But you're not calling the shots forever, man. Not on your fucking life!

These are animals we're talking about here. Dumb, ignorant beasts! What the hell's the difference how many you kill? Tully remembered AceArrow, himself, ridiculing the hairy assholes.

"Hey, Tully, you're going to love this assignment. Did you

ever want to take the world's most precise fighting machine and aim it at the biggest piece of shit around?"

"Doesn't sound too bad, sir. In fact, it sounds as if we definitely have the advantage."

"Oh, we do, Tully. We do! You see, the world of domestic service needs a general cleansing. It's polluted at the moment with the stink of primate flesh. Those brute bastards, the DoRights, have contaminated the industry. Every time they take a dump, it's one more load of shit the country doesn't need. They're unclean, Tully. Morally offensive, because they're scientifically impure."

"Gee, sir, I never thought about it that way. I just figured they were kind of expensive broom sweepers, but still sorta harmless."

"No Tully—harmful, not harmless! They're tainting the entire service industry, like a piece of rot that keeps reproducing everyday, defiling scientific beauty. You know what science is, Tully? It's control over your environment. It's the precise running of a handsome machine that operates with accuracy again and again and again. Like my robots: exact, perfect, dependable."

"Well, I gotta admit, sir, that I always preferred the power ya get from a weapon rather than a human arm. You do have a point there."

"Of course, I do, Tully. Because mechanical power gives you control—over your home, your work, your life—everything! And we have that control in my robots. Wait till you see them. You'll fall in love. And I want you to use them, Tully. Use them to eliminate the country's greatest enemy. Their enemy! Right now, their biggest obstacle is that scientifically unstable, bare-assed, shit-producing half-breed of a monkey. Think of him as unfriendly fire, Tully, a parasite eating away at the bowels of research."

Jesus, the guy had a way with words, thought Tully. AceArrow plainly had a bug up his ass about the DoRights. But crap, he was paying the bills! Let him vent his spleen. An assignment like this came once in a lifetime, and who knows? Maybe, in some fateful way, Tully was also advancing the surge of science. If he believed everything AceArrow told him, they were a couple of well-meaning Einsteins changing the world forever. One thing for sure, if might meant right, he was wielding the biggest sword around.

Scientific discovery happens only through a leap of faith: someone, somewhere, veers away from customary dogma and dares to challenge the old-line orthodoxy. A BrickWell believes so strongly in his sixth sense that he's willing to sacrifice years, maybe even decades, to prove his hunch is correct. It took many starts and stops before TriCubed finally succeeded in developing a rather tame species of beasts, genetically engineered to stand upright much of the time and be amenable to household service. Since these animals did not have to forage for food anymore, they had a new sense of reality as well as a chance to turn their attention elsewhere. They were ready for the next rung up the evolutionary ladder, and BrickWell was there to take them by the hand, one step at a time.

These apes could be taught repetitive tasks and enjoyed the company of humans. In fact, since their entry into the labor force six years ago, there had never been a case of a lazy or disgruntled DoRight. TriCubed scored a winner with their popular product, and sales kept increasing 20% a year.

Of course, there were some drawbacks, but these seemed tolerable compared to the service the DoRights performed. If you baked with a DoRight in the kitchen, you had to be particularly careful when you used vanilla, unless you wanted a lethargic chimp lazing around your mixer. DoRights imbibed the odor of vanilla with the zeal of a drunkard guzzling his first drink of the day. The apes tried to whisk the scent out of the air by inhaling long, deep breaths, hoping to snare every molecule of the delicious fragrance. They were completely captivated by vanilla, and a busy baker cautiously worked around her hairy domestic helpers if she still wanted their assistance that day.

BrickWell wasn't surprised at the chimps' response to vanilla. Recent research into the human nose-mind connection showed that certain smells aid in relaxation. In fact, the University of Arizona had just published the results of their spiced-apple study, indicating that the stress response, including elevated blood pressure, reduced 50% when subjects sniffed spiced-apple.

Other studies, he found, validated vanilla's effect on humans, whereby anxiety levels dropped drastically when a person perceived the vanilla scent as pleasant. But the DoRights not only became less anxious, they became downright inattentive, led by the vanilla to some distant Shangri-la where they luxuriated for the duration of the irresistible aroma.

Besides hampering your baking a bit, it took some getting used to when you walked into a house and saw a creature covered with resplendent blackish-brown hair pushing a vacuum cleaner. These female apes were big, powerful animals, and you had to remind yourself they weren't violent, even though they had the strength of a 450 pound man. They were there to help, not harm. Still, you had to overcome your initial reaction which was often a mixture of shock, fear, and sometimes simply plain revulsion. What helped calm your imagination was watching the DoRights take care of their young.

They were the most caring mothers on the planet, and they snuggled their babies to their chest with pure delight. Child and mother blended in each other's arms like the Kollwitz painting and could melt any nonbeliever's heart once he saw the look of utter tranquility in the mother DoRight's eyes. She'd lick the baby, pick its hair, stroke the child and actually dominate its presence, so that the infant was enfolded in a security few human children experience.

And the babies were part of the package. When TriCubed sold a DoRight, they sold a mother and child. In fact, they sold a clan of four adults and four children. Research proved the female DoRight needed to care for her own child to be content. In all the experiments where a DoRight was separated from her baby, the chimp could perform the tasks but grew more despondent each day.

During the investigative stage, the DoRight mothers flourished in fresh learning situations as they completed their individual tasks, responded to their child, and then set about accomplishing a new feat. But the single females grew morose with each passing day, suggesting they had nothing or no one to live for. They seemed to give up and would die in their sleep for no visible reason. They just stopped wanting to live. So TriCubed packaged their DoRights in twos: mother and child.

But another requirement came with the product. DoRights had to live with other DoRights in order to thrive. Take them away from their community, and they cried every night. The crying grew to wailing, and the child joined in. Consequently, a lone DoRight became an intolerable situation. Even if you bought yourselves ear plugs, the neighbors would complain.

A sad DoRight is a lamentable creature, and her sobs pierce your soul. Too much sadness, too much hurt, too much pain comes through those moans. Therefore, the best circumstance was to create a clan and have four DoRight mothers with four DoRight children live together in one room. If you couldn't use four DoRights, you could rent out their services each day. So buying a clan was a bit like starting a business. You either put them to work at your home, your friend's home, or your neighbor's home. Moreover, you needed a big enough place to house them, for you had four powerful apes sleeping side by side accompanied by four frisky growing apelets.

TriCubed provided a service contract guaranteeing the exchange of a DoRight clan every five years. The new clan arrived at the house, ready to start work. And the old clan returned to the compound, where the mothers mated, and the children started school. At five years old, they were ready to be separated from their mothers for long periods of time, and

TriCubed started to train its next generation of DoRight helpers. In another five years, the females, fully trained, reached reproductive maturity and, once pregnant, became part of a newly formed clan.

Of course, TriCubed kept enough male apes around to act as studs. But that's all they were needed for: their sperm. The human family now afforded the safeguard originally offered by the male. With little effort, the DoRight, devoted to her new kin who sheltered her from harm, gladly switched allegiance. The male was a means for breeding and could be discarded after the act as easily as tossing a banana peel aside after the sweet, creamy flesh was eaten.

Women who worked at TriCubed never tired of reminding their male colleagues how expendable they were. Sexism with a feminist twist trickled through their daily dialogues.

"Stan, what do you get when you cross a DoRight with a CEO?"

"Well Alex, even if I don't know, I'm sure you're going to tell me."

And Alex replied, with mischief lurking behind her smile, "A female chimp who meets her stud for lunch, sets her Rolex to beep in five minutes, and announces, 'Put out or pack off, buster! Time is money.' "

Stan tried to stifle his laughter but couldn't. The workplace humor seemed well-intentioned, and he didn't mind a chuckle or two, even if his ego became wrenched a bit in the process.

But Ben remained fixed, unwilling to respond to the crass jokes skimming the tops of the coffee cups. When asked by Sharon, "What's the difference between a DoRight and a DoBetter?" Ben refused to answer. He blinked and looked at the wall clock, trusting this momentary irritation would soon pass.

So Sharon pressed on, "Okay Ben, since your feelings are mighty fragile, I'll tell you anyway. A DoRight does anyone, but a DoBetter has her personal assistant administer a gene screen to see if he ranks high enough before she accepts his deposit."

That was Carol's cue to blurt out, "Sort of like a sperm credit rating, Ben. A genetic TRW!"

Still, Ben's demeanor continued its uninterrupted impassivity. He seemed determined not to encourage the office wittiness at his expense. Then Debbie joined in, speaking in the most somber tone she could mimic, and pronounced, "Ladies and gentlemen, let's take this a step farther and market this innovative concept. We'll have sperm stations on every corner. And we'll label the donors as Regular, Super Plus, and Premium. That's the only way the DoRights can make an informed decision about their bodies!"

By this time, Ben gave up all pretense of annoyance and laughed with the rest of them. The women probably would never admit openly that they enjoyed making the men feel uncomfortable. Instead, they called it joking, office-variety humor. But there were a few women who confided in each other, and they firmly agreed that they liked the taste of revenge. They even intimated to each other that they were looking at men through different eyes—quite possibly the eyes of a primate.

The somewhat tame ridicule continued to erupt within the walls of TriCubed as Meagan stopped by Eric's desk and asked, "Say Eric, why do DoRights buy sneakers with steel tips?"

Before Eric could respond with any decent retort, Meagan rushed ahead, chuckling before she finished the sentence, "It's simple, Eric, really easy. She wants to kick the sperm-spewer out of bed when he's finished, so she can get back to her tennis game!"

Although the jesting remained good-spirited, more than one male employee winced every time he became the object of a sperm joke, knowing—or maybe slimly hoping—that certain human habits would remain uncompromised. DoRights were still different. After all, *Homo sapiens* had engaged in long term partnerships for thousands of years. It couldn't possibly change overnight, could it? And that disquieting thought went unanswered as men felt the undercurrents of sexism sail shamelessly through their workplace.

What BrickWell observed along with his research team was that DoRights needed the affiliation with other females, not males, when the day ended. Manifestations of a united womankind, they affectionately huddled together, energetically ranted in ape chatter, gustily ate with each other and familiarly lay side by side in their sleep. They protected their sisterhood and could even be trusted to hug or reprimand each other's young. But that group companionship was vital for the DoRight's survival. She needed her species' company—she needed to belong. Assured she could go back to her clan at night, she performed her duties with vigor. In isolation, she never left the room, but sat in a corner with wide frightened eyes, holding her baby and refusing to eat.

Most interesting of all was to watch the adaptability of humans to their new-found living time-savers. Certainly, those people with greater flexibility were the ones who bought the clan in the first place. They were the kind who adjusted to their hairy, humanlike creatures quickly. They were the type who loved animals and didn't mind the extra noise before bedtime or the occasional mishap a DoRight toddler might get into. They were usually people who appreciated the additional assistance so much that they couldn't help but be nice to these creatures.

The presence of the DoRights in the home seem to tame the humans as well, for the DoRights brought a certain protection to the hearth. They were fiercely loyal and any intruder would be up against several powerful brutes, who bared their teeth and scared the interloper away with their fierce verbal pandemonium. Although aggression had been bred out of them, they acted as super-sensitive burglar alarms drawing attention to any misfortune with the shrill of their voices.

By 2006, DoRights were found in homes across America

and were being exported to countries around the globe. TriCubed was destined to become the next Coca Cola. Of course, the animal rights activists were starting to kick up their heels and scream accusations about brown bondage. But it was hard to take them seriously because the DoRights appeared quite content in their man-made environment.

There were some rather strong arguments suggesting that this was the best thing yet to happen to man and beast. If they lived together in a compatible setting, they would get to know each other better and improve on Nature's original intent for harmony. And there were statistics to show that in households with DoRights, child abuse and wife beating were non-existent.

As TriCubed's profits continued to soar, those who could afford a clan grew to understand and, perhaps, even love their extended family of brutes. Little did they realize that a small but growing voice of discontent was spreading like a virus through the ranks of unemployed service workers.

Seven

When BrickWell introduced the DoRights to the country, he hoped to generate more leisure in people's lives. But sometimes good intentions gravitate wayward. While some found extra time, others found themselves out of work, dispossessed by altered apes. Five years ago, on March 9th, an anniversary commemorating anguish, Angie worked her last day for the WonderWinds. The family became proud owners of a DoRight clan, and they didn't need a live-in maid anymore. Five years ago, and still Angie hadn't found steady work.

She found part-time jobs here, temporary jobs there, but, by and large, she was dependent on her welfare checks, the Church, and the City Enabling Agency. There just seemed to be fewer and fewer opportunities for unskilled labor. At 55 years old, Angie needed to keep working, she wanted to keep working. But she certainly couldn't walk into a company and operate a computer. She always helped people, either by cleaning houses, caring for children, or working in fast food restaurants. She never asked for much, just enough to get by, enough to make her feel like a real person again—not a leech.

Angie liked to work. It gave her a reason to get up every morning, a place to go, and people to see. When she worked, she felt she belonged. And she wanted so much to belong. She never belonged anywhere.

Her dad walked out when she was six years old. Her mother (God rest her soul) tried the best she could, but with Angie, Douglas, and Carver, it had been too much. The poor woman couldn't earn enough money for the needy family, even though she traveled from town to town looking for jobs. So she just gave up. She stopped. She stopped talking, stopped bathing, stopped combing her hair or dressing, and finally stopped eating. She lay in bed and stared. All day long, her glassy eyes gazed out, hiding the turmoil within.

The three children tried to feed her. "Please, Mommy, you've got to eat."

"Aw, Angie, she ain't gonna eat nothing."

"Don't say that, Douglas. She's got to eat."

"Angie, can't you see? She doesn't even hardly know us."

"But Carver," Angie gulped through her child-tears, "we got to get her better. We just got to!"

"Don't cry, Angie," Douglas murmured, as he tried to pry his younger sister off the bed. "We'll figure out something."

But no amount of youthful deliberation could induce their mom to swallow food, and in the end, Carver told his fourth grade teacher about the family's dilemma. The next day, some doctor-looking men came into the apartment and put their mother on a stretcher and then left. Just like that. No Mommy. Poof! Vanished! Angie never saw her again, but she saw those eyes her whole life. Those bulging eyes haunted her, blaring that it was her fault Mommy gave up. Maybe if she had been less trouble, maybe if she had learned to cook at six years old, Mommy might not have gone away. And if Mommy had gotten better, she'd never have to see those eyes. They darted in and out of her memories, accusing her of not being a better child.

After that, Angie remembered the orphanage, the foster homes, and finally being on her own. But she always missed her Mommy. She missed sitting by the bed, brushing the long black hair, smoothing the curls with her little fingers, and then brushing some more. She missed resting her head next to Mommy's shoulder, even if Mommy didn't say anything. Those were the best moments of her life, when she took care of Mommy. And those were the moments she longed for most of all.

Then she lost touch with her brothers. The last she heard, Carver went to Alaska in `98 to find work, and Douglas was killed twenty years ago in a drug raid. She always knew Douglas would get into trouble. He went wrong in high school and never got right. So Angie was all by herself, and she wanted very much to be part of a family, any family—she wanted to fit in somewhere.

Last Monday at the Employment Office, she saw a flyer haphazardly posted outside the door. In big letters was the question: **WHY ARE THE DORIGHTS STEALING YOUR WAGES?** Then in smaller letters, it read: **Do something now. You can make a difference!**

Angie was curious. In a way, the paper was right. The DoRights were stealing her jobs. Look at the WonderWinds. They went and bought a clan and could care less about Angie. Mrs. WonderWind told her they were sorry, but the DoRights were cheaper in the long run. Besides, the children took a shine to the little chimps. Then the missus said they'd like to recommend her, but many of their friends were considering buying clans also. What could Angie say? How could she compete with biotechnology? Either machines or animals displaced the workers, and the unemployed were left helpless. Nobody needed her anymore, and she felt black and blue, sort of bruised, like a discarded blanket you don't use ever again.

But this flyer intrigued her, so she called the phone number. She figured she had nothing to lose since she had nothing anyway. The woman on the other end of the phone answered,

"UHLF, may I help you?"

Tentatively, Angie offered, "I seen your flyer, ma'am, and I was calling about it."

"That's wonderful, miss. Just for our records, what's your name?"

"I ain't gonna get in trouble, am I?"

"No, no, we just like to get everyone's name, so we can keep track of our callers. We get a lot of interested people."

"My name's Angie, ma'am. Angie Cutler. All's I wanted was to find out what the flyer means."

"And my name's Ellen. Well, Angie, UHLF is the Union for the Human Labor Force, and we represent people. All the people who work or were working in the service industry."

"That's me, Miss Ellen. I used to work for Mr. and Mrs. WonderWind, but lately, I just can't find work nowhere!"

"Angie, you've called the right place. We're here to help you. It's unemployed people like yourself that make up a large part of our membership. This is what we're trying to change. You deserve work!"

"It's just that my job is now being done by DoRights, Miss Ellen. How can I get any work when DoRights are there first?"

"But that's what we're about, Angie. The urgent reform we want to put in effect calls for eliminating the DoRights. Get rid of them. Those job-stealing apes don't belong in the labor force!"

And Angie felt her prayers had been answered when she replied, "I couldn't agree more, Miss Ellen. I couldn't..." But her voice cracked, and she didn't want her five years worth of collected tears to embarrass her in front of such an important person, so she remained silent, leaving her unfinished sentence floating somewhere through the receiver.

"Come to our meeting tonight, Angie. You'll like the people there."

Beaming, Angie hung up the phone, her empty world suddenly filled with promise. She let loose a deep sigh, permitting her psyche to temporarily burrow in the fleeting instant of anticipation. Maybe she found a group who wanted her, who wouldn't fire her. Maybe, after a long lifetime, Angie finally found a family.

But Tully wasn't concerned about Angie's hopes or the plight of displaced workers wanting to belong again, wanting community, where shared joys balanced gently in the midst of exposed sorrows. Euphoric, Tully pressed the gas pedal harder as he left SeaBank, vacating the stains of his abundant devastation. His body drove the van, but his mind reran the night's mission in glorious detail.

Ten miles out of town, he stopped at a pay phone. "Job accomplished, sir!" he buoyantly whispered through the instrument.

"Perfect, Tully. Perfect. This is the beginning!" exclaimed AceArrow. "But Frank, are you sure you weren't seen?"

Jesus fucking Christ! What does this guy take me for? A novice? "No sir. It went off as planned. When I execute an invasion, I choose the best moment to strike, and I'm sure we spent only a few minutes at each siege. The men were beautiful: fast, efficient, thorough."

AceArrow's pleasure seeped through the phone, "Good work, kid. Good work."

Tully never heard the compliment. Instead, he responded to the word *kid*. Was AceArrow serious? *Kid?* Is this bastard shitting me? *Kid?* Tully was a fucking general, a leader, a king. *Kid?* AceArrow had no idea who he was actually talking to. And with that knowledge blanketing his scratched pride, Tully hung up the phone, suddenly lost in the fantasy of future raids, AceArrow's disrespect slowly decomposing into some retrievable slot of Tully's brain.

Unwarned, Francie and Reba walked up the stairs, taking for granted that their privileged sanity was still secure. They had carefully carved out their shelter in the universe, but neither one questioned its fragility. Neither one knew that Tully had silently encroached on their asylum. Not even Josh, when he blurted, "Hurry up, Mom. I have to go to the bathroom."

"Hey Josh, there's a spider crawling over there. Watch out!"

"Oh no, there isn't, April. You're lying."

"Yes, yes, there really is. Look, you can see it. Now there's two of `em."

Amid the taunting, Francie was fumbling for her keys at the front door. Everyone crowded around, ready to spring toward their own private space. Real family meant playing together but also letting go. The past few hours had been spent in the kind of dinner discussion that ranged from soccer games to boyfriends and from TV shows to Rockazz music, whatever tantalizing topics might interest ages that spanned six years old to seventeen. Usually, the younger ones were cast out of the conversation, but somehow belonging to this group helped them get on with the business of growing up. So they watched and imitated and worried about getting their share of pizza, french fries, identity.

But now that the evening was used up, the movie over, the older kids were anxious to retreat to their sequestered territory and touch their personal lives once again. The little ones hovered a bit closer to Francie, not yet ready to accept the pronouncement of "Bedtime!"

Francie pushed the door open, and a whiff of vanilla hit her nose. A scent so strong, she felt she was standing in the bosom of a giant sponge cake and would have to eat her way out to civilization. But the air was quiet—strangely quiet—and the quiet was smothered by the smell.

"Hey Mom, what's that smell? Can I have some?"

Before Francie could respond to Sara, Reba asked, "Francie, did you bake a cake before we left? Boy, you sure used a lot of vanilla."

"Reba, I don't know what the hell that is! After the phone call, I dashed out of here 'cause everyone was waiting. I'm going to look in the kitchen."

As she started to walk toward the kitchen, Francie noticed the door to the enclosed porch where the DoRights slept was wide open. That was strange. They constantly kept it closed. Although the DoRights were faithful to their human hosts, they relished their privacy when the clan came together for the evening, and they punctually closed their door. It was their time, their room, their right. But, Francie reasoned, the alluring bouquet of vanilla probably enticed them to surrender their seclusion. After all, a lullaby sniffed is just as soothing as a melody hummed. Tonight, the DoRights must have smelled themselves to sleep.

"Reba, why don't you go into the kitchen and see if something spilled. I'll be right there."

While some of the kids followed Reba, others ran upstairs, uninterested in the bewitching aroma. They had to resume real life. Their mothers could manage the mundane.

Hurriedly, Francie walked over to close the connecting door between the living room and the darkened porch lit only by an nearly full moon. Convinced that the floating fragrance emanated from a kitchen calamity, she wanted to get on with the evening, put the kids to bed, have a cup of decaf, and go over notes from today's sessions while the issues were still fresh in her mind. Perhaps one of the babies had pushed the door ajar. Sometimes a DoRight youngster didn't realize its own strength; without a doubt, the animals were pure muscle.

Absentmindedly, Francie reached out to shut the door. She wasn't even looking into the DoRight room as much as she was purely operating by rote. You see an open door, you close it. But somewhere with that trivial act, her eyes shifted as her nose picked up the pungent vanilla odor, and in that imperceptible movement, Francie entered a netherworld that scraped her vision raw. Go back. Go back three seconds. Go back, eyes, to the innocence that was minutes ago. Return, brain, to my unspoiled optimism of faith. Don't let my mind be raped like this.

But there was no returning to moments passed. There never is. For a second, Francie wanted to vomit, cleanse her body of food, of sight, of feeling. Quickly, the instant nausea subsided when she realized she wasn't alone. There were children in the next room, thirty feet away, and Francie willed herself to step inside.

She knew she wasn't prepared for the scene that slashed her eyes, but she also knew she had to play the warrior, the protector, the shield. She, alone, stood between her children and the visual terror that gouged her sight. All she saw was blood, blood everywhere, splotches splattered on the walls, the windows, the ceiling, and more blood lying in pools on the floor. Vanilla blood. That's what she smelled. Vanilla blood.

As Francie's eyes cut through the thick red, she distinguished bodies heaped around, lifeless, contorted, gnarled bodies of DoRight mothers and DoRight children—bodies that looked like they were gnawed and slashed and ripped. And then Francie realized she wasn't only looking at bodies, but also at body parts. A gore-soaked arm was tossed in the corner; a mangled leg was flung against the wall; a head, grotesque in its angle, with eyes popping in shock, was hanging by a tendon, ready to roll along the floor. Battered, bloody pieces, hallowed sockets, spilled brains, torn, deflated, emptied intestines—breath cramped, crushed, crimped. Life wrung out like a soaking sock, squeezed, and then squeezed again to remove any drop of vitality.

No nightmare came close to forewarning Francie of a scene such as this. The brutality of her vision was beyond any horror film she ever watched. Stiff, misshapen forms sprawled where once affectionate, energetic, chattering creatures used to play. The smell of the vanilla blood fused with the hairy ripped bodies assaulted Francie's senses.

She wanted to plug her eyes, her nose, her ears to the grotesque art of savagery. But she couldn't seal her mouth, and she whimpered—no scream, no shout, no roar—just the whiny, shivery sounds of a frightened little girl, broken sobs spluttering from her throat. For the moment, Francie felt like a lost child who had opened the door to Hell, the door to ultimate damnation, where the reality of her eyesight would scorch itself indelibly on her brain.

Lost innocence was not in the surrendering of your virginity, or in bearing the economic pressures of a large family, or in fighting aggressive lawyers. One's sense of self always remained in touch, and you could get on with life. But at this moment, Francie knew she had lost a part of her soul she'd never regain. She confronted pure evil—unadulterated, squalid, violent evil—and she'd never be safe again. Whoever or whatever committed this atrocity could get to anyone, to her, to her children, her friends—anyone.

Francie understood what her English teacher years ago used to preach: "Nature is indifferent." Never before had a fact been made so clear. If the most savage act of brutality could befall the most loving of creatures, there was no benevolent force in the universe. The DoRights were kind, they were gentle, they were caring—they were motherhood at its finest. The chimps lived an uncomplicated life of service, responsibility, and attachment. They labored, they parented, and they remained fiercely protective of their clan. The DoRights took care of their babies; they took care of each other—and they bestowed the rare gift of joy upon their human home.

What kind of human being or animal would enter this serenity and contaminate it with the disease of bestiality? The DoRights harmed no one. They worked, they played, they loved. And yet, some horror out there crept in, uninvited, to rip their bodies to shreds, and they died a gruesome death—no dignity, no mercy, no hope. Just pain, pain for themselves, pain for their children, utter agony in their last breath.

Before Francie could calm her mind, she heard a few of the family crossing over to her side of the room, and like some distant echo, Reba's words were trying to penetrate her isolation. "Francie, the kitchen's fine. The vanilla's coming from here. Can't you smell it?"

"Oh, Reba," Francie whispered to herself. "If you could smell what I see, you'd run away—forever."

They knew from her hunched shoulders that something was wrong. They saw her turn convulsively, trying to tell them something with choked intensity. But, for moments, no sounds stumbled from her mouth. Instead, her face reflected the pain of a thousand year old woman trying to interpret the incomprehensible. Francie never recognized who saw what, which children's eyes registered the mutilation and opened their sleep to the nightmares of inevitable fear. She quickly slammed the door and yelled, "Away! Everyone away from the room. They're dead. They're all dead. They've been murdered!"

EIGHT

What Francie didn't know, along with nine other uninformed families, was that certain DoRights were placed randomly in ten clan households. These were special DoRights who had been taught the rudiments of human speech. They could speak English. Granted, it was a broken English, somewhat like the language of a two year old, but they had jumped the infinite verbal gap between human and ape and could now communicate with words. These special creatures were called ChangeOvers, and they were TriCubed's brainchildren.

The reason regular chimps couldn't speak was twofold: they were born without a voice box. And they didn't have the brain wiring that was required for language acquisition. The genetic engineering responsible for creating chimps with an anatomical box, capable of producing speech, and brain circuits, capable of learning language, was far easier than teaching the chimp its first word. Even though the altered species was biologically ready to speak, the animal remained mute during the teaching sessions.

The researchers tried every which way to encourage speech. They pronounced a word and then shaped the chimp's lips, trying to get it to expel air through its compressed mouth. When that didn't work, they opened the chimp's mouth, inserted a tongue depressor and pushed the tongue against the back of the throat. At the same time, the teacher held the ape's nostrils shut, so the creature had to expel air through its throat. That burst of air always approximated the sound of *c* in *cup*. The chimp uttered the syllable while its anatomy was distorted, but never repeated it without a gag in its mouth. The babies still continued to gibber away in their own ape talk, vocalization unfathomable to the human scientists.

However, one ape-child was fascinated with a gold necklace worn by Elaina SunRise. Each day, Elaina would come in, hug her adoring chimp, and let it play with the pendant. Every time the ape did something correct, Elaina rewarded it with sixty seconds of pendant play. But one day, the gold chain broke, and Elaina left the necklace overnight at the jewelers. The next day, without the gold treat, the little chimp refused to participate in any of the learning directives for the entire session and just scampered away from Elaina after each command.

When she walked in the next morning, Elaina hugged the chimp and continually repeated the word *hello*. The baby, forgetting about yesterday's loss, expected Elaina to have the necklace and kept jumping on her to find it. All Elaina did was repeat *hello* till some semblance of the sound popped from the chimp-child's mouth. Immediately, Elaina produced the gold pendant. After sixty seconds, she hid it and repeated the process.

By the end of the day, the chimp pronounced ten words, and history was made. A fascination, an accident, the right animal, the right teacher—everything miraculously came together at that moment, and TriCubed had its talking chimp. One vocal DoRight gradually led to another, since apes are great imitators, and BrickWell had eighteen talking apes after two years.

Still, the great mystery remained. Would these gifted primates give birth to babies who could acquire language in their early years? No one knew because the initial eighteen ChangeOvers had not reached reproductive age yet. Some of them were close. Thirteen of the females were over nine years old, and BrickWell knew that within the year, all thirteen of those adolescents might become sexually active.

So he waited, waited for time to touch these energetic chimps and endow them with the biological beauty to create another living creature. Certainly, he was anxious, but at the same time, he amassed a tremendous amount of patience with this project. He had to. Primates were not machines. They responded in their own way, on their own time, and if they felt unpressured yet loved, there was no telling the rewards they'd grant their human researchers.

BrickWell was willing to wait, for he had tapped into his ancestral treasure chest. He suspected golden opportunities that man could not have fantasied thirty years ago. Now these opportunities were literally days away, and Adam BrickWell, Science's eager emissary, would hear the impressions of an animal fifteen million years old. How did they perceive the world of humans? What did they think about their closest, hairless, blue-eyed cousin? Did they have any primitive memories stamped into their DNA that would shed light on the dawn of Civilization?

BrickWell would be there to take a voyage back in time, and he would hear, firsthand, how prehistoric man must have viewed his earth as he searched for food and shelter. The new Columbus, BrickWell stood poised, ready to discover primitive patterns of human thought. Most definitely, not space, not the ocean's floor, but the brain was destined to be the next New World, the untapped region that could give birth to an unequaled human renaissance of precious ideas, solutions, explanations, interpretations. This is the territory of invention and prediction. This is the territory of kindness, generosity, and morality.

If this unexplored country was the key to man's civilized survival, BrickWell wanted to be there at the beginning, helping the humane prevail in our humanity. Now he felt closer than ever in bringing about his life's purpose: the human-chimp reunion.

"It happened, Bette. One of our ChangeOvers gave birth today. A healthy, wide-eyed baby boy."

Bette grabbed BrickWell's hand, "Adam, that's the next step! You're nearly there. I get goose bumps thinking about this new chimp generation coming into being. We're like their grandparents."

"That's funny you should say what you did, Bette. When I watched the birthing of the infant, that's exactly how I felt. You know I try to stay objective when it comes to my research, but each new baby captures a place in my heart. Many days, I walk out of the lab feeling like the grandest father around. In some unique way, I'm related to these glorious primates."

"You'd better stock up on birth announcements, dear, because you have several other ChangeOvers ready to go into labor soon."

And BrickWell smiled, thinking of a future where he became the teacher, the student, and the observer at the same time—a future filled with revelations he had yet to hear.

But neither press nor public received the forgotten birth notices because the ChangeOver project remained classified. It was too soon to tell the world. Data on the ChangeOver's adaptability to clans and human households needed to be collected. So the research team opted for home trials and placed ten ChangeOver mothers with their infants in homes across the country.

The scientists postponed the teaching of language to the babies in favor of observing the infants interact with speech-producing humans. Would the chimps, now owning the physical apparatus capable of voice, acquire language naturally like our own toddlers? It was a compelling theory, worthy of being tested in the field. Unanimously they let the marketing department place their new breed of ape in selected homes and watched.

During periodic visits, the researchers would pull the adult ChangeOvers aside and talk with them. But so far, no infants had spoken their first word to the researchers or the clan owners. Nor had the adult ChangeOvers ever communicated verbally to their human families. If speech spilled from the creature's mouth, certainly one of the owners would have called in or relayed this information to a company rep. But, as of yet, none of the DoRight homes reported anything unusual to the visiting evaluators. Assuming, or at least earnestly anticipating, that the young chimps knew speech, the examiners concluded the toddlers were keeping the words to themselves. But every scientist on the project believed, or hoped, or even prayed that when the youngsters returned to the lab, they would show language mastery. It was there. It had to be. But the chimps didn't know the gift they had yet.

Since the experiment was only eleven months old and still fraught with more questions than conclusions, TriCubed remained reluctant to release its findings. The scientists weren't sure if the ChangeOvers would become restless with their community of DoRights, now that they acquired another language. And if the ChangeOvers couldn't work side by side with the DoRights, they'd have to stay at the lab till more ChangeOvers came of age.

No one was familiar with where this specialized knowledge would lead, so the few in the company privy to this classified information thought surveillance for the time being offered the best procedure. As long as their team made recurrent visits, they'd rather act cautiously for awhile—at least for another year, when they could trade the ChangeOvers for regular DoRights and study their prized species in a controlled setting.

BrickWell had no problem keeping the ChangeOvers a secret, for he was not the kind of man who craved celebrity. He only desired bio-replacement, his theory for scientific renovation, a sort of regenerative remodeling that put the earth back on track. And with a loud segment of animal rights activists rejecting DoRights, he was pretty clear that the ChangeOvers would intensify their anger even further.

Until he was sure that language acquisition would benefit the singular species man/chimp, absolutely no one but his select research team would know of his talking apes. Premature publicity might sabotage the entire project, and he didn't want his ChangeOvers carelessly catapulted into the spotlight. They'd be on talk shows across the country, and for some reason, imagining a ChangeOver being interviewed on *The ToNight Show* was not the type of future he wanted played out for his whiz kids.

A myriad of assorted dreams was taking place at TriCubed now that the government had released permits on Applied Physiological Engineering. One research team set out to prove that if chimps had additional leisure time because they didn't have to continuously find food or fend off rival chimps, and were given paints or other artistic materials, these animals would draw—and they would draw magnificently. In fact, they had several primates who mastered brush painting, finger painting, and pencil, chalk, and crayon drawing. Pierre-Picasso, their most prolific artist, produced 33 paintings in one day and threw a tantrum when his brush was taken away.

In order to prove that this was more than an experiment waiting to be written up for some esoteric journal, the scientists frequently sent the art work to major exhibits across the US. Of course, the judges didn't know the artists were apes. Neither did the human buyers. But a handful of chimps was making quite a name for themselves in the art world, and soon, TriCubed was going to reveal their true identity.

Another research group worked on the body hair, trying to develop a much shorter and lighter haired creature. They wanted their apes to resemble humans as much as possible. There were even plans on the drawing board to restructure muscle, so that the ape would have shorter arms and longer legs.

BrickWell felt the closer chimps came to their human counterpart, the safer all primates would become. Even though man kills his own, it becomes, at least, an ethical consideration. We don't think twice about hunting, fishing, or chasing. It's our recreation and, possibly, our food. But so far, not too many humans have stalked or eaten other humans. Perhaps, BrickWell hoped, he could get man to also include primates in that protected zone. Perhaps, he could get man to see the ape as his closest and, therefore, most defensible relative.

Of course, the practical goal was to provide as human an ape servant as they could. This way, they'd have a competitive edge over robotics and the use of robot helpers in the home. Although that industry had been around for many years, it never captured the hearts and minds of people the way the DoRights had. It must be that link we have with our evolutionary roots, but America and the world took to the DoRights the same way they took to their dogs, their cats, and their horses.

Inside each human is an affinity for other living creatures, and the chance to live side by side with a species so closely related to humankind was an adventure whose time had come. Now that TriCubed was the market leader, their continued superiority depended on research and development: a better product meant an even more endowed DoRight. They had carved out their particular corner, and no one was going to take it away from them.

Nine

Francie wanted to run away, run from reality, from responsibility, from that bogeyman in the shadows, that huge mouth of danger ready to devour any unsuspecting soul in its midst. What ogre lurked behind her lightless closet door? As a child, she could readily escape her nightmarish torments by crawling under the covers and hiding from the evil. Although she outgrew her fears of the darkened room, the murky corners, the unknown under her bed, she never remained a hundred percent sure that something, someone, wasn't out there, ready to pounce when she was most vulnerable.

She would have traded places in a moment for the two year old's luxury of being able to run into her mother's arms and feel safe. But she had nowhere to run. She was the mother now, she was the safety zone, and she was damn scared. Somehow, her several horrific fantasies never came close to the stomach-turning facts she now faced. What caused this carnage? Who wanted to butcher these gentle creatures? Why would someone destroy Good and create chaos, create hurt, create sorrow?

Francie never understood why anyone intentionally harmed a living thing, human or animal. She hated the wince of pain that a sarcastic remark wrought. She, who loved most sports, frowned upon boxing. When Francie heard about parents who battered their children, her first thought was that these adults ought to be incarcerated till the child was 21. Then the psychologist in her took over, and she reluctantly succumbed to behavior modification theory.

She attributed wars, executions, viciousness to a less evolved human state because it wasn't natural to hurt your fellow human. She had watched enough babies to know that a child comes into this world full of trust, full of love, full of grace, and something outside that child distorts his affection for others. No, it definitely wasn't natural to harm.

Reba took the kids into another room to try to talk to them while Francie phoned the police. After the call, she experienced an uneasy feeling. Is that all? Just stand here and wait? Do nothing? Pass time? Hope? Somehow, that was impossible. She had to act now. Passivity was not part of Francie's framework, and she felt compelled to do something, anything.

Intuitively, she realized she needed to talk to someone immediately, not hours later. Because her fears would grow to gigantic proportions if she didn't share her tragedy with some person who had been there before, who had seen death, violence, nature's underbelly, firsthand. But who? If she called her parents, they'd be so traumatized, she'd end up taking care of them. And Reba was best at what she was doing right then, calming the children. There was Sam, her close friend from graduate school. But, at this moment, she didn't want a theoretical explanation of her fear—she wanted strength. Someone else's strength. Someone else's shared experience. Another rather large shoulder to lean on for just a minute.

In an instant, his face blended into her horror. Why not? He would know. He had been there before. Why not call him now? She was going to anyway, right? He might have been her next racquetball match, so why not call him as a friend? He was a kind of friend, sort of. Even if their comradery merely revolved around their parleys at the racquetball court, she knew him enough to joke with. And Francie believed that when two people could create humor between them, they already had the start of a healthy friendship.

Besides, she could never explain to anyone who wasn't a part of it, but the devout racquetball players shared a community among themselves. They were the particular competitors who played year in and year out; consequently, their familiar faces guaranteed a certain loyalty when help was needed. She couldn't say why, but Francie knew she could call any one of her partners, and they'd respond. They were those kind of people. But right now, the only person she wanted to talk to was FD. He'd know what to do.

In addition to his celebrated professional reputation, he was a first-rate racquetball player, fast, precise, and indisputably a true sportsman. Francie heard more than one person comment on FutureDick's modesty, remarking on his ability to make you feel like a winner, even when you just lost the match. That was assurance enough for Francie.

You could tell a lot about a person's character by how he played ball. Was he fair? Was he generous? Courteous? Or did he complain when you won and gloat when you lost? Inevitably, the inner self demurely exposed its quintessence on the court. Francie usually found out if she could trust someone by how they acted inside those high white walls. Instinctively, Francie knew she could trust FD.

Although she understood she must be strong for the children, must somehow role model bravery, she wanted to translate this terror to someone else. And that someone else had to know about crime. She sure as hell had no experience in that area. But she needed to draw strength from somewhere. Otherwise, she'd be no good to herself or her children.

Never had there been an obligation she walked away from.

All through her life, she assumed the full load for herself, her family, her career, but every once in a while, she wanted to stop playing Wonder Woman and play normal. She wanted a reprieve from total responsibility. She wanted to enlist someone else's help because, this time, this weight wasn't about money or a broken car—it was about a broken life, many broken lives—and she had no guarantee that the killer wouldn't return to slaughter the rest of the household. She'd be willing to die for her children, but she wasn't willing to have her children die for anyone—or anything.

As he thought about Tendra, Bounty, his destroyed dreams, the blare of the phone jolted FutureDick out of his reverie. He knew the phone would ring. He knew someone on the other end would be asking for help, and once again his consciousness jumped into challenge mode. He would be tested, as he had been tested his whole life, to find answers. He never minded the perplexity. Wasn't that the essence of existence, the reason man had been given a brain? In fact, he rather enjoyed pitting his wits against what initially seemed the unsolvable, the hidden.

Yet with each new case, his pursuit of the intriguing puzzle grew increasingly frigid, his sensibilities blunted by some uninvited arctic blast. FutureDick's continual encounter with malevolence gave him what he called "frostbite of the soul." Over the years, violence perpetuated greater violence. Brutality, like an art form, sought higher, more intense levels. And each year, his stomach turned a little more sour as it confronted the inhumanity of our race.

"Hello, FutureDick speaking."

"Hi, FD, it's Francie Franks." She hesitated briefly, as if she had trouble formulating her words. When FutureDick didn't respond, she tossed out dispiritedly, "You've seen me, FD. I'm the woman who kicks you off the racquetball court on Wednesday nights." Oh God, let him remember. Give him some inkling of the me who's behind this telephone call.

"How ya doing, Francie? Sometimes I wonder if you walk

around with a stop-watch. I've been meaning to tell you how accurate you are with your knock on the door."

But Francie didn't pick up on his humor. And FutureDick's words floated through the maze of fiber optics, unchallenged and unrequited. Murmuring she had been meaning to call him for a game, she caught her breath and then splashed out with, "Something's happened. Something terrible has happened!"

"Go on, Francie. I hear you."

"I've just called the police, but I wanted to talk to you personally. I know what type of work you're in, and to tell you the truth...oh damn it, FD, I'm scared. I'm really frightened for my family, and I need someone I can trust. Someone who might know what to do. Can you come over immediately?"

At that moment, the buzz for call-waiting bleeped into FutureDick's ear, and he responded quickly, "Sure, Francie, I'll be there—hold on a minute."

"Hello, FutureDick speaking."

"FutureDick, it's Adam BrickWell calling."

Switching between calls, FutureDick took Francie's address, assuring her he'd be there soon, and turned his attention to BrickWell, the famous SeaBank scientist. "What can I do for you, Dr. BrickWell?"

"You come highly recommended, FutureDick, and I'm not going to mince words. I need your services pronto. I'm in the middle of a catastrophe and..." BrickWell caught his breath, needing to pause before uttering the next words: "My DoRights are being murdered! They're being torn apart!"

"You're speaking in the present tense, Dr. BrickWell, like it's happening right now."

"It is! It sure as hell is! The police just called, and they're responding to five different clan slayings tonight. There's been a mass murder, a goddamn bloodletting. And I'm numb, completely numb. I feel like someone's just punched me in the stomach."

"Let me get more information from the police, Dr. BrickWell, and I'll be there at ten tomorrow."

"Thanks, FutureDick," BrickWell said shakily as he hung up.

FutureDick stared at the receiver in his hand. The silence had been broken, the peace polluted, and depravity raised its ugly head—once again. The chase now began, but this time, he felt he was miles behind in the race. This was a new one. An animal killer? Violence had a funny way of shifting faces, and nothing was immune to its vengeance, not even dumb beasts of burden.

As he drove to Francie's, he wondered if her call was connected to BrickWell's. Francie Franks, the woman with the ever present smile. On the hour, she would knock at the court door and say, "Time's up, guys. It's mine now!" They'd joke about who was going to take who to the cleaners and then switch places. She'd walk in, he'd walk out. But she had a nice way about her. He knew that under those big protective eye glasses and sweatband resided an agreeably cute face, which seemed to perpetually smile—except when she was in the midst of a game.

FutureDick would go upstairs to the balcony every once in a while and watch Francie play. She was a strong player, not as powerful as him, but quick on her feet. She played an intellectual game, continually trying to place the ball where her opponent would least suspect it. The only recourse some of her competitors could use was to overwhelm her. They'd get so frustrated with her cunning that they'd hit the ball as hard as they could, and Francie's genius was no match for their raw strength. But she never gave up. She simply raised her racquet, convinced she would demolish her opponent on the next rally.

FutureDick liked that in a person, particularly in a woman. He appreciated determination, but he respected tenacity. To never give up showed a certain constancy in your character; you were willing to go to the ends of the earth for what you believed. Consequently, you could be trusted because you could be depended upon to never walk away.

Perceiving this strength in Francie, FutureDick thought more than once about asking her out. But it was awkward.

Usually he was walking out, and she was walking in. The timing was all wrong. He'd go to shower and wind down. She was just gearing up. And by the time he strolled out of the sports center, his mind was on work or at least a hundred light years away from initiating a friendship.

So FutureDick looked forward to meeting Francie off their athletic turf. Who was the woman behind the player? She sounded tense. She sounded scared, not like the usually confident woman who relished kicking him off the court at exactly the right time. With her high top basketball shoes and fierce glint of competitiveness, she looked ready to face Genghis Khan and his hoards. Whatever it was, it had to be something quite devastating to knock the spirit out of Francie Franks.

And BrickWell, who blazed through several exhaustive years of trial and error, never letting the uncertainty prevent him from bravely walking into his lab each morning, also received a punch to his equilibrium. Nearly paralyzed with incredulity, he pondered the *who* and *why* of the crime. But the scientist, unknowingly, had made enemies, antagonists he never knew and probably would never meet: opponents such as Angie, who suffered from his success, or employees like Harold, who crumpled under his requirements.

Harold knew he shouldn't have done it. He had been with TriCubed for two years, and he knew the rules. But lately, he couldn't seem to control his need to drink. What started out as a happy hour after work grew to an evening with two six packs, then a shot before breakfast, drinks at lunch, and before he knew it, he was drinking all day long. Lunch had come and gone, and he wanted a drink. He needed a drink. So he went out to the car, grabbed his hidden bottle, and was about to return when he decided to sneak the bottle in. Who would know? It was two in the afternoon. Three more hours and he'd be finished working. Just in case he got thirsty toward late afternoon, he could grab a little nip.

Harold, no stranger to the company's regulations, was well aware that alcohol was forbidden at TriCubed—for anyone. If a janitor or secretary were caught drinking, they might get a warning. But any employee who worked in sensitive areas, particularly those areas that dealt with ape handling, was subject to immediate dismissal.

As a consumer chaperon, Harold was in charge of escorting potential customers through the DoRights' residences. It was a somewhat tricky job because you didn't want to bring too many strangers into the compound at any one time. The DoRights loved people, but they liked a few at a time. If one of them felt threatened, she'd set up a ruckus that ran through the entire compound and sometimes took days to diminish. This tension then affected the DoRights' capacity to learn, their sociability, and their willingness to meet customers. Thus, two days of closure meant two days of lost customers and potential damage to TriCubed's image as experts in the field of animal engineering.

In his job as liaison between DoRight and buyer, Harold had to make sure he closed each gate because the babies loved to wander off and explore new ground. After he showed the MerryMarks around the inner compound, he brought four DoRight mothers and their children into the outer compound to meet the couple. This way, the eight DoRights could become acquainted with their potential family before the actual transaction took place.

The outer compound sat on top of a small hill about a block from the parking lot, so it was removed from the front entrance that led out to the main road and, eventually five blocks later, to the freeway. While the MerryMarks were watching the DoRights practice folding laundry, Harold excused himself and went into his office for a drink. It was a slow day, and he figured since the MerryMarks was his last appointment, he could afford to finish the flask. All he had left to do was return the DoRights to their life station and bring the MerryMarks to the Customer Care Department.

Harold was feeling pretty good as he walked back to the compound. The liquor always had that softening effect. It just seemed to last shorter and shorter these days. He greeted the MerryMarks, left the DoRights to continue their chores, and walked the couple out of the compound to the Corporate Center. Then he returned to lead the clan back to their life station, blessing the saints for his cushy job. It couldn't get any better than this.

As he went to open the gate, his heart lurched. It wasn't completely shut. There was a foot and a half between the gate and the lock, the door wedged ajar by some phantom force, just enough room for its shadow to ease out, just enough space for a baby DoRight to leave the compound.

Don't panic, he thought. The clan was pretty engrossed in what they were doing. They probably didn't notice. He prayed they didn't notice. Where was his mind when he escorted the MerryMarks out? How could he have overlooked such a simple task?

Like a wild man, he ran to the DoRights, who looked as industrious as ever. One baby remained, sitting close to its mother. "God, my God. Where are the rest of the babies? Where the hell are they?"

Then he spotted another ape child playing with blocks in the grass. "Okay, Hal, you got two. Only a couple left. Look. Look by that tree. Don't forget the bushes near the work tables. Goddamn it, they've got to be here. You just aren't looking in the right place."

But all he continued to see were six DoRights. "Come on, guys, where are you? I know you're hiding. Don't panic, man. Control. Keep control."

Still, he only counted six, six goddamn DoRights. He couldn't stop the agitation in his brain as his mind washed in and out. For a few seconds, he'd be confronting the terror of his reality, and then, he'd go blank. His brain shut off—totally dark. No thoughts. No awareness. No sight. A blink of the eye, and the light bulb once more snapped on. Again the anxiety repeated its jolt through his veins, his heart, his gradually weakening legs. Like a wind up toy whose mechanism has malfunctioned, he redoubled his same steps around the outer compound, repetitively, monotonously, vainly looking for the two babies.

After a while, the DoRights stopped their task and looked at him. They started following him, not knowing what they were looking for, when one of the mothers realized her baby was gone. She began to moan while the next DoRight, aware that her baby was also missing, chimed in as well. Sensing their sisters were extremely upset, the other two mothers clinging onto their own babies, joined the commotion. It didn't take long till the dirge traveled to the inner compound, and anguish enveloped the heart of every DoRight in the facility. By this time, some managers headed into the area, and all Harold could say is, "Two babies are missing!"

"Are you kidding, Harold?"

"No sir, I can't find them. I've looked all over."

"What'd you say? I can hardly hear you."

Harold raised his head, looked PeakMarsh in the eyes, and with the utter boldness it takes to admit you've blown it, you've failed, clearly announced, "The babies have left the compound."

"How, Harold? They can't climb over the wall. Where could they have gone?"

But Harold couldn't speak. He had used up his courage when he mumbled his last few words to PeakMarsh. The shame he felt at that moment suppressed any syllables he could issue in his own defense. What could he say? He was supposed to close the goddamn gate, and he forgot? These things happen? What's the big deal? He wanted to scream with every ounce of sound he had left, "Ya know, sir, I'm human. I forget just like anyone else." Instead, all that floated from his larynx were silent phrases. He was mute. And the babies were gone.

Harold might not have been fired if the two babies had been

found alive, but with the company situated so close to the freeway, their chances were slim. Rush hour had started, and the babies scampered up the ramp to an army of speeding machines, each soldier weighing two thousand pounds. They crushed the little apes in a matter of minutes, without even realizing that living matter had entered their jungle of rubber, steel, and ferocity.

He never had a chance to explain himself. The managers immediately smelled his breath, brought him to GoldWorth, the division director, and Harold was terminated instantly. Although he knew he had made a mistake, Harold was angry. Very angry. They could have given him a warning. Jesus, these were babies, two trivial babies. How much could it matter? They weren't worth anything yet. Shit, he had been a reliable employee for two years, never complained, always came to work on time, and he was good with the DoRights. They liked him.

Yet that bastard GoldWorth looked him straight in the eyes and told him he had a drinking problem. Him? A drinking problem, just because he enjoyed taking a nip during the day? Of course, he denied it. He didn't have a goddamn drinking problem. He just liked to drink. That's all. Besides, it was none of GoldWorth's damn business, but he kept that last thought to himself. When the Director suggested he go to Alcoholics Anonymous or a treatment program, Harold bit his tongue till it bled. But he didn't answer back. He just wanted to get the hell out of there. He sure as shit wasn't going to call any more attention to himself now. He had lots of time for that.

"Look, Harold, you've been a good employee, but we have strict rules here. You know that."

"Yes sir, I do. But it'll never happen again."

"After you've been in AA for a year, come back here. I'm sure we can consider rehiring you then."

"But you don't understand, Mr. GoldWorth. I don't have a problem with alcohol. I had a beer at lunchtime. I'm sure that's what you smelled. But I was sober, sir. You don't get drunk from one beer."

"Sorry, Harold. Those are my terms. Get yourself into recovery, and we'll talk in a year."

That was it. His best job, ever. Finished. Kaput. The goddamn fucking nerve of them wanting him to go to AA! The hell he would. Who does GoldWorth think he is, interfering in the privacy of a man's life? He'd get the hell out of there, but they'd see him again. They sure would. He never took that kind of abuse from anyone before, and he'd be damned if he'd take it now.

Even after the story dropped out of the newspaper, the mistreatment Harold felt lingered for weeks. It wasn't fair. He deserved another chance. What right did they have to humiliate him like that? He'd show them. He'd show them all right. He wouldn't just get angry. He'd get even! And as he raised his drink to his mouth, visions of the compound writhing in flames danced through his whiskey-soaked brain.

TEN

FutureDick tried to stop staring at Francie. He never saw her dressed in anything else but gym shorts. With her full face revealed, not hidden behind the thickly rimmed plastic sport goggles, Francie looked beautiful—frightened, sad—but beautiful.

"Thanks for coming over, FD. God, am I glad to see you. I need help. I need it now, and I don't know where to go. I've called the police, but they're not here yet. And I wanted to talk to someone who, who..." Francie never finished. Instead, she looked at him and whispered, "Oh hell, FD. I'm frightened for my family. In fact, I'm terrified, and I really..."

Again she suspended mid-sentence as her voice choked, and the tears streamed down her face. She looked so forlorn, FutureDick would never have guessed that this was the same woman who ran circles around most of the other racquetball players. She touched him where no human had touched him for nineteen years. And as he put his arms around Francie to comfort her, he felt an ache in his heart, not the crushing weight of grief, of bereavement, but the tinge that reminded him he still had a heart. He still had a center that could be moved by feeling, by tenderness. He had kept the wall up for so long, he simply forgot that the heart was more than a muscle that pumped blood. It could also commiserate with another's urgency. It could respond.

Although he offered his strength mixed with whatever masculine protection went along with that offer to Francie, he realized that she would never know what she opened up for him. He had put his feelings to sleep. They weren't needed anymore. All they did was hurt his insides, and his goal was to stay as far removed from emotional ache as he could. No involvement, no passion or compassion, no response. Keep the little beating machine efficient but aloof. Keep the bloody bastard silent.

But something in Francie's need, in her willingness to share her concealed self with him, an almost stranger, resuscitated his hibernating heart, and he felt a strong desire to shield her. He knew her physical strength. He saw her power on the court. Yet she showed him her vulnerability as well and struck a prescient cord he thought had shriveled up years ago. He wanted his arm around her shoulder. He wanted to be needed by her as much as he wanted to defend her from harm.

Breathing deeply, he realized these were the first full breaths he had taken since his loss. They felt good. They felt whole. And he felt human as he stepped back into life once again, for this is what Francie offered him: the opportunity to vibrate, to feel, to live. Up to now, he pretended not to notice that his was a half-life, devoid of caring. Francie pulled his mask off. Unawares, she created the possibility for him to resurrect his emotions.

He didn't know where his awakened warmth would steer him, but for the first time in uncompromising years, in countless days and nights of shutting himself off, of shutting himself out, he was willing to let his heart take the lead instead of his head. He was willing to try feeling again.

Did you ever notice how the leaps in a lifetime take merely instants of our immediacy? A few seconds, and we find ourselves sitting atop a fresh emotional or intellectual plane. Yet FutureDick could neither examine nor luxuriate in his newfound universe, for Francie pulled away from his comfort and beseeched him with her frightened eyes.

"FD, I can't go back there. But see that room across the living room, the closed-in porch? We had a clan of DoRights sleeping there. Please go look."

"Francie, were you baking tonight? It smells like a cake factory in here."

"That's from the porch, FD. There's vanilla in there, but go see first."

FutureDick watched enough movies and participated in enough reality to be prepared for anything. He even fantasied a dead body lying in the middle of the floor or a room torn apart by a group of undisciplined apes gone on a rampage. For some reason, BrickWell's conversation didn't connect with him. Maybe he assumed that BrickWell's dead DoRights were at TriCubed. Maybe Francie's anguish momentarily blinded him. Maybe he still couldn't comprehend the senseless killing of innocent things. But he never imagined the unadulterated savagery that bashed his mind when he walked through the door into the sweet smell.

The ferocity with which this massacre took place had to come from the seeds of pure hate or pure madness. Why else would anyone invoke this sort of torture on another living thing? He stood there, trying to get his private investigator analytic gaze to work, but his objectivity remained remote. He couldn't distance himself. The violation of life was too complete.

And then he heard, "Help me. Please help me."

Where was it coming from?

"Help me. Please help me."

The voice was dim, but the words were clear. They were

emanating from a pile where one ape lay on top of another.

"Francie, come here. You've got to come," he called as he cautiously walked over to the mound of mutilated flesh. He had to be careful. The floor was slippery with blood, and he didn't want to destroy any evidence. Although, from what he could see, there was only death, not clues.

He noticed that the lock on the door to the living room had been broken. One of those cheap hook latches dangled from the side, and it looked like an arm had been thrown against the door with such fury that it bashed the hook. At the same time, the strong aroma of vanilla persisted in blatantly attacking his nostrils. Francie appeared at the broken doorway, and FutureDick motioned for her to come in.

"Help, help me."

Francie's eyes opened wide. Her look of disbelief convinced FutureDick that she was also a stranger in a strange land, a land of animals turned domestic, but also a place where apes had learned to speak. What had he called them? "Dumb beasts of burden?" At this moment, he was more the dumb beast, not this revisionist chimpanzee.

FutureDick looked at the ape on top of the pile. Her neck had been fractured and was hanging to the side, angled like a puppet whose master relinquished the strings. She was dead. She was definitely dead. He shoved her away with his foot and looked at the ape underneath. Blood covered her hair, creating the illusion of a slick, glistening body suit custom-tailored to fit over her hairy sheath, but her eyes were open. Pupils rigidly fixed, paralyzed with fright, they stared in alarm at FutureDick. Francie, who had been standing behind FutureDick, tentatively approached his side and called, "Emma. Emma, is that you?"

FutureDick remembered that these apes were helpers. They had names. Their owners knew how to tell them apart, knew how to recognize the individual features that distinguished one DoRight from another, the way we know which dog or which child belongs to us. Francie bent down and put her hand on

Emma's head. It was still warm. And Emma blinked her eyes. But there were no tears. There was only disbelief. Her brush with terror shocked her eyes into an appalling stare that would forever be afraid to close again. She looked at Francie and barely whispered, "Help. Please help."

Francie wanted to question Emma, to explore with her the ability to speak, to break the barrier between man and beast—actually communicate mind to mind. But Francie suppressed her curiosity for the moment. This was the wrong time and, most certainly, the wrong place to construct a dialogue. As curious as Francie was about this intellectual breakthrough, there was no way she could or would muster her examining skills amid the blood and brutality. Emma was alive and Emma needed help.

"FD, the police are coming, and I don't want them to send Emma to some strange hospital where she'll be probed by doctors and reporters. I don't want her taken away. We've got to hide her."

FutureDick's initial impulse was to reject Francie's suggestion. The ape was wounded, maybe critically, and he was afraid to move her. Who knows what additional damage the two of them would do the frightened animal? But he understood Francie's intimation and couldn't conceive of a worse fate for the battered chimp than the impersonal environment of SeaBank Veterinary Hospital. Emma would be picked to death there.

"Okay, Francie, let's do it. Do you have anything flat? I don't know what's broken. I can't even conceive of how hurt she might be. If we move her, it's got be very, very carefully."

Francie thought for a moment and then realized that the leaf to her oak dining room table might work. It was around three feet wide and might be long enough to support Emma while they carried her to Francie's office next to the kitchen. But how could they lift her? It would be impossible for just the two of them.

When Francie came back with the dining leaf, she also carried two skate boards. With seven children, there was enough athletic equipment in her home to outfit a small village. Her eyes gazed upon FutureDick soothing Emma with the most gentlest of tones.

"It's alright, Emma. We're here, and we're going to help you. We're going to take care of you and fix your hurting. Just wait, Emma. You'll be all better soon."

He had taken out his handkerchief and was wiping the blood off her face. Watching FutureDick's sensitivity toward the bleeding, broken ape confirmed Francie's choice. She had made the right call. If anyone could help them in this emergency, it was that man over there, that kneeling man trying to save her poor Emma.

They painstakingly slid the leaf under Emma's back. Then Francie held the chimp's head up while FutureDick straightened the board under Emma's neck. Dispassionately, Francie tried not to watch Emma grimace with each push, but Francie was mesmerized by Emma's face. That's where the words came. Right from that mouth. What else can she say? What does she know?

Cautiously, they maneuvered the dining leaf supporting Emma on top of the two skate boards. Then slowly, so very slowly, they rolled her to the office. Francie used to daydream about recarpeting the living room or refurbishing the oak planks sitting under the shabby rug, but they couldn't afford it. When she and Reba moved in, there was some type of tropical woven grass mat covering a needed-to-be-refinished wood floor, but the women left it there, as is, a testament to what Francie called *desensitization*. What you see with regularity, you can always get used to, even crummy carpeting.

Now Francie congratulated herself on her frugality. The cheap floor matting was flat, and the two of them were able to roll Emma over it. What if she and Reba had installed thick, two inch wall-to-wall? Pushing the chimp's stout body through lush broadloom pile would have surely wrenched one of their backs. Francie swore to herself that she'd never complain about the damn floor again. Tonight it had been worth its weight in flimsiness.

When Francie and FutureDick were near the office, the bell rang. Both of them were solid athletes, and yet, both of them were straining for breath. "Just a minute," Francie whispered. Knowing the visitors couldn't hear her, she continued exerting her waning effort till they rolled the huge bulk into the smaller room. Then she slowly heaved herself up to answer the door.

As she left FutureDick, their gaze met. Nothing needed to be said. Their eyes understood and silently made a pact: they were in this together. Their sense of decency, their sense of boundaries, and their sense of safety had been so violated that they shared what perishable humans share in moments of crisis: inspired alliance. Cooperate or die. And at this moment, they felt like the last two human beings left on earth.

But Francie or FutureDick never confronted an Angie or a Harold, the rejects who roamed through their same city, unseen, unsatisfied, unheard. Nor had they faced Clarene, another dissident in the middle of the crowd, who saw the propagation of DoRights as dangerous. These chimps were not harmful to humans but rather the other way around. Humans were desecrating the temple of existence by tampering with the animals' souls. Altering the ape's genes was stepping on God's land. These scientists didn't belong there. Clarene knew that for sure.

In her heart, she believed she was right. She was on the side of good, of morality, of beneficence. And they were wrong. They were evil. They were mistreating God's creatures—the apes. Shouldn't the apes have rights like humans? Weren't these chimpanzees living things, entitled to their own simian destiny? Did man have the prerogative to distort the ape's genetic inheritance and turn the animals into slaves to do man's bidding, man's dirty work, just because men or women were too lazy to do it themselves? There must be a way to stop this genocide.

God wanted her to be his agent for goodness, to thwart the incarnation of Satan—to destroy TriCubed.

Clarene was certain it was her consecrated fate to intervene in the devil's work. No divine plan would allow a corporation of sinners to defile His creation. If she didn't halt this unholy abuse, who would? For years, she felt lost, with no direction, no goal, no purpose, and then one night, she opened her heart to the Lord. That's when she heard His message loud and clear. That's when His spirit infused her with the moral energy to fight evil. As an instrument of justice, Clarene knew it was her duty to rally the forces of good around the DoRight cause. And saving the apes from a life of slavery would be her way of giving thanks for her redemption. Besides, wasn't she offering everyone else who helped her a ticket to salvation?

Clarene lived day and night with these thoughts racing through her mind, jubilant that she had walked out of the fog and now began to see with exceptional clarity. She'd physically be in a checkout line at the supermarket, but mentally she'd be trying to develop some scheme to sabotage TriCubed's computer network. Or she'd be pulling off the freeway exit to go to work and then start to figure out a way to frighten TriCubed's customers. Even when she'd be on the verge of falling asleep, in that twilight space between consciousness and void, she'd create her forever fantasy: she'd steal into TriCubed, free the apes, and lead them onto the evacuating ship that would take them back to Africa.

Clarene dreamt up various scenarios of industrial disruption, and each one became more outrageous, more risky, and more expensive. Although she enjoyed constructing elaborate schemes of subversive strategy, she needed a simple plan, something that would be low cost, low risk, and precipitate the failure of TriCubed. So she worked hard at devising doable operations.

When Clarene tried to bring up feasible resolutions at the HEART meeting, the group either ridiculed her for being too radical, scolded her for not working within the system, or ignored her for being too unrealistic. What were they afraid of? Weren't they ready to walk down the path of righteousness? God would care for them because they cared for God's living creatures. But none of her HEART friends went along with her proposals. She was a lone voice trying to bring justice to a world gone crazy for profit at the expense of its defenseless beasts.

The HEART meeting was over, and Clarene was dejected once again. Why did she bother coming? She had carefully elaborated on what she called a foolproof plan to inject viruses into TriCubed's central computer, and nobody seemed to care. They were politer than usual, but the vote ended up the same way—negative. Except this time, she noticed she had another supporter, a new member, Kevin, who showed up at the last two meetings.

As Clarene was walking down the stairs, Kevin caught up with her. "Clarene, you were great. I'm sorry the group didn't listen to you. Personally, I thought your plan was right on. It sure made a lot of sense to me."

"Thanks, Kevin, but it doesn't make me feel any better. I go through this all the time with the group, and the only thing they wanna do is walk around with picket signs. Surely, there's gotta be a better way. I get so tired of them."

"Hey, Clarene, why not come over Friday night? I've got a few friends who feel as strongly as you do, and I've got a hunch they'd like to meet you and hear what you have to say. I know they'd agree with you!"

Sometimes you turn right instead of left, or you leave the house five minutes earlier, or your letter gets lost in the mail—small acts which seem inconsequential at the time. But that shift in direction, switch in plans, or lost communication can alter your destiny. A mere side-step in ordinary action, and your life changes immutably. "Why not come over Friday night?" Six words, common words, and Clarene's raison d'être was conceived.

She did go to Kevin's a week later; she did meet his friends, his glorious, committed friends; and they did listen to her. In fact, they devoured every word. That's all it took. Clarene, riding on the heels of Saint Joan, had finally found her audience. On that moonless night, when everyone else was starting their weekend, their drinking, their dating, their 48 hour work break, Dark Friday was born.

Its inception aroused none of the neighbors, stirred no countrymen to action, and certainly inspired none of the DoRights. But this small, exalted group locked arms and pledged themselves to the liberation of apes now. Each member then placed their right hand on the Holy Bible and swore an oath to place their lives on the line for God's creatures, great and small. Dark Friday's imperative was to exterminate TriCubed along with its profiteering moguls. And its dignified leader was Clarene.

Eleven

After she showed the police in, Francie pointed them in the direction of the blood bath and then ran upstairs to check on the children. She briefly explained the state of events to Reba and walked into the bedrooms to see what the kids were up to.

This was going to be one of those long nights. She knew she would hold each one individually and try to let them know they were okay. She told them the police were here, and she'd be up later.

"Give Mom a hug, April. It's really going to be okay. Mommy's here."

"But Mommy, the DoRights? Josh says they're dead, all dead. Does that mean I won't see Edmund jumping up and down? And what about Shirley? Won't she be anymore?"

With that last query, tears hovered momentarily in April's eyes but eventually lost their lodging as they burst upon her cheeks. The child shuddered with cries of confusion, of loss, of bewilderment, too young to be acquainted with the world's dark side, but old enough to be altered forever. Bruised innocence, when reality scars the once-upon-a-time faith we all wanted desperately to hold on to.

April, picking her head up from Francie's chest, muttered, "It's not fair, Mommy. It's not right."

"I know, sweetie. I know. It's not fair. And these things shouldn't happen. But they do, April, and I can't explain why. I don't know why myself. I only know I love you, my little girl, and I'm here to take care of you, to hold you while you hurt."

As Francie held her youngest child, she cried the silent tears every mother sheds, the quiet tears of helplessness. If she could, she would grab April's pain for herself. She would gladly fill her being with her baby's anguish rather than allow her daughter to ache. But Francie couldn't. No mother is capable of crawling inside her child's heart and snatching up the pain. Therefore Francie's soul throbbed with the indescribable suffering of maternal impotence.

When the sobs subsided, Francie kissed April's forehead, saying, "I'll be back here soon, sweetheart. And you keep remembering Edmund's and Shirley's funny faces, so tomorrow you can draw lots of pictures of them."

Francie slowly left April's room, her mind a mix of fear, of love, and possibly vengeance. She hated whatever or whoever brought this disaster upon their household, upon their children, upon their DoRights who were no more. She wanted to lash out with all her force, flinging the invisible menace off the planet, left forever to float in space till it disintegrated into dust. But she restrained her rage. She was the go-between. She was the armor. And she separated the horror from the warmth.

Thank God Reba was here. She'd protect the upstairs, their life's reason for being, while Francie grappled with the downstairs, the dreadful business of death, destruction, and details.

Francie haltingly described her evening to the police. Her mind was on Emma, her children, FD—and her brain fled from the ordeal of having to relate the grisly details to anyone. A Detective TigerTail introduced himself and tried to pacify her.

"Your's isn't the first report, Ms. Franks. We've had four other calls this evening, and we're spread thin. We don't know how many murders there were, but every house we've entered looks like a war zone."

"But why, Detective? These are docile creatures. What can the police do?"

"We're trying our best, I assure you. I'll have my men here as soon as I can to dust for prints. Ms. Franks, I'm here to help you. And I want you to know that I'm determined to get to the bottom of this. But I can tell you one thing. Every house we've seen has that strong vanilla odor, and we're trying to find out what it is."

Francie wanted to be friendly to TigerTail. He seemed efficient, he seemed sincere, and he certainly seemed committed. Still she didn't want him to notice how anxious she was to join FD and Emma. So Francie thanked the detective as she walked him to the door.

"By the way, Ms. Franks, didn't you have four adult apes like the other households? Or was yours a special situation?"

Francie blushed, as she frequently did if she was about to embark on an embellishment of the truth. But the lights were dim, and she hoped TigerTail was too distracted to see the hint of color burnish her cheeks.

"You're right, Detective. We did own four adults. But when we came home, I called TriCubed immediately because one of my DoRights was still breathing. And they sent their medics to bring her back to the infirmary. They wanted to help her as fast as they could."

"Well, I hope she makes it. I really do." Flustered, TigerTail hastened his step out the door, wondering what the world was coming to when he started confusing chimps with humans. By the end of the night, he was certain he wouldn't be able to tell the difference.

Francie released a heavy sigh of relief. She hated to lie. It felt miserable, so out of place with the image she set for herself of the honest, courageous mother. But Emma took precedence over her pretense. It was Emma who had to be saved.

Interrupting her self-castigation, Francie shouted the chimp's name inside her head. *EMMA!* That was the clue. Her talking ape. There was the eyewitness. She knew she should inform TigerTail about Emma. Would he even believe her? If he did, she knew his mouth would water to be able to talk to Emma. Could Emma help him? Maybe? But Francie couldn't. She just couldn't impose that harsh human world upon the fragile creature Emma had become. She was hanging on to life with the thinnest of threads, and Francie couldn't push her into the spotlight. There was too little of Emma left.

Moreover, Francie had to admit she felt imperceptibly better when she found out other households were also involved. It was callous of her, she knew. Why should she wish this catastrophe on anyone else? What kind of person was she that she felt relieved because other DoRight clans had been slain? But she knew why. It didn't take her degree in psychology to explain her feelings. It took her nurturing sense as a mother to understand why she could breathe a bit more freely. At first she thought her home was singularly selected. Some malignant force out there had entered her island and proceeded to destroy part of her family. Did that mean it would return for the rest? Would it swoop down one unsuspecting night and devour what remained of them?

Now Francie found out neither her family nor Reba's were of interest to this cancer. It's aim was the obliteration of DoRights—humans were irrelevant—and it had metastasized over the entire city in one night.

Of course, Francie felt sympathy for the innocent animals who had perished. They were the best of the best, only there to help make other's lives easier. But Francie's compassion could be measured, could be doled out, now that her brood was safe. She'd fight vigorously to find the killers, but she could restrain that inner reserve of rage and fury she kept under wraps if anyone or anything advanced threateningly toward her children.

Sharing a kinship with the other mothers in the animal kingdom, Francie was the lioness, the doe, the she-bear. Like the wolf or DoRight, she'd confront any enemy who'd attempt to assault her offspring. She knew she would die in their defense. What surprised her even more is she'd also kill for their protection as well.

As she walked into her office, she saw that FD had retrieved some kitchen towels and was trying to bathe Emma gently, so that he could see the extent of her wounds. Francie locked the door and walked over to the broken creature. She bent down on her knees and cradled Emma's face in her hands, stroking her head, her cheeks, soothing her with assurances that she was okay. They would take care of her. She was safe.

Francie knew there was no way they'd be able to determine if any of Emma's bones were broken or how much injury her body sustained. She realized she'd have to call TriCubed sooner or later. They'd have the proper emergency equipment to help Emma. And Francie wanted answers. Could all the DoRights talk or just some of them?

But before she entered the world of corporate care, of explanations, of cover-up, she wanted this time with Emma. She wanted to hear more. "Oh Emma, what happened? What happened to you?"

Emma moved her gaze to Francie and answered, "Me hurt. He hurt me."

"Who hurt you, Emma? Who?"

"He did. It did."

"What was it? What did it look like?"

"He big. He strong. He hurt. It smell good, lots of good."

"But, Emma? Why didn't you scream, make noise, cry?"

"The smell. It just come. We not know. We smell! We smell!"

As Emma started to get agitated, FutureDick asked, "What did he look like? Can you describe him?"

"Like me. He look like me. He big. Have brown hair, like me. It look like me."

Then Emma moved her eyes wildly, straining to remember something, something that was part of life, something that belonged to her. "My baby! My baby! Where my baby?" She paused, she knew. And she felt the waves of wretchedness all mothers fear. "He hurt my baby. It kill my baby!"

The sadness that came over Emma's face brought tears to Francie's eyes. She held Emma's head, but what could she say to this mother who had lost her child? Francie's words couldn't bring the baby back. Francie's touch couldn't stop the throb in Emma's heart. Francie's soothing voice couldn't remove the scenes piled up in Emma's brain, scenes of madness, of murder, of complete annihilation of sanity and safety and self. Desolate, both females shared a requiem of anguish, one mourning her lost past, the other cowering before her frightened future.

When BrickWell hammered out his hopes for saving the chimpanzees from extinction, he proceeded on the precept that his bright new world would promise a better future for primates. They were being tossed away, hunted, hacked, homeless, in the name of man's modern greed. Surely his novel approach influenced their captors, causing a moment of reflection, of reevaluation. The chase would never be the same now that he had initiated the era of equality.

Moreover, the monies didn't matter when BrickWell built his compound to breed the chimps. Foremost was his concern for adaptation; he purchased security in the form of similitude, paying little attention to the dollar amount. And the result was a constructed environment so closely resembling the apes' familiar habitat that their adjustment seemed effortless.

In order to simulate their lost African homes, the chimps were kept in a compartmentalized compound, dense with trees and separated by large ponds. Since chimpanzees do not swim and, in fact, fear playing in the water, the ponds served to divide the various chimp communities. For breeding purposes,

TriCubed would sometimes move the females in estrus from one colony to another, but the males always stayed together in their own colony, continually rivaling each other for dominance. They were more interested in their male relationships while the females were more interested in their babies and each other. The apes, quite clear about their sexual roles, seemed entirely satisfied spending most of their time with those of the same gender.

And, as far as TriCubed was concerned, this worked out perfectly because once a DoRight gave birth, she and her child became part of a clan that was sold to a household. In five years, the female would be exchanged. She'd return with her first child, mate, give birth, and then leave again with her new baby. Her first child would remain at the compound. This was the toughest transaction, the separation, and here is where good, sensitive human teachers became crucial. They had to replace the primate mother.

Although the child would be with its mother at their half-year reunions, which lasted one day, the parting remained the most ticklish aspect of BrickWell's perfect plan. The children missed their mothers, and he was sure the mother missed her children, even though she was distracted with a new infant. To ease the sense of abandonment, all four children from the original clan were kept together, where they could continue to play with each other. They were like brothers and sisters, having lived together for five formative years, and this familiarity gave them some solace.

TriCubed also kept them busy learning domestic tasks the entire day till they were old enough to sire or bear children. Then the females created their own clan, and the males eventually became part of the adult male colony. TriCubed's goal was to keep all four clan females together for the forty to fifty years they lived. First, they worked in a human home for five years. Then, ideally, they mated and conceived at the same time, and after giving birth, the sisterly four moved to another human home. This cycle would continue till they were ready to retire and return to the compound.

The hitch was adaptation to a new human family, but the DoRights usually adjusted quickly. They enjoyed the company of humans, and if they felt loved, protected, taken care of, they didn't mind their new home or their new parents.

But TriCubed's carefully planned time clock was still being tested since the company had been selling DoRights for only six years. So far, their regulated mating schedule worked. Yet the body, like nature, is unpredictable, and TriCubed kept alert for the exception, not the rule. The theory was wonderful, but could they make sure all their females conceived at the same time?

TriCubed actually had a choice in the matter. Once exchanged, they could house the original clan back on the compound for as long as they needed, either to conceive and give birth or to be bought. Still their ace in the hole, which they hadn't had to use yet, was removal, then implantation of a fertilized egg back into the female.

Biotechnology was a precise science, but the company held true to establishing as natural a chimpanzee life style as they could. They wanted their females to conceive the way they would in the wild—except for the ChangeOvers. These specialized chimps did not live with the other DoRights.

When they were in estrus, a male ape was brought into each ChangeOver life station and closely monitored by experienced handlers. Of course the male was oblivious to his chosen position. He just lumbered in, eyes darting, ears listening, intent on scrutinizing his new surroundings. There, the panting primate sat and watched, not knowing whether to search out competing males or immediately enjoy this unexpected windfall of four females in heat. The system seemed to work well, and maybe all four females could become impregnated by the single male.

But TriCubed left no room for doubt. The ChangeOver females were offered the chance to copulate with six different males. After one session, the handlers would wait two hours and then introduce a new male to the group. They called their method "assurance mating," and, thus far, it worked for each female in the ChangeOver community. However, they only tried it on the original eighteen apes, too small a number to be certain they could systematically predict results.

In fact, every once in a while, one of the ChangeOvers would reject the male. Why it happened, the scientists weren't sure. Maybe her sense of smell or sight was offended, maybe she was too independent, maybe she just didn't like the male. Usually when that happened, the male would stomp away to mate with a more receptive partner. He was horny, and if she was disinterested, it was her loss. He'd find some other appreciative recipient. BrickWell couldn't help but wonder whose loss it really was, for the female could mate unceasingly. She never became tired like her masculine counterpart.

During one mating episode, the male didn't leave. He tried every which way to mount the female, and she wasn't having any of it. She simply shook him off and walked away. But he came back for more, *rejection* not a word residing in his vocabulary. Finally, he annoyed her so much that she started bearing her teeth and clamoring to enlist the aid of her fellow ChangeOvers to ward off this intruder.

The male tried to swish away the other females to get to his prize, and the screeching accelerated whereby the entire camp was going to be affected. The ape handler realized it was time to stop the procedure and had a devil of a time separating the male from the defending wall of ChangeOvers. All the handler could do was distract the male, while he called for help to herd the indignant macho beast back to his life station. His concentration was bent on squelching potential chaos in the compound, and he never looked in the male ape's eyes. Otherwise, he would have seen the pure hostility emanating from the pupils. The male wanted that particular female, and he'd do anything to get her.

"Could that be?" thought BrickWell. "Do I have a renegade ape on my hands?" He remembered the abortive mating episode and wondered if the ape he sold to the zoo escaped. But no one had called him, and the newscasts didn't indicate such an incident.

Can't be. One ape couldn't destroy that completely, that viciously. Never. He refused to consider any type of feral chimp psychosis that would lead to the brutal mania graphically repeated to him in the course of the evening. Marauding apes could be seen, could be heard. Yet this catastrophe was done in silence, the sorrowful silence of savagery. And he sipped his glass of wine, wondering if the logic in his brain was unraveling at the night's frantic nausea.

TWELVE

"What if they want to search the rest of the house, FD? What do I say?"

"Sit tight, Francie. I'll think of something. But it's late already, and they might call it off till morning."

"I tell you, FD. I may not be running out of steam, but I'm having a hell of a time with the deception."

"Patience, Francie. Patience. Pretend you've just scored the fourteenth point."

With FutureDick's allusion to racquetball, Francie grinned—the first light moment of the evening. But the joke withered abruptly when she gazed at Emma. Poor Emma. She needed medical attention now, yet the police were still probing the death scene, the ruined room that a few hours ago bubbled with life and love and babies.

While the officers tried to translate the terror into evidence, Francie went back and forth between Emma, her children, and the investigating team. Tomorrow was Saturday. She had the whole weekend to pick up the pieces of existence and try to make them fit again.

At the same time, FutureDick was sitting beside Emma trying to sort out the fragments of horror and see how they connected. Francie told him that four other clan homes had been demolished so far. Someone, something, some well-organized group wanted vengeance. These were not amateurs. It was too slick. The homes were precision bombed, quick entry and exit, preplanned. They knew which shelters to target, and then they vanished. He knew he should have gone out to see TigerTail, but that might have compromised Emma.

He looked at the pathetic chimpanzee, the sadness, the pain, the helplessness written over her despondent face. What motivation would lead someone to kill a defenseless animal? Hate? Anger? Envy? Insanity? TigerTail could wait. Emma couldn't.

FutureDick was anxious to get the languid ape to a hospital. He didn't know what internal injuries she might be suffering, and he felt useless just sitting there, not able to do anything to ease her distress.

Finally Francie dashed in and said the police were gone. When they left, they said they'd be back tomorrow to look throughout the rest of the house. "No use spending a sleepless night over monkey murders, those guys said. It could wait till morning. Besides, they had another DoRight call to investigate. Can you believe that, FD? They think the DoRights are just pets, mindless, domesticated brutes!"

Although he clearly understood the cavalier attitude of the officers, FutureDick tactfully answered, "Well, let's score ourselves a point, Francie. Forget their insensitivity. We didn't want them hanging around anyway. They probably don't own any DoRights and quite possibly never met one before. All they see are the remnants of chimp corpses. Forget them because now we can get Emma the attention she deserves."

Instantly the issue of DoRight awareness evaporated as Francie and FutureDick focused once more on the talking ape.

But it was a slight hint, an indication of police priorities, that the killing of chimpanzees might not rank as high as humans on their values chart.

Since every DoRight owner received a 24 hour emergency number, Francie contacted TriCubed immediately. When she told security one of her DoRights had survived, he put her through to BrickWell. The guard was screening incoming calls, but he knew this was one the CEO would gladly take.

"Dr. BrickWell, Francie Franks here. I have a DoRight who was involved in the killings, and she's been beaten pretty badly. Can you help?"

"Certainly, Ms. Franks. Let me take care of it. After what I've been hearing, I don't know how she survived. You can't imagine how relieved I am that she's holding on. We'll get there immediately."

"But I've got another problem, Dr. BrickWell—a crucial problem."

"Hold on a minute, Ms. Franks. Let me get the ambulance going."

Francie remained on the phone while BrickWell made arrangements for an ambulance. When he returned on the line, she pelted him with questions about Emma.

"Dr. BrickWell, my ape speaks! She communicates in English, and I'm sure you knew that. Why didn't you tell me when I bought the clan? How could you cover up that sort of information? And why the hell would you? I feel cheated—completely cheated."

BrickWell tried to pacify the young woman and get her to realize that he wasn't trying to deceive her. "Ms. Franks, our silence was strictly for the benefit of the apes. There was absolutely no fraud and no intention whatsoever to be cagey with the owners. I swear to you! Your Emma belonged to a special control group we call ChangeOvers. And they're still in the experimental stage."

"But Dr. BrickWell, a talking DoRight, for God's sake!

Think of how my family and I might have responded if we knew."

And she swallowed for a brief second, nearly choking on the lost moments of contact never to be lived. Then she whispered, "Oh, Dr. BrickWell, I wish I would have known. Just think of how my children's lives would have been changed if they had the chance to speak with Emma."

"But Ms. Franks, it was too soon. I'm truly sorry, I am. Still, we have to protect the chimps, and we had no way of forecasting the ChangeOver's ability to adapt. We didn't want to jeopardize the chimp's natural relationship with her owners or her clan. This was a wait and see proposition."

Conscientiously, BrickWell explained the ChangeOver experiment to Francie and elaborated on how only ten ChangeOvers were placed in random homes. The researchers simply couldn't predict what would happen, and they didn't want to encourage unrealistic expectations from the owners or pressure the ChangeOvers in anyway. BrickWell asked Francie to come to the infirmary tomorrow and assured her that they would do everything they could to save Emma. He wanted the chimp to live as much as she did. His chimps meant an awful lot to him.

Francie was somewhat placated. At least, she saw the dilemma from the scientist's vantage point. Yet she still felt deceived, taken-in, conned by a company who wanted her coffers but not her collaboration. She certainly wouldn't want to contaminate the experiment, but she *was* the owner. Right?

FutureDick listened in on the portable phone so Francie wouldn't have to repeat the conversation. Besides, he wanted to hear BrickWell's voice. He wanted to start getting his sixth sense in action and see if he believed this guy. BrickWell sounded concerned, he sounded sincere, but FutureDick remained wary.

When they hung up, FutureDick told Francie about the scientist's call earlier that evening. So, almost officially, he was legitimately working on the case. But he hadn't met with

BrickWell yet. The relief showed in Francie's eyes when she found out that FutureDick would be investigating the murder. Taking a deep breath, trying to get the oxygen to alleviate her anxiety, she sighed and said, "God, FD. I'm so grateful you're involved. There are certain people you just get a good feeling about, and you're one of them."

For some reason, FutureDick felt particularly pleased about Francie's comment, and he wondered while driving home why he cared if Francie liked him. He thought he had canceled those kinds of concerns years ago. Maybe not? Maybe this was part of feeling again.

What Francie and FutureDick didn't know, and what BrickWell failed to mention, was that Emma was the particular ChangeOver who had rejected the aggressive male stud. Why should BrickWell worry them unnecessarily? He was quite certain that angry ape remained in captivity. Chimps don't break steel bars, do they?

Near morning, as BrickWell, Francie, and FutureDick tried to close their eyes and blot out the noxious nightmares of reality from reaching their bedroom doors, the day began brightly. Partners in crime, the sun never revealed what the dark endorsed. Yet Friday evening became the night of infamy. Seven clans were demolished in less than five hours. After a few hours sleep, FutureDick went down to the station to see TigerTail. They liked each other and over the years formed a friendship that became tighter with each case they worked on together.

In fact, TigerTail was glad BrickWell had called FutureDick. With seven different attacks, his force was going to have to spread out, and he could use any help he could get. He talked to BrickWell that morning and had him fax the list of DoRight owners to the station. TigerTail contacted the police in DoRight service center cities across the US, but these locales remained untouched. Isn't it funny how the identical blue sky can look so tragic in California and so peaceful in Illinois? This must have been a local incident because TriCubed's corporate headquarters was located in the same southern California city as the murders: SeaBank.

So far, the only clues found at the scenes of the crime were some synthetic material and a sticky substance. The nylon-like strands might have come from a sweater or blanket. They were brownish-red in color, about the same shade as the DoRights. The investigating team also scraped off a moist residue that smelled like vanilla. The lab was busy analyzing these two items this morning. Otherwise, there was nothing else to go on. The murders had been meticulously carried out, and the police were baffled at the intensity of the violence.

BlackArm sent his men out to any possible places where someone might be implicated. Six TriCubed employees had been fired in the last three years, and they were being questioned right now. TigerTail and ScoreMore were going to meet with the president of HEART to see if the animal rights activists had any leads. BlackArm dispatched detectives to all the neighborhoods where the DoRights lived to see if anyone saw or heard anything. Something? Some sound? Some vehicle? Some obscure incident? He even sent his people to the union halls and unemployment offices to see what they could hear from the many dissatisfied workers who had lost their jobs to the domestic chimps. BlackArm didn't have any other ideas right now, but he told FutureDick to search for whatever might bring in additional evidence.

Before his meeting with BrickWell, FutureDick went back to Francie's and looked around. Francie wasn't there. Her son, Josh, answered the door and said his mom went to TriCubed. He seemed like a nice kid, eager to help, but FutureDick didn't want to bring the nine year old into the room splashed with unwashed blood and chalk outlines of dead bodies. So he thanked Josh and went into the clan's quarters with a much fresher eye than last night.

What caught FutureDick's attention was how easy it would be to get into the enclosed porch. The outside door had a single lock that was easily picked. No broken windows by the door. Therefore the DoRights couldn't hear the intruder. They were probably sleeping peacefully when the killer entered the room.

FutureDick would have to go to the other six homes, but he suspected that the clans were typically housed in flimsily secured places. They weren't really human, but they weren't dogs either. Why should anyone keep these loyal creatures in a bolted shelter? Just like dogs are kept outside in an open house, FutureDick surmised that if the clans' residences had any locks at all, they were probably negligible pieces of hardware.

What bothered FutureDick was the lack of noise. Although Francie explained briefly how the DoRights were mesmerized by the smell of vanilla, it didn't make sense. They were in danger. And the DoRights were known to make a considerable commotion when they perceived threat. Even the smell of vanilla wouldn't silence them. He was sure of that.

The little reading FutureDick squeezed in this morning suggested chimpanzees engaged in a sophisticated system of communication and called attention to danger in two ways. Most likely, they would deliver an SOS scream, a clear, high-pitched call, relatively long and drawn out. They'd repeat this shrill steadily. Chimps who are severely threatened will definitely send out this obvious appeal for help.

And infants will cry in a way that suggests trouble. A combination of tantrum screaming interspersed with repeated bouts of whimpering becomes louder and more frenzied as the child's anxiety increases. Chimpanzees talk to each other. Why didn't they talk that evening?

But TigerTail said no calls came in from any of the neighbors the whole night. Certainly out of seven different areas, there should have been one irate neighbor who was awakened by the din and called the police to complain.

FutureDick knew the DoRights were chimpanzees, but they were altered chimpanzees. Might it be possible that in gene modification, the sense for survival gets shifted also? Perhaps sacrificed? Or was he jumping to hasty conclusions? Were the DoRights actually becoming too content? The only experiences they had with humans were favorable, so why should they fear people? People had always been kind to them. Consequently, they were secure. Fat, happy, much too secure.

Was their instinct for self-preservation waning because it wasn't called upon anymore? Like a muscle that's never used and then atrophies, had the complacent DoRights lost their SOS scream? Or didn't they ever have a chance to use it? More than likely, they were all sleeping. Perhaps they never perceived the approaching danger because they never saw it. Perhaps they never had time to open their mouths.

What had Emma said? "Like me. He like me." If the *he* were like Emma, then the *he* was not a human being. And wouldn't a DoRight be more terrified of an aggressive ape-stranger than a benign, beloved people-person? Where were your screams, Emma? Where were your cries?

FutureDick stepped outside the porch and looked around the trampled lawn. How do you find the answer to over fifty murders among a blade of grass? He found nothing. As he walked to his car, he was concentrating on one aspect of the case: a motive. What was the motive for killing apes? He could figure out why TriCubed's executives would get killed or the handlers or the scientists, but not the apes. Who would be disgruntled enough or deranged enough to kill a colony of chimps? It couldn't have been devil worshippers or some secret cult. They would have taken body parts with them. The killing was murder for murder's sake, some sort of testament to a larger cause.

FutureDick walked across the street to his car and happened to glance down at a silver fragment lying by the manhole cover to the sewer. He picked up what looked like a metallic plate and stuck it in his pocket. At this point, he'd put Popsicle sticks in his pocket if he found one lying around. Anything might be a clue at this stage of the investigation. He realized he had very little to go on, and he'd better get some knowledge quickly. He needed to find out more about the DoRights, the industry, and its competitors. He needed to meet with BrickWell, now.

"Just call me Adam," BrickWell told FutureDick after they shook hands. The scientist had a firm handshake, FutureDick noticed. He liked that in a person. It was a small hint to the measure of his self-confidence, his ability to grasp another's palm solidly, silently saying, "Intrinsically, I'm worth something."

They settled the business arrangements up front. Then FutureDick told BrickWell about his night at Francie's with Emma.

"You know, FutureDick, I wasn't being secretive about the ChangeOvers for any kind of profit motive. I have to protect my chimps."

"But what if one of the chimps would have started talking to its owners?"

"That's fine. I was willing to take the chance. I just didn't want to set up any unrealistic expectations ahead of time. I couldn't predict how the ChangeOvers would react in their human setting, and I had to play a wait and see game."

"I can't argue with the scientific method, Adam, but I can tell you it was the shock of the century when words came out of Emma's mouth. By the way, how's Emma doing?"

"Still critical, FutureDick. I talked to the doctor a half hour ago, and she seems to be resting more comfortably, but she's listless. When I saw her this morning, I got the impression that she's balancing whether to stay or leave."

Then BrickWell stopped speaking and looked toward the window, lost momentarily in his thoughts about Emma, her abilities, her life.

"Excuse me, Adam. Is there anything I should know about? Anything at all that might point me in some direction?"

"This is silly, but the thought crossed my mind," said Brickwell, a faint flush appearing on his cheeks. "Sometime ago, a male chimp got too aggressive with one of the ChangeOvers. She wouldn't mate with him, and things got a bit out of control. We sold him to the zoo and thought that was the end of it. But it turned out that Emma was the female who wouldn't mate. Of course, I called the zoo this morning, but they sold that male to the Cleveland Zoo nine months ago. It was a thin hunch, the idea of a rampaging male chimpanzee, but so highly improbable given the circumstances, I knew it wouldn't hold up."

"Do you possibly have any other ideas about the motivation behind the crimes? Have you personally been threatened? Made an enemy? Have the DoRights made some enemies?"

"FutureDick, my whole life has been science. I look for ways to solve problems, genetic problems, biological problems, and I'm drawing a blank here. Why the DoRights? They're innocent. If someone doesn't like me—and I can't think of anyone right now—why not come after me? But why the DoRights?"

"That's been bothering me too, Adam. Last night was my first chance with a DoRight, and I've got to tell you, they're wonderful animals. Of course, I'm dealing with limited experience here, but if Emma represents the rest of your handiwork, you brought a marvelous creature into our lives."

"You've got to help me, FutureDick. I'm worried about my chimps."

FutureDick stayed a while longer to find out about TriCubed's customers, the company's marketing plans, its management, and some of its new research. He had no reason to doubt BrickWell. The researcher seemed committed to his work, his employees, his dream of bringing man and primate closer together, and to running a quality operation.

In fact, BrickWell came across as the benevolent scientist rather than the greedy entrepreneur. Of course, FutureDick never let the image dictate the possibility of innocence, but at his gut level, he felt BrickWell loved his creations and could never conceive of harming them—at least, not in a brutal, intentional manner. The moral issue of whisking the chimpanzee out of its natural habitat and changing its internal structure was an irrelevant consideration for BrickWell. The man sincerely believed he was making the world a better place to live for humans as well as for apes.

FutureDick drove home from TriCubed, his mind flitting among possibilities. Now was the catch-up time when he learned the background of the case. BrickWell gave him loads of reading material about TriCubed. But FutureDick needed to learn about the domestic services industry as a whole. He needed to become an expert overnight. And this initial step toward accumulating knowledge is what he loved best about his work. Every case offered an opportunity to learn, and he considered this a prime benefit of the profession. He got paid to study. Each new problematic situation made him feel like a college freshman all over again.

If his body was a sanctuary, his mind was the altar. He honored the brain's ability to integrate information, so much so, that he trained his intellect harder than his legs. Sometimes, he'd read till three in the morning. Then he'd get up again at six to continue. Not often. But if FutureDick was absorbed with a subject, time lost its relevance. So did weariness. Learning re-energized him, and his body easily adapted to three hour nights, if necessary.

In the back of his mind, he carried a statement made over twenty years ago. Who said it, he forgot during the passage of time. But the essence remained. When divorce was flagrant among movie stars, his bygone friend made the observation that whenever you fall in love, you feel reborn. "That's why they keep having affairs. It's the only way to access the fountain of youth."

"But," thought FutureDick, "there's got to be other ways. The impracticality of falling in love over and over again seemed like chasing your own tail."

Then he realized that when he starts a new case, he also

feels young, he feels fresh, a novice wanting to find out more. Rejuvenation could be found with the brain as well as the heart. And he jumped into the gathering of pertinent information zealously, knowing every time he filled his brain up with knowledge, it would grow a little bit stronger, just as his biceps expanded when he did his curls. He had no doubts that the act of learning made him feel youthful, but he wistfully admitted that the additional knowledge also made him feel older.

Still he looked forward to starting this case. Francie, Emma, the DoRights—definitely, his was an emotional involvement. Yet he wasn't worried about the answers. They were there. They always were. It was the circuitous route leading to the explanations that sometimes proved worrisome.

Besides, who knows what insights might occur following an afternoon at the library? Better yet, he'd go for his run first and clear his mind. The jogging generally rubbed away mental debris, leaving his attention unusually acute, his focus more formidable. A cerebral shower, he called it. Instead of shampoo, he used his running to cleanse his brain, making it ultra-sensitive, and thus readily receptive to information.

FutureDick knew that solving puzzles required facts, but he also knew that deep within the human mind resided a fertile field of intuitive knowledge. He based his investigative success on being able to tap into this inner wellspring, and he knew that a run along the beach was one of his best shortcuts to comprehension.

Thirteen

Francie, anxious to see Emma, raced out of the house. She hoped against hope that Emma would survive. But the battered creature looked so tired, and seemed too weak by the time they transferred her to the infirmary, that Francie knew Emma's life teetered like a one year old taking her first steps. Wobbly. Quite wobbly. Emma had to help the doctors. Her will to fight was indispensable to the surgical team, and Francie feared that Emma had lost her reason to be because Emma watched her child being ripped apart. Why should Emma want to live in a world where insanity reigned?

When she entered TriCubed, after showing the guard her pass, Francie heard the clamor of a crowd. The hallway buzzed with reporters who came to the company for firsthand news. With seven clans so ruthlessly murdered, the media knew they had a sensation on their hands. They were just looking for the angle they would pour their afternoon's energy into.

Francie managed to skirt around them to get to the hallway entrance that led down the sterile corridor of the infirmary. She stood by the door of the recovery room. In trying to be unobtrusive, Francie didn't notice a small young redhead start to follow her as she slipped quickly through the medical wing door.

Opening the door, Francie gasped as she saw Emma lying in bed with tubes and bandages and monitors—a far cry from Emma's roots. This was surely a science fiction nightmare out of some late night movie where modern technology lovingly embraced anthropoids. Francie always thought she was part of a great experiment that would bring man closer to his cousin, the chimpanzee. Now, at this moment, she felt aligned with the Grand Inquisitor who was issuing a harsh judgment against humans and an even harsher judgment against their simian associates.

Francie, caught up with Emma's precarious condition, didn't bother to close the door completely. Immediately her concentration was on Emma and what she could do to help. She went over to the bed and bent close to Emma's face. "Hi, Emma, it's Francie. How are you doing?"

"Hello, Francie." Emma spoke with such pathos in her voice, that Francie had to clench her teeth to stop the tears from falling on Emma's cheeks. "I hurt. I hurt all over."

"Hang on, Emma. The doctors are going to make you all better. You'll see, Emma. You're going to get better."

"He hurt me, Francie. He hurt my baby. Sad. I much sad."

"Oh Emma, we love you. All the children miss you, and we want you to come back. We want you to get better. We want you, Emma."

Francie thought she saw a glint of a smile quickly pass over Emma's face. Emma tried to say more, but she was having trouble breathing. So Francie bent close to her moving mouth to hear what Emma whispered. Barely hisses of breath, the words trying to punch their way through some invisible opponent, wrangling to get themselves loose, "I love you, Francie....I want my baby....My baby...My baby...My baby, he hurt bad...."

Amid the buzz of the monitors and her rapt attention with

Emma, Francie never saw the young journalist standing by the door. There was a struggle going on between life and death, and strangers were not invited. She couldn't conceive of any intruder eavesdropping on this beleaguered moment as she tried to compel Emma to live. This was Francie's personal vigil, and the remnants of the outside world ceased to exist. Live, Emma, live. Don't let go.

The redheaded reporter, Dariel Grey, was stunned. She had walked into the story of the century—a talking chimp! Edging quietly to the infirmary door, she heard the two females talking: the human woman and the DoRight beast. Although the chimp had problems catching her breath, and Dariel wished that damn medical equipment would run more quietly, she caught the gist of the conversation. Then the woman bent over the broken primate and put her ear to the creature's mouth. At that point, Dariel couldn't grasp what the ape said to her concerned visitor, but she knew the DoRight was moving her lips.

Dariel quickly stepped out of the doorway, already structuring the Pulitzer Prize story swimming through her brain, when the door flew open and the woman ran out screaming for help. "Doctor? Where's the doctor? Somebody, come quick!" The staff rushed out of the white emptiness and bolted into the room. At the same time, the guard came running down the hall and stood in front of the door. Behind him, you could see a flurry of journalists jogging through the corridor, anxious to scoop up the next bit of news. But they didn't have to wait too long. Twenty minutes later, the door opened and the doctor announced, "We lost her."

While he walked down the hall, Francie caught up with him. He knew who Francie was and offered her whatever explanation he could. But it only amounted to, "Sorry, Francie. We tried our damnedest, but the creature suffered way too much internal bleeding, and the force of the blow to her chest just broke her body in two. Her lung was punctured, and we couldn't save her. I really wanted to. She seemed quite pathetic."

Francie wanted to scream, "No, no Doctor, you don't understand. How can you? You're a man. You'll never, never understand. Emma didn't die from a hemorrhage. She died because she saw her baby split apart, broken, torn, shattered. The fruit of her womb, graced with the most ugliest of deaths. That's why she died. She gave up, mister. She just gave up."

But instead of challenging the weary, stale looking man, Francie clutched some residue of courtesy and thanked the doctor.

"Before you go, Francie, I wanted to tell you something. When Emma died, we removed her ovaries, and we're going to use her eggs for reproduction. I don't know if this will help, but Dr. BrickWell has promised her first child to you."

Francie tried to blink back the tears, create a levee before the flooding threatened to pour down her cheeks. Almost inaudibly, she responded, "I know I should appreciate everything you've done to save her—even her future babies. But Doctor, I only wanted my Emma. I wanted her to live so much."

Then, from somewhere deep within where she kept her cache of reserved energy, she increased her pace. Move feet, move. Remember, one foot goes in front of the other. Fast. Faster. Get to the car. Get to the car so you can cry and cry—and cry. So you can cry about the lost innocence of your children and the twisted, ruptured bodies of your DoRight family. Get to the car so you can cry about how you rationalize a life where the harmless, the virtuous, the good are made victims regularly. Get to the car and cry for yourself, Francie, for your pain, for your children's pain, for the world's pain.

By the time Francie returned home, she had wept some of the sadness out of her soul. She knew there would be more days of grief, but she also knew that the sobbing helped her. In the despairing moments of her life (there may not have been many, but they were enough), she climbed into her gloom and rolled around in it like a mud bath, allowing it to envelop her completely. She instinctively knew that the only way to relieve sorrow was to walk into its vortex and feel its severity.

In college, when she broke up with a boyfriend, she'd go in her room, light a candle, and play "The Moonlight Sonata." She called that her depression concerto. During the tough nights of the divorce, she'd sit by the window watching the tree sway back and forth, back and forth, from the ocean breeze. And somehow, she'd get through those times of despondency that allowed pain to play freely and fiercely with her heart. What Francie couldn't understand is why the pain hurt harder the older you grew. Isn't there any skill or trick or shortcut we learn as adults that takes the heaviness and heals it faster?

But Francie knew the answer even while she asked the question. The only thing you learned as the years leaped by is that you must cherish what you love because you can lose it in an instant—or in a night of terror.

Gleefully, Francie's terror became Tully's torch, and he laughed loudly into the phone. "We're all set, sir, for our next ambush. Are you still sure that you don't want me to reconnoiter TriCubed while they're disorganized?"

"Keep to the original orders, Tully. Let's play it out. I need time to evaluate how much attention the press will give it. I'm still toying with the idea of switching to a few human targets." AceArrow was already devising an alternative approach.

"Sir, they're not the enemy. They're your market. Shouldn't you treat them differently? At least, be alerted to their possible panic?"

But Tully's words withered in the lengthy pause that followed. Till AceArrow's voice exploded menacingly through the wires, "Just remember who's financing this deal, Tully. As far as I'm concerned, apes and people occupy the same space. It doesn't really matter who gets hit."

Yet it mattered to FutureDick. All human harm counted. And he was beginning to categorize DoRights as near-humans. As he ran, FutureDick thought about the events of the last 24 hours, assassinations, talking apes, Francie's tears. For a while, he let Francie's face float around his mind.

Unexpectedly, he realized somewhere between his holding her and the present, he let go. He had finally released his demons. Surely he had grieved enough.

Still, as he said goodbye to the comfort of isolation, he tried to understand why he had grieved for so long. Perhaps it was easier that way. Perhaps holding on to the past, which was known, prevented him from starting a future, which was undiscernible. But why should he have been afraid? He walked into danger constantly, professionally as well as athletically. In fact, fear rarely entered his consciousness.

Be honest, FutureDick. Don't bullshit. This is you you're talking to. You've been afraid because it hurt. It hurt too much when Tendra was killed that you decided not to get involved. The independent man, you called yourself. No time for women, strictly one-nighters. You had work and sports and reading. A full life, man. A full life.

But Christ, buddy, admit it. You were hiding, hiding from your emotions. How full is aloneness, FutureDick? No matter how busy you get, do you always want to eat by yourself, sleep by yourself, play by yourself? Which male myth have you bought into? John Wayne? The Lone Ranger? Superman? Isn't it about time you gave up these security blankets? Isn't it about time you let your heart out of its foxhole? Aren't you ready to gamble your vulnerability?

Hurt is part of the human language. You know that. But so is love, man. So is love. How long do you deprive yourself? It's over, man. The mourning's finished. Tendra's dead, and she's not coming back. You can weep forever at her memory, but the mourning's finished. Give yourself permission, FutureDick. Give yourself permission to exercise your emotions. Lord knows, your feelings could use an aerobics class.

FutureDick's laughter escaped spontaneously, merely to be muffled by the aria of a six foot wave. But he looked into that wave and realized he set himself free, for he alone could give himself leniency. Only he could permit himself to walk into the emotional expanse and take the risk of rejection, of anguish, of happiness.

Such a simple comprehension, permission: permission to love, to feel, to care. Yet, for FutureDick, the moment proved profound, for he tapped into the simplicity of life. You are allowed. He was allowed. He was the ultimate arbiter. And the exhilaration of understanding spread through his body, entering the souls of his feet.

Unawares, his step quickened, and he flew along the shore, enjoying the time out, feeling lighter than he had in many years. Every once in a while he shared an intimacy with the sea that reminded him he was part of Nature's munificence. When he experienced this solidarity, like he did today, he felt such a keen sense of personal power that he could have traded places with Atlas and held the world on his shoulders.

He breathed the grey-green water, he absorbed the salty air, and he guzzled the blue of the cloudless sky. This was the oneness that children claimed more often than adults. And FutureDick celebrated this feeling of unity, for it happened rarely. Still he was pleased it happened at all.

He habitually chuckled when he heard pundits proclaim that men were adept at spatial reasoning, and women were especially intuitive. FutureDick was sure that there were women who reasoned like men and men who possessed the feminine insight. He should know. He was one of them. If not for his sixth sense, he would have abandoned private investigation years ago. Yet he felt his hunches so strongly that he knew his mind-body connection was working overtime.

Through the years, he learned to trust his inner sense, sometimes more than his intellect. His brain dealt with facts that he pieced together. But his instinct operated on its own, awakening his perception to a deeper understanding of problems, of issues, and of people. Furthermore, he had spent years reading people, sometimes to his own discomfort. Maybe that's why he enjoyed so much time alone. It became too unsettling for FutureDick to feel the intensity of another person's covert hostility, hidden fear, sheltered anger, concealed duplicity, as it permeated the conversation like the grating smell of a bad cigar.

Consequently, he chose his friends carefully. Rather than select them, he felt them, psychically X-raying their hearts to see if they were good or bad. What an elementary way to understand people he often thought. But he couldn't help it. As much as he criticized his impulsive sensibility, he couldn't ignore it. Every time he tried to squelch it, call his insight a hasty generalization, it rebounded more sharply, intensifying its message and calling attention relentlessly to its impression. So FutureDick listened to his inner voice and heeded its judgment. It was usually right.

Besides, in his attempt to constantly grow better, he enjoyed improving the third side of his human triangle: body, mind, heart. With his body, he moved. With his mind, he thought. And with his heart, he saw. He tried to balance all three parts of his being, and not until last night had he acknowledged something was missing. Not until last night had he admitted to himself that he tried too long to stop feeling love. And with his newfound awareness came added energy as he bounded up the stairs to his house, ready to grapple with these monstrous murders.

During the next few days, FutureDick investigated anyone who might be related to the case. He questioned the TriCubed employees, even the six who had been terminated within the past three years. Each had an alibi. One in particular, by the name of Harold, was quite vocal in his dislike of TriCubed. He complained about their stubbornness. "I'm glad the company's in trouble. None of those bastards would listen to me. You see, they got these rules, mister, and that's all they know. Just go by the rule. Little people like me don't count!"

"What rules are you talking about, Harold?" responded FutureDick. "Company policy or something more subtle?"

Harold quickly stopped FutureDick from probing further. “You know. The sort of rules that have to do with your own personal life. The company don’t belong there. It’s my life, and those assholes can’t tell me how to live it. Where do they get off dealing with employees that way? Besides, mister, they don’t treat you nice. Think they’re better than you. I hate ‘em, hate ‘em all.”

“But murdering DoRights, isn’t that a harsh punishment to impose upon TriCubed? Certainly you don’t condone that, do you?”

“Hear me, mister, and hear me well. Those bastards deserve everything they get. I hope to God they lose their shirts. The only thing I’m sorry about is I wasn’t there to see their faces when they found out about their precious DoRights. That’ll teach ‘em to care more about apes than they do about people. That’ll show ‘em they got to treat their employees better.” And Harold grinned as he silently considered the guardian angel who was carrying out his desperate dreams.

When FutureDick investigated Harold’s account of the unholy night, Harold had an airtight alibi. He got drunk in the neighborhood bar and passed out. The police took him to detox downtown, and he didn’t leave the center till ten the next morning.

FutureDick met a couple of times with the president of HEART and found out about a splinter group, Dark Friday. This new activist organization made itself heard by putting up flyers at the usual places: the university, the health food stores, the bus station, and the coffee houses. They even pasted the all-night laundries and public toilets in SeaBank, resolved to impress people’s minds when they were least expecting it.

Determined to speak to anyone slimly connected to DoRights or animals in general, FutureDick called Dark Friday’s president, Clarene Wishman. She invited him to a meeting the next night. From what he could tell, the group did more talking than protesting. They were trying to figure out how to raise money in order to fly to DC and storm the Congress.

He couldn't be completely sure, but they looked woefully unprepared to engage in any kind of terrorism. And FutureDick knew that without a bankroll, terrorists lost a lot of their terror. He hoped they might be able to give him some clues as to who would benefit by killing DoRights. But they were as baffled as he. They couldn't conceive of anyone, unprovoked, who might hurt these defenseless creatures.

FutureDick thought he might have a lead when he went to the UHLF meeting and heard a brash, disgruntled unemployed construction worker take the podium and speak. He was angry. The audience was angry. They were angry at months of unemployment, sometimes years, and the lack of any help from the government, the church, the corporation. Nobody, no agency, no aid came from anywhere, and they felt stranded.

But their anger focused at trying to operate within the legal framework. For how long they would remain peaceful, FutureDick couldn't estimate. But right now, they were preoccupied with building a grassroots organization that would erect an amendment to the Constitution: *No person shall be without a job. If any person is competent and willing to work, and such person is not employed in the private sector, the Department of Labor must hire such person for the public works sector.*

This organization had its hands full with trying to channel the hostile energy emanating from hopelessness and redirect it in a constructive way, a way that would enable UHLF to make a difference.

First they wanted to devise a case that would go to the Supreme Court. Then they could target their greater goal: the establishment of a people's party that would enter the next presidential race.

The meeting seemed more a means to vent frustration, so that the participants felt some sort of emotional support. They were displaced, outside the mainstream, and the Union was trying to create community. Obviously, massacring DoRights didn't promote that purpose. UHLF was trying to formulate a practical method whereby these disadvantaged could still hang on.

Baffled, FutureDick approached the case from another angle. What was there about the DoRights that made their elimination beneficial? Who or what would gain with their disappearance? Certainly not their owners. And, decidedly, not TriCubed. But who stood on the periphery of the DoRights' success? Who watched these docile apes develop a following of owner-patrons and cringed, crippled with enough loathing to kill?

For every action, there's a reaction, and for every winner, there's a loser. But for every success, does someone else have to fail? FutureDick couldn't provide the answer to his thoughtful question. He hoped to God that such a theory was illogical, but it was clearly possible that someone or something toppled as the DoRights innocently set the world on fire. He had to speak to Adam BrickWell—soon.

Fourteen

Days went by, one blending into the other, as Francie resumed her routine. There were the children to wake and send off to school, there were her clients to see and restore, there was a family life that started when the classroom let out: lessons, practice, competition. The children engaged in those fertile activities after school that added an enhanced dimension to their sense of self and kept Francie racing to pickup points before and after dinner.

And usually there was her hour, her private hour, the sixty minutes she stole each day to run or play racquetball. She guarded those minutes ferociously and only relinquished them for emergencies. Even in times of high stress, like this past week and a half, she snatched her sixty minutes and played FD on consecutive Mondays. In fact, she reasoned, what better time was there to work out than when you were under stress?

Francie remembered when her youngest, April, was small enough for a stroller. She'd wheel the child to the track, plunk the carrier in the middle of the field, and run her twelve laps around the sitting baby. Like a clown, she'd yell, wave her hands, make faces—whatever it took to engage April, and whatever it took for Francie to get her running accomplished for that day.

When it rained, those few precious southern California days, Francie would run through the house, prancing from room to room. Soon April joined her, then Josh, and maybe Sara and Lanie, if they were around. After ten minutes, the family found themselves wending through chairs, tables, and beds, asking, "When do we finish, Mom? We're getting tired." But Francie continued for at least thirty minutes, till the boredom of the shortened path finally vanquished her. Then she'd run an extra mile the next day when the sun once more appeared.

Francie learned that athletics were her salvation. They kept her going when her emotional life was pulled. The more she increased her physical stamina, her breath, her sense of well-being, the stronger became her determination to get through this life with grace, with dignity, and most definitely, with a full heart. Those last years with Alan were a strenuous test for her. But she ran, and she ran, and one day, in the middle of her jog, she knew she could go it alone. She could walk into life with her children, challenge fate, and say, "I can do it!" The awareness, the confidence, that flashed through her body that day never left her as she vowed to end the marriage and start again.

Once Francie went through the process of renewal, she would be able to share the experience with her clients-to-be. Because once you've walked around in hell, you become comrades with everyone else who has endured the depths of loneliness, pain, rejection. But Francie learned well from her stroll through despair. She learned that the human spirit is indomitable and fights to survive. She learned that the tears lessen. And she learned that out of death, comes rebirth. For every ending, there is a beginning, and Francie began again.

That was the miracle she made for herself. She created a second time around. An older, seasoned, emotionally experienced

Francie started school, started her family as a single woman, and started a new game: racquetball. She glided through school competently, she reared her children with the nurturance of unlimited love poured out on their sprouting lives, but the athletic challenge of mastering the game of racquetball became her obsession.

How could hitting a ball against a wall be so formidable? She'd aim in one direction, and the ball would fly in the other. She'd swing, and she'd miss. She'd go for a backhand with all her might and never get the ball across the court. Instead, it weakly limped along the floor. The game dared her to succeed, and she took up the war cry with the fury of a baby gasping its first breath. She would beat this physical opposition. She would learn how to artfully maneuver her body around the empty, huge, sterile cell and hit that evasive blue ball with pinpoint precision. She would conquer her body's clumsiness.

So Francie practiced in between classes, when the children were in school, when the children were asleep. She practiced in every spare moment she retrieved. She even practiced in her sleep, dreaming intricate shots in that twilight zone before heavy slumber. The ball would smash into the corner and die, deflated, overcome.

But the game's defiance became her deliverance. Instead of incessantly concentrating on her poverty, her aloneness, her 26 hour day, she broke up her persistent terror with her desire to master a game, a simple game, a small game, but an athletic diversion that empowered her to stay alive. And Francie became good. She gripped her racquet with authority, caressed the mindful rubber ball, and proceeded to overpower her opponent. Male as well as female, she didn't care. She just wanted to control that small three-inch irrepressible ball.

Like Francie, FutureDick also found himself enticed by the siren wail of the seemingly silent racquetball court. Temptation emanated from the plaster walls, daring its occupants to perfect their game. The closer they came to controlling the erratic rubber ball, the less slack they allowed themselves for error. And that might be where the grand deception took place.

The game seduced you into thinking you could control anything. After all, if you could regulate a ball speeding over seventy miles an hour, why couldn't you manage the caprices of the universe? For a few brief seconds, racquetball players play God, till they open the door at the end of a match, and life slaps them in the face.

But at this moment, FutureDick's investigative approach was taking a severe pummeling. He had control over nothing and sorely needed some direction, yet BrickWell wasn't able to furnish any leads.

"Adam, you've got to replay TriCubed's development for me. Is it possible you or one of your executives stepped on the wrong toes? Perhaps when you began importing chimps from Africa? Maybe a government official, some agency, some group took exception with your plans?"

"FutureDick, I've been mulling it over myself. Everything we did was aboveboard. It's not often you get a vote of confidence from the preservationists and the hunters at the same time. But we did! We kept the chimps from becoming extinct and paid their pursuers more for hunting less. By the end of the nineties, the countries themselves had set up strict protection laws for their primates. I can't imagine dissatisfaction from those groups. We all won in the final transactions."

"But someone, something, some group must have lost as you and your company gained success. Otherwise, there's no motive here. And I'm hesitant to call this random violence. It was too well planned. If it were some type of hate crime, Adam, the organization's certainly supported by big money."

"If our hate has reduced us to killing innocent chimps, we won't be able to walk out our front doors. No one's safe in that sort of society."

"Hold on, Adam, I haven't reached that kind of conclusion yet. It would be easy to blame it on drugs, youth gangs, or even devil worshippers, but something's gnawing at me to look for a more practical reason. If we find the reason, we find the logic. Who do you know who hates chimpanzees?"

"That's a tough question to ask me, FutureDick, because I see the world through my own lenses. I've given a lifetime for their survival. They're good, they're kind, they're loving, and they're fun to play with as well as teach. In a sense, they're the closest I've come to moral perfection. How can I slide into the consciousness of the deranged? And that's the sort of aberration it would take to torture and kill these animals. For the life of me, I can't seem to intellectually get anywhere near that kind of hate."

"Well, think about it, Adam. Just try to envision who or what loses when you gain. It's there, right in front of us. We just can't see it yet. But those households were selected as targets for some particular advantage, some message, some warning."

"I agree, FutureDick, but I never learned how to speak the murderer's language."

Yet Francie forced herself to study a new language: SportsSpeak, the lingo of the court, a vernacular grounded in the game of racquetball, the game that offered her another lease on life. Eventually the diversion became her new school, the University of Existence, as her induction into competition taught her lessons she never learned in college, or in child-rearing, or in marriage.

Francie discerned that the rules in the athletic arena are different from ordinary affairs. She recognized that it's appropriate to be aggressive, to challenge, and to win. Consequently, Francie liberated a part of her personality she never knew she owned. The nurturing component of her being was only one aspect of her totality. She also owned a fierce competitiveness that flourished in a contest of physical skill.

She realized that once your athletic competence is expanded, it's your intellect that controls the game. That newly-found knowledge increased Francie's respect for quick decision-makers who chose correctly. Those were the geniuses of the world. They saw a problem, a riddle, an opportunity, and their brain evaluated the options at heightened speed—then they proceeded. They ran the choices through their mental encyclopedia, a compendium that swiftly amassed information from sight, from experience, from intuition, and they acted. And Francie acted. She knew her options on the court, and she executed the best of the alternatives instantaneously.

She perceived the court as a microcosm of human ethics. Who a person is, their sometimes hidden self, becomes exposed during the course of the fast paced game. Honesty, courtesy, intelligence rise to the surface in those sixty minutes when two opponents enter the white-washed plastered rectangle, shut the world off from interrupting, and proceed to bash a seamed rubber sphere against the wall. The superego takes a nap, thereby unleashing the basic impulses of the person's genuine identity. And in this time and space, the real warriors show themselves.

But the rule that illuminated Francie's comprehension and boldly underscored all her previous lessons was the Tenet of Territorialism. When a woman enters the field of male gladiators, she treads on sacred ground, ground that has rarely been stepped on by the female of the species. The male will fight to the death to hold his position. Simply, a man does not want to be beaten by a woman on his athletic turf. And Francie was certain she brought out some kind of inner strength that her male opponents kept in reserve for life or death situations—because they would do anything, climb the walls, dive for the ball, bash their elbow, anything, to not lose to a woman.

Yet as hard as they played, Francie subdued them in many, many games. She was sure she changed their lives as much as the competition changed hers. It wasn't the academic or business world where equality needed to evolve; it was in the sporting theaters, where male and female of like ability and fortitude could challenge each other as equals. This was the true test of person to person; this was the key to the executive washroom.

Moreover, Francie's athletic enlightenment allowed her to gain confidence in her opinions, her mothering, her body, and, at the same time, posed an ache in her heart. Would she ever meet a man ready to accept her as she is, strong, determined, uncompromising, and fervently maternal? Had she turned into a package of dynamite too volatile for any male partner?

"They're stronger than dynamite, sir! These troops annihilate their targets in minutes. Pure precision. Like they've been soldiers for years."

"Good, Tully. That's the way I wanted it. No hesitation."

"Are you kidding? These robots are better than bullets, and they don't swerve when they hit bone. They're always on the offense, and when finished, they just walk away, ready for the next raid. Beauty in motion!"

"Well, that's how we programmed them. Good machines are hard to beat, my man." AceArrow actually had some lilt to his voice when he mentioned his robots. His one permanent pleasure, the CEO took pride in everything his machines performed—even if their atrocities betrayed nature with the most brutal of acts.

"Wish you had been there, sir. Tonight was outstanding!" And Tully glittered with the satisfaction of the victor, forgetting that the spoils were a composite of flesh, fear, and broken body parts.

But the private knowledge owned by AceArrow and Tully became public domain when FutureDick turned on the late evening news. Expecting to hear about the commonplace robberies, drug busts, and accidental homicides that repeated night after night, he listened halfheartedly to overly-perfect announcers, who blared their disasters with disarming half-grins. If crimes were hamburgers, McDonald's might have a serious rival.

Nonetheless, his sarcasm soured five minutes into the program when the newscaster reported that Chicago had been hit by a series of clan killings that evening. FutureDick felt a phantom boxer deliver a right to his belly, and he tried to suck in the air that had just evacuated his body. So far, five clans had been killed, but the count wasn't in yet.

"Why are you shocked, man?" he asked himself.

"You know violent crime has been increasing," he answered.

"But these are animals. Innocent, defenseless, and kind."

"Since when did killers become concerned with ethical considerations?"

"But why Chicago?"

"Why anywhere, man? Something's wrong, terribly wrong!"

FutureDick's inner dialogue wasn't merely a game he played. It was a mental test, a serious question and answer parley he performed when he desperately wanted some understanding.

Ten days had passed since the murders in SeaBank. Psyches were still numb from that rampage, and now the killer struck again. At least this time, FutureDick knew what he was up against. It wasn't a local inhabitant or hate squad. It was a well-organized, well-financed operation. Someone or some group was able to quietly move from one city to another in a short amount of time and precisely pinpoint their targets.

What did Harold say that stuck in his mind? "I'm glad the company's in trouble." FutureDick had never bothered to ask Harold what do you mean by trouble? He figured that the company would have to replace the clans at their own expense, and anytime there's a chunk of change taken out of profit, it's trouble for the business.

But this was trouble on a grander scale: this was trouble for present clan owners as well as potential clan owners. This was big trouble if you had a serial killer on your hands that could freely roam from state to state and, possibly, country to country.

As his mind weaved its way through devious criminal schemes, the phone rang. Francie was calling to theorize about the new state of events. "I'm relieved," she said, "that these assassins are gone from SeaBank. Even with the 24 hour police watch at the house, I've never felt completely safe. I've had trouble sleeping every night, and for some reason, I'm still concerned about the kids."

FutureDick wanted to say, "But Francie, they could return. You know as well as I do that SeaBank is corporate headquarters."

Deliberately, he smothered his first response and said, "Francie, your kids are tough. I think they've separated the crime from themselves, and now with this latest series of murders, they can see it's all directed toward the DoRights."

"I want to believe you, FD. God knows I do, but it seems I've generalized the fear. I can't help feeling that it's not over yet. Chicago's just not far enough away for me. I suppose Mars wouldn't be either."

"Don't worry, Francie. You don't think I'd let anything happen to my blossoming racquetball opponent, do you? I need your competitive cleverness to keep me on my toes or at least chasing the ball."

They bantered back and forth for a few minutes, and Francie asked how the case was going. "Do you have any leads at all?"

"Nada, Francie, nada!"

But he wanted to take her mind off the massacre and never mentioned tomorrow's appointment with BrickWell. Perhaps this latest series of killings might spark a faint memory from the scientist. Somewhere along the way, the guy made some enemies. He had to. We all do. Still Francie was smart to remain defensive. It kept her alert. It kept her safe. So he said, "I know what you did, Francie. You got me to come into your life under the guise of wanting my professional expertise. What you actually wanted was an athletic partner you could try to humiliate in the court."

"Oh, FD, I didn't need to deceive you for that. I could have cornered you at the gym and shamed you into playing me. If I had asked you in front of enough people, you couldn't afford to say no. It would look like you were afraid you'd be clobbered by a woman!"

"Francie, your being a woman doesn't scare me. It's the precision of your game that terrifies me into chasing the damn ball."

"Seriously, FD, I do appreciate everything you've done to help. If you hadn't been there that terrible night, I would have buckled. I know I look strong to you, but honestly, it felt good to have someone else to depend on for a change. I really thank you. It meant a lot to me."

Then Francie, suddenly embarrassed, quickly said goodbye. And FutureDick slowly hung up the phone, thinking, even though he had been pulled into a nightmarish world of savage casualty, he had also walked into the universe of Francie Franks, and he didn't want to leave.

Stunned, BrickWell sat before the TV, replaying in his brain the newscaster's descriptions of murder. Somewhere off in the distance of his stuccoed, three story California-modern home, a phone rang, trying to pierce the stupor hemming in the scientist's consciousness. Somewhere normal life still continued outside his mind, but he was imprisoned with visions of his babies, his trusting, loveable chimpanzee babies, ripped, bleeding, mutilated.

How could anyone do this to a DoRight? These animals were human-helpers. They hugged, they kissed, they patted, they groomed—they were man's closest advocates. They were bred to do almost anything for the human species. A DoRight clan was the nearest we came to witnessing cooperation, love, and loyalty on a sustained basis, a testament to what a civilized paradise might be like. The apes nurtured, worked, played and cared for each other. There was nothing in their activity to provoke outside hostility, and yet, they were being murdered, systematically, as if they were the country's worst enemy. But there was nothing antagonistic about them. Why? Why the hell why?

Instead of an answer, all his query did was bring up face-flashes of the many DoRights he had known over the years. Swimming in and out of his mental photo album was the special countenance of Viva, the first DoRight he saw born. Eighteen years ago, he still remembered the date: December 23, 1988.

It was raining, one of those rare unending eight hour torrential downpours. He'd just returned home from the lab when he received the message to come back. Lillianne was going into labor. BrickWell rushed over to his familiar work place and sat with Lillianne for the long evening, watching her give birth.

The act of giving life was in itself a marvel to BrickWell, but the baby DoRight's ability to survive its initial shock with the outside environment was nothing short of miraculous. The first thing a baby ape must do when it is born is to cling tightly to its mother's fur. It does this instinctively as it holds on with both its hands and its feet. BrickWell was so moved by this three pound creature's fight for life, for protection, for its mother's body, that he named her Viva: for life. And as he watched Lillianne lay back nestling Viva to her warm body, BrickWell thought this is the image that should be painted on the Sistine Chapel. This is where life and love originally started.

For the next few weeks, he crammed every free moment he had with watching Lillianne's maternal behavior. A recipient of nature's profoundest gift, the bonding of mother and child, Lillianne guarded her infant zealously. The baby, its eyes large but bright, with a small wrinkled face and oversize ears pressed flat against its head, covered with thick black hair, stayed tightly clasped to its mother's body for ten weeks and went everywhere with her. Never once in that time was the infant separated from its parent, while she nursed it, cleaned and groomed its fur, and hugged it closely, hugged it continually throughout the day.

Even though Viva started to crawl by herself when she was three months old, Lillianne remained intensely protective of her child, and it took one more month till she'd let another chimp touch her newborn. BrickWell knew from his research that a chimpanzee mother would die for her child, and that children intervene to protect their mother. But it was his firsthand experience with Lillianne and Viva that made the written words ring true, for his eyes saw how strong and enduring the mother-child relationship truly was. They were one. Genetically united, they were responsible for each other's well-being and created a symbiosis that lightning couldn't sever.

Although he certainly felt secure in his masculinity and couldn't imagine himself being anything other than a man, a husband, a father, BrickWell sometimes speculated on what Lillianne and Viva experienced, or for that matter, his own wife and children, a tenacious tie he would never know. He'd shield his family, he'd fight for his country or his friends, but what kind of connection breaches your individuality and binds you forever to its life? Could he pledge his loyalty forever to anything? He doubted it. Yet, as he watched Viva grow and Lillianne protect and care, he knew theirs was a forever promise. And again, he asked himself, "Why? God help me, why?"

These are helpless, loving creatures, unprotected in today's sophisticated weapons environment. Admittedly BrickWell knew his anguish not only stemmed from the blaring bestiality of the crime but also from his culpability. He endangered the DoRights in the first place. He introduced them to the world of humanity—or as far as he was concerned, the world of inhumanity. As aggressive as their ancestral society was, there remained a spirit of cooperation and play. The ape community did not intentionally murder its females. It was biologically programmed not to. Who else would perpetuate the species?

But now, because of him, the females were being ripped apart. It was more than just a criminal offense. It was an outrage, an abomination, because anyone who interacted with these chimps and created a relationship knew of their unrestrained love. He saw it all the time, between the chimps themselves and between the chimps and their human teachers. Even he experienced their emotional generosity.

Since Viva was the first baby born in the compound, BrickWell spent part of his valuable research time playing with the one year old chimp child. Viva was his prodigy, and he would show the world what a fine piece of animal craftsmanship he had wrought. For three years, BrickWell became Viva's human father. Then his schedule grew too demanding to spend additional time in the compound. He had to direct the introduction of their new product, the DoRights, to the country. He had to make it happen.

Months went by till he walked back into the compound to see Viva. He suspected she'd be happy to see him, but he never anticipated the uninhibited welcome he received. When the little ape spotted him, she let loose a smile that engaged her face from ear to ear, and with earsplitting shrieks of excitement, she pounded the ground with joy for close to three minutes. Then she ran up and leaped into his arms, giving him a tremendous chimp embrace.

After they hugged each other for a few moments, Viva pulled away and started to groom him. She sifted slowly through his eyebrows and then the hair on his head, looking for some foreign body she could pull off. When he squatted to set her down, she gently but firmly ripped open the buttons of his shirt and continued to groom the hair on his chest. Then she scrambled over to his sock, pulling it down, and inspected the lower part of his calf.

BrickWell learned that grooming permeated virtually every aspect of chimpanzee social life. Besides its functioning to help care for the skin, it provided for long bouts of relaxed, friendly physical contact, which consequently reduced stress in many situations. It restored harmony in the wake of aggression, and it expressed fondness, particularly between mother and child, siblings, and now in Viva's world, between herself and her human family.

But BrickWell never tired of the experience of being groomed. It was the most liberated greeting he knew, and he steadily felt that chimps were much more culturally advanced than humans because of their sessions of social grooming. So he groomed back, carefully picking through Viva's head and back and chest.

When Viva had groomed and hugged for fifteen minutes, she grabbed both his hands to play their game, the ancient childhood romp BrickWell's grandmother had taught him: *Ring Around the Rosie*. Enchanted by the repetition, by the opportunity to frolic, by the singularity of their private pastime, Viva bobbed with delight at each recurrence of "all fall down."

Deeply moved by her honest, exuberant, unsuppressed show of affiliation, BrickWell kept turning his head so she wouldn't see the accumulated tears. When an ape loves, it really loves, and it really loves in perpetuity. It would have to take a pure psychopath or non-human, which in his mind were one of the same, to harm these creatures. It would have to take an act of insanity, done by someone who never loved or never was loved in return, because the sane do not destroy the only thing the world has going for it: benevolence. The DoRights were the most charitable living things around, and what devil incarnate wanted to spit in the face of their unselfishness?

Fifteen

The night was lost, and he was going nowhere. Every lead dried up. The police, trying to pierce the impenetrable, ran into dead ends and they found nothing. No clues, no motives, no prints—not one damn fingerprint.

Feebly, offering a practical explanation of the vanilla odor, the lab's conclusion (a suggestion those familiar with DoRights presumed anyway) pried loose a phantasmagoric vision of languid apes being dazed to death. Apparently, a spray or time-released aerosol bomb emitted the sweet-smelling extract in such large quantities that the chimps were literally drenched into dullness. Overcome by the tranquilizing effects of the scent, the softly-sedated, muted DoRights sluggishly fell into a vanilla bog, where every last one of them was annihilated.

This analysis supposedly explained the chimps' silence, but FutureDick disagreed. When self-preservation squares off against a soporific, the urgency for survival has to strike the stronger blow—unless genetic tampering eventually tempered the DoRights' epinephrinal obligation to struggle for life. Still, the instinct to live was basic, emerging from the core of Nature's endowment. Where was the shriek? Who heard the cry?

No, FutureDick reasoned, there had to be another component to their submission. Someone stronger, someone smarter, someone faster, nimble enough to slaughter eight listless apes in an instant. Who, what, how many could carry out noiseless extermination in the blink of an eye? As his answers withered with the onslaught of more questions, FutureDick squinted out his window and tried to glimpse the recent brutality. But he saw only shadows, dark spots where killers were supposed to be.

Yesterday, FutureDick took the metallic plate he found by the sewer to his friend, Saxony. As a metallurgist, she would be able to identify the constituents of the nondescript fragment. But he could see that this case was taking on a national dimension, and he had no motive to work with. Tomorrow morning, he had an appointment with BrickWell. The single avenue to finding answers would have to be through TriCubed's contacts, and since the corporation did business all over the globe, FutureDick felt he was looking at the stars and trying to find which one of the billions would shoot across the sky at this precise moment.

On the brighter side, he had been getting to know Francie better. And that felt good. They went jogging together and even played a couple of racquetball matches with each other. Although he was a stronger opponent, she was a feisty little player, and he found if he let down during a game, she'd capture enough points to nearly beat him.

There was nothing romantic between them—yet. He was taking this very slowly. But so was Francie. Most importantly, they both wanted to develop a friendship, to get to know the insides of each other. He remembered the other evening, Francie swiftly kissing him goodnight, barely brushing his lips, and saying, "That's all you get, FD. I want to really know you, and I don't want all that other stuff to get in the way."

That felt fine to him. If he was going to open himself up once more, FutureDick knew it had to be a day by day process, a painstakingly slow development, because if he ever loved again, he wanted some sort of surety that he could amble into old age with the woman. As everlasting as our modern inconstancy would allow, he wanted a for keeps relationship. He wanted to stroke the white hair of his beloved and brag with pure joy that she was his best friend.

Though he went with a few women since Tendra's death, he knew it would never amount to anything. He knew that before he asked them, before he rang their bell, before he slipped under the covers. He supposed he dated occasionally to make certain he was still male, needing some vain verification that he could be attracted to the female, that he could spend an evening or afternoon talking, touching, easing out of his pain. But it never actually worked. He distanced himself, and no woman ever pressed close enough to penetrate his hermetic shield.

Even in the act of sex, FutureDick felt alone, untouched in a universe of pain, physically spent, but emotionally barren. So he put extra hours into work, into sports, into activities that would burn up the unused, seething energy that kept replenishing itself at a rapid rate.

Not till Francie opened her door the day of the massacre did FutureDick feel like initiating a connection. Maybe it was finally time, that elusive commodity which works its own way with the mind and the heart. Or maybe, just maybe, he had been waiting for the right woman, the like woman, the only woman who could make him forget what he once loved lifetimes ago—and make him want to begin again, wiser, older, and definitely more tentative.

When FutureDick walked into BrickWell's office, the next morning, he saw the strain on the scientist's face.

"I'm still dazed from last night, FutureDick. It's tearing me apart. Math is so easy for me to understand, but murder so unintelligible."

"Adam, you've got to help me here. It just doesn't make any sense. Surely it's larger than DoRights. There's a message here—one of power, one of persistence. Someone's trying to tell you something. Think. Who gains when you lose?"

"Wish I knew, FutureDick. I'm the only one in this business."

After FutureDick left BrickWell's office, the words "only one in this business" played on the edge of his mind. That was true. When he studied the domestic services industry, FutureDick learned that TriCubed had no other animal competitors. The company was too far ahead in its research and development program for any other biological engineering firm to catch up. But what about the competition outside the animal market? As he sipped his cup of coffee, he recognized the possibility of competition. Who or what competes with the DoRights? What was left? Humans, machines, or aliens?

Immediately, FutureDick discounted aliens. He was convinced that the first visitors to our planet wouldn't want to harm animals or, for that matter, disrupt the service of cleaning homes. Although he was being facetious with himself, he admitted that he shared a somewhat idealized notion of extraterrestrials. Perhaps he had been brainwashed by E.T. or Isaac Asimov, but he knew that aliens would be of an inquisitive rather than destructive nature.

If they traveled so far to explore other worlds, why would they want to destroy what they've just found? It's man who destroys, man who kills. Animals usually wound their own and solely in special circumstances, such as leadership combat or territorial dispute. They're not out to kill their species. Man is. His aggressiveness supplants his rationality and any kind of sensitivity toward preservation of the species. Isn't man the only animal capable of genocide? What other earthly creature plans and carries out mass extermination? Didn't Asimov write in *I ROBOT*...

And with that, FutureDick never finished his thought. His

brain pounced upon that word: *robot, robotics.* That was the other serious industry competitor to the DoRights. Robots were being used worldwide in manufacturing, research, medicine, and certainly for the past ten years as domestics. But when TriCubed hit the domestic services industry, robot sales dropped. People preferred living things within their households. They collected plants and dogs and cats—and now DoRights.

Although the robot could service a home efficiently, it lacked the gentle humanity a DoRight immediately instilled. So the home robot sales had plateaued. Those who worshipped machines continued to purchase domestic robots, but from what FutureDick recalled, the sales kept growing thinner. He must find out which companies were still in business.

Now for the first time in days, something made sense. If he looked at the brutality with economic vision, the possibility of a motive began to take shape. If the murders were hate crimes, the assassins would have killed more. They had that capability. They wouldn't have waited ten days when they could have lynched a hell of a lot of DoRights in the meantime. They wouldn't have traveled cross-country either. There were too many peaceful apes between SeaBank and Chicago to spare the expense.

On the other hand, if the murders were committed out of fear, he'd have to discover who or what a DoRight had frightened. And if any suspects were frightened, they'd have to be absolutely terrified. Nothing FutureDick read or heard substantiated a DoRight's ability to instill that kind of alarm, that particular brand of panic which warranted genocide. Possible. Possible?

But not as probable as vengeance generated from Wall Street. The fight for power, for position, for money, created its own kind of magnetic mystique. So hypnotic, so heady, that men forgot they must be moral. Too many times their motivation clouded their rules of conduct, and they failed to ask, "Is it right?" Instead they demanded, "Can it be done?" Bottom line: Can we? Not, should we? These little Machiavelli's stepped on anything or anyone who stood in the way of their profit or potential. Had the DoRights inadvertently become a deterrent to someone's dreams of becoming a king?

And with that thought, FutureDick went to call Saxony about the metal plate he had found. But when her answering machine picked up his call, he assumed she was still on vacation. Up to this time, she'd uncovered nothing, and now she was probably in Cancun, drinking margaritas while the DoRights slept soundly in their quarters, oblivious of encroaching danger.

But Tully thrived on danger. Walking the precipice was the only experience that energized his life so completely. The more he tasted the thrill of tempting death, the more he craved that adrenalin rush. Ordinary life was just that: ordinary. But going to the edge, holding power over what lives and what dies while protecting your personal vulnerability, that was the height of intoxication. And Tully wanted to quaff the nectar of aggression till he reeled in its drunkenness.

Sixteen

Research compels time to pass slowly. As you sift through your facts in the morning and continue the word journey while the sun goes down, information piles up till you reach the end or the breaking point. For FutureDick, there wasn't any breaking point. He never allowed himself that luxury. Instead, he plodded through financial reports, business magazines, *Wall Street Journals*, and industry directories till he found out what he needed to know. Five days had gone by since he last met with BrickWell.

Five days of trying to figure out corporate culpability. BrickWell thought his hunch was farfetched. "I wish it were some CEO, for Christ's sake. That narrows down the search."

"Why not, Adam? What would make a CEO cleaner than a common thief? They're both after money."

"Possibly, FutureDick. But a CEO's got a hell of a lot more to lose. He's got a business at stake."

"That's just the point, Adam. Big bucks, bigger risks!"

"I don't know. I keep thinking it's some crazies out there,

some type of eco-terrorists who don't like genetically manipulated animals."

"I don't disagree, Adam. You may be right. But my gut tells me this is a well-financed operation, and I haven't found any fringe groups dealing with that kind of cash. They'd rather buy Birkenstocks."

What FutureDick discovered was that many of the blossoming robotics companies, blushing with entrepreneurial lust twenty years ago, closed within the last five years. There were a few survivors who appeared to be holding their own in this highly competitive global market. Their stock increased or at least remained steady. But one company, Robomaids, clearly looked like it was in a spasmodic financial struggle to keep its doors open. Its profits declined each quarter along with the value of its stocks.

FutureDick tried Saxony again, but still no response. It had been five days since he left his last message. Every other day, he'd return to the houses where the DoRight slaughters had begun. Every other day, he'd comb the lawns, searching for missed revelations from days before, but no other clue ever jumped out at him. The grass sat there, silent, ignorant, uncaring.

When he left the library late in the afternoon, he drove to Francie's. She invited him for dinner that night, and he realized he had been pleasurably excited all day about spending the evening with her family. FutureDick was an only child, so he tended to romanticize large family meals, where brothers and sisters sat around, joking, talking, smiling. Intellectually, he knew he created a fantasy, that big households didn't consistently equate to contentment. But emotionally, he participated in the myth. The little five year old, who perpetually wanted a sibling to share his secrets with but now remained hidden in the adult's sentimental memory, thrilled whenever he had a chance to be part of a big family on a holiday or special occasion.

Francie's spirited meal was no exception. The words flew faster than flies around the table, and FutureDick relished every minute of the clamor that seemed quite natural to the blended family boisterously enjoying themselves. Different conversations erupted at various spots around the table, amid the passing of platters and interspersed among the gulps and chewing of food. Between Reba's brood and Francie's, they almost had a football team. They definitely had a baseball team, and they had no problem getting someone to play Risk or Monopoly whenever the desire arose.

The kids were bright and energetic, but FutureDick grew particularly fond of Josh. The young boy had a softness about him. Even though he was a first-rate gymnast as well as a strong student, he exuded a modesty FutureDick rarely came across in young men. Josh was genuinely friendly, and FutureDick spent a good part of the evening recounting experiences to him about his work. The boy was intrigued. When he said goodnight, he shook FutureDick's hand and thanked him for spending time with him. FutureDick wanted to grab the kid and hug him for making him feel unequivocally accepted, but instead, he shook his hand and said, "Anytime Josh, I really enjoyed talking with you."

FutureDick hung around while Francie put the younger ones to bed. He realized that a great deal of her world revolved around her children and her commitment to them. And he couldn't help but admire the juggling act she played. She passionately wanted to make their reality a positive occurrence, filled with enthusiasm and opportunity, but Francie knew, as he knew, that her grasp could extend just so far. She couldn't stop the bruises that the children would confront when they walked out their front door. Hell, she couldn't even stop the brutality from intruding on her perfectly planned communal home.

When Francie came downstairs, they sat for awhile drinking decaf and talking. FutureDick told Francie about his own family. He glossed over the tragedy, but from the way Francie seemed to be studying his eyes, he knew she felt some of the torture he had been through. She didn't press him. She could wait till he was ready to say more.

Now, FutureDick felt like talking about her children. He wanted to know who they were, how they were. What was the face that company didn't see? This was a topic that Francie could probably write a thesis on, and she grew so wrapped up in talking about the kids that when she glanced away and saw the clock, she cried, "Whoops, FD. See how you get me going! I wanted to see the news, and it's 11:01."

"Francie, the news is always there. It never goes away, sort of like a sinus headache lingering in the background."

"But FD, there's a mighty world out there to learn about."

"No, Francie Franks, there's a more magnificent world in here to learn about."

She turned on the TV, ready to be hypnotized by some tragedy, some environmental disaster, some civil war, some politician's posturing. And the color drained from her face when she heard the announcer say, "Stand by! Another mass slaying of DoRights in Phoenix, Arizona."

Francie looked at FutureDick with a wild shine in her eyes and whispered, "They're coming closer, FD. They're coming back!"

FutureDick didn't answer. He was miles away, traversing the distant regions of the mind, where the brain valiantly tries to fit the next digit in the equation so it makes some sense. Some goddamn sense. He wasn't worried about the proximity of Arizona to California. No state was either near or far with technology's recent ability to provide hyperspeed to any destination in the world—if you could pay for it.

He was worried about the frequency of the crimes. The killings were happening closer together, now only five days between this massacre and the last. But he had nothing—just dead, mutilated bloody bodies.

For a few minutes, FutureDick remained quiet. He was thinking. He talked to TigerTail everyday, but the detective had scoured SeaBank and reported no new leads. Chicago also had nothing. Invisible clues and torn bodies, the crimes were committed by barbaric ghosts who descended in the middle of the night and then disappeared. Only FutureDick knew these crimes were committed by flesh and blood organisms, living things who killed cleanly, mercilessly, and now, way too frequently. The deaths were unbelievably violent with ripped ape body parts flung around the rooms, but there were still no clues.

Since the Chicago murders occurred several thousand miles away, TigerTail called off his 24 hour police security from the original SeaBank homes. FutureDick couldn't argue with this decision. The teams could be catching criminals instead of watching tomblike, saddened homes. But his reverie dissipated abruptly when he realized he would rather not be solving a crime at this moment. Any case could wait, for sitting next to him was a beautiful but frightened woman, a woman he wanted to know completely.

FutureDick put his arm around Francie and firmly held her. Maybe he could transmit some of his strength, some of his safety, some of his warmth. He wanted to say, "Don't worry, Francie. I'm here. I'll watch out for you." He wanted to offer countless assurances, a fail-safe immunity to harm, but he knew from experience there was no such word as *assurance*. He'd do what he could, but he couldn't give guarantees anymore (even though he wanted them for himself), so he sat there and held her, listening to the gruesome details of the Arizona massacre.

As he encircled her, she pressed closer, trying to bury herself in FD's flesh, trying to escape the demons about to grab her and tear her apart. FutureDick stroked her hair, stroked her face, and raised Francie's chin so that their lips met. He kissed her softly, fully, silently communicating his desire but also his affection. He wanted this woman. He liked this woman. And what he knew from the depths of his soul is he needed this woman. He needed to join the race of the living again, committed to a partner, a soul mate, a reason for smiling.

Francie responded. Her passion leapt out before she had a

chance to squelch her flame with propriety, with *should's,* with the *do's* and *don't's* she had a lifetime to learn. She wanted this man and she didn't care. Let the world judge her tomorrow. At this moment, she wanted to join her body with FD's, move to his rhythm, breathe his smell, and devour his lips, his face, his neck.

She hoped everyone was sleeping upstairs. At last check, all was quiet. But just to be sure, she put her finger on FD's lips, grabbed the blanket off the couch, and led him into her office where she locked the door. Then she spread the blanket on the floor. As the moonlight drifted through the blinds, Francie took off her jeans, her shirt, her pants and bra.

Slowly she walked over to FD, open, vulnerable, giving, yet unhesitatingly joyous. Francie felt comfortable in her body. It didn't resemble the emaciated shapes that drenched the popular pages of fashion magazines. And it didn't approximate the voluptuous movie stars that intimidated her as a teenager. Her figure was solid, well built, rippling ever so slightly with the hint of worked muscles. But the sensuousness that oozed from her healthy body was as much a challenge as an invitation.

She smiled. Looking at FutureDick, she seemed to float as she neared his side. This was their moment, that brief anticipatory interlude before fusion. She became Everywoman, strong, passionate, desirable. Her womb, which had borne four healthy children, was ready, even anxious, to receive this Samson of a man.

As she moved toward him, FD took off his clothes, and when they met, two vibrant, muscular bodies embraced in the colorless night, capable, confident, and eager to fuse their energy into each other. FD kissed Francie on her lips, on her face, on her neck, her arms, her breasts, gently, warmly—guilelessly, his love taking a leisurely stroll through infinity. The more unhurried FD kissed, the more fiery Francie became. She clutched his hair, bit his neck, pressed her fingers into his back, massaged his arms, his shoulders, digging her fingers deeper, deeper. His restraint stimulated her frenzy, till she growled into FD's ear, "Take me. Please take me."

With those words, FutureDick lifted Francie up and placed her on top of the blanket. He enveloped her in his arms as he mounted her quivering body seething with desire. As powerful as he was, Francie was his match. Her exercised legs wrapped around his back with the pressure of an iron vise, swaying, caressing, titillating, and their bodies moved in harmony to some distant biological beat which had been drumming for eons.

The strength of her body merged with the fervor of her passion. And Francie's total abandon excited him into a shivering that whisked him away, swept him up into an ethereal never-never land of ecstasy. He was lost, completely lost, and for a moment, he thought he'd lose touch of any sanity that kept him real. Then he exploded, a coming apart of all his senses and a coming together with a woman who opened a universe of bliss FutureDick had walked through centuries ago.

While he crashed through the gates of unexplained rapture, Francie also allowed herself to let go, to be overwhelmed, to open, open to this man, open to her fire, her zeal, her enthusiasm—and joined with FD in touching the heights of furor she'd never let herself explore before. Perhaps she had been too afraid of her own intensity, her raw power, her real strength, but with FD, she didn't hold back. She didn't have to. He was strong enough for the both of them. And he allowed her to reach inside the very core of her being and let go.

For that brief moment, her defense, her resistance, her protection melted, and she was transported to another place, another time, a brief kiss with eternity. Her euphoria lasted for seconds, but it changed her assumptions permanently, for Francie found out what it meant to transcend your earthly body on your own terms. Whatever energy she imposed on this incomparable mate, he was man enough to receive. Her strength encouraged him and, at the same time, imbued Francie with the courage to discover more about herself, her body, her desire. She didn't have to keep apologizing for her vitality. Knowingly, she opened her eyes to gaze at FD.

But there he was looking at her, with such an expression of wonderment and love, her voice caught in her throat, and she barely whispered, "Thank you, FD. Thank you." FutureDick enclosed her head in his arms and held her against his chest, held her as if he were afraid he'd lose her to some malevolent force he couldn't control.

When FutureDick arrived home that night, there were two messages on his answering machine. The first was BrickWell wanting to meet him at eight in the morning. FutureDick could guess what that was about. Tonight's carnage was going to impact the company tremendously. These were not mysterious accidents anymore. There was a methodicalness at play here that threatened to wipe out a large number of DoRights and, consequently, a company which had spent eighteen years perfecting its product. What could he tell BrickWell in the morning that would ease the scientist's sense of dread?

The second message was from Saxony. She found something and wanted to talk to FutureDick right away. Oh Saxony, I could kiss you for this. Anything is better than what I've got now.

When she picked up the phone, he knew he had woken her, but she dismissed his apology with, "Gad, FutureDick, am I glad you called. I've got your metal plate figured out. It's a piece of trilium. That's an alloy of titanium, which is high strength, light weight, and flexible. A metal that's used in planes, spacecraft, and robotics. In fact, that plate you gave me had some small markings on the edge indicating a series number. I don't know what the number means, Detective, but its coded for an American company."

"I owe you, Saxony. Anything you want, except my new racquet. Thanks a lot, kid. Bye."

He knew it. He had been on the right track all along.

Retaliation was coming from robots, domestic robots who had become displaced homemakers, usurped by a dangerously loveable DoRight. Furthermore, according to Saxony, it was probably an American company. That bit of information narrowed the field considerably. Holy shit, was he lucky. What if he had to check out the scads of robotics companies in Japan and Europe? By the time he'd return, the entire DoRight population would be decimated.

Okay, FutureDick, get to work. That's what you're getting paid for. It's a long shot, but you're going to visit three robotics companies, the only three companies in the US still manufacturing androids. What do you have to lose, man? There's certainly nothing coming up roses around here.

After he booked his reservations for Minneapolis, Secaucus, and San Ramon, it was two in the morning. He could get five hours sleep if he could fall asleep now. But his mind kept filling up with pictures of renegade robots on the march from town to town. Unstoppable. Each one possessed the strength of ten men, yet there was FutureDick holding off the robotic army with a lance and shield. Whose form was he protecting behind him? Who was he trying to screen from harm? Francie? It *was* Francie! There she stood, his formidable Francie, in his flickering reverie, defenseless, alone, vulnerable.

Seven a.m. arrived too early, but he was alert immediately. He finally had a lead. How did that piece of metal end up so close to Francie's house? No plane had crashed. And no space ship had touched down in the middle of the night. The final answer flew through his brain as he whispered the word *robots*—robots from some company, some garage, somewhere. Certainly, this had to be more than coincidence.

At least FutureDick was able to project some scant optimism to BrickWell. With dark circles propping his eyes, the man looked like he hadn't slept in days. Ashen, he held his cup of coffee with two hands. BrickWell's field was biogenetics, so he had little information to offer on the field of robotics. But he did say that at one of the service industry conventions, he met a Mr. AceArrow, and he didn't like him.

BrickWell, usually reserved about people, surprised FutureDick with this comment. It appeared AceArrow came up to BrickWell during the cocktail hour, while BrickWell was explaining how a chimpanzee's mind works. The scientist passionately, and probably with a bit too much bravado, praised the human-like apes because they were able to solve new problems by themselves without being shown how to do it. BrickWell, then, related the anecdote where grapes were hung from a roof in a room with some small boxes and a chimpanzee. "The chimp will pile one box on top of another to get the grapes. But the gorilla and orangutan will just sit there."

AceArrow, who happened to join the group at the beginning of the story, responded, "Climbing on top of boxes doesn't mean the chimp can adequately perform housework."

"No sir, no, it doesn't. But chimps are comfortable using tools. They can actually invent new games. If they find a rod, a pole, or a box, they'll test it out as something to be jumped over, swung around, or squeezed under. These creatures are quite innovative and seem to enjoy using equipment."

But AceArrow came back immediately, "That's hard to believe, mister. What I know about chimpanzees is they either fuck or shit. And I can just imagine those hard up monkeys taking a crap in the middle of the living room while they're learning how to pick up a broom."

No, BrickWell didn't like the guy at all.

Nor did BrickWell care for the snippy journalist who wouldn't leave him alone. He usually enjoyed talking to the younger generation. They kept him in touch with time, reminding him that the only constant in life was change. But this reporter, Dariel Baker, was a nuisance, a damn snoop trying to interfere with one of his most important experiments.

Of course, Dariel didn't see herself in such a sinister light. In fact, she imagined she was serving the side of truth, freedom, and her chance for journalistic honors. Patiently she waited. Dariel had her story fully written, and it was good, very good. Still, she needed to hit the public just at the right time. Timing was everything in life. It made for good jokes and good sex. And it definitely made for good public reaction.

In her article, she vividly described the meeting in the infirmary between woman and ape. How the woman cried at the DoRight's bedside. How the chimp spoke softly, and so sadly, to her human owner. How the grieving mother bent over to kiss the animal and hold its head. The communication, the love, the bonding—the sentiment was explosive. Why, by the time you got through paragraph two, there wouldn't be a dry-eyed reader left.

Best of all, Dariel had the exclusive. She was the only one in that hospital room. She had tried to interview Francie later that day, but Francie refused anyone from the press. Still, Dariel drove out to her house and studied the place, the family, the tranquil setting that had been a participant in this latest 21st century drama.

If Dariel hadn't been there, she wouldn't have believed her ears, but her facts were verified. She interviewed BrickWell and found out a little bit about his talking DoRight program. He wouldn't say much, simply enough to validate Dariel's experience.

ChangeOvers, BrickWell called them. As far as Dariel was concerned, they were more than changed over, they were downright spooky. Of course, she didn't express her reservations to the scientist. The man was in a state of shock. You'd think these apes were his children or something. Nope! Dariel was an able journalist. She knew when to keep her mouth shut. She knew when to listen so she could retrieve information. And she had to listen mighty hard with BrickWell.

"It's too new, too early," he kept saying. "We need to be sure that these talking chimps will adapt to human homes as well as their DoRight clans. That's why we haven't gone public."

"But, Mr. BrickWell, don't you think the public has a right to know?"

"Young lady, not when there are tentative conclusions and lives at stake. Why should we jeopardize the ChangeOvers' adjustment period? They still need to be studied."

"I'll write that in my article. This gives you free publicity. By the time I'm done, your phones will be ringing off the hook with would-be buyers."

"That's not what I want—profit at the expense of safety. I want to know my ChangeOvers work well within their human setting. Please, I beg of you. Don't print the story. Please wait. For all our sakes, please wait till we know more."

"Well, I don't know, Mr. BrickWell. I believe in telling the facts to the people. And these are pure and simple facts."

But BrickWell blocked Dariel's appeals, and his tone grew harsher as he growled loudly, "I'm asking you nicely, Miss Baker. This is just the wrong time. If necessary, I'll have my lawyer contact your editor. I'll get an injunction. Don't force me to silence you."

"Okay, Mr. BrickWell. I'll wait. But—just for a little while."

Sure, that's what she told him. A little while. And she did. She waited ten days till the next slaughter. Then she called BrickWell again, saying it was essential to tell the story. She'd be missing the mark as a journalist if she remained silent. But she had no idea that BrickWell was a friend of WriteWord's, the editor-in-chief. When she submitted her story, he handed it back, responding, "Not now, Dariel! Just wait a bit. Let's give BrickWell the benefit of the doubt. Work with him."

The bastard. The goddamn bastards. Both of them. BrickWell had reached the newspaper first. But she'd show him. Yes, chimpanzees can talk, and within a couple of days, the whole world would know. She'd be damned if the *SeaBank Sentinel* or BrickWell would stop her from making journalistic history.

No one could obstruct the people's right to know for very

long. There were other ways to get your story printed. Once it was out there, once another publication staked out a claim for her copy, those chummy conspirators were powerless to conceal the truth. Sorry boys, the facts found their way around your muzzle. And when she heard the news that night about Phoenix, Dariel knew her time had arrived.

Seventeen

After his meeting with BrickWell, FutureDick checked in at the police station. If there were any new developments, he wanted to know before he flew east. TigerTail was beaming, well, not quite a glow, but his haggard, sallow expression definitely looked lighter. Still, it was the first time FutureDick saw any hint of a smile since the DoRight case began.

"We got a break, FutureDick. You won't believe this, but some engineering-type character hooked up a camcorder in his DoRight's pen."

"Are you serious, TigerTail? We've got a video of the murderer?"

"Somewhat. The lens was focused toward the door. So you can see the entry and parts of the slaughter. Hey buddy, let me warn you! It gets real gory when you see body parts fly through the air."

"I'm ready, Detective. Show me what you've got. I may skip lunch after this preview, but I'm catching a plane soon. And I've got to see this."

"Oh, you'll see it alright, pal. You'll see apes killing apes!"

The video turned out to be quite fuzzy. It was dark, and the only light seeping into the room came from outside the pen, emanating from the moon. Movement appeared on the tape, but you couldn't tell what it was—a shadow, a something at the bottom of the picture. Then you heard a hiss, a spray. For over a minute, the sound continued its steady, barely heard fizz.

After sixty unremitting seconds, the apparition grew a little larger, but you still couldn't make out the silhouette through the slats of the gate. Again the hiss faintly reverberated against the silence of the night. Gradually the black figure grew larger, nearly to the top of the gate, and once more, the recurring snake-like resonance was heard from the video. No other movement appeared on the screen, just the low sizzle of what FutureDick thought sounded like deodorant spray.

Now the dark configuration reached over the rim of the gate, and a black arm holding a canister slowly dropped in front of the screen. You could clearly see the arm and the can in front of the opening, but the rest of the shape behind the slats was undefined, its blackness blending with the wood. The old, penetrating hiss hurried forth from the lone, black arm. Then, suddenly, the arm was gone.

For close to two minutes, all remained quiet. Unexpectedly, the arm reappeared, reaching over and quietly unhooking the gate. When the gate swung open, a form that looked like an ape, but stood more upright, froze momentarily in front of the screen. At first glance, the creature looked like another DoRight—the hair, the face, the body. But as you studied the animal, although somewhat bent, it plainly was too straight to be an ape. And when it began to move, there was a flexibility missing in its walk. It looked too perfect.

Almost otherworldly, the shadowy specter was soundless. FutureDick strained to hear it sigh or take a breath, a gasp, anything. The quiet was terrifying. You saw five ape-like forms enter the gate, but you heard nothing. Resembling a circus where you see a dozen clowns spill out of a Volkswagen, the image kept walking through the door, one after the other. You had to keep count or you'd lose track with the repetitive reappearance of the form.

When the last creature stepped inside, FutureDick thought he saw a smaller image outside, a human image standing near the gate. He couldn't tell for sure because of the poor quality video, but the form lingering outside the pen looked like a man, a darkened man, partially obscured by the half-opened gate.

Then total hell broke loose. You heard a momentary shriek, but it was stopped mid-scream, as if the voice had been instantly clutched out of the victim. The abrupt screech crescendoed so quickly, you weren't really sure you heard it at all. Reality would have demanded a replay to make certain. Otherwise, the instant shrill was lost in a dream, an angry cat, an imagined echo, for it never repeated. Nullified. Deleted. Blipped out. But FutureDick's brain improvised what his blinded vision lacked. And he knew at that moment, a DoRight's life had been destroyed.

The camera was only focused at the gate, but the sounds of bodies being snapped and bashed would cause revulsion in the most hardhearted viewer. Instinctively, FutureDick wanted to rewind back to the silence. He knew the staccatoed thuds, the crackling rips, the yanking, pulling, twisting would remain in his memory for years to come.

Once in a while, a limb would fly in front of the camera, but the carnage happened too quickly. With five assassins, they were able to do a lot of butchering in a short amount of time. Actually, FutureDick never saw them leave. All he saw was a fountain of blood hit the screen, and the lens became blurry as the thick liquid clung to the glass. Then there was nothing. The silence of the massacre gave corroboration that life could be taken away in a flash, while once more the screen reduced to soundless black.

"Is that a gas or what?" TigerTail asked. "Pretty spleen-wrenching stuff, guy. How do we go about looking for five apes? Certainly someone should have spotted them by now. They kind of slither in and out without a trace."

"I don't know, TigerTail. Are you sure they're apes—or imitations? Go back and check it again. What's human, what's animal? What's real, man? Are those ape things that walked into the pen really apes? I'm not convinced, but I've got to go. I'll call you later. You can bet on that!"

What FutureDick didn't have was time to discuss his theories further. He had to catch the 10:03 flight to Minneapolis. If only he wasn't so rushed, he would go back to the ape's entrance into the pen. Who or what was that darker figure who never entered the torture chamber? FutureDick needed to freeze the frame and study it.

But his mind was already on his plane and the possibilities of information waiting to be uncovered. When he called Francie from the airport, her answering machine responded. As he boarded his plane, he was sorry he hadn't reached her. He just wanted to hear her real voice and say he was going to miss her. It never dawned on him that he hadn't said that to anyone for nineteen years.

It also never dawned on AceArrow that his irreverence inflamed the most moderate of men. If sensitivities were jostled, the sap deserved it. The guy should have learned how to harness his feelings in the first place. Besides, AceArrow didn't give a damn. If the moron paid more attention to machines instead of succumbing to intellectual laziness, he would appreciate the rhythm of their controlled beauty.

Perhaps AceArrow should have paid more attention to his audience. Then he would have noticed the grey-haired stocky man standing near BrickWell. And an especially empathetic AceArrow would have seen this same man, Bruce TreadHard, wince when AceArrow spun into his harangue against the DoRights. For TreadHard, a staunch supporter of the DoRight participation in human life, owned a clan as well as a large percentage of stock in TriCubed. He knew BrickWell from the project's beginning because he was especially fascinated with chimpanzees. More than once, he confided to BrickWell, "Adam, my friend, if I wasn't exceptionally busy earning a living, I would have been there with Goodall and loved each minute of it."

But TreadHard had poured his energies into transforming a modest salary into a fortune, a bonanza built from thermal-lined slippers. As a teenager, he worked part-time in his father's shoe company. When he graduated from the University of Michigan, captain of the wrestling team and a degree in anthropology, he went back home to help his father run the small factory.

After persuading his dad that there would be a market for a slipper that kept the foot warm as well as cushioned, TreadHard designed a classic piece of footwear whose time had come. Recognized by Macy's, Bloomingdales and a host of other large department stores across the US as a hot item, TreadHard's slippers were an instant success. Yet for TreadHard, they were merely the stepping stone, the launchpad to real wealth.

With one eye on slippers, he watched the opportunities of the sixties parade before his eyes and invested every pay check, every bonus, every commission in stock or land. Everything else, such as his own apartment, his own car, his own love, was postponed for four years. A particularly patient man, he deferred his life for 48 months, the longest months a 21 year old ever experienced. He didn't mind suspending independence for a while, but putting his hormones on hold was a true test of endurance only a handful of young men could pass. If his sacrifice bought affluence, then any drive could be diminished—temporarily. Perpetual prosperity was his goal, and he wasn't taking any time out for testosterone.

So TreadHard studied technology, observed people, and interpreted trends. He was there when Xerox started, along with IBM, McDonalds, and Pampers. And he invested in paper, the necessary ingredient that fueled America's obsession with instantaneity. He bought stock in the papers used in machines, the cartons used for milk, the wrappings for hamburgers and french fries, and the liners for disposable diapers—all one of a kind products. As the manufacturers became rich, he became richer.

He contacted urban planning offices throughout the US and bought land where freeways were proposed. He watched, he waited, and he created an investment portfolio that would have been the envy of kings. His little slipper company still produced warm, fuzzy foot holders, but his private interests allowed him the independence he wanted: the freedom to travel, to surf and ski and climb, and to give something back.

Bruce TreadHard received a great deal of pleasure by helping struggling entrepreneurs get started. If he believed in the individuals and their dreams, he was there with money, encouragement, and a listening ear. His capital oiled the project, but his ability to listen sustained the doer through the worst of times. Even though his philanthropy was based on the financial feasibility of the young venture's success, TreadHard sometimes felt like a guardian angel, giving someone a new lease on life.

"If you help the idealists make their dreams a reality, Adam, isn't that giving them a new life? Or at least, a different life?"

Certainly BrickWell couldn't disagree. He was one of the recipients of TreadHard's generosity, and he often wondered "what if?" What if Bruce TreadHard hadn't called him? What if he couldn't have found any backers? What if his dream had stayed just a dream? But TreadHard *had* called him, excited about his project, eager to talk with him. And at their first meeting, TreadHard discussed his curiosity about chimpanzees, how he read about BrickWell's research, and why he wanted to know more.

As TreadHard listened attentively to BrickWell's explanations, predictions, and goals, he nodded his head in agreement, smiling, intrigued by the scientist's glimpse into the future. By the end of their meeting, TreadHard, who had become a full-fledged believer in DoRights, also shared the researcher's vision. Moreover, TreadHard's involvement in TriCubed allowed BrickWell to continue his work during the lean, exploratory years, and the benefactor never failed to squelch BrickWell's anxiety with a pep talk at three in the morning. "Come on, Adam, it's just a slow period. Hang in there, Doctor."

"Easy for you to say, Bruce. I just can't seem to find the right combination. I either splice the gene too much or not enough. Can you imagine me sending lackadaisical zombies into those homes? The project wouldn't last a month."

"But your idea's right. You know it is. I know it is. Jesus, Adam, you're not cutting paper here. You're dealing with a living organism. And you're trying to do something that's greater than both of us. Thank God there's people like you who see the world and say, 'I can make it better.' You'll get it right, Doctor. I know you will."

"Thanks, Bruce. I appreciate your faith in me, but goddamn, some days are killers. My calculations take extraordinarily long to work."

Many conversations later, TreadHard found himself hugging BrickWell when the breakthrough came. Although they never spoke about it, the men shared a silent bond with each other. BrickWell owed his career to TreadHard's faith and financial support, and TreadHard owed BrickWell his gratitude for a kind of personal fulfillment. After all, BrickWell allowed him to be part of the project from the start, and it was the closest TreadHard would ever come to the immediacy of scientific discovery. For a brief time, he tiptoed with the gods, and he devoured every ecstatic minute of it.

Consequently, when AceArrow's cynicism peppered the interested cluster of conventioneers, TreadHard subdued his urge to belt the pompous bastard in the face. Ridiculing the DoRights demeaned one of the most spiritual episodes TreadHard had ever experienced, and he didn't take the derisive remarks lightly.

In fact, TreadHard indisputably felt a man was his words. Once he spit them out, he'd better be ready to fight for them. And, holy shit, did he want to battle with this contemptuous pygmy of a human being. But he restrained himself—not because of propriety or manners or fear—but because of Adam. This was BrickWell's day in the sun, and lucky for AceArrow, TreadHard didn't want to eclipse any of the brightness.

EIGHTEEN

After FutureDick scrupulously researched robotics companies, he added another linguistic dimension to his vocabulary. Fascinated, he looked forward to meeting with the CEO's and discussing androids, cyborgs and artificial intelligence. What he had gleaned from his reading was that androids looked and behaved like people. If that were the case, then couldn't androids be constructed to look like DoRights, too? Wasn't it possible to merely change the human-like flesh to hair or fur?

But the robotics companies built more than androids. Their robots resembled diversified forms that fit the function. Most popular were the mechanical arms or mobile devices, controlled by computers, sensor equipped, and now in their eighth generation of artificial intelligence. A robot didn't have to look human to act human. A mobil device could take the configuration of a three foot high, polished metal apparatus that might resemble a vacuum cleaner, but could react the way a human would in a problematic situation. The quick-witted machine would see, hear, walk, think, and act with its environment.

More marvelous were the possibilities of the 21st century. Plans were on the drawing boards for moon mining units to ship raw materials from the moon back to earth on space shuttles. Imagining robotic devices wearing red, white, and blue and digging for ore on the moon made FutureDick realize his was an antique world already. Man must have some innate urge to explore, and he had peeked into most of the corners of the earth. What could he conquer and use next? Venus? Mars? Robots would roam all over the galaxy retrieving resources. And for a brief moment, FutureDick visualized neon signs floating through space, blinking their offering: ***Shuttle Lube and Oil in 10 Minutes—Turn Left at the Next Star.***

FutureDick's research also provided a glimpse of what the industry would perfect during this decade: devices that crawled along the sea bottom collecting precious metals; rescuers that scrambled over mountains helping skiers, back-packers, and anyone lost or hurt in rugged terrain; and the world's first universal mobile soldier. Designed as impenetrable lexan-spheres which could be parachuted into dangerous situations, these human replacements were equipped with TV camera, sensing devices, and tank capability.

A new soldier for a shrinking global village. Sort of a dichotomy of terms, thought FutureDick. The closer we get to each other, the more sophisticated our weaponry becomes. Science fiction has become fact, and man watches from the side lines, hoping his lust for land, power, or patrimony won't involve his children. Still FutureDick believed the robotic soldier would symbolize the end of war because no side would ever win. Yet, if the world ignored its truculent technology, it was going to be the beginning of a brutal, barren century.

But FutureDick reluctantly brought his research to a close and concentrated on the three US companies, in Minneapolis, Secaucus, and San Ramon, that could offer some answers. He was certain one of these firms might provide the rationale for the crime. Except, after two days of walking through miles of rooms collecting scads of information and watching robots rise from dead, pallid metal, he wasn't any closer to breaking the case than he had been in his comfortable chair at SeaBank City Library. Discouraged, and as frustrated as he had ever been, FutureDick wandered through a night that kept getting darker every minute.

In Minneapolis, he explored Supernomics. The thriving company offered no clues to his killers. The last place they dreamed of placing their machines was in a home. They sold their drones to cities as street sweeps and guides for the blind. Their specialty, SuperSavers, was used by fire departments to save lives, by police departments to remove and dispose of terrorist bombs, and by recreational areas as 24 hour life guards. The state of California was the chief consumer of their superb SuperSaver forest fire fighter, and it would order more any time it passed a budget increase.

Supernomics was swamped with orders since the floods occurring four weeks ago in Louisiana. Their autonomous life boats had been used by the state to rescue disaster victims, and every water-edged country and state seemed to be placing an order they wanted filled yesterday. Self-propelled vehicles were not a novelty. They had been around for a while. It was the comforting android in the vehicle that made Supernomics a sure bet. He soothed his rescuees as he dried them off. The Minneapolis-based company was more interested in Mexico or Australia than in the small US market wanting humanoids to sweep their kitchen floor.

As FutureDick toured the high tech facility, he became enthralled with the replication division. There, industrial robotic workers stood in assembly lines reproducing themselves. StandTall, Supernomics' CEO, explained with pride how efficient his machines were. "Precision, that's the key. We have designed the ultimate in quality control. My flexible manufacturing systems do not make mistakes."

FutureDick smiled at the boast. You're so right, Mr.

President, but don't you ever get bored walking through your company and not being able to ask how the family's doing? What do you serve at the Christmas party, Valvolene? For some unexplainable reason, FutureDick sensed an eeriness in this huge facility, an eeriness that came from the huge amount of steel and the tiny number of human beings. He had walked into a distant time already arrived, where humans rather than robots seemed to be the by-product. He couldn't help wondering who worked for whom.

But Supernomics was definitely not hurting for business. They were only hurting for time, not enough of it. While pressing to fill back orders for their robotic nurses and gas station attendants, they also ran 24 hour shifts to meet the increasing demand for their specialized SuperSavers. Supernomics welcomed competition. As far as they were concerned, there were enough customers to go around. "The world's a very large marketplace," beamed StandTall.

"We've nearly got the marketplace to ourselves. I can feel it," crooned AceArrow to his merciless mercenary.

Eagerly, Tully agreed, "Just a few dead DoRights, and pow! we teach people a large lesson. Now that I'm heading back west, why don't we really drive the lesson home and hit the TriCubed compound?" Tully kept trying and AceArrow still resisted.

"Why bother, Tully? The random DoRight attacks are scaring the shit out of people. Think of what a couple of dead humans would achieve!"

So they deadlocked, Tully thirsty for a DoRight doomsday, and AceArrow, enamored with his ability to wipe out whatever or whoever he wanted.

"Adam, what the hell's going on? I can't believe the shit I'm hearing on the news."

"Believe it, Bruce. There's some crazies out there who went on a rampage."

"But the DoRights, of all targets. They're absolutely harmless, not to mention pretty well isolated."

"I agree. For the life of me, I can't figure it out. Goddamn it, Bruce, I keep asking why."

"What's going on with the investigation? I want to know everything."

Unaware of the strain revealed in his voice, BrickWell proceeded to tell TreadHard the grisly details, what happened with Emma, how he had hired FutureDick, and how literally clueless the police seemed to be. The most baffling crime of the century they were calling it, and all he knew was he had a lot of dead DoRights on his hands.

"Adam, do me a favor. Let me know when FutureDick calls you. I want to help you through this thing, and I've got to know what's going on. If you don't mind, I'd like to be on top of it as much as I can."

"No problem, Bruce. I'll do whatever it takes to get to the bottom of this. Between you and FutureDick, I have the best brains in the world on my side."

After TreadHard hung up, he waited a while, contemplating the insanity that had crept into his consciousness. He pictured Baby Romeo jumping on Rosemary's back, and he smiled. Romeo never sat still. The little ape was constantly wired and terribly inquisitive. One of TreadHard's greatest pleasures lately was to watch his DoRights. As Carolyn folded laundry, she hummed an ape song that gave a faraway look to her eyes. But she snapped to the here-and-now the minute her daughter, Tracy, bounced into the room.

Sometimes TreadHard sat and read near his simian helpers, simply to feel their rhythm. They moved quietly, at ease with their work, in touch with their surroundings, and quite content within themselves. Their peacefulness spilled over onto him, and he felt connected to his clan—a kind of father who protected each of them. Let some bastard come into their pen. He'd show him, alright. The guy wouldn't know what hit him.

But reality broke into his reverie as he looked at the phone, and pictures of his affectionate chimps faded while he dialed Security Systems Inc. He wanted extra protection for his DoRights immediately. Otherwise, he'd set up a mattress outside their pen. He'd protect his own, no matter the cost to his pocket, his sleep, his safety.

When TreadHard replaced the receiver on its stand, he considered his response to the tragedy. Throughout his lifetime, he envisioned himself as a charitable person, a reasonable man who operated within a set of moral rules that required he treat others fairly. He was ready to play any game, whether it be on the business field or the tennis court, but he demanded two things: he wanted to know the rules and he wanted all the other players to abide by them. "Fair is fair," he would remind the people involved in his financial deals.

If he encountered any cheating in his sports, he just stopped. More than once, he had walked off a tennis court when his opponent shortened the boundary lines. His tendency to withdraw from a situation, especially if he suspected fraud or deception, was usually his first option. But sometimes, evasion didn't always feel right to him. Sometimes, the cheat became a challenge, the unfairness became a foul, and that's when TreadHard decided to get even.

Although he was physically strong, his muscles reflecting years of wrestling and mountain climbing, he never used his strength as a threat. He preferred to improvise mentally, planning ways to teach a lesson that might allow the liar to reflect. And now, he thought quietly, could there possibly be any sort of lesson you'd effectively teach a killer of DoRights? Perhaps this offender was immune to morality, unencumbered by the rules of rightness that charge men's lives. Perhaps this was the sole exception that called for retaliation rather than reprimand?

Nineteen

In Secaucus, TechnoHelp re-echoed the prosperity of Supernomics. The CEO, a Mr. StarFire, blustered with self-satisfaction when he showed FutureDick around. His company serviced the medical industry, and TechnoHelp was constantly refining its robots' accuracy. After all, these precision machines were not only used for hospital maintenance, but his select group, Surgeonetics, was put to work in the operating rooms across the United States. In any kind of complicated surgery, where steadiness was key to the success of the procedure, his doctor machines took over and performed flawlessly.

StarFire glowed when he explained the skills of his mechanized medics and said he looked forward to a boom year, since he was finally able to fill his international orders. He commanded the market, alright, but he didn't have enough robots. His people worked night and day shifts trying to accommodate the demands of a world market, straining to deliver a consistently high quality product, and attempting to stay one jump ahead of the Japanese.

StarFire was wed to his company. Using terms like *cherish, adoration, devotion,* he spoke of it the way a groom describes his bride. The business, which started in his garage twelve years ago and reached world renown in a matter of months, clearly consummated StarFire's theories of robotics exactitude. Unquestionably, he let FutureDick know that if his life were at risk, he'd select a mechanized scalpel over a human hand—always—no matter how expert the flesh and bone doctor was reputed to be.

But his confidence proliferated from his work ethic because he demanded exceptionally tight quality control. No robot left TechnoHelp without myriad hours of assurance testing. Apparently, self-replicating robots hadn't agreed with StarFire. As much as he lauded his product's superiority, he still wanted human beings to give them birth.

When FutureDick shook StarFire's hand and left to catch his 3:30 plane for the West Coast, he wondered if his cross-continent investigation was worthless. What was he looking for? He had just visited two firms who couldn't supply their markets fast enough; the only contracts they signed were for manufacturing, not murder. Apparently, there was enough business out there for everyone. Certainly these firms, particularly their CEO's, weren't interested in destroying TriCubed, much less the kindly DoRights who proved to be the most cooperative animal yet to inhabit a home.

But his gut told him differently. There were apes or ape-like things killing their genetically altered sisters. Why? Some mastermind had to be behind this unnatural eradication. The single conclusion FutureDick consistently arrived at was that someone wanted the DoRights out of commission. Someone wanted to scare the hell out of the buying public. Without DoRights, a share of the domestic services industry would open up again. But was it only market share or was there more? Had BrickWell made an enemy he forgot about? Or worse, someone he never suspected who hated him enough to ruin him?

At the airport, before boarding his flight, FutureDick reached BrickWell. After describing Supernomics and TechnoHelp, he tried, unsuccessfully, to cheer the scientist up. "Look, Adam, it's really in the process of elimination. As we keep narrowing it down, we get closer to the solution. I'll get the killers. I promise you."

"FutureDick, I have no doubts you will. It just may be too late. That's what I'm worried about. The dead DoRights and the possibility of a dying company."

"But we've got the video I told you about. And we've got a more alert customer base." As soon as he said that, FutureDick was sorry. All it did was remind BrickWell of his potentially frightened buyers.

So FutureDick immediately added, "The rampage has got to stop soon, Adam, or those murderers are going to walk into a host of hand guns."

"Thanks for calling, FutureDick. My optimism has taken a vacation at the moment."

"Well, I'll call you from San Ramon. I'm meeting your old friend, AceArrow, there."

FutureDick could swear he heard BrickWell's tone pick up a bit, if for no other reason than the familiarity of a name with a face. Even if it were a nasty association, BrickWell could visualize who FutureDick would be questioning. Any recognition, dim as it may be, helped at this moment.

Next FutureDick called Francie to let her know how his investigation was progressing. He thought he could lessen her fears about the Phoenix tragedy. But truthfully, he wanted to hear her voice, hear her say his name, hear her smile over the phone. As the call went through, he felt his heart quicken in expectation.

"Hi FD, how's it going?"

"Francie, I'm out here on the East Coast when I'd rather be jogging at my ocean. What's happening there?"

"Reba's taking the next two days off and going to the mountains for the weekend. She's taking the kids hiking. Except for Josh. He's got a sore throat. Boy, FD, is she a brick. I can't go, but what a relief to know the family will see some different scenery for a while."

"Don't worry about anything, Francie. I'll be back soon, either tomorrow night or Friday morning. And you know what? I challenge you to a game of racquetball. So start getting your strength up!"

"FD, one of these days, I'm going to beat you at that game, and you'll be eating humble pie, Investigator!"

"My charming athletic nemesis, you may be 190 years old by then. See you soon, Francie."

"Bye, FD. I know I don't need to say it to you, but be careful."

When FutureDick hung up, he still felt her warmth; it had managed to course through the phone receiver into his fingers and hijack his body completely. He thought about their last evening together and couldn't wait to get back. He wanted her nearness, her affection, her excitement. And he wanted to make sure that she existed, that she was there for him—and that when she said hello, he heard his heart respond before his voice.

Francie was delighted FD called. She never had time for men in her life or, actually, never let herself have time. She didn't mind some brief interlude now and then, away from the house, the family, the job, where she might have a two or three week fling. It would start instantly like a match but then fizzle out just as quickly. As of yet, she wasn't willing to get involved on a long-term basis because she recognized that time spent with a man was time spent away from the children, away from her friends, and away from herself. And these three areas were critically important to her.

The demands of her profession left her too little time, and time was quite precious right now. She constantly seemed to be dividing the minutes, giving the bulk of her stored pantry of moments to her children. She'd fit in her sports but eliminate her reading or her movies. She'd fit in her friends but shorten the minutes in their candid conversations. Yet she gave her children as much of the clock as they needed, even if it meant less sleep or unfinished lists of things to do. She knew her children required her now, not tomorrow, not next year, but now, because youth measures time by the preeminent present: the past is long gone and the future too far away.

All too often she saw parents put their children on hold, thinking that the emotional life of the young would remain fixed indefinitely. But the psyche never worked that way. The mind, a delicate piece of machinery, is attached forever to the heart, and this fragile connection must be nurtured frequently, or the adults who grew from children would be stunted.

Francie knew her children would only be young temporarily. Thus she had too little time with them. But Francie also understood if she ignored the importance of their emotional growth, she'd send individuals into the world who would be nothing more than grown-up babies, unable to think and act like strong, independent, fulfilled human beings.

Francie realized if she made any impact on her environment, she hoped it would be through her children. She intended to give good people to a society that could surely use it. And she also desired to do something for herself. She wanted her children to be her friends; yet she knew if her children's self-development were thwarted, she'd have a hard time playing with them as adults. We seek our own level of acquaintance, and ever since her frustration with Alan, Francie set her expectations of friends high.

Again, it was a time thing. She'd work with emotionally anemic people the entire day, but she wasn't going to spend one of her few cherished moments away from the office in an unsatisfying friendship. It never worked, and she had all she could do to nurture her own children. So how could she nurture the rest of the world in addition?

Therefore, Francie was surprised to find how easily FD

slipped into her life. Before she knew it, she found herself looking forward to their conversations, particularly their racquetball word play. Crafting their own verbal game, they fashioned their special sort of familiarity, and they had fun. When was the last time Francie remembered she had fun with a man?

Besides, her attraction to FD was more than enjoyment. It was her passport to constancy. He, their relationship, their intimacy, their intellectual concurrence provided her with the feeling of safety. She so rarely felt safe with anyone, but with FD, he was the bulwark, her sanctuary. She could let down and yet he'd remain there—like Gibraltar. Undoubtedly it was his steadiness she admired most. He could be counted on. How could she help but notice when he and Josh became acquainted that night? There was a mutual communication between them that filled Francie's heart with joy.

She worried repeatedly about taking Josh's daily father (in name only) away from him, but she felt no role model was better than a poor role model. Still she silently applauded when Josh made a friend with a decent male adult. Francie wanted her son to see the best that men can become, and she was convinced that FD was unparalleled.

Furthermore, if she were going to be completely honest with herself, she'd have to admit that the night they slept together was overpowering: pure pleasure. She certainly wouldn't mind more of that in her life.

Initially, she diminished her emotional reaction to FD every time she saw him. After all, she had called him to help her through the anxiety. He was a crime consultant, and theirs had started as a professional relationship. Yet she recognized her euphoria when they remained friends even after the terror had settled down. So that jolt to her belly, when she'd first see him or hear his voice on the phone, was a challenge to be reckoned with. In spite of her well-planned life and inner rational discourse, FD moved her. He kind of crawled inside her heart and refused to leave. How could there ever be time for this added exhilaration in her life?

"Bruce, it's a long shot, and I doubt if anything will come of it, but you'll never guess where FutureDick's going tomorrow."

"Adam, I can't imagine there's anything left. He's checked out everything."

"Our only competitors—robots! So he's visiting those guys connected to the domestic services industry. And he's got an appointment with that asshole we met at the convention a while ago."

"What was his name? Ace? AceArm? No, AceArtist? Shit! AceArrow! AcefuckingArrow. You've got to be kidding. Mr. Big Mouth."

"You've got it, Bruce. Remember? The guy makes domestic robots. I wonder how his business is doing now. I bet he's chuckling all the way to the bank! You know our sales are down, way down. Not a customer for ten days. I'm being honest with you, my friend. You've got a lot of money invested in the company."

"I'm not worried about the money, Adam. It's a strong company. It always has been. And the product is outstanding. I know that from personal experience. This will blow over—if for no other reason than the tightening of security. But I can't stand the thought of anyone purposely harming a DoRight!"

"I agree, Bruce. I surely do. The viciousness of the murders has left me so horrified, I'm questioning man's climb on the evolutionary ladder. Perhaps he, too, deserves to go by way of the dinosaur. A species capable of such bestiality makes its accomplishments pale."

"Yet we all have some sort of rage kept smothered inside. That's also troubling. I can't conceive of hurting an innocent creature like a DoRight, much less ripping them apart. Damn! It makes me want to puke just visualizing it. But the wrath I feel toward the killer is seething. I want to shatter him, just break him into pieces. Holy shit, I don't know why my response is this vehement! It puts me on the murderer's level, and I hate that.

But I've got to tell you, it's there—inside me."

"Sometimes I wonder, Bruce, if we're all capable of destruction. It might depend on our personal limits. Any one of us can get pushed too far. I don't see that as degeneration. Rather, more like self-preservation, our way of ridding the species of evil, pure evil. No one ever said man wasn't an aggressive animal if he had to be."

"Aggression, sure. But Adam, the hostility I feel toward the killer has such a strong component of brute force to it. I never knew I was capable of this type of emotional intensity. An eye for an eye isn't good enough. I want the killer to suffer pitilessly. Shit, I'm just as shocked at my lack of compassion as I am at the crimes! Kill the bastard slowly, painfully, horribly. Wow! Did I say that? Where's it coming from?"

"I don't know, Bruce. As a scientist, I don't pledge to have all the answers to the human condition. But I bet if you strip away the thin film of communal conformity we adhere to, each of us is susceptible to some pretty harsh retaliation. Just push us hard enough! It boils down to personal limits and their connection to justice or morality. Right or wrong, friend. Isn't that what all civilizations are about?"

"Put that way, Adam, I feel somewhat exonerated. Except, I've always prided myself on being a reasonable man, and now I want nothing to do with that kind of moderation. Instead, I'd prefer my emotions to feel their full rage. Just let me soak in this anger till I become raw because the crime is wrong, just goddamn wrong."

"We'll get the bastard, Bruce. We'll get him."

"We'll get the bastards, anyway," thought Tully. He didn't need AceArrow to tell him what to do. The guy sat at a desk devising war plans. How could a CEO know what it's like to be on the battlefield? He sharpens pencils and pushes paper. You need a soldier, a true fighter, to map your most effective strategy. The veteran's been there before. He knows the ropes, not like some fag from the front office. And the more he rationalized his taking matters into his own hands, the more anxious he became to reach the Pacific where the largest cluster of enemy lay, unwarned of their extermination.

What part do innocent bystanders play in aiding and abetting felons? Certainly the pundits of the press would never admit their accommodation to the criminal mind. Yet the killer inevitably plays a catch-me-if-you-can game with the reporter, each wanting a bit more succor from the other. The newshound wants the inside scoop, the exclusive, the chance not only to regurgitate the whole bloody story, but also the opportunity to mold events so a bit of sensationalism seeps in.

In the meantime, the lawbreaker gains his celebrity status by using the reporter as his press agent without even having to pay the contractual ten percent fee. And as the crimes grow more heinous, the press releases grow more generous. Yet it costs the criminal nothing but his bad deeds and a continuous craving for notoriety. In effect, he becomes a front page junkie.

Except Dariel was untutored in criminal complicity and immune to BrickWell's petition. A story is a story is a story, and it had a right to be told. She knew she'd get her article published. She also knew she was risking her job at the *Sentinel* by going against her editor's wishes. But hell! She had a strong story, didn't she? She had a winner! If the *Sentinel* didn't want it, she'd find another newspaper. BrickWell couldn't manipulate the entire US press, could he?

After ten years of free-lance writing, Dariel could tell when she had a marketable piece of material in her hands. What she didn't know is who would jump at her exclusive. Newspapers had carried the tragic events of the DoRights across the front page for nearly three weeks. Still, her new information was valuable enough to pump another ounce of adrenaline into a story that could capture the public's attention again, even if it might be for a limited amount of time.

Dariel realized that readers were like baby dogs in a room of bouncing balls. They were fed massive amounts of information daily, and you had to attract their attention. Get in their brains quickly with your newsworthy item and get out before the next piece of information bombards you from the number one position. Yes, the public was curious, but they were also fickle. They would just as soon move onto new news, a new fad, a new celebrity.

Over the years of instant hamburgers, instant calculation, instant replay, people lost their patience along with their desire for details. If yours was the lucky or notable (one never really knew which spot it claimed) article to lure common consideration, you attained a brief bit of glory: your writing was heard, transmitted to a file drawer in the inner recesses of the mind, and probably remained irretrievable, unless you had touched an emotional throb in your reader.

"Well, why not go for the big guys?" Dariel asked herself, and she placed a call to the *New York Times*. If they weren't biting, she'd contact *The Washington Post* or the *Los Angeles Times*. But she generally had a preference for the *New York Times* and admired their consistency. The paper persistently kept faith with its mission of wanting the public to know.

When Evan SageSon, the news editor, said, "Fax the article immediately," Dariel knew she had made a sale. The story would hit the stands in two days. But what Dariel never stopped to consider was how her investigative report would affect the remaining DoRights, BrickWell, or Francie. Dariel only saw information, not lives.

TWENTY

FutureDick arrived in San Francisco that evening, rented a car, and drove out to Robomaids in San Ramon. He had an appointment at nine the next morning, but he thought he'd look over the facility first. Otherwise, the night ahead of him was going to be too long. He had to get something going on this case. He was due. The law of averages used to prove that with enough attempts, some hint, some discovery, some damn answer showed up. How many more tries were necessary?

When he drove up to the gate, a security guard stopped him and said the company was closed. Nevertheless, FutureDick noticed lights blazing in the left wing of the main building. He remembered that the previous companies he recently toured, Supernomics and TechnoHelp, were both on double shifts in order to fill their purchase requests. But the parking lot at Robomaids was practically empty. He saw three vehicles, one with the license plate ACE-A, and he knew that had to be AceArrow's car. Yet when he tried to engage the guard in conversation, the watchman remained tight-lipped.

All FutureDick learned was that AceArrow came into work quite regularly in the evening. Immediately, FutureDick found himself forming silent questions in his mind, "Why would a CEO work every night? Wall Street was closed. Didn't he trust his controller? Wouldn't he hire supervisors to eliminate managerial problems? Or technicians to solve technical difficulties?"

From the research that FutureDick plunged into prior to his arrival at Robomaids, he discovered that the company had been the only serious domestic robots competitor to the Japanese. It took a specialized robot to clean up homes, one able to grasp equipment but less precise than industry required. A machine that could sweep, fold, vacuum, wash, and still appear pleasing to the human eye. Japanese robotics, in business for 31 years, crafted such a machine, and they were world famous for their quality control.

But Robomaids had been able to nudge the Japanese aside in the US market by capitalizing on the theme of American know-how. The company came into existence in 1988, just before the Great Lay Off, when cost-conscious corporations discarded a host of skilled engineers. These out-of-work, trained and tried technicians eagerly joined Robomaids, grateful to have a job and pleased to be part of an energetic rather than dying industry.

Their willingness to work hard, work well, and work overtime gave birth to a quality product. Proudly as well as patriotically, those in the country who could afford it responded with encouragement by buying a made-in-the-USA domestic robot. So the company, created with a faith in mechanized, menial assistants, was able to grow over the last eighteen years by producing a good-looking, low-maintenance, efficient, computerized servant: a heavy-duty Robomaid.

However, in the past two years, profits remained even: no increase in sales had occurred. And FutureDick wondered how this lack of growth affected their research and development program, which had to remain strong in order to challenge the

Japanese. Their robots didn't have to be bigger, simply better, a goal that took constant effort together with funds. Those lights on in the building indicated overtime for certain employees, and FutureDick had the feeling this labor was out of dedication rather than time and a half.

The next morning as FutureDick walked across the parking lot to Robomaids, he noticed that the company grounds didn't look as clipped as he would have expected. Corporate lawns usually had that look of precision, announcing all was right with the world. Manicured grass reflected well-managed firms, neat, clean and full of controlled vigor. But these grounds reminded FutureDick of a house that looked in order till you inspected the corners and sills and noticed dust, spider webs, and mouse droppings. There was some maintenance going on, but it definitely seemed reduced.

The minute FutureDick shook hands with AceArrow, he knew he didn't like him. Maintaining the masquerade he used at the other two companies, FutureDick posed as a possible investor wanting to see the business firsthand. But the tone in AceArrow's voice annoyed FutureDick. He had heard it before, a sound that suggests impatience with the world and any human being who comes across your path.

FutureDick called it the Chicago sound. As a child, he used to spend summers visiting his grandparents in Chicago, and he heard that same sarcastic intonation when he met kids in the neighborhood: a mild disgust mixed with rudeness or gruffness. You never knew if they were slightly angry with you or with life in general. But the vocal intent always managed to put the listener a step down. FutureDick knew now that the sarcasm covered up a greater insecurity than the speaker was aware of or would even acknowledge, but as a child, he frequently felt an odd man out kind of syndrome because the tone implied you're wrong, buddy, and I'm right.

So every time AceArrow spoke, espousing the growth potential of Robomaids, FutureDick braced himself against the beginning words till he grew used to that hint of hostility in the voice.

"But what about the negligible increase in profits over the past two years?"

"No problem. We've been putting the money back into the company, particularly some new projects, so our robots can expand their usefulness."

"Such as what?"

"Space travel and weapons."

"But those fields are highly risky when you had such a dependable domestic market before."

"Certainly, Mr. BrightBurn, you can see that a company can't stand still. Given our precarious environment, Robomaids wants to be the first to populate alternative planetary living systems."

"That's quite commendable, Mr. AceArrow, but I'm interested in your domestic services division. Is it worth investing in now when it's coming up against US competition?

"And what competition is that?"

"I'm referring to the DoRights and TriCubed. If I invest in a company, I want to know who its competitors are and what sort of growth I can expect. You see, Mr. AceArrow, I do my homework. But I still prefer machines to animals."

"I can assure you, Mr. BrightBurn, that TriCubed is not a problem. We build a reliable robot. And even though the DoRights captured a part of the market, I'm convinced they were just a fad. People will tire of the animal attraction and return to the machine. I can guarantee you, there's nothing to worry about. We're working on some exciting innovations."

"You speak about the DoRights as if they're past history. My understanding is that their company can't process their orders fast enough."

"Well, Mr. BrightBurn, I'm just going by what the newspapers print, and I'd venture to say that TriCubed is in a bit of trouble. As I said before, the DoRights have run their course.

Ask my customers. My machine can out-perform those monkeys any day of the week!"

FutureDick saw that AceArrow could not be pushed out of his arrogant smile, and he was pleased that after the meeting, the CEO asked him to go on a plant tour with the customer relations coordinator, Ms. Smythe. They went through the manufacturing facility but stayed clear of last night's well-lit section. Smythe explained that the south wing was the research and development lab and was off limits to visitors. She smiled when she said, "You know, trade secrets and all sorts of high tech stuff. We're very careful about industrial spies."

Smythe brought FutureDick to the front door and thanked him for coming. But just as he prepared to walk out, he said he wanted to freshen up before he caught his plane. Since it was close to lunch, Smythe gave him her card, told him to call her if he wanted additional information, and made sure to inform him to have a nice trip. Then she excused herself. The timing couldn't be better. FutureDick enjoyed playing the role of the affluent Mr. BrightBurn, who had money to dispose of and wanted to invest properly. Still FutureDick knew if you catch employees close to lunchtime, their scrutiny falters. All he wanted was to be by himself for awhile, and he knew all Smythe wanted was to say goodbye and bask in her sixty minute break.

So FutureDick walked over to the men's room, past the entrance receptionist, and hoped that she wouldn't be looking when he walked out. After staying in the washroom for ten minutes, he opened the restroom door a crack and saw that he would be in the receptionist's peripheral vision if he stepped out. This was the tricky part of his trade: when to go for the fast move. He couldn't stay in the restroom the whole afternoon; someone was bound to use it sooner or later.

A break. He needed a break. And there it turned up, twenty long minutes later. A tour bus of high school students came in for their once-a-year field trip. They were Future Engineers of America, bestowed with the opportunity to see technology at its finest. Enthusiastically, they flocked around the receptionist, giving FutureDick the cover he needed to shoot down the hall to the elevator.

When he reached the third floor, he saw a set of double doors to his right with a *No Admittance* sign posted very, very clearly. Inside the right-hand door was a slit glass window, large enough for FutureDick to look through and see men in white lab coats bending over a desk, studying some type of blueprint. He knocked. One of the researchers glanced up and shook his head. FutureDick knocked again. The younger of the bunch frowned as he walked over. He peered through the small slash of glass, then reluctantly opened the door.

"Excuse me, sir, but I'm Mr. PinPoint with the FairField High School Engineering Club, and I've sort of lost one of my teenagers. I just wanted to make sure he hadn't wandered this way."

"As you can see, Mr. PinPoint, we have a no admittance policy for this lab, and no one except technicians or researchers is allowed in this part of the building."

"Gee, you know how kids are. Their curiosity kind of gets the best of them at times. And these are all future engineers, so I wanted to make sure one of my students hadn't broken any company rules. They're just too excited about robotics. They'd love to get some hands-on experience."

"We've seen no one, Mr. PinPoint."

"Well, thank you. Perhaps I can explain to my class what you're working on here. They'd be most interested. You'll think this is funny, but my guys and gals are convinced that giant robots will someday rule the world. They have vivid imaginations. Even more hilarious, they're sure that some secret mission is taking place where an army of robotic soldiers will be let loose in each country."

The young man remained unmoved, no smile, no crinkling of the eyes, no acknowledgement whatsoever.

"I'm sorry, Mr. PinPoint, I'm busy, and you can tell your

students, we build maids—Robomaids."

Before FutureDick could counter the last bit of information emerging from the sober, white-coated, would-be scientist, the door closed in the investigator's face. Finished. End of conversation. Don't bother me. But FutureDick had engaged the technocrat in enough small talk to let his eyes scan the premises for any hint, any minuscule suggestion, that Robomaids was hiding something.

And FutureDick found what he was looking for. Back in the corner, stacked against the shelf, were limbs—not the realistic limbs you'd find on a human-like robot—but hair-covered limbs with long, claw-like fingers. He counted them: four hairy arms and five hairy legs, waiting to be attached, waiting to be fitted into possible killing machines that were programmed to rip apes. He definitely had to run this concept by BrickWell.

FutureDick knew his discovery was more yearning than truth. Maybe Robomaids was designing a museum exhibit or building robots for a theme park or possibly a movie. Those limbs might belong to any number of robots who could be used in a variety of places, but FutureDick didn't believe his list of logical choices. The confidence that AceArrow exuded looked too genuine for a firm which remained profitless for two years. Some sign of concern should have appeared on AceArrow's face, but he acted pretty flippant for the CEO of a company whose market share had steadily decreased.

AceArrow devoted his working life to robots. He believed in them. He knew these electromechanical wonders were more dependable than people, and all he wanted to do was supply the world with service-oriented humanoids. So what if he made money doing it! Shouldn't he? He wasn't greedy. He just wanted America. Let the Japanese have the rest. They had enough competition among their own.

AceArrow deserved his US market. He had worked damn hard to develop a machine that excelled in the home. Did anyone truly understand what it was like to create an android? The senses and abilities humans take for granted were enormous tasks for his scientists to build into a plastic-metallic-electronic expert system. The man-hours they spent in perfecting a robot who didn't drop glasses or walk into walls seemed endless.

He remembered the early stages when they worked on their successful development of Robo-vision. They had to translate a video image into numerical values that a computer could understand. Each shade of grey between black and white was assigned a number: the darker the shade, the higher the number. Robo-vision interpreted a picture by breaking down the image into dots and assigning an appropriate number to each dot. When the robot looks at a slice of watermelon, it sees the darker seeds and skin and the lighter rind and meat. A digital image of the watermelon might take 80,000 numbers, since the computer identifies all dots associated with the various shades in the watermelon slice.

The enormous task of giving his robots eyes was nothing compared to their hypochondriac problem. The robots kept shutting themselves down. State of the art machines are designed to monitor the condition of their health or proper functioning. If any internal problems occur, the robot diagnoses and corrects. Good robots are good doctors. They know in which subsystem to look for the trouble: electronic, hydraulic, electrical, mechanical, sensors, or software. Competent metal-medics, they continually monitor their entire state every few seconds. If these fabricated automatons find anything abnormal, they shut themselves down, address the problem, and hopefully self-correct.

But their robots kept shutting down. Too self-absorbed with their functioning, they couldn't do any work. AceArrow was baffled. So were his researchers. Then one night, GreenGrass touched a robotic arm and received an electrical shock. That's when they realized their hydraulic filters were not adequate. The mesh needed to be larger to prevent clogging. When you pump hydraulic fluid through a filter at high speed, static electricity is produced, building up a charge, and the charge signals the computer to shut down. Although the problem was trivial to correct, the amount of time it took to solve added up to months.

And what about the beautiful sensors they had built into their Robomaids? No matter what scooted in front of their machine, be it a baby or dog or marble, their robots were equipped to stop on a dime—no worries here about a few hundred pounds worth of artificial intelligence going berserk.

But AceArrow was particularly proud of his preventative maintenance program. Cars get their oil changed every three thousand miles. Humans see their doctors once a year for a check-up. Therefore Robomaids came in for an annual spring cleaning, a physical with a lube and oil tacked on. For three years, his customers received free service; then they could sign up for any number of maintenance plans. Thus the company profited from selling their product as well as supplying its parts and service. As far as AceArrow was concerned, he was in the best of all businesses: he made money and added to the country's well-being.

Surely AceArrow deserved his profits. After all, it was his dedication and perseverance that brought Robomaids into the home. Of course, he had to give credit to his gifted research engineers. They stuck by him. So weren't they entitled to some privilege also? It had taken years to produce these powerful and intelligent entities.

Yet people seemed to view their humanoids with some degree of uneasiness. It never failed that machines made many people uncomfortable, even though Robomaids were guaranteed not to harm humans. How could they? Each robot was programmed with the Three Laws of Robotics promoted by Isaac Asimov over half a century ago: *A robot must not harm a human being, nor through inaction allow one to come to harm; a robot must always obey human beings, unless that is in conflict with the first law; a robot must protect itself from harm, unless self-protection undermines the intent of the first or second laws.*

His mechanical babies were as harmless as puppies. Yet he had a difficult time convincing consumers that these heavy-duty machines were completely accommodating, completely safe, completely reliable. People were still apprehensive around them. From the beginning, AceArrow had been amazed at the subtle suspicion evident in their voices. Where their misgivings originated from puzzled the CEO. Didn't these dullards know anything about technological elegance? He, who loved machines, looked forward to walking into his home and being greeted by his PAL (power-driven automated laborer).

"Hello, Mr. AceArrow. How are you today?"

"Great, PAL. Just great."

"I'm glad to hear that, sir. What can I do for you?"

"A glass of white wine, please."

"Certainly, Mr. AceArrow. I'd be happy to serve you."

See that. Whatever you wanted and they jumped. What better option was there than to surround yourself with non-complaining staff? No headaches. No colds. No gripes. None of his wives ever said I'd be happy to serve you. Shit, they never said anything except what can you buy for me now. His marriages didn't last, but his PAL did.

His PAL was always there, listening to him, touching him, taking care of him. He could tell his PAL anything, and the robot would understand. His PAL was sympathetic to him, a sterling kind of friend. AceArrow certainly couldn't say that about most of the human beings in his life. People usually wanted something from you: money, feelings, answers, attention. If lucky, sometimes they gave back, but then they usually wanted more. They continually wanted more. Didn't his potential customers see that Robomaids were clearly more human than most people? And you never had to give anything in return.

AceArrow had generally been disappointed with the sales department. Originally, he expected instant success the year he marketed his first generation of Robomaids. But the business never really exploded onto the home domestic service market. It grew slowly, but it grew. His buyers were mainly the children born in the seventies, babies accustomed to machines: TV's, VCR's, PC's, CAT scans, copiers, calculators, machines for the mind, the belly, the sky, the earth. The power generation. Push *Power* and it gets done—instantly.

They reached voting age when the country used a machine for nearly everything, machines to clean your teeth, clean your car, clean your carpets, clean your dishes. He frequently wondered when a machine to clean your brain would be developed because he knew if such a device came into being, people would function better, physically and emotionally.

This generation and its babies understood that machines were faultless—people weren't. But AceArrow wanted a larger slice of the market. He craved that huge senior citizen piece of the pie, and they remained more hesitant, harder to persuade. They were the ones who needed their brains cleaned. If only they weren't so pigheaded. Couldn't they see how their lives would improve with an android around?

He thought of several marketing schemes: two-for-one, RoboRaffles, summer inventory sales, swap a car for a robot-thon, 10 day free trial, buy a home/get a robot—even an institutional program where vouchers for individual robot purchases could be accumulated, then redeemed for the rugged model Robomaid designed especially for schools, orphanages, and rest homes. Yet the year 2000, when he was confident Robomaids would have their best sales yet, turned out to be a disaster. That was the year the DoRights were introduced to the American public. That was the year of his ulcer. That was the year he'd like to repeat, so he could stop the first DoRight from ever making it out of TriCubed. If he could have prevented the initial sale, could have sabotaged the monkey research, could have frightened the customers, Robomaids would never have gone into its present slump.

"Bruce, you're going to think this is crazy, but wait till you hear FutureDick's prognosis. Robots! Robots who look like chimps are slaughtering the DoRights. I'm not kidding you. He's serious."

"If I hadn't heard of his reputation, I'd say he's doing LSD—or caught in a science fiction time warp! But I know he's on the level, Adam."

"It sounds too bizarre when I run the scenario through my mind, but I know it's technically possible. If you can teach chimpanzees to talk, you can certainly program machines to kill. But Bruce, the madness of it all leaves me empty."

"I've got to agree, Adam. The legacy of the 21st century is going to provide future historians with a mouthful. It seems more popular to destroy than to discuss. And the money spent in creating killing machines is absurd. You know the people behind this have got to be sick. Really sick."

"This, you're really going to love. FutureDick's implicating AceArrow. In fact, he just called from San Ramon where AceArrow has his Robomaids company. Can you believe it? What if that bastard masterminded this whole situation? What if he built a murder machine?"

"Hey, wait, Adam. Be careful. That's a strong accusation. Would the man be crazy enough to risk his reputation, his company, and possibly, even his life?"

"Right now, it's just a theory, Bruce. Just a theory. I've got to speculate something. My babies are dying."

"You know, I never liked that asshole, AceArrow. Anyone who doesn't like chimps is questionable as far as I'm concerned."

"Now that I think about it, he was pretty rude, wasn't he?"

"Rude, Adam, is not the exact word. Obnoxious or obscene might be better! I still feel distaste when I recall that outburst at the convention—and my pure restraint. The bastard deserved a punch in the face."

"If he's behind this, Bruce, he'll be getting more than a black eye. But for the life of me, I can't think of a punishment severe enough."

As each man hung up the phone, their minds tried to retrace AceArrow's face. "Could he really have done it?" thought BrickWell. "Is he that crazy? That angry? That desperate? Why? My DoRights, my beautiful DoRights. Why the hell, why?"

"I bet the cocksucker did it!" thought TreadHard. "He seemed like that sort of guy. Nasty. Foulmouthed. Hostile. That's what I remember most about him, his suppressed anger. He didn't speak. He snarled. If he's really guilty, the bastard deserves the death sentence. But in our justice system, that would never happen. Humans don't die for killing animals because animals are expendable. Men are not! Still I'd be goddamned if AceArrow had one tenth as much intrinsic value as any one of the murdered DoRights. Could he really be guilty?"

TWENTY-ONE

FutureDick drove to the airport, wondering how he could break into the lab and get the evidence he needed. If he called his man right, AceArrow had the lab wired for security, and FutureDick felt that time was not on his side. More delay meant more dead DoRights. He'd have to convince TigerTail to pull strings. At least contact his officers' network in northern California to get him a search warrant, so he could surprise the security guard in the evening after everyone went home. But FutureDick knew that only picked people had the key or combination to that lab door, and he'd lay odds the lonely sentry wasn't one of the chosen.

Going through search scenarios in his mind, FutureDick walked passed the airport newsstand. He had almost rounded the corner when it registered, and he doubled back. There on the front page of the *New York Times* stacked across the counter were the words: **"LAS VEGAS—Latest DoRight Massacre!"** This must have happened last night. FutureDick, too anxious to get to Robomaids, never stopped for a morning paper, and here were two mass killings side by side in the Southwest: first Phoenix, then Las Vegas. Systematic extermination planned correctly every night could potentially be a Holocaust. The butchers moved from city to city, and every police force in the country would have to be on alert. What were the chances of sparing extra officers to protect apes when humans would then be left alone?

FutureDick never caught a chance to answer his own question because at the bottom of the front page was a four inch article with the heading: **"Talking DoRight Reveals Secrets To Owner!"** How the hell did the press get wind of Emma? Certainly BrickWell didn't say anything, and FutureDick knew that Francie wouldn't divulge a minute of that extraordinary night. In fact, she had been extremely careful about communicating to the press. She said nothing. Anonymity, not celebrity, was her inclination, and she wanted her family excluded from the limelight. So she refused any interviews, hoping the tragic event would be pushed back into distant memory. The pain, still raw, still able to bring tears when she least expected, wasn't something she wanted to share with the public.

Engrossed in the story, FutureDick sat in the waiting room and read about Emma and Francie in the hospital. The reporter, with descriptions as graphic as a photo, recreated the scene of the frail, bandaged ape, the concerned owner and confidante, and the struggle for the ape to reach Francie's ears with her last words. Although the journalist never wrote the dying chimp's exact confession, she intimated that Francie knew secrets, secrets about the ape and secrets about the murder.

A stranger would come away from this article believing that Francie was the key witness in a murder trial. If an outsider could be influenced, what would a killer think? Considering every TV news station across America must have picked up on this recent turn of events for today's news, his logic would be preordained for him by the press. Who knows how many hours the broadcasters had been having a glory day with their talking apes?

FutureDick couldn't wait to get back to Francie where he could take precautions for her safety. Las Vegas was a bit too close for his comfort, seven hours drive from SeaBank. But when he looked up at his gate, departure time had been delayed 45 minutes.

What FutureDick hadn't seen, because he arrived at the airport early, was the thick, murky fog beginning to roll over the city: San Francisco, buffeted by its notorious fog that usually stayed west of the Presidio, was about to be socked in. Tonight was that once in a while opportunity when the impenetrable fog would gain momentum and bully its way over the entire city, over downtown, over the 101 freeway, over Candlestick Park, and sink into the Bay. And the mist attacked unmercifully while the airport lay in its siege.

Anxiously, FutureDick went over to the gate assistant to inquire about the delay, but she had no idea when they would get the all clear signal. FutureDick didn't like this. Something didn't feel right. He sniffed the air for one brief second, and there it was: merging with his uneasiness was that foreboding smell, a slight variance in the scent. It didn't smell right. It smelled danger. It smelled terror. And what he feared more—it smelled death.

As his anxiety mixed with his intellect, FutureDick started to replay the scenes of murder. It continually bothered him that the DoRights never seemed to sense the intruders. Vanilla or no vanilla, how could living killers act so quickly that the DoRights were offered no time to scream? Could an odor actually blot out a self-preservation response? Wouldn't a screech naturally escape on its own? The video showed five hit-men, one for each female and one for the babies. Yet, there had been no prints, no prints anywhere.

All he had was a picture of ape after ape entering the pen. They had to be masterly trained to attack so efficiently, some kind of super-simian. The DoRight apes were strong. Pure muscle. Some could be five times as strong as a person the same size. Yet these primate assassins were stronger. They not only killed their fellow creatures, they lifted the DoRight up, twisted, ripped, and smashed, certainly not characteristic of ordinary chimpanzee aggression.

But the video apes were not ordinary. FutureDick couldn't recall reading anywhere of one chimp lifting another over its head and smashing it to the ground. Each animal weighed close to two hundred pounds. Could they so easily heave their own weight? Doubtful. Definitely doubtful.

Who or what could possess that Superman type of strength? It had to be a Superman type of ape, one created by man, not nature—one forged from metal into a machine. It had to be a robot. And he'd stake his last buck it came from Robomaids. He was sure of it. If AceArrow were manufacturing machines for a theme park, he'd want to show them off, not keep them hidden from a potential investor. He'd want to portray Robomaids as fiscally sound as possible.

But it didn't make sense. How do you transport an army of killer robots cross-country to the backdoors or backyards of each house? Yes, they operated at night, under the cover of dark. Still, you just don't march down the street near midnight without someone seeing you. The world's not blind. There's constantly a night person around somewhere.

Then a penetrating glimmer, and click! the light bulb exploded in FutureDick's brain. The flash. That moment of awareness when you know you've correctly answered your query, and your perception is altered forever. Those maniac marauders didn't get out of a van. They climbed out of the sewer. That was where he found the metal plate, near the manhole cover.

Of course! The buried walkways! The National Eco-Waste Transport System! Anyone could traverse an entire city under the surface of the streets if he were willing to navigate through the narrow subterranean highways. Since the federal government funded construction of municipal sewage and waste transport systems in the late '90's, most US cities had modernized their sewers. They needed very little urging. A market for recycled sludge promised hefty returns, environmentally and financially, and cities nationwide took advantage of free money offered by the government. Everyone was happy: the feds witnessed the construction of a national underground infrastructure; the states smiled at their cities' ability to help others while helping themselves; and the cities celebrated the additional jobs that creation of the conduits generated for their unemployed.

But the real winners, the killers, thought FutureDick, must have howled for hours when such an accessible transportation design plopped into their plan. They only had to figure out which houses were situated close to the covers. That's it! The manhole covers. Climb out, commit your bloodletting, and escape. No trace, no tire marks, no fingerprints, no clues. Why the hell hadn't he realized it before?

I got you, Mr. Mastermind! The age of technology cuts both ways. For all of Robomaids' engineering superiority, you never calculated the widespread use of the video camera or man's unending ingenuity. Who would have expected a camcorder mounted in an animal's pen? Anyone who loved animals, FutureDick theorized. What AceArrow hadn't factored in was that the DoRights were not animals to their owners: they were family.

The van sped down the interstate, its destination SeaBank. At the last moment Tully received orders to change his route. Double back. Now he knew it was meant to be. Why else would he be returning to once-worked territory? He didn't mind giving into AceArrow's misguided whim because he could carry out his own mission that night also. It was a damn sight better than any plan the CEO would have devised. Tully was about to tangle with greatness, and his fingers twitched upon the wheel as they readied themselves for the invasion.

He loved this assignment because he loved unbridled

power. He was captain of an invincible army, and all Tully had to do was transport them to the enemy every night. With each ambush, his men, his mighty machine men, rose magnificently to the occasion. They zeroed in on their targets and operated in synchronization with their well-programmed commands: *Break! Slash! Rip!* That was the essence of their software. Those three little words, *break, slash, rip,* which meant swift elimination of their adversaries, their competitors: the DoRights.

Ever since the Gulf War, which was over way too quickly for Tully's tastes, he wanted to command a fighting unit. Wasn't that what soldiering was about? You weren't supposed to fly into enemy territory and demolish it in three days. You were supposed to engage in fighting—real fighting—hand to hand combat like the old days. The only time he ever saw genuine assault anymore was in the classic film clips from years ago, and his copies of *Apocalypse Now* and *Platoon* were wearing thin.

He wanted action, live action. And today, his dream had come true. He'd gotten his troops, the best soldiers money could buy. Shit! They were the best in the history of warfare, and they were under his control.

Who knew what would happen after this assignment? The men listened to him, not AceArrow. He, *Bisonballs* Tully, was their commanding officer. If he didn't want to go back to Robomaids, he didn't have to. He could go anywhere with this killer team. He could rob banks, he could take over a city, he could take over a country. Executed properly, he could use his men to get whatever he wanted.

Tully had no obligation to AceArrow. In fact, AceArrow could be eliminated with the smallest order to his machines. Right now, Tully trusted the CEO, and they enjoyed an equitable working relationship. However, he wasn't sure he wanted to put his future in the hands of one man, even if that man was quite powerful. Tully also bulged with power. Wasn't he plainly in the driver's seat? Wasn't he literally pushing the army's buttons? And every time he thought about the raw energy he controlled, he grew excited about the direction he was heading toward.

Retracing his steps worked to his advantage. He could ambush a shit-load of DoRights and test his warriors on human beings. He knew that people would react quicker. Although initially, he rejected human targets, he was still curious to see what kind of opposition they'd put forth. Ultimately, they were goners. No one could go up against these metallic musclemen. They'd mow down anything in their path. Tully couldn't wait to set his army loose on those owners of the talking DoRight.

Francie loved moments like this. Every time she happened to be with one of her children, alone, she felt she was granted a rare opportunity to get to know the child better. She tried to arrange special times with each youngster throughout the year so she could spend a few hours one-to-one. Happily, here was an extra, she and Josh home for the evening, unexpected, unplanned, and unhurried.

She knew he wasn't feeling too well, but the mushroom-onion-avocado pizza they ordered in, along with the four videos Francie brought home, perked him up a bit. The entire evening was planned: watch one video and eat pizza, take a break and read two chapters of *Watership Down*, talk, watch another video, eat frozen yogurt, popcorn, or peanuts—whatever Josh felt like. This was his night, no compromises with his sisters. He got to call the shots. If he didn't like one video, there were three others to choose from.

Francie enjoyed talking to Josh about world issues. Although he was only nine years old, he already had a keen grasp of right and wrong. He owned a compassion for people that had always been unique to him. Consequently, his teachers, his friends, and even strangers gravitated to him for relationship. They liked being in his company because he remained genuine, radiating good will toward whoever was with him. And, somehow, this generosity of spirit made his fellow companion feel special, feel good, feel alive. What spark Josh ignited in others,

Francie couldn't quite grasp. She just knew, over the years, notes and comments came to her about her son with the good heart. He made people feel like people.

Of course, his sisters ignored this trait in Josh. They argued about TV programs, who won the chance to pick the restaurant, the movie, the front seat of the car. They laughed at Josh's irrational fear of spiders. But in their soft moments, they also remained protective of him, realizing he was their brother, their only brother, and a rather nice person at that.

So Francie and Josh sat side by side on the floor pillows, eating pizza, drinking diet Cokes, and watching one of their all time favorite videos: *Harold and Maude*. With the tension and turmoil that surrounded the past month, the tears, the sleepless nights, the panic, this was one of the first moments in melancholy days when Francie touched a part of her inner peace. It was still there, the ability to be content, to be at one with the world, to sit next to your child and enjoy sharing the same universe with him, to know that this offspring is part of you and has a wealth of adventures ahead of him and a lifetime to become.

What the hell is going on with those planes? Certainly they can fly above the fog bank. As FutureDick looked at his watch and saw the readout of six p.m., he realized that SeaBank, only ninety minutes away by plane, was somehow evading his reach. If he rented a car, he would be on the road for nine hours. Too late. Much too late.

Too late for what? How did he know he should get there in three hours? He couldn't answer. He just knew. He knew that somewhere around nine was the bewitching hour. By nine, it would be dark. By nine, violence could once more walk the earth. By nine, death troopers could storm another house. Whose house? Whose house? Francie's house. Why not? Her house had been hit already. She owns no DoRights. She owns nothing.

But in the back of his brain whispered the horror he had

been fighting back. She does own something. She owns information. She supposedly owns information that could implicate the killers, the machines, Robomaids. AceArrow wouldn't. There's no way he'd attack humans. He knew murdering animals would be criminal yet, at least, defensible. But humans. No, not even AceArrow could be that bloodthirsty.

Automatically, FutureDick replayed the CEO's face in front of his mind's eyes, and he knew the answer. There was no humanity left in AceArrow. Maybe there never was. His whole demeanor told FutureDick that bottom line was what AceArrow lived for. Profit. And his company was losing money. Destroy the obstacle standing in the way of his increased revenue, and he becomes a happy man. Simple logic. Black and white, no grey. Destroy Francie and any evidence, then Robomaids surges higher on the stock market.

That's when FutureDick realized AceArrow was going for broke. The moment he unleashed his mechanized terrorists on the country, he claimed his vision. Nothing, no one, no thing, no body would stand in the way of his company's success. Therefore, Francie was expendable. Francie was in danger, mortal danger, and FutureDick was ninety minutes away. Actually so close, but by airline standards, perhaps the distance of infinity.

FutureDick had only one choice: TigerTail. He couldn't call Francie. He'd scare her too badly. And where would she hide? Eventually, AceArrow would catch up with her. What if he were wrong? He'd traumatize Francie and Josh with hypothetical theories, and they'd still remain sitting ducks. He needed to stop the mysterious murderers, not send Francie away. So TigerTail was his best option.

"TigerTail here."

"Hi man, it's FutureDick. I've got a problem, a big problem."

"So what else is new, FutureDick?"

"TigerTail, you've got to get back to Francie's house. Tonight. I smell DoRight trouble."

"Oh, come on, buddy. The last killings took place in Las Vegas. We were hit weeks ago. Her house has already bought it."

"No, TigerTail, she's in danger, man. Think about that video. Remember how straight those apes stood when they walked in?"

Twenty minutes later, which seemed like two and a half lifetimes to FutureDick, he had convinced TigerTail to get some men over to Francie's. He begged TigerTail to enlist the SWAT team, but the detective wasn't buying it. Those officers were on call for real action, not hunches. BlackArm would never go for it. If FutureDick were wrong, it would be TigerTail's ass on the line, not to speak of the demerit on his record. Let FutureDick fool with his own career, not TigerTail's. But he did promise FutureDick he'd go there with four other officers and at least some specialized rapid-firing weapons. They'd stake out the house and stop any intruders from entering.

"You've got my word, FutureDick. If you're wrong, I get six months of work from you, free. If you're right, you're a goddamn hero, and I owe you. But geez, buddy, I hope you're wrong. Going against killer robots is not what I call an evening of fun."

All FutureDick could do was go back to his seat and watch the gate. Departure time was now scheduled for seven, 45 minutes from now. "Please don't change it again. Whatever's out there, I'm begging you, please let my plane leave at seven. Please don't take away my life once more."

Tully's mind wandered as he drove. Should he spend the $120,000 from this job on setting up a base camp in Los Padres National Forest, or should he wait till he accumulated more cash? Although $120,000 would go a long way, $500,000 would go even farther. He needed more soldiers. Five robots did not constitute as substantial an army as he had intended.

And who knows what jobs AceArrow had planned for the future? Tully enjoyed this sort of work. No, *enjoy* was not quite right. He loved these attacks. He thrived on them. Why give it up so soon? Maybe in a few years, but right now he was in a dream-come-true situation, and the entire country lay before him.

He had big plans and he needed time to develop strategy. That was the link between execution and success. It was completely in the strategy. If Tully were going to take over anything, it had to be properly organized. He didn't worry about getting caught. He worried about preparation, alternatives—design. The operation design must be flawless, and he was the man to do it.

So Tully daydreamed his drive away, as he smiled through fancies of his own city, his own country, and, possibly, his own world. Why not? Neither Napoleon nor Hitler had what he had: the perfect army, immune to bullets, immune to disease, immune to life. They'd last forever, and they'd be under his rule—commander in chief, General Tully.

Why was he perspiring? The airport was air-conditioned, and yet, his whole body felt clammy. Close to seven, FutureDick saw one of the assistants approach the flight board. "Don't change the time. Please don't change the time." His mind whispered pleas to some unknown authority, some corporate craftsman who held the power of life and death in his choices.

Instead of reaching for a new number, the assistant picked up the microphone and announced that Flight 231 to SeaBank would now be boarding. The wave of relief that swept through FutureDick made him feel giddy for a moment. Perhaps it was his missed dinner, but he knew it was more than hunger pangs. He was going home. And more importantly, he was going to Francie's.

By 7:20, the plane was filled, passengers strapped in, and the aircraft remained motionless. But FutureDick's mind raced through the history of the DoRight murders. He counted on past performance. All the DoRight killings had taken place after eleven in the evening. Surely they wouldn't attack early, particularly if their target were people, not apes. These terrorists counted on the element of surprise. This way, you could grab the sleeping body and demolish it. If they were really coming to Francie's, and that was debatable, they wouldn't take the chance of being seen by neighbors, would they?

As FutureDick played these mind games in his brain, he tried to reassure himself that he was letting emotions cloud his logic. "Look at past patterns, man. Why should they change now?" But his mind didn't win the argument with his heart, and he sat there, white-knuckled, breathing deeply, staring out the misty window. By 7:40, the pilot announced they were given their place in line for take-off. They were twelfth. "So how long could that take?" FutureDick asked his shadowy dialectician. Jets are powerful devices. They could be airborne in a matter of minutes. But he didn't have minutes. He only had seconds, and they were slipping by—too quickly.

He never knew where those twenty minutes went, but they were the longest moments of his life. He talked to himself, drew pictures in his mind of worst scenario, best scenario. He tried to empty his brain completely and just see grey, but Francie and Josh's vulnerability imposed itself on his consciousness, and clips of their broken, bloody bodies whirled like fuzzy images before his eyes. Twenty endless minutes threatened to squeeze out any sense of equilibrium. He thought about going up to the cockpit and intimidating the pilot. "Get your ass airborne or else!" he would bark. But he had no weapon with which to enforce his demand. His gun was lying in the glove compartment of his car at the parking lot, and FutureDick was sitting quite helpless in seat 7A.

At eight, the pilot firmly announced, "We're next," and when FutureDick looked out the window, the plane was two feet off the ground, unknowingly in a race with a van going 65 miles an hour between Las Vegas and SeaBank.

TWENTY-TWO

At 8:30, TigerTail and his men were just about to leave the station, when his two best undercover narcotics agents, Polonsky and Greene, came walking in with ten gang members from the Hell Hawks. TigerTail could see that the two lone detectives needed help with the bookings.

These kids were tough. They respected no one except other gang members. Authority had little meaning to them, for they had lived too long in disposable neighborhoods, areas with poor schools, poor law enforcement, poor parental attention, and just plain poverty, as plain and as poor as you could get.

How do you look up to positions of power which emanate from a political system that keeps you on the outside looking in? These young men and women saw their parents, if they still had a parent or still owned a residue of respect for any kind of kinship, forever economically oppressed. What's more, their vision of the future was filled with few options and even fewer material joys. So they decided to build their lives by their laws, not the regulations handed down from the silvered-spoon plutocrats.

The gap between the *haves* and *have-nots* had widened too far in the last twenty years, and the underrepresented young finally lost their tolerance with text book explanations. They weren't buying any of it. As far as they were concerned, everyone and everything out there was on the other side, not their side, but some side that couldn't give a shit if they lived or died. They would show them. If they were going to be outcasts, untouchables, they'd create their own opportunities, and they'd create them now, under their rules and their people.

The Hell Hawks had been caught in a drug bust somewhere on the south side of the city in the back of a bakery. These youths had a cottage industry thriving among the muffin tins and cookie sheets. Their customers would sneak in the alley and do a deal at the service entrance door. Little light, little traffic, but lots of cash passed through those sugar-cinnamoned portals. And the drug of choice, the latest incarnation of blended dope popular on the streets, was called RoundHouse.

RoundHouse, a combination of cocaine, crystal, and THC, was a new version of long standing drugs, blended in particular ratios to create the latest, but greatest, high. The three narcotics were mixed together in a liquid. Then the elixir was combined with a soft drink or orange juice, whatever the user had on hand. The dope had to be administered through the digestive system, as it was too potent to be injected right into the bloodstream. It would cause immediate cardiac arrest if introduced all at once into a vein.

Ever since the use of needles received such a bad rap in the eighties, drug users became more creative with their abuse of chemicals. They wanted their high, and they wanted some semblance of health. Although Roundhouse took an hour to travel through the bloodstream, the wait was worth the effect. Once flying on a hit of Roundhouse, you walked around buzzed for twelve hours. Even the underworld was teaching its addicts one of life's little but important lessons: Go for the long-term pleasure, not instant gratification. You'll gain more by waiting. Patience as a virtue had finally entered the ethics of those men and women unable to face the harsh reality of life straight.

This new derivation was creating havoc with teenagers. School, work, purpose was irrelevant while drunk on this drug. Even if you discounted the increase in the school dropout rate, you couldn't ignore the rise in petty crime. Roundhouse was not cheap, and junkies were robbing anyone to get money for their habit.

TigerTail looked at the clock and decided he had enough time to help Polonsky and Greene. What he didn't foresee was one of the hoods freaking out in the middle of the station house. The guy grabbed a pen, jabbed it into Greene's arm, and tried to back them both out the door. After he was eventually subdued by three officers, the rest of the gang was taken downstairs and put in a cell.

TigerTail sent Greene to the emergency room and told Polonsky to call FireFace at home. Get him to the station to help her and make sure to book each person individually. So what if it would take the whole night? TigerTail wanted no more mishaps this evening, and he had to leave.

He looked at his watch. It was already 9:30, and he had promised FutureDick he'd get to Francie's by nine. He'd never forgive himself if anything happened. TigerTail lived by one creed: all a man has is his word. When he gives it to someone, he's obligated. His integrity is on the line. His self-worth is on the line. He was on the line. TigerTail never went back on his word, and he was thirty minutes late already .

Tully eased into a parking place at Fourth and Madison. The second time around was easy. He knew where the sewer was, and he knew how long it would take his super-soldiers to travel to their confrontation point. But his real genius resided in his ability to effect a silent ambush. Get in and get out, quickly. Do the job, round up your troops, and evacuate.

The toughest part of the assignment for Tully was hearing

the rats scurry out of the way as he marched his troops through the pipe-lined passageway. He hated rats. They never let him forget his nightmare. When Tully was five years old, living in the tenements with his mom, his father must have been off on one of his routine binges, a huge black rat bit him on his leg while he was sleeping. He woke up in pain, screaming, blood spreading across the sheet, wondering what he had done wrong to deserve this suffering. He thought he was having a bad dream, when he realized the gnawing he felt was not a fantasy. A rat was actually chewing on his calf.

He hated rats. He would have killed every goddamned rodent he found in the tunnel, if he weren't afraid of blowing his perfect cover. But by sewer, he could traverse the city at night, go wherever he wanted without being seen, and all he needed was his remote control to unleash his supreme military might upon the world.

The five year old may have conquered his fear of rats and turned it into pure anger, but his rage at his father, who failed, who fled into the oblivion of alcohol and died when he was nine years old, remained on simmer. He always drew upon its seething heat when he was approaching danger or being threatened. "I'll show you, you fucker! I'll show you what a real man can do!" What he really meant was, "I'll get you back for hurting me, Daddy. For loving liquor more than you loved me. For leaving when I needed you most."

But Tully had given up his tears long ago. It felt ten times better to hurt back, at anyone, than confront the intolerable apathy his father inflicted upon him years ago. Maybe his father was a fuck-up. But not him! Certainly, not Frank *invincible* Tully, the living dynamo.

Francie and Josh were talking about hunger. Uganda had undergone a severe drought, and the news continually carried stories of the starving population.

"You know, Mom, it doesn't seem fair that we have so much to eat, and they have nothing."

"It gets too complex, Josh. It's more a matter of distribution and selection of crops. The country decided to grow items to export instead of food. Then they were going to use the money they received from selling their coffee to put back into their country and help the people."

"But Mom, you can't eat coffee. It's not like lettuce or carrots or grapes."

"True, Josh. Their theory sounded feasible. But somehow, it didn't work, and the people had no food because they didn't grow any. Then the soil became depleted of minerals, which made it unusable for crops. And the drought was the final straw. Nothing could be planted."

"But Mom, why bother selling to other countries? Why not take care of yourself?"

"I wish I knew, Josh. From your eyes, it sounds so possible, and I agree with you. But I think the smaller countries want greater clout in the world markets, and they think they can give more back to their people that way."

"But it doesn't work, Mom. Those babies are dying."

"You're right, Josh. Somehow power and greed get in the way, and the good intentions never filter down to the people. They go hungry."

"If it were left up to me, Mom, I'd create a government for the people. I'd tell them to grow crops they could eat, and if they have any left over, then they could sell them in Uganda. This way, all the food would be kept in their country."

"But Josh, how would they have gotten the money to improve their country? They wanted to enter the 21st century with some of our tech-luxuries."

"I don't know, Mom. They don't really need VCR's. They need milk and bread for their stomachs. Couldn't they wait till their people were all fed?"

The conversation between Josh and Francie continued for another ten minutes. She was frequently caught off guard by Josh's intellectual simplicity. What he said made sense. It smacked of good judgment, but it was also spoken without the knowledge of human guile and deceit. Oh my son, you will have so much to give the world.

Finally FutureDick arrived in SeaBank. Six and a half hours ago, he had started out on what was supposed to be a ninety minute trip. If he believed in the fates, he'd say they were against him. But he had no time to contemplate the meaning of life. Charging to his car, he nearly collided with a family of four, who were probably on their way to Disneyland. The little girl stepped into his path just as he was running around the side of the group. "Great reflexes, FutureDick," he murmured, as he jumped two feet off the curb to avoid hitting her. No one was going to get in his way, even if he had to risk a speeding ticket.

He'd be at Francie's in twenty minutes—twenty minutes and he'd be able to offer her the protection he promised. But in the back of his mind rang the refrain: "You may be too late, FutureDick. You may be too late."

He had to get there. And there was no faster route than Farragut to Main and Main to Lifton. If he could put his car into *fly* or Mach speed, he'd be there already. Often he wondered what would happen to traffic congestion if cars could fly for a block or two. But right now, he had to contend with the law of gravity and practice psychokinesis: he'd try to get all the stop lights to remain green. Of course, his logic knew he couldn't exert any supernatural force over a computerized timing system, but his intuition liked to think he could. Besides, if the light turned red, he didn't care. He'd go through it anyway. Sometimes the laws of man supersede the rules of the State, and this was one of those moments—he had to get to Francie's.

Tully slowly slid the sewer cover aside. Perfect. No cars, no activity. He and his men could get in and out like clockwork, no complications. This was the real thing. No more fooling around with one clan at a time. Now he had a dual opportunity: first, a human target, the most cunning competitor of all. Then, the little haven of TriCubed, where the greatest number of DoRights were housed. His stalwart soldiers were about to be baptized through fire. And they were now reprogrammed to rip humans as well as apes.

It was so much easier for a commander to deal with mechanical men. They listened, never questioned, never talked back, never failed: the perfect fighting machine—no emotional involvement, neither lean nor mean. Nothing. Just performers. And that's where it mattered. A good soldier had to perform, had to get the job done cleanly.

Tully held on to his control box, his protection. This black plastic mechanism was the single barrier that separated him from his men. Otherwise he'd certainly become their first victim. The lightweight apparatus created a low level magnetic radiation shield, so that Tully could stand unthreatened among his warriors without being hurt. Yet he could safely watch their assault and switch to another program if necessary. But Tully knew that wouldn't be required, not with this team. They always obeyed—they always won.

Quietly, he hoisted himself onto the asphalt and watched as five indomitable brawny beasts climbed stealthily out of the street. Black apparitions blending with the night, silent, smooth, and deadly. Tully, operating his controls, accurately guided them to the tree near the curb. There, under cover of the tall timber sitting next to its all-embracing neighbor's high shrubbery, he could regulate the onslaught. Nothing got any better than this!

TigerTail sped along Barker and took a right on Lifton. It was 9:50, and he wanted to get to Francie's where he could station his men in strategic positions. According to FutureDick, if they climbed out of the sewer, TigerTail would have to wait till all five robots made it up onto the street. Of course, that's assuming that the same number as in the video would still be used. Hopefully, that was a pretty safe assumption, because if there were more robots added since the video, TigerTail was too weak. He hardly had enough men to take on five machines.

Additional assailants might really complicate the situation.

As he approached Francie's house, his headlights caught some shadows in the grass. He could swear he saw something move near the tree. It was too damn dark. He couldn't tell for sure, but the tree trunk looked wider than it should. He decided to continue past Francie's house and radioed the two men in the other car to wait a block away. "Stay out of sight, QuickEye. I think we've got potential trouble, here."

After Tully collected his men by the tree, a car wove its way down the quiet street. He knew it would pass in a moment, so he grouped his men closer together, hoping they would be camouflaged by the almost moonless night and the shrubs. He didn't think the car would turn into the adjacent driveway because there was a car parked there already. But if it did, he'd switch to surprise attack. He had more than one offense up his sleeve. A good commander prepares for all contingencies, and now, nothing would halt his advancing army.

He had time, all the time in the world. There was no other rendezvous but here. If it took the entire night, he had time, and he had patience, but no one or no thing had more patience than his impregnable SWAT team. They could wait years—they could wait lifetimes.

When TigerTail drove past, he saw that the manhole cover was lying slightly to the right of the sewer opening, and there was sufficient room for someone to squeeze out of the opening. In fact, there was sufficient room for a band of killer robots to crawl out silently and position themselves around the house. He drove to the end of the block, turned the corner, and jumped out of the car with his binoculars. He was right.

There was something near the house. He could see several dark shapes congregated around the tree and a smaller shape, a man, standing among them. He was holding some kind of control in his hand, and his lips were moving. "Count, TigerTail. How many of those black things do you see? Man, is it dark.

But, shit, it looks like five hairy apes. Five large robotic apes. I don't believe it! Just like FutureDick warned. With the little guy, it'll be six to five odds."

TigerTail wished they were more even, but with their refined weapons, it was doable. He ran back to his car, radioed his men to park their vehicle, approach the house on foot, and close in now. Quickly, but very, very quietly.

Tully decided to wait five minutes after the car passed, just to be sure there was no other activity on the street. Patience, man, patience. That's the key to surprise attacks. You've got to pick the right minute, move at the appropriate time. Tactician Tully was waiting for that best of all moments.

Now! Right now! Tully left three of his men by the first tree and proceeded to the next tree, the one closer to Francie's house. There he situated his last two robots. The house stood alone, braced against the murky shadows, unaware of the violent rites of initiation it was about to participate in.

Tully looked at the house, looked at his men, and then bent his head down to strike the word *attack* on the keypad of his portable control. As his fingers spelled out the six letter word, he anxiously savored the anticipation of following his fifth gladiator up the stairs into the unsuspecting residence, into the blood.

For Tully, this was the height of ecstasy. Being in the middle of an ambush beat fucking a woman any day. The sexual climax was over in seconds, but the fight, this fight, lasted for minutes, maybe even hours. It was sustained rapture. And the beauty was, you didn't have to capitulate to some dumb bitch. You didn't have to yield to anyone.

It was all yours, the bliss, the frenzy: a total transport to pure power. You decided who lived and who died. Tully felt himself getting erect. He always did right before battle, his body manifesting its potency for the whole world to see.

He watched the front soldier start to move, slowly, steadily, a bomb about to explode and tear apart the lives of the defenseless family: Their Enemy. He watched, a gleam in his eyes, a fullness in his soul, every inch of his body aroused, and he enjoyed his first of the many electrifying spasms that would follow.

TigerTail saw his men running toward the house from the opposite end. The four of them converged on the shadowed lawn at the same moment and edged toward the tree where the little guy was standing, replete in camouflage gear. The bastard was completely unaware of TigerTail, and the detective saw why. Walking away from the make-believe soldier toward the house were two gigantic apes, robotic apes, hundreds of pounds of exotic metals, wires, plastics, lubricants, programmed to kill. The ferocity of the future revealed in the very certain present, his men were going up against a new type of enemy without a clue about its vulnerability.

FutureDick had warned him. But how do you honestly tell someone what it's like to face a foe who may be unstoppable, whose bones don't break, and who is probably immune to ordinary weapons? How do you teach someone to go hand to hand with a mechanized zombie?

And while Tully dreamed his erotic dreams and admired the sleek, sensuous motion of his first warrior, he felt a rifle butt press against his back.

"It's all over, creep. SeaBank police. Call your thugs off. We've got you surrounded."

Where the fuck did they come from? Who were they? How did they know? Tully couldn't turn around to see. He just felt the metal jabbing his lower back. Think pal, think. His men have already begun their advance. These losers will never stop them. It's too late.

"Not on your life, dipshit. We've started."

"Stop it now, mister, or this bullet goes right into your spine. I won't kill you, buddy, I'll just paralyze you for life."

"Go ahead, copper. You think I'm scared. My men will

grind you, pig. They'll step on you like ants."

His threats struck their mark because Tully felt the barrel swipe his back with an irate shove. But the swing of the rifle arced and hit his left arm, which was holding the control. The instrument flew from his fingers and landed in the hedge near the tree.

Tully's eyes convulsed with shock before he lunged toward the bushes. His shield, his impenetrable armor, gone, in the flick of a moment. An urgent, uncanny squeal escaped his lips as he wildly went down on all fours, trying to crawl into the foliage. He had to find the box. It was his protection. It was his life.

Tully's sudden movement alerted the first robot, who turned toward the bellied figure. With two strides, the creature caught up to the crawling man and unhesitatingly grabbed his left leg. But just at that moment, Detective FearLess kicked the robot's elongated limb, trying to dislodge Tully from its grasp.

Instantaneously, the mechanical beast dropped Tully and latched onto Fearless's shoulder. With the ease of a body builder lifting a brick, the ape-like machine whisked FearLess above his head. In a matter of seconds, the brute had raised both arms around FearLess's torso and snapped it.

The man's dying shrieks penetrated the air. But the hapless tones never moved into the computer's sensors, for there was no programmed receptor for mercy in the electronic brain. FearLess appealed to a void, where any kind of emotion was non-existent, and a human cry was measured by intensity of decibel rather than the power of its plea.

Tigertail watched in astonishment. It had all happened so quickly that he was stunned. In one moment where there was life now lay the fractured remnants of a human body, a body that used to house a mind Tigertail depended on, that joked and smiled and placed service above self.

My God, FearLess, where did you go? Man, you were with me a minute ago. Tell me, for whom did you die? That little fuck-face! That shit! Wildly, TigerTail looked around, ready to chase Tully, trying to restrain the command in his brain that decreed he kill the punk. Blast his brains out. But he needed the little shit. God damn it! He needed the asshole. This little prick was his link to the country-wide slaughter. And before Tigertail could grieve his colleague's untimely death, he saw the monster turn and start toward him.

Then time stopped. Abruptly, the seconds started to stretch into hours. A new dimension set in, a crisis dimension, where you see your death approaching, and you seem positively impotent to stop it. It's bigger than you. It's better than you. And your mind starts to race, like a magnet attracting steel filings. Every option flees through your brain, in and out, in and out, and nothing works.

TigerTail faced his menace, and his mind faced the prospect of annihilation—extinction—death, in the worst of all possible ways. Agony. It would be pure torture to be touched, to be ravished, to be torn apart by this unswerving machine, his bones ripped free, his nerves exploding in raw, impeccable pain. An instant of negation, nothingness, and then Nature took over.

But without warning, the slow motion frame fractured and a gush of adrenalin shot through his body. That's the precise moment the fight instinct clicked in, protection, the preservation of the species, fight or flight. And TigerTail chose to fight. "I'll kill you, you bastard," he shouted. "Crazy. Who am I talking to? A goddamn machine. A fucking robot!"

But he relished screaming at this hunk of metal and yelled again, "Say your prayers, big boy. That's the only thing you got left."

TigerTail moved closer to QuickEye and yelled, "Go after that motherfucker. I'll take this one. Just shoot, man. Just shoot. Whoever downs one, get to another son of a bitch. Quick."

His remaining men were struggling to stop the ape robots from advancing toward the house, but the bullets merely retarded their progress. They wouldn't stop.

There stood TigerTail, shooting with his semi, from left to right, trying to obstruct the would-be monster from moving forward, and all he could do was stall it. He couldn't knock it down. It might as well have been wearing a bullet proof vest. Nothing seemed to penetrate.

All of a sudden, TigerTail dropped to the ground and rolled over quickly to the nearby bushes, where he took momentary refuge. The advancing robot stopped, moving his mechanical eyes from side to side, not able to focus on its distinct human target. Then, it swung around to its right, heading toward QuickEye.

Meanwhile, Tully had reached his life support system, the black box. And crawling into the brush, he directed the nearest robot to follow him. Tully slithered through the grass, a human snake bent on destroying whatever blocked his path, till he reached the curb. Glancing back, he saw his warrior close behind, while the four other stalwart, devoted soldiers were being rammed with bullets, noisily lighting up the darkened night.

Tully crept on all fours to the manhole where he slid through the opening. Guiding his sole beloved robot through the cavity, he edged himself down into the sewer, preparing for Plan B. All was not lost. Not yet. There was lots of killing left to do. Soon, he would enter his finest hour. Even with only one robot, he could single-handedly eradicate the entire DoRight compound. One metal soldier was worth a whole platoon of humans. And with Tully's expert directions, they would wipe out every fucking ape that BrickWell owned.

When he reached the van, he positioned his man in the rear, then climbed into the driver's seat. Destination: TriCubed. "Let's get that shitload of DoRights sleeping there, my beauty. Just you and me." Now's the time to depopulate the pen. Why couldn't that bastard AceArrow see that? He could kill more there in fifteen minutes than nights of roaming the country. He'd show that wimp CEO what a real commando could do.

Twenty-Three

Josh and Francie thought they heard gun shots outside the house. Since they were watching the old time thriller, *Dirty Harry*, they weren't sure if the shots came from the TV or from their neighborhood.

"Let's check, Mom. Turn the video off."

"Okay Josh. But why would anyone have machine guns on our quiet little street? The only thing you could kill would be flowers."

"I don't know. That noise sounded pretty close. Like it was right by the door."

And when they heard it again, they knew it wasn't coming from the silenced TV. Francie's first instinct was to grab Josh and hide. Find some little nook, even a kitchen cabinet, crawl in the back, and wait till the terror passed. But before she could devise any sort of deceptive action, Josh had run to the front door to see what was going on.

QuickEye, unaware of TigerTail's predicament and

engrossed with trying to thwart the artificial killer-ape ten feet away, didn't notice the new robot heading toward him. So TigerTail scrambled from the shrubbery to distract QuickEye's aggressor. The robot turned and started to walk toward TigerTail, except the detective could see that the mechanical gaze directed its sights not on him but at the light emanating from Francie's porch.

"Hey, you bastard, come get me! I'm right here!"

Still the robot ignored him. A human fly that didn't exist, TigerTail stood there, protecting some invisible no man's land that kept the monster at bay. But the monster was leaving. It didn't want to play anymore. Instead, the capricious demon wanted to do battle with Francie's steps. TigerTail ran after him, hoping he was humanly faster than the robots he left fighting the rest of his men. His only hope was to deter the advancing menace—then he saw why the robot had decided to march upon the solitary house.

There in the dim light of the opened front door stood a little boy gaping at the muddle of apes and cops. A child. Innocence personified, and yet the perfect human target for the oncoming missile of a machine. "Get back, kid! Get back!" TigerTail beseeched the boy to get away, close the door, run, but his voice died in the volley of bullets flying from his men to the undefeatable machines.

He had a single choice. Aim at the fiend's back. The front sure as hell didn't work. TigerTail focused on the skull and shot a line from head to foot down the supposed spine.

"Die, you son of a bitch, die!"

TigerTail emptied twenty rounds into the back of the unrelenting beast and finally hit something. Where he hit or what he hit, he had no idea. But some spot in the heel or the back or the neck was soft enough to receive a bullet and block the message running from the computer software.

The machine slowly went down, crimping into a pitiful heap, like a puppet whose strings were cut. TigerTail was jubilant. He had destroyed in a few seconds what seemed omnipotent a few minutes ago. By cutting off the line of communication to the brain circuitry, he overpowered pounds of superior strength. But his exhilaration was short-lived. He had to get back to his three officers and tell them where to shoot.

"Get in back of the bastard. Just keep shooting till you hit the spot. It's somewhere down his spine."

So TigerTail ran to each man, explaining how to stop the robot. Yet as he was helping his team, another metal demon started to approach the house with accelerated speed, heading right toward Josh. The boy stood in the doorway, watching a movie become real.

Getting into the inner compound had been easy. Almost too easy. Didn't TriCubed know there was a war going on, and it had to defend its position? But Tully took advantage of the company's negligence and quietly glided like death's cohort into the first DoRight life station.

"Attack, my love, attack!" And as his emotions reached their ecstatic crest, he watched, entranced, engorged, near bursting, wooing his almighty soldier to destroy further. Wave after wave of pleasure ransacked his body, while scream after scream permeated the blood spattered pen.

The DoRights hugged their infants, hysterically trying to break through the plastered confines, but where could they go? Tully had secured the gate, so they ran around confused, desperate to find an opening, frenetically trying to escape the killer's reach.

It was breathtaking to watch his Herculean assailant raise the unruly, shuddering chimp above its head and crack her back. The robot would sling the limp, broken body against the wall and immediately grab another would-be victim. A baby would break so quickly that its blood spurted high in the air, geyser-like, raining down a shower of red upon the intransigent mechanical brute.

The blood, the gore, the beauty of the massacre made Tully

hard repeatedly. And in the middle of his third orgasm, he thought he heard his father whisper, "You done good, boy. You done good." But then his fury exploded, and his vision drank in the sight of a baby's eyeball being hurtled across the room, as the raging robot slammed the frail corpse into the wall with heightened intensity.

Swiftly, Tully moved his combatant to the next life station, oblivious to the tremendous din threatening to envelop the earth. By now, two security guards had reached the first life station and stood witness to the slaughter. They stopped, unwilling to proceed further, while one watchman called the police on his cellular phone. They wanted to save the DoRights, but they wanted to save themselves more. And the scene revealed a massacre so complete that they knew they were outnumbered before they penetrated further into the compound.

FutureDick was rounding the corner to Francie's house, when he heard the shooting. He knew instantly the terror had begun. He tightened his fingers on the wheel, while his mind repeated its own mantra: "I hope I'm not too late. I hope I'm not too late."

As he pulled up to the curb and grabbed his gun from the glove compartment, he saw men on the lawn shooting at apes, the same straight apes he remembered from the video. Then his glance sped rapidly to Francie's house, and he saw a blackish-brown robotic brute going up the stairs. There stood Josh, somewhat hypnotized by the approaching weapon. Josh, all alone, perfect prey for this programmed annihilator.

FutureDick thought he could hear Francie screaming in the background, when his instincts propelled him to run from the car as if he were zipping over the finish line of a 10k race. Trying to cover the hundred feet in seconds, hidden energy, he never knew he had, emerged to accelerate the sprint. But his speed seemed sluggish, for his snail-paced steps couldn't overtake the mercurial automaton. As fast as he was going, it wasn't fast enough to get there to save Josh. The killer robot darted there first and, in a split second, yanked Josh off the ground by his waist.

The boy was a feather in the claws of this massive machine, and his little legs and arms looked like they belonged to some forlorn rag doll whose fate was in the hands of a petulant King Kong. The beast lifted the child up, possibly expecting a heavier object. As it flung the boy into the air, its grasp must have loosened temporarily because Josh's body flew into the house, where his head hit the bannister, and he dropped, collapsed, in a heap of what was once the living flesh of a vibrant, beautiful boy.

And as FutureDick ran his heart out, still seeming to be miles from the assault, Francie suddenly materialized to confront the robot.

"Oh Francie, what are you doing? Get away, get away, my love."

But, of course, Francie never heard FutureDick's thoughts. Her rage was unstoppable. She placed herself between her crumpled pile of son and the nearing terminator intent on killing anything in its path.

"Take me, you son of a bitch! Take me! But keep your filthy hooks off my child. Stay the hell away from my baby!"

As she screamed at the unhearing machine, tears streamed down her eyes, for she could see no movement coming from Josh. His eyes were closed, his body limp. The little form lay there like a deflated balloon, all his air having swooshed out in the unyielding impact.

The robot immediately swept Francie up and started to raise her above his head. FutureDick had reached the steps and began pummeling the metal backside with bullets. But his ammunition was no match for the trilium-girded frame. He couldn't stop the monster. Still, he kept shooting. Clip after clip, he prayed, "Die, you bastard. Die," when he connected. Somewhere in this technological marvel was a spot that could be touched, that could be breached, and when one of FutureDick's bullets penetrated this susceptible area, it jammed a circuit. Convulsively, the machine holding Francie in the air began to fling her from side to side.

The arm, like a palm tree caught in a hurricane, swayed back and forth. When it flared to the right, Francie hit air, but when it swooped to the left, Francie's body hit the wall. Every thud against the wall set up an explosion of wrath that FutureDick didn't know he owned. He wanted to climb aboard the monster's back and tackle it, but he might crush Francie with his maneuver if the machine fell on top of her.

Meanwhile, Francie was squirming inside the robot's grip, struggling to turn her body so that the same shoulder wouldn't receive the impact. She cleverly tried to provide a new spot to absorb the blows from the wall, but her resilience was failing with each painful knock into the plaster. Back and forth, the beast rammed her body into the wall.

Just when FutureDick had decided to go for the brute's leg, TigerTail joined him with his semi-automatic and ripped a spray of bullets down the fiend's back. It crumbled. And as it went down, it dropped Francie. She fell on the floor, bruised, bleeding, but relieved that her devil incarnate had let her go.

What was once a seething component of wires, metal, software, commanded to exterminate, lay there helpless, innocent, harmless—it couldn't raise a finger to kill a flea. And next to it lay the only two human beings who had revived the life's blood left in FutureDick's heart.

FutureDick glanced at Josh and saw how white the child looked. He wanted to lift him up, but he realized that the emergency crew would be more skilled in handling the little body which, if not dead already, was teetering on the edge of a chasm we all reach—the bleary border of life or death. FutureDick went over to Francie, bent down and held her head.

"Don't die on me, Francie honey. Don't die. Don't take away my chance to live again. Hang in there, for God's sake. You can do it. I've seen you in the racquetball court. I know how you never give up. Sweetheart, please don't give up now."

Francie looked at FutureDick, gazed into his eyes, and with a whisper, she weakly said, "Please FD, stay with Josh. Please... don't let them let him die. Please take care of him."

Then she smiled, just a glimpse of a smile, and said, "I never knew you watched me on the court." With that, she closed her eyes, yearning to sleep for a long, long time.

TigerTail walked over and put his hand on FutureDick's shoulder. "The ambulances are here, man. They'll take over. We really nailed those bastards, didn't we?" But he never mentioned his lost man to FutureDick. What good would it do? The poor guy was waging his own competition with death, and right now, it was anyone's game.

As the crew in white walked in with their stretchers, FutureDick stood up. "Thanks, TigerTail, for being here. You saved their lives!"

"Hey FutureDick, thank you. You have an uncanny feel for getting to the heart of a crime. It's like you smell trouble right before it's about to start, man. I'm sorry about the kid and his mom, but we'll throw the book at the bastard who's behind the whole thing."

"Give me a minute, TigerTail. I'll be there soon. Let me just see what's happening with the family."

FutureDick watched as the paramedics checked Josh's and Francie's vital signs. The child and mother were still alive. Francie was banged up a lot, but her strong body would sustain the attack. She'd be plenty bruised, but for the moment nothing seemed broken.

Josh, on the other hand, was barely breathing. The way his head was angled indicated the possibility of a broken neck. His color was poor, but he had his age going for him. Perhaps his youthful body might be able to overcome the damage done to his slight frame. Children seemed to own this incredible ability to renew their tissue, their bones, their blood, their life. Josh had to be one of those fighters. The world was waiting for him, and his candle had much more flame left in it. Although the blaze was spluttering right now, it couldn't go out. "Please Josh, don't give up, my child. Feed your beautiful fire. Keep it going." And with that prayer, FutureDick walked out as the paramedics ever so gently wrapped Josh and lifted him onto the stretcher.

Breaking through his bliss, Tully heard the sirens amid the screeching in the compound. He switched commands and started guiding the robot between the scattered dead apes. When he reached the last pen, he saw the two guards standing by the opening, yelling to the police.

Carefully, Tully took aim and shot the first watchman in the chest. Before his cohort could react, Tully fired a shot to the second guard's head. As the man tumbled over his partner, Tully edged to the gate with his worthy warhorse. Through the cacophony of chimp shrieks, Tully peered out at an advancing line of patrolmen, guns raised, aimed toward the pen.

Moving behind the robot, Tully trailed his protector out the gate, hearing the bullets whiz past his ears. They splattered off the metal body as it haltingly shuffled away from the compound. "Just ten more feet," thought Tully, "and then I can run for it." While the police would be aiming at the mechanical ape, Tully could break away and race toward the van.

He knew he could beat the bullets if he drew near enough to the entrance of the compound. Of course, he'd have to sacrifice his beautiful warrior. Inevitable. That's what a good soldier did: protect his commander. And his gutsy troops were the best. They'd gladly place themselves in the line of fire for their leader. It was their charge! It was their mission! Safeguard their general at all costs! Besides, there were a hell of lot more of them back at Robomaids, but there was only one Tully.

Three—two—one. Break! Shadow-like, Tully bolted from behind the robot toward the parking lot, flinging the black box when he lunged forward. As he ran, spewing forth saliva, gasping for oxygen, one of the patrolmen, the youngest and the fastest of the municipal blue convoy, broke loose and started racing after Tully. The youthful officer's verbal warnings died in the moonless air as Tully dashed to his four-wheel-drive savior. But he was no match for Officer FleetFeet's pace. The pride of the academy, this young policeman won medals for his speed, and like a gazelle, he was gaining on Tully when the culprit neared the van.

Trapped in the time warp of immediacy, Tully bulldozed through the *now,* that involuntary wink waffling between life or death. He knew he was going to make it. He had to. He was impervious to human weakness. Like his premier automatic army, he could outwit the frailty residing in ordinary men. He was special. He was above men, above death. The vehicle waited out there, offering him refuge, offering him escape, and he reached out to grab the door's handle.

But he never clenched the metal. Just as his fingers bent to embrace the steel curve, his brain exploded into a million polychromatic, flashing flares. Then all went black, lightless, blank, and Tully's body slid along the side of the unopened door, smoke lilting out the hole that used to be his neck.

Dispirited, the two men who had been tied to the DoRights since their genesis mourned their loss later that evening.

"I think the world's gone wild, Bruce. And I swear to God, my heart hurts worse than my head."

"How many did that son of a bitch get?"

"38. Oh, Christ help me! 38 innocent DoRights." And BrickWell stopped, choking on his sobs, unable to continue the conversation.

"I'm sorry, Adam. Really sorry. The utter malice of it all leaves me speechless."

Composed, BrickWell added, "Somehow I feel responsible, Bruce. Not only for the chimps, but for the injured mother and child. In fact, the boy's critical."

"Cut it out, Adam! There's no way you can hold yourself accountable. We have a nut on our hands. You're not the creator of world sanity—just DoRights, my friend. Just DoRights."

"But Bruce, it's an unbelievable situation. Such complete cruelty. Why didn't they come after me instead?"

Softly, TreadHard whispered through the phone, ignoring BrickWell's last question. He had no answers. He never would. Because only cowards go after those weaker than them. And in the robot's arms, each DoRight was as breakable as a matchstick. "Let's pray it's over, Adam. Enough is enough. Some raging evil has exploded into our lives and refuses to leave."

The phone remained silent for a moment, and then TreadHard hissed, "Who's responsible, Adam? Who's behind it? If it's AceArrow, I want to know immediately!"

TWENTY-FOUR

When he walked into the hospital the next morning, after what must have been an hour's worth of sleep, FutureDick inquired about Josh. He held his breath while the information assistant went to look up the boy's name. Let his name be listed. If there's any sanctity left in this world, let this child still count. Please, let him matter. She glanced up and said, "Room 236." Unacquainted with last night's outrage, she never heard the sigh of gratitude that swam through FutureDick's body. For a moment, he thought his knees would buckle beneath him. The boy was alive. He was still fighting.

FutureDick went to Josh's room, but he wasn't allowed to go in. Listed as critical, the child had sustained a head injury and was in a coma. Oh Josh, where are you right now? Where have you gone?

"His breathing is weak but stable," the nurse offered. "In a way, he's lucky. His instincts kicked in when he was thrown against the stairs, and he knew how to protect himself. Fortunately he fell the right way, so there's no broken bones, just a massive amount of bruised tissue. But he was knocked unconscious, and so far, the X-rays can't pinpoint the trauma to the brain."

The woman, experienced in disarming dread, tried to reassure FutureDick, salving him with terms like *youth* and *time* and *energy* and *determination.* Surely her consolatory tone was meant to mitigate his anguish. But lady, this is Josh we're talking about here. This is a heart, a mind, a soul that caressed my spirit and made it smile. And his very core, his center, his link to life is wounded. Can't you hear me? He needs his brain. Get in there and fix it. For God's sake, bring him back.

Still somewhere deep in that vital organ, in that complex compacted grey matter was an injury fighting with Josh's soul, and the battle was raging at this very moment. Yet FutureDick was forced to crouch helplessly on the outside and wait. He could watch, he could possibly hope, but he definitely couldn't mend the child's broken mind.

FutureDick kept trying to swallow as he walked out toward the elevator. Some sinister organism had invaded his throat and was squeezing it from the inside, squeezing every ounce of air out of his lungs. He never realized how much the little guy had touched him, but his thoughts replayed Josh's impact with the bannister. The thud droned away in his head. Clearly, the boy's athletic ability probably saved his life. It was that blessed gymnastics training that came through during the crisis, and Josh, even in the twilight between life and death, managed to fall correctly. What a guy. What a warrior.

Next, FutureDick went to Francie's room. At first, he stood by the door and watched her. She seemed so small, so frail in the hospital bed, dwarfed by the white sheets, white blankets, white walls. As he approached, he blinked back the strain of the past 24 hours. Rather than flesh colored, her neck and arms were black, red, purple, blue, and her face was swollen. He could tell that she hurt, badly. And he was sure that the pain roved through every part of her body.

Gently taking her hand, he kissed it. Then he repeated to her what the nurse had told him about Josh. She didn't say anything, but he sensed the wave of relief through her fingers. He felt her instantly relax and could see a serenity enfold her, even though her lips remained still.

Lost in her own world for a while, she stayed silent, quiet, wanting the news that her child was alive to sink in and comfort her like a down blanket. Clenching FutureDick's hand, she still remained motionless, attempting to hold the moment dormant, where she could luxuriate in the perishable peace. After lounging in the long interlude, calmly she looked at FutureDick and smiled. Her eyes welled with tears as she beamed with complete pleasure.

"You know, FD, this is just a minor setback. As soon as I'm out of here, I'm getting a reservation, and I intend to show you no mercy on the racquetball court."

FutureDick fought back the tears as he cupped Francie's face carefully in his hands and blurted out, "My love, I never want you to show me mercy. Francie honey, you're a fighter, and you've got to keep fighting. Don't you dare lose your spirit. That's who you are, and I love it. Your zeal, your grit, your fire. You never do things half way, and I want you to hear me. I adore your determination. I felt sorry for that robot when I saw he was going up against you."

FutureDick bent over and kissed her softly, sweetly, knowing he had come home once again. And his heart spilled over with feeling as his eyes finally filled with tears. Yet with the tears came the words, "Francie, I'm so glad you're here."

The clean-up after a crime goes unnoticed. First, there is innocence, then defilement, and finally, the effort to erase the desecration. But somehow, the scene never looks the same. You can't go back to the original because the location has become tainted. There will be bloodstains on the leaves, bullets buried in the ground, pieces of flesh or metal flung throughout the blades of grass, and the serenity becomes changed forever.

Francie's front yard had lost its chastity.

And in the face of this moral profanity, people had changed and would never be the same. So it went with TigerTail. He had confronted his mortality last night, and for a brief moment, he was certain he was going to die. Psst! Over! Gone! This made him angry, not frightened, but mad as hell at the Frankenstein responsible for his panic and the country's savagery.

It was no problem identifying Tully. He wore his dog tags around his neck like a badge of honor, a soldier to the end. His perforated body lay in the morgue while TigerTail tracked down the next of kin. Hopelessness sat alongside his resentment; he had come so close to finding out the *who* and *why* of the case. And what he called acid indigestion was the sour taste of futility. Why couldn't he have had a few minutes to question the little shithead?

TigerTail had come back to the station to do some long-distance fact finding about Frank Tully. But his all-night vigil turned stale when he was unable to gain any information worth pursuing. How could there be so few clues and so much crime? The detective remained puzzled. Murder upon murder, and the link to the entire mystery left no papers, no address book, no notes. The closest TigerTail came to any strategic plan were the maps he found in the van. Their routes were inked in with an orange marker. But TigerTail knew where they had been—he wanted to know where they were going next. No clues. No goddamn clues!

The only bright spot that entire day was the explanation he learned from RainRock, their computer expert. Apparently, TigerTail had struck the death knell or at least the circuit breaker when he shot at the robot's back. Located between the power-driven beast's neck and upper back was an open two-inch square covered with aluminum filament. This filament, woven into a mesh covering, protected the robot's core, the heartbeat of its operation: the software chamber.

Through this opening, miniaturized discs could be inserted,

so that the machine responded to the many commands issued by its owner, or its commander, or its creator. In those four square inches, that tiny but vulnerable aperture, TigerTail's bullet had hit its mark and cut off the robot's life blood—his orders. When the bullet severed the complicated web of microchips, it stopped the messages being sent to all the electrical circuits in the metal body, and the machine froze. It was no more. Some died standing, like Tully's sequestered offender, drilled gangland style by an angry, anxious blue line of trained executioners. Others were badly damaged, and they just collapsed. Either way, the robot gave up the fight and waited for some cure to rehabilitate its badly beaten body.

But TigerTail was less interested in the robot's demise and more anxious to find out who owned these electromechanical monsters. Whoever owned these automated criminals crafted the crime. Except there was no title deed in any of the robots' pockets. They were clean. Tully was clean. These mechanical mishaps could be any entrepreneur's private invention from some hidden garage, some underground lab, some college experiment gone awry. Evil emanates from everywhere, and it doesn't need a corporate stamp of approval to make it complete—or even marketable. Yet Robomaids still remained the prime suspect.

TigerTail agreed with FutureDick. He felt in his gut that AceArrow was involved. He just knew it. But they could prove zilch. The CEO's story looked legit. He's been creating ape-like Robomaids to compete with the DoRights. They're about to launch their new product nation-wide. America, the land of the free market, the home of healthy competition. The best widget wins.

With help from the San Ramon police, TigerTail and his men meticulously searched Robomaids' lab. They found nothing. AceArrow had taken his domestic robots and encrusted them with hair. He reconstructed the face so that the new mechanical man looked like a chimpanzee, an artificial

DoRight.

Now AceArrow was about to initiate a costly marketing campaign. No doubt his career was on the line. At the very least, his company was dancing between life and death. With three years of stagnant profits, they had hocked everything to mount this program. TigerTail knew it. FutureDick knew it. And both of them were powerless to stop this grinding entrepreneur. AceArrow had covered his tracks—beautifully.

"He's clean, Bruce. The police found nothing."

"That's hard to believe, Adam. What's left? Or should I say, who's left? Tully single-handedly couldn't have designed this coast to coast killing spree. Too much money involved. He needed a backer. Where the hell did he get his robots from?"

"That's the curious thing. AceArrow has all those damn electromechanical creatures who look like DoRights sitting around, and he has the perfect alibi. Healthy competition! Sort of like camouflaging a Ford to look like a Rolls, wouldn't you say?"

"And the police bought that?"

"What else could they do? They searched the entire place. Clean, Bruce. Let's face it, nothing out of order."

"I'm not convinced, Adam. The guy's as crooked as a three dollar bill. He's sitting there with his mechanical apes, flaunting the evidence in our faces, and pleading 'not guilty'!"

"Well, you've got good company. FutureDick doesn't believe him either. But in order to prosecute, we need some demonstrable proof or corroboration. And with Tully dead, we have no leads. Nothing to implicate the bastard! If I knew for sure, Bruce, I'd be sick about this. But I can't condemn an innocent man, can I?"

"Are you kidding, Adam? Who the hell else would have any reason to destroy the DoRights? It gets clearer every moment. With our chimps out of the way, AceArrow corners the market. And he provides his customers with two models: human or animal. I've got to hand it to the asshole. Brilliant marketing! But if that's all it were, hell, I wouldn't care. There's enough room in the industry for competition. But, Christ, Adam, we've got a sicky on our hands."

"You sound so definite, so completely sure."

"I am, damn it, I am! It just doesn't make sense to not connect the DoRight massacres to the introduction of his new product. He had to have planned the whole bloody thing! Butchery—pure and simple. Next thing you know, he'll be handing out business cards that read, 'Carnage by AceArrow. When it comes to biolocide, we do our best!' "

"Everything you say sounds right. But how do you convict someone without evidence?"

"Sometimes, there are higher laws, Adam. Even in the jungle, there's always a bigger or better predator. Although the DoRights might finally be safe, this isn't over yet. Not by a long shot! I doubt if there's any expiation good enough for the crime. It was wrong, just way too wrong."

"I couldn't agree more, my friend. They were like my children."

TWENTY-FIVE

Those little shits. Were they serious? Did they really think he'd be dumb enough to operate out of his own factory? Let them search all they wanted. He was running a legitimate operation, a beautiful operation. AceArrow was unduly proud of his new generation of Robomaids.

Why hadn't he thought of it earlier? The perfect competitor to the DoRights: DomesticApe. It could do everything a DoRight could and probably do it better. Furthermore, its owners didn't have to worry about DomesticApe taking a shit, making noise, or taking time out for chimp brats. His machines did their work quietly, efficiently, and, if necessary, 24 hours a day. That was his gimmick. DomesticApes don't turn off. When you buy one, you buy a perpetual helper that will work for you day and night.

What fascinated AceArrow was how easy the modifications to his existing Robomaids were. Just by covering the bodies with synthetic hairlon, refining the finger dexterity, and adding lullabies to the speech repertoire, he moved his electromechanical product into its next generation. The only snag the company ran into was the redesign of the face. He remembered the session when WinSome said, "I think we should leave the face as is. I like our Robomaid's face."

And AceArrow replied, "But this is another option to the DoRight. We want to make our product as similar as we can."

Then SilverStone piped in, "But Mr. AceArrow, who wants to come home and have the face of an ape greet you at the front door?"

"Apparently, a hell of a lot of people 'cause the DoRight sales keep going up."

Frowning, RedField spoke up, "Why can't we give them an ape-like body with a human-like face? That way, we've got the best of both worlds."

AceArrow stayed firm. "I don't think so. I think it's the ape-like face that fascinates the public. Did you guys ever notice how people stare at the chimp's face in a zoo? The face resembles a human's, but the whole front protrudes into that very wide mouth. I think people try to imagine how their faces developed from the ape's face and think if they stare long enough, they might be able to find the missing link."

Quickly SilverStone interjected, "But that's just the point. We have evolved, and don't we want DomesticApe to reflect our evolution? It's not only like us—it's better than us."

The researchers went back and forth with AceArrow, each one voicing his objection to the duplication of a primate countenance. But in the end, AceArrow won. He knew he would. Although he might listen to other opinions, he made the final decision. Why shouldn't he? It was his company, and he was willing to take the risks associated with ownership. Therefore, he also wanted the ultimate power as well. He paid for it.

Besides, he knew he was right on this one. For whatever reasons resided in the fickle heart of customers, they loved their animals. And AceArrow wanted to be sure he produced the most animal-looking robot he could construct.

More than that, he intended to destroy TriCubed. He wanted

them to share sleepless nights, the drop in sales, the day after day reminder that a whole life's work can diminish because a new product hits the market. What better weapon did he have than his own brand of bomb—the work-around-the-clock DomesticApe.

When TigerTail located Tully's mother in San Ramon, he flew her son's body up to northern California, courtesy of Police Aviation Support. TigerTail had been on the force for nineteen years, and the biggest improvement he noticed in law enforcement was the cooperation he received from PVS, Police Volunteer Service. He never thought he'd see the community become their ally during his career, but it happened.

A few years ago, when she was transferring a prisoner from the county jail to a police van, a young officer, Patricia Martino, was shot in the back. The criminal pushed her, promptly grabbed her gun, and shot her as she tried to grab him. He was eventually captured, but Patricia's life flitted in and out of consciousness for days. When she finally came to, the prognosis was that she would live. But, and that was the big *but,* she'd be confined to a wheel chair for the rest of her life.

There are some people who make every defeat another beginning. Patricia was one of those intrepid souls. Undaunted, she sat for hours in front of her computer and crisscrossed the US with her telephone, setting up a web of volunteer services. She called companies, she called professionals, she called families—she called everybody. And when she was finished, Patricia had organized a tremendous network that helped police officers enforce the law. Yet the masterstroke of her accomplishment was that this assistance was free. Time, services, and equipment were donated.

TigerTail knew police were overworked, underpaid, taken for granted by a society that wanted their law enforcement officers to risk their lives in the defense of their community. And he often wondered when these dedicated men and women would simply walk out. If the cities didn't wake up and pay their cops the money, respect, and gratitude they deserved, how could these municipalities prevent desertion? But the impossible happened. And in his lifetime.

With PVS firmly established for three years, life on the force became a bit easier. It was still hazardous. It always would be. That's probably what attracted many of the officers in the first place. It still paid low wages and demanded longer hours. But finally, it was more productive. Their communities now supported them with extensive help, and TigerTail's ability to solve crime grew as he enlisted all the support he could get.

After TigerTail deposited Tully's body in the San Ramon morgue, he drove over to Tully's mother. He usually never tried to second-guess his suspects, accomplices, or collaborators, but he was surprised at her response. When he saw Mrs. Tully, she appeared frail, a wisp of a thing, this small, elderly woman. But she received the news of her son's death without a flinch.

Stony-eyed, she listened to TigerTail, put on her coat, and drove with the police down to the morgue. When they slid the long drawer from the wall, she stared at Tully's face for five minutes, brushed the top of his hair away with her fingers, and softly whispered, "I always told him to be careful." That was it. She turned away and asked to go home.

TigerTail thought Mrs. Tully might have been in shock. Give her time to absorb the news. Let her be. So he waited till the next day, when he dropped by to question her further. He needed answers. Goddamn it. He needed something. But her self-control remained intact. No tears. No sobs. She was proud of her son. He had served his country in war and in peacetime. He had been a good boy, and she would give him the burial he deserved, a hero's farewell.

TigerTail found out nothing, at least not from the mother. Tully's career in the marines had been unremarkable. He never reenlisted after the Gulf War. Instead, he had odd jobs till he started working for the San Ramon sewer department as part of their maintenance crew, five years ago.

After four years, he became a supervisor and was doing fine. But he quit unexpectedly three months ago. Tully had evidently been the silent type because none of his men really knew him. He came to work, did his job, consistently performed the tasks quietly but efficiently, and left, befriending no one. He commanded a certain kind of respect, the kind of admiration that is born out of exclusivity. You can't judge what you don't know, and no one truly knew Tully.

The personnel manager was baffled when Tully quit. No explanation, no remorse. The guy just walked in one day after five years and said I'm giving two weeks notice. Then he walked out of the office without so much as a sorry. No one knew him while he worked there, and no one ever knew why the tight-lipped Tully left. Just packed up his things and split.

TigerTail contacted old teachers, old neighbors, old military buddies. No one could say anything bad about Tully. But no one could say anything good, either. He was there. He was quiet. He always completed his work and then went home alone. Sort of stayed in the background and watched.

The single constant running through Tully's life was his height. He was short, and he was self-conscious about it. If anyone would comment or joke about his 5'6" stature, he would stare that person in the eyes and say, "Would you like to do something about it?" Usually, the joker backed off with, "Just kidding, Frank. Just kidding." But when the guy didn't refrain from harassing Tully, a fight would occur. And two marine recruits had their noses broken in a bar brawl by this *little* guy, Tully. Even his mother told TigerTail that "her son may have been small, but he was mighty. The mightiest of all."

TigerTail swallowed hard at everything Graceland Tully said about her son. The person she knew and the person he was trying to discover seemed like two different people—a murdered Dr. Jekyll and Mr. Hyde. Apparently, the mother knew very little about Tully's life. But nobody else was on intimate terms with him either.

When they searched his apartment, it was immaculate, everything in its place. Where were the normal doodlings of everyday life? Where were Tully's phone numbers, books, letters, diaries, remnants that a life was lived within these four walls? The guy was a monk, obviously sworn to a pledge of silence, for nothing, not one clue from the flat leaped out to guide TigerTail.

Sitting next to the alarm clock, which was set for 5:30 a.m., was the latest copy of *Soldier of Fortune*. The nightstand drawer contained a revolver and the picture of a young boy around ten years old. There was a look in the boy's face that vaguely resembled Tully. But the child had a dull stare, his thoughts apparently in some cryptic dreamland, and the camera captured just the shell of a person. It could be Tully when he was younger, but the vacant eyes spoke otherwise.

In the corner of the bedroom, a set of barbells stood guard, testifying to Tully's physical demands on himself. No letters, no books, little food, little clothes, and only two other mementos: a picture of his boot camp company on the wall and his honorable discharge in the dresser drawer. Whatever Frank Tully knew, he carried in his head because there were no remnants of a past life in his apartment.

With Tully dead, FutureDick was stymied, the case stalemated. How could he provide the evidence he needed to implicate AceArrow when the search at Robomaids turned up nothing? Josh had been in a coma for 48 hours, and Francie slept fitfully. TigerTail arranged for constant surveillance of AceArrow, but FutureDick knew that would turn up empty. The man was crafty. He knew how to cover his tracks, and nobody was talking.

Even though the killers had been eradicated, FutureDick was still dissatisfied. Perhaps there were more hidden away in some secret stockpile. If AceArrow did it once, he could do it again. What would prevent him from contemplating some other genocidal plot once he decided he didn't like dogs or babies or men with green eyes? FutureDick wanted the real murderer apprehended. He wanted the brain behind the unflinching, metallic brawn.

BrickWell calmed down a bit. The possibility that no new attacks would take place allowed him to turn his attention to the drop in sales. FutureDick suspected it wasn't the monetary loss that bothered BrickWell as much as the death of his chimps. He knew each one individually. They had become his foster children, and he felt responsible for their well-being. Somehow, he let them down when he wasn't able to guarantee their complete safety. BrickWell was coping, meagerly, but he looked relieved when FutureDick saw him yesterday, his nightmares finally over.

Yet the demons lingered for FutureDick. Josh lay in a coma, Francie seemed withdrawn, and that bastard, AceArrow, would get into his car everyday with a smile on his face. Life always had a funny way of smacking you in the face. It was never completely good or thoroughly bad. Right and wrong fused together at some point, and so much of our living took place in that undefined limbo.

FutureDick would like to crawl into AceArrow's bedroom in the middle of the night, tie him up, and coerce a confession by any means necessary. He thought of the movies and books he had come across over the years. In a somewhat disquieting, yet enjoyable meditation, he graphically reminisced the torture techniques that tyrants used quite willingly, and, in his mind, he applied every abomination he could think of to AceArrow.

He pictured the CEO's torment when he crushed his testicles, bored through molars till the pulverized nerves were plasmatic dust, leisurely pulled out twenty bashed fingernails, forced water down his swollen nose and up his skinned anus. In FutureDick's imagination, no cruelty was too harsh for his enemy, and the only restraint that kept him sane was the knowledge that Francie and Josh were still breathing. Their life gave FutureDick hope, and for that reason, AceArrow remained alive.

FutureDick went back to the hospital that night, still puzzled about who to squeeze for information. When he went up to Josh's room, the doctor was walking out. He reassured FutureDick, saying, "We don't know for sure, but the boy's young, and because of his youth, he has a good chance of snapping out of this. A coma is the body's way of handling excessive trauma. He's healing from within."

FutureDick wanted to believe the physician. But Josh looked helpless lying there, scarcely breathing, hooked up to modern man's technological nutrition: tubes and machines.

Decisively, FutureDick went over to the child and spoke softly. "Come on, son. You're strong. You can lick this thing. There are so many people in the world who love you, Josh. And there's so much for you to do."

As the older man sat there, holding Josh's hand, trying to force some of his own vitality into the boy's fingers, he didn't realize that there were tears falling onto the sheet, his tears, traces of sorrow FutureDick needed to shed for his heartbroken history—and possibly his aborted future.

When TigerTail confronted Tully's mother with the singular photograph found in the night stand, she coldly answered that he was her other son, Thomas, Tully's younger brother. He lived in VictorVillage, location of the 1950's Good 'ol Days theme park and home for 180 mentally retarded adults from across the country.

The residential center was started by a teacher, Mrs. Worthington, whose own mentally-handicapped daughter inspired her to build a community where these potentially productive adults could live, work, and function somewhat independently. Her vision of independent living escalated to total self-sufficiency when they embarked upon their first-of-a-kind recreational replica: Good 'ol Days. The park was a 1950's town, replete with soda fountain, Elvis, dial phones, white bucks, and 57 Chevys.

Worthington's blueprint for runaway success turned out to be her underestimation of the market. She thought the park would slowly attract tourists traveling through Arizona and eventually bring in enough revenue for each resident. With diminished expectations, any return is a windfall, and Worthington's miscalculation exploded into instant prosperity. People flocked to this pretend present, anxious to be transported back to a time when all appeared tranquil, happy, innocent.

Good 'ol Days was a pre-computer age, penny-candied dream, and those who lived through the close of the twentieth century yearned for the idyllic days of long ago. They never saw the skeletons left over from the McCarthy witch hunt, the lost soldiers from the gagged Korean War, the young black men whose lynching evoked unacknowledged tears, or the housewives who imbibed tranquilizers, diet pills, and booze to lift them out of their chains.

What captured the attention of the tourists was a world of yesterday, a world where violence was still taken seriously, where virginity was valued, and where time progressed at a controllable pace. Worthington met an unfulfilled need. She gave her customers what they wanted, but she also gave her mentally-limited residents a life, an opportunity to be needed and earn their own way. These handicapped adults worked at the theme park and depended on themselves—not welfare. They paid their own way, whether they knew it or not. Worthington's VictorVillage was a model followed worldwide, and all she wanted to do was help her daughter. This was Thomas Tully's home, the only person his older brother, Frank, ever loved.

TigerTail had Tully's driver's license and registration from the van. He had Tully's mother, ignorant as to who her son actually was. And he had a photograph of a mentally incompetent younger brother. Is that all a life can be measured by? Your ID and your two blood relations? Billions of people exist on this earth, yet, nothing remains once the air escapes the deflated body?

Tully had definitely made an impact the past few weeks he lived. Now, he had become the invisible man. Who the hell did Tully talk to? What was he about? Didn't he ever love, ever share a secret with a friend? TigerTail had this uneasy feeling he would never find out, for Tully, it seemed, had fled human discourse long ago.

If he confided in anyone, it was probably his brother, his solitary brother. But no one would ever uncover their secrets because Thomas Tully, very much alive, with his half-opened smile, his light blue clouded eyes, and his oily platinum blonde hair, lived in a world all his own.

TWENTY-SIX

FutureDick walked into Francie's room. She briefly smiled at him and then let her head drop, so he wouldn't see the tears. She was trying hard to be optimistic about this whole ordeal. Hell, weren't she and Josh still alive? But the rationality she confronted in her mind never made it down to her heart, for her heart felt the tremors. Her heart heard the shallow breathing of her young son, heard the struggle of his small damaged body trying to hold on, trying to break through the coma's grasp.

No matter how much Francie thanked some supernatural fate for saving their lives, the tears still came. What good was a machine that beeped your child alive, when, in reality, he was lost in a nether world of famine and fog, bereft of all human contact.

Still there was FD. Every time she saw him, she experienced a small shock, much like surprise, surprise that he was there, surprise that he kept coming back, surprise that he cared and maybe even loved just her. She wanted to be strong for him, to hide her vulnerability. But it was no use. She couldn't put on a front, not with him. In fact, he had a way of bringing the real Francie out of her. For some reason, every time he was around, she let her guard down and showed him who she honestly was.

She had never experienced that type of joy before, the freedom to be whoever you are with a man. And the more she showed him, the more he wanted. For Francie, this validation was renewal, a kind of rebirth. So many men were threatened by her strength, her outspokenness, her uncompromising attitude, her wit. Not FD. He seemed to relish everything about her, and she sometimes had to stare in the mirror to make sure she still existed. How could this treasure of a man have walked into her life and stayed?

But at this moment, Francie couldn't preserve the smile on her face, and she wept silently, head down, shoulders scrunched. She wept for her baby, his innocence, his pain, his life.

FutureDick didn't say anything. He just walked over and held her. They sat that way for over an hour, silent, bonded, sad. Then FD unwrapped his arms and said, "Francie, I'm still bothered by the DoRight case. It's just not over for me."

"But FD, you've got your murderer, don't you?" And quickly she spluttered, "There won't be anymore, will there?"

"No, no," FutureDick whispered reassuringly. "Tully's dead. The robots destroyed. But what bothers me is that guy, AceArrow. I'm sure he's the specter behind this sordidness. And we can't pin anything on him."

Francie's gaze clasped his eyes for a brief instant, "But what can you do, FD, with no evidence? If you don't let go, you're creating a living hell for yourself."

Francie was probably right, but FutureDick, quite used to the torment that had touched his dreams, murmured, "I need closure, Francie. But more than that, I need some sort of justice."

With that, he gently kissed Francie on the forehead and neck and left. Francie, still feeling the tickle of his lips below her ear, watched him walk out of the room. She stared at the empty doorway for a few moments and then put her head down and cried again, for herself, for her son, and for the man who had carved a permanent niche inside her soul.

Known only to the two men, Tully and AceArrow, was a financial bargain sealed with a handshake. After the elimination of the Franks' household, Tully was to be paid $120,000 in cash. The clandestine meeting had been prearranged, and AceArrow was given specific instructions concerning delivery of the money. If Tully didn't show up, AceArrow was authorized to deliver the bounty to Tully's mother. She would know what to do with it.

All the preparations and arrangements between AceArrow and Tully had been done in private, away from the company, the apartment, the public eye. Any directives were delivered orally, person to person or through a pay phone. AceArrow wanted no record keeping of their visits or their purchases: no Visa—all cash, no phone card—all quarters. In essence, avoid the luxury of the instantaneous modern age. What might be fast may also be revealing because it merely takes one machine transaction to track a human trail. Nothing, positively nothing, must be written down. AceArrow demanded that plans be etched into memory. Tully agreed.

They shared a philosophy in common that revolved around one major tenet: trust no one. But they never spoke about their distrust of one another. Instead, they scrutinized each other warily and waited for the one false move of betrayal that would justify revenge. AceArrow and Tully were not tweaked by the pangs of conscience which determine retribution. Moral doubt never entered their nightmares either.

Although they were born worlds apart and grew up in social environments so disparate that you'd think they could never clearly communicate with each other, they were much more alike than different. They agreed in perspective, for they both viewed the world from the *me first* stance. These men were ultra-egoists, and the earth, its peoples, and its resources existed to please them.

They may not have acknowledged their life's schematic to each other, but they both resolved at an early age to accumulate as much power as they could in any manner possible. Neither ethics nor lives would stand in the way of their self-serving goals because if you didn't act, you'd be acted upon. And nothing or no one was going to fuck with AceArrow or Tully.

FutureDick couldn't stay at the hospital any longer. He had to do something—anything—even if it meant retracing his steps. AceArrow kept coming up unblemished, and yet, FutureDick knew he was the center, the mastermind behind the murders. Still, there was no way to link him to the crimes. As far as the police were concerned, Tully could have worked for anyone. AceArrow wasn't the only robot manufacturer in the US. "Hell," they said, "some nut could have produced those things in his garage." But FutureDick knew, absolutely, that AceArrow was the killer. It was that particular CEO's fantasy the hired henchman made into reality.

Yet with no leads, no proof, FutureDick had nothing to go on, and no way to forge a link between Robomaids and mass murder. The search of the premises uncovered no clues. Yes, they were constructing robots that looked like apes. Yes, they were just about ready to market them. Yes, these computerized systems were designed as servants, helpers for the home. And, yes, the plate found near the scene of the crime could belong to any one of a number of robots because the licensing number is stamped on all automated machines manufactured in the US. Studying the financial records, the inventory, and the company's operations offered no hints of foul play.

The closest FutureDick and TigerTail came to smelling something rotten was the robbery that occurred nine months ago. Someone had broken into Robomaids' lab and stolen robotic parts, software, and various tools. AceArrow reported the theft to the police, but they never caught the thief. Where were they supposed to look? The heist was slicker than oil, no prints, no tracks, nothing.

Graceland Tully wasn't surprised when she received AceArrow's call. In fact, she had been expecting it. Her son left implicit instructions, in case he became sick, hurt, or dead. She knew exactly what to do: take half of the money, fly to VictorVillage, and make arrangements for Thomas—lifetime arrangements. Therefore, if Thomas ever became incapable of working, he would always have a home, a VictorVillage home.

Frank thought of everything. What a good boy he was. He always looked out for Thomas. From the time he got his first job, he helped pay for his brother. Even now that Thomas was earning his own, Frank always sent a little something extra to Worthington. "I want my brother to get special treatment," he would tell his mom. What a good boy.

And he looked after his mother, even though she hardly saw him. He'd check in every once in a while to see if she was okay. He'd send her additional money each month to fatten her social security. She had no complaints, not Graceland Tully. Her boys were good boys. She'd always taught them there was no room for tears in this life. You just lived it as best as you could, without whining.

God never liked losers, and He certainly didn't want to hear any crybabies. "Get on with it," she'd repeat to Frank. "Remember, don't ever tell your secrets to anyone. Only you can take care of you." Oh yeah, she had raised her sons proper and practical. She made sure that Frank never made a mess of things, and she told him, till she was blue in the face, "Through thick and thin, Frank, thick and thin, you got to keep a stiff upper lip!"

Yet, even in his passing on, he thought about his mother. His letter said to take half the money and put it in the savings account he had opened for her. He took care of her, alright, that son of her's. He took care of her!

Since she had been told of his death, Graceland slept about

two hours a night. So much to do, so little time. It was necessary to get everything in order because she had to prepare his room, his special room. When the police left, the little woman went over to Frank's picture and stared at it the rest of the afternoon. She sat, she stared, she never moved till two in the morning. Somewhere, she lost a day, as her mind relived the memories of her baby, her boy, her very good boy. No tears, Graceland. No tears.

Unblinking, the dry-eyed mother knew exactly what she had to do as she took out the boxes of Frank's past. Graceland saved everything he did without Frank knowing it. Furtively, she hoarded his yesterdays in the corner of her cupboard, caressing his childhood memories whenever she felt lonely. Her hidden cache: school report cards, letters, vaccination records, even clothes. Frank's whole life lay organized in two by three foot cardboard boxes, and she was solely responsible for resurrecting her son, her very good boy.

During the next few days, Graceland worked frantically, eating little, sleeping less, for she was building a shrine to her son, Frank, the warrior. First, she painted his room. Then, the driven woman constructed a life collage around the four walls, covering every inch with his papers, his grades, his pictures, his clothes, his life. She considered pasting items on the ceiling, but she couldn't reach. So Graceland covered the windows instead.

But she had to get the lighting just right, soft enough to let his spirit dance among the candles. With considerable care, she strategically placed her holders in different corners of the room. However, the crowning glory of her temple was the bed. His bed. The hardy piece of furniture that held his body for many years. There atop the cover lay Frank's uniform. He never knew she had taken it when he got out of the service and came home to visit. But while he packed to move into his apartment, he tossed out what he called non-essentials. And she promptly retrieved it from the garbage pile.

His uniform was one of her very prized possessions, and

today, she finally had the opportunity to display it! Up till this time, the furtive mother was relegated to sneaking off to the closet to take a peek at her warrior's clothing. No more. Now she could show off her pride and joy, her son's uniform, for all the world to see. Now she could pay tribute to what a very good boy he was.

Graceland had to work fast. Any day now, Frank had written, she would be getting a call. She had to finish. So little time and so much to do. At the end of the fourth day, the phone rang, and the man on the other end told her what to do. She was relieved she had a couple more days till the key arrived because everything was not yet right. It had to be perfect. Her son was perfect, and now he would remain alive in his perfect room.

When she stood in the doorway 48 hours later, twenty candles blazing in adoration to Frank Tully, Graceland knew she had done well. What she ignored were the increasing heart palpitations she'd felt ever since she started creating her memorial. What she forgot was that she had to eat, had to sleep, had to rest.

TWENTY-SEVEN

FutureDick had no doubts that AceArrow designed the Robomaids' break-in. In effect, he stole from himself and probably collected the insurance money to boot. But FutureDick couldn't prove it. Even searching AceArrow's home produced zero, nothing. Every potential lead led to a cliff, which spilled over into nothingness. And TigerTail had informed him last night that all surveillance was called off, not enough evidence.

When he phoned BrickWell, he apologized, "I know the murders are probably over, Adam, but somehow, I feel the case isn't finished yet. If you don't mind, I'd like to keep working on it."

"That's fine, FutureDick. We still have enough money to allocate to the problem. But if this dry spell lasts much longer, I may have to cancel. As you know by now, our sales are way down."

"I appreciate it, Adam. I'm certain I can get to the bottom of it. Somewhere, someone erred. It's still a human-manufactured crime!"

"Do me a favor, will you? Please call my good friend, Bruce TreadHard. He's a major stockholder in the company. But more importantly, he's involved. He seems to have taken this very personally, and I know he'd like talking with you."

"No problem, Adam. If he's got a suggestion, I'm all ears."

The call to TreadHard revealed no alternative theories, but FutureDick enjoyed talking to him. A no-nonsense kind of guy, TreadHard asked pertinent questions and listened intently to FutureDick's conclusions. The robbery at Robomaids particularly interested TreadHard.

"Is that a kick! Rob from yourself. You know, FutureDick, I met AceArrow also. He struck me as the sort of guy who would do anything for a buck. But rob from yourself! Cunning. Really cunning."

"Bruce, I've got to be blunt—professional or not. I don't like the guy. I don't like his looks, his tone, his whole being. I just don't like him!"

"FutureDick, I couldn't agree more. He struck me as a pompous asshole when I met him, and I've never had occasion to revise my estimation. It looks like you and I certainly see things the same way."

When FutureDick hung up the phone, he felt invigorated. There's nothing that packs a punch as solid as validation. The unanimity that he and TreadHard shared not only confirmed his insistent intuition, but also aroused his desire to win this wicked game, a game where lives are scored instead of points. He didn't have to sit in SeaBank, hoping for a confession. He could act. He had to!

In his world, people did not construct a massacre and walk away free. Certainly over the centuries, man learned to temper his aggression and live in an ethical manner. Man learned to cooperate with larger and larger groups, till he had to co-exist peacefully with the entire world. Wars were diminishing, and countries were catching on to global rather than national thinking.

Man had evolved. FutureDick knew the process was slow,

but, at least, there was progress. There was change. And the hopes for a peaceful earth lay within reach. However, every time an AceArrow came along, every time violence occurred, every time man lifted his arm against his fellowman, FutureDick realized how hesitantly human beings took their stunted steps toward harmony. It was possible, but so painfully slow.

Yet FutureDick had not developed any kind of patience as he grew more aware. Instead, he wanted swift justice with every new criminal apprehended. He wanted crime not to pay, and there was AceArrow in his white collar and power tie, sitting in his easy chair, smoking a cigar, and chuckling all the way to the bank.

FutureDick must have missed something. There is no perfect crime, just imperfect people. Tomorrow, he would again contact Robomaids' researchers, its marketing director, and Frank Tully's mother. Maybe he overlooked some minute clue the last time around. Maybe AceArrow screwed up somewhere.

Except sometimes you don't have to screw up to get caught. These are the times someone else screws up for you, or worse yet, someone gets tired of screwing around, waiting for justice to prevail. The only people who can afford to wait for *right* to hang *might* from the scaffold are those not bothered by time. And time was the one commodity running out for TreadHard.

He watched the rain, the never-ending downpour, a sign that the heavens were angry with man and could vindictively vent their frustration by pelleting the earth with billions of weepy water drops. It rained. It poured. It splashed upon the trees, the roofs, the grass, and sometimes slipped through the chimney, looking for a dry surface to sop. The rain was crafty, all right. It had a mind of its own and slithered into every corner, every particle, every area it could reach.

But TreadHard also had a mind of his own, and the time had come. He had been more than patient with his fury, and he watched, for he was a careful man. He hoped the culprit would be caught, that sense would prevail. Still with each DoRight murder, he understood that insanity reigned, and the power to destroy had provided a certain pleasure to its masters. The terror had terrorized long enough, and he must put an end to it.

It didn't matter to TreadHard if he were taking the law into his own hands. He was dead already. The biopsy results showed that his cancer had spread. For five years after removal of his prostate tumor, he had been clean. For five years, he had dared to hope, dared to plan for another quarter of a century that would give him more time to read, to travel, to play, to watch his grandchildren mature. But the recurring pain up the front of his right leg and across his lower back revived the old dreams, the visions of him swimming in black, drifting in nothingness, the door being shut, ending, his ending, the overness of life.

And every morning he knew he was getting closer to confronting his horror: the dread of non-being. Sooner or later, he would have to see the doctor. Sooner or later, he would have to submit to tests. And then, wait. The long, lonely wait till the results arrived that verified or denied your viability. Yet ninety days ago, in the morning's grey, before the sun burst upon the day, he opened his eyes and knew. He was ready to face his adversary. That's what his cancer had always been: a worthy opponent, who also had patience, who could wait days, months, years, and then pick the precisely correct moment to capably invade his body—the moment he thought he was finally cured.

He saw the doctor, he had his bone scan, he received the pronouncement, and he even underwent biopsy surgery. But he knew. He knew before the lab knew that his attacker was back. Only this time, there would be no clemency. This time, the cancer had declared all-out war on his body and would accept nothing short of total victory. TreadHard realized it would spread, sprout throughout his body by attaching itself to his bones and looting their marrow for its nourishment, depriving him of necessary red blood cells.

He had done extensive reading five years ago, and he found

out that prostate cancer was malicious. When unleashed, it zoomed to the bones and grew tumors, tumors that pressed painfully against the nerves, frightening the victim into unconditional surrender. The stark, gnawing pressure could break the mightiest of men, transforming them from warriors to whimpering children, begging for mercy or relief—or death. The longer the invalid fought, the larger the tumors grew, weighing him down while sucking his blood. The twentieth century's own vampire had entered his body, uninvited.

But TreadHard would fight. He would defy every malignant cell till the pain obliterated his reality, for he had one advantage. He still had time. He had six months, maybe a year, to prepare himself, to watch, to wait, to do whatever he felt ought to be done to make things right with the world. His body was undeniably sturdy, testament to his years of wrestling, skiing, climbing, and surfing. He had built more than muscle. He had built inner discipline, as he waited for the right wave, climbed the steep precipice, or leaped the side of the mountain. TreadHard had used a lifetime learning how to wait, how to watch, and how to challenge.

So now, as he considered the rain, the tears that God shed at the DoRights' tragedy, he smiled, for he was still strong enough to act. And modern medicine was generous enough in the proliferation of its pain management. He had amassed enough tranquilizers, antidepressants, painkillers and narcotics to help him escape, not days, not months, but years of pain.

And years of power were peeking their way through AceArrow's fantasies. He had done it! He and his machines, the best of all combos. Once he completed the final details of his obligation, he was free from any connection to Tully. And that's what he wanted. No witnesses. No links. No partners.

AceArrow wasn't sure if he was being followed, if his phone was tapped, if he was under surveillance. He just knew he had to get the money to Mrs. Tully. Who could surmise what the steely Tully had set up? AceArrow wasn't taking any chances.

Even if Tully hadn't completed his assignment, he'd pay the mother the full amount. AceArrow wanted the affair done. Over! Kaput! His market reposition program had accomplished its mission: DoRight sales certainly plummeted as he predicted.

Now all he had to do was introduce his DomesticApes to consumers and wait for the cash to roll in. AceArrow figured he had seven more days. By then, the memory of the murders would fade, and the novelty of simian robots would grab hold of a public frightened of live chimpanzees. Seven more days, and he could breathe again.

So what if he lost his five supra-prototypes. It was worth it. He couldn't take the chance of anyone tying him to the murders. Whatever that Franks woman found out apparently wasn't strong enough evidence to arrest him. Here he was, walking around free, impossible to implicate, and ready to make millions—well, at least, thousands.

Personally, he was glad Tully was out of the way. The guy went berserk, absolutely bonkers! Best that the psycho's gone from the picture. He never really liked the little schmuck to begin with. The man served him well, no doubt about it. But the less people around remotely involved in his scheme, the safer he felt. And he sure as shit didn't want a crazy asshole deciding to use his own private army whenever the desire hit him.

AceArrow comforted himself with his well-planned security. If the police had been able to connect any of the murders to him, he wouldn't be sitting in his study drinking coffee and strategizing the future. They were weak, feeble, impotent, and he was going to be laughing his way to the vault, every last goddamn step of the way.

After he went to a public phone and called Mrs. Tully, he returned to his safe to pull out the $120,000. For months, he had been cashing close to a thousand dollars a day until he accumulated his pay-off. The only thing left to do was put it in the bus station locker and mail Tully's mother the key. Then he was done. Finito!

He waited till three in the morning and drove his car within a mile of the station. Deliberately he walked a rather circuitous route to the depot. When he approached the entrance, he stood by the door for fifteen minutes. No one came in, no one went out. Just him, the money, and the shabby-looking passengers immersed among the even seedier-looking derelicts who came in to escape the cold night air.

As he turned the key, "It's over" flew from his mouth. Then he scurried to the closest mailbox where he dropped Mrs. Tully's envelope in the slot. He would have felt more secure personally placing the key in Frank's mother's hand, but there was no way in hell he'd get within fifty feet of the Tully household. He wanted to stay as far away from those people as possible. Once he confirmed with the mother that the key had arrived, he could get on with making money, lots of money.

"Adam, how are you doing? Is it getting any easier?"

"Thanks for asking, Bruce. We're picking up the pieces, but let me tell you. I feel I'm in mourning after World War Three. It's the strangest thing. I never realized how connected I was to my DoRights till their demise."

"I could have told you that. The pleasure I get from watching my clan is immeasurable. I can't put my finger on it, but these innocent chimps enter your heart, somehow. Particularly, the babies!"

"Funny thing about human emotions, Bruce. You think we'd show greater fidelity to man rather than to brute. That our sorrow would be more manageable and, perhaps, less consuming when an animal dies. Still, I find myself absolutely grief-stricken. It's mind-boggling to admit that I'm as attached to the DoRights as I am to my own children. And I haven't decided if this is good or bad yet. Am I crazy or just sentimental?"

"Neither, Adam. I'd call it *evolved.* Your ability to love, to feel, makes you what you really are: a human being. Perhaps you're used to seeing male and female zombies who have lost their capacity to feel walking around. They look like you, but they're minus a heart, a center, whatever it takes to respond with emotion. Consider yourself one of the lucky, Adam. At least, you're not among the walking dead!"

"Jesus! When you put it that way, Bruce, I ought to be ecstatic I can still cry."

"You're damn right, buddy. You're goddamn right!"

"Listen. Thanks for all your concern throughout this affair. You've been a brick. I know I've told you this before, Bruce, when the DoRight research stalemated, but your ability to be there for a friend during the rough times is a blessing. I really mean it, my friend. You'll never know how you've enriched my life."

"Goddamn it, Adam! You're the one who let me have the joy of discovery in the first place. And for that, I shall be forever grateful. Listen, I'm taking off for a couple days—time to hit the wilderness and commune for awhile. Take care, pal. I'll call you as soon as I get back. It'll all get better. It's got to!"

TWENTY-EIGHT

Graceland worked furiously for five straight days, and now she turned her attention to VictorVillage. She had to retrieve the money, deposit half, and arrange a meeting with Worthington. How could she think about sorrow or grief? That was for fools. So much to do, so little time.

But one crowning touch must be merged into her composition: Frank's final words. In his instructions, he told her to destroy the letters. How could she? She never destroyed anything he did, least of all, his very last words. She needed to hold on to them. They were a tangible reminder that her son thought of her till the day he died. Her good boy took care of his mother and brother—even in his last breath.

Graceland, trying to discover a prominent place to position the two letters, looked at the room. Not on the walls. They wouldn't stand out. But on the bed. That's where she'd see them every time she walked into the room: one letter on each pillow. The first note explained what she should do after receiving the money from a Mr. AceArrow. The second letter instructed her to go to the police if Mr. AceArrow didn't call. She never read the whole thing. It was way too long. Anyway, it wasn't necessary. Mr. AceArrow did call.

Had Graceland read the eight page detailed report, she would have learned about her son's very last job, who his boss was, and what he did. But Graceland wasn't much for long bouts of reading, and she had so much to do. She couldn't be bothered making out all that stuff about robots and business arrangements. Besides, she didn't like the police. She followed her son's instructions. That's what any good mother would do.

It was time to go. The key arrived that morning, and she was scheduled to meet Worthington tomorrow at ten. Just enough time to make reservations, get to the bank, and pack a box for Thomas. He loved receiving candy. Those palpitations again. What a nuisance. She'd just ignore them. If she didn't concern herself with those loud, hammering beats, she knew they'd go away. Pretty soon she'd be able to take it easy. Didn't her body know that?

FutureDick went to the hospital early the next morning. He wanted to see Josh before he went back to his investigation. Hoping to send some type of message through the boy's fingertips, some encouragement, some affection, FutureDick sat by the bed holding Josh's hands, talking to him about his own life as a child, his dead wife, his dead daughter. And as he talked, he opened his soul wider to this silent child and to the world. He spoke of his dreams, of Francie, of life, as if he were writing a book and Josh had become the computer into which FutureDick poured his thoughts.

"Come on, son, the world is yours. You've got things to do, sports to learn, girls to meet, people to help, people who love you. Josh, you've got to go through the teenager's torment, not that I'd ever want to do it again, man. But you've got to experience it. It's a trip! And the girls, Josh. You've got to see what it's like to fall in love. You'll immediately give up any ideas that people can control their emotions. You must feel what love is like."

It was at this point that FutureDick's voice broke for a second, as Francie's smile flew across his brain, and the real fear of losing her to desolation, depression, sadness became all too real for the moment. But then he continued, "The times get better and better the more you experience the world, your world, man. Your world. We want you back, Josh. Your mom, your sisters, your friends, me. We all need your happy face here with us. In fact, your sisters swore they wouldn't kid you about the spiders. They said..."

That's when FutureDick felt the little hand graze his fingers. Gingerly, those slim fingers grasped his thumb and held on. FutureDick knew he wasn't imagining things because he looked down and there were Josh's fingers twisted around his own, holding on for dear life, dear sweet life.

"Come on, buddy. I feel you. I hear you. Come on, Josh. I know you're there. I know you can hear me. I know you want to come back, to come home. Fight Josh, fight. You can climb out of there. Just open your eyes. You can do it. Come on, man. You're a fighter. Show that son of a bitch robot that you won and he lost. He's lying in a junk heap right now at the police station. But you're here. You're alive. You're nearly home, and you can beat that monster, Josh. You're so much bigger than he is. You're the winner, not him. Come on, Josh. You're so close, so close."

And with those words and those tears, FutureDick never heard himself begging. All he saw were Josh's eyelids fluttering, opening, staring, capturing FutureDick's gaze. When their eyes connected, Josh's pale lips stretched into a broad grin and he whispered, "Hi FD, what's going on?"

FutureDick started to answer, but only the merest hint of a gasp escaped his mouth as his throat choked the sound back into his belly. He felt like shouting, screaming to the world that Josh was back, bellowing his joy to the universe. Yet nothing came out but tears, tears of happiness at this child's battle to recover.

Then FutureDick carefully raised Josh's hand and kissed it. He wanted to grab the boy and hug him, enfold him in his big body to convey his euphoria, his love. But all he could do was hold his hand and stutter through his tears how proud he was. FutureDick pushed the call button and launched into a nonstop narrative about what a fighter Josh was, how he had been in a coma, and now he was back. He had beaten that killer robot. He had won.

The relief at the boy's recovery jolted FutureDick into uninterrupted talking, his rush of words a safeguard preventing Josh's return to the shadow world. The doctor arrived fifteen minutes later, and by then FutureDick's continuous chronicle had recounted the history, the mayhem, and the demise of the menacing robots. Josh and his mother were heroes in the eyes of the country, for they were the only two humans to ever go up against these killer androids and survive.

When FutureDick walked out of Josh's hospital room, he walked away from the lively eyes and exuberant smile he had known in the past. Overcome by the rush of his explosive emotions, he stopped in the visitor's room and sat for ten minutes. He needed to savor the regeneration that spread through his veins and kept him smiling, even though his cheeks hurt from the prolonged grin.

Impatiently, he raced up the three flights to Francie's room, never considering the ease of the elevator, but defying the dimensions of time and space as he flew through the stairwell. Bounding into the doorway, he stopped suddenly. Francie lay still, composed, hushed in the momentary slumber her body needed to mend itself.

FutureDick deliberated waking her, grabbing her in his arms where he could roar the wonderful news. But instead, he stifled his enthusiasm, the compulsion to tell repressed by the greater longing for Francie, his Francie, to heal. So he left a note by the side of the bed.

See you later, my love. I've just spent the morning talking to your wonderful son. He's back, Francie. He's back. And he's as bright as ever. When you wake up to this joyful news, remember I love you. I love you both. For keeps, FD

Now it was time to go to work—real work. For every action there is a reaction, and FutureDick wanted to finish what AceArrow had begun. It was time to react.

It seemed like years since she left the house, and yet, Graceland had only been gone for 38 hours. But they were 38 long hours. She took a Greyhound to VictorVillage just yesterday. Of course, Frank would have wanted her to fly, but she hated flying. People belonged as close to the ground as they could get, and the trip to the airport just seemed too much, too far, too scary. A bus could get her to Arizona just as well, slower perhaps, but who cared? It simply meant less time with Thomas, and after two hours with her handicapped son, she always started to get restless anyway.

Graceland arrived in the small desert town at seven in the evening. She went to the cafe across the street from the bus station and ordered a grilled cheese sandwich and coffee. But after her first bite, she realized she wasn't hungry. She was nervous. Her stomach, still tied in knots, couldn't forget the frenzy of the past five days. And her mind, mad with the delirium of detail, relived the construction of her beautiful memorial: her tribute to Frank.

She needed to get back home where she could stand outside the bedroom door and survey her mastery. She had been too rushed. Maybe there was something she forgot to do. Although, at last glance, it looked just how she wanted it: every one of Frank's items in its special place, candles shedding their glow around the room, his uniform ready to get up and move, as if Frank would walk in any moment, don the regimental blues and salute.

That night, she couldn't fall asleep. She stared at the splotched motel ceiling and viewed her brain reeling through pictures, pictures of *what had been*. Her mental movie drifted over the years with Frank, the years alone, the frustration with Thomas, her husband's death: in rapid succession, the memories bounced around in her head as she watched the bedside clock change from two to three to four.

By seven, she had showered, dressed, paid for her room, and walked back to the cafe. Her nine o'clock appointment with Worthington went splendidly. Why wouldn't it? It's not often a parent comes in with sixty thousand dollars for a resident's upkeep. Sixty thousand is real cash money!

The director offered her condolences on Frank's death, but Graceland shook it off. Somehow Frank wasn't really dead. He was very much alive in her mind, and as soon as she got home, she could breathe his essence right in her own house. So she politely changed the subject when Worthington started to talk about her older son.

Graceland wanted to get down to business, sign the necessary financial papers, see Thomas, and get back on the bus. Worthington would never know how unburdened Graceland felt now that Thomas would eternally be taken care of. She had just been set free. Whatever guilt she repressed at her son's deformed birth was released when she handed the sixty thousand in cash to the director. Wasn't that payment enough for her stunted son? What more could he have wanted from her? Or from Frank? Hadn't they both given a major portion of their lives for Thomas to live in his incomprehensible universe?

She was never sure if Thomas really recognized her. He certainly seemed happy to see her and fired off a steady stream of phrases about his room, his roommate, his work, his portable radio, and his goldfish. To Graceland, her son was as beautiful as ever, but he belonged to a world she could never enter, a private world which spoke another language, a child's language. A world where time and emotions and responsibility and happiness were measured by different standards, not her standards, not adult standards, but different standards.

She tried to fathom Thomas's planet, but it eluded her. His mind heard the music of a divergent drummer from a faraway land, and Graceland never understood how to get there. Yet Thomas looked well. Worthington said he was one of their best workers and always seemed so pleased when he helped the tourists at the park. Well, he should be one of their best people. Just like his brother. They did what they were supposed to do. She taught them properly: get the job done no matter what the cost. That's what was important—to finish.

Graceland and Thomas went to Good 'ol Days. He was excited about his park, and as they walked around, Graceland sensed his pride of ownership. When it happened, she wasn't sure, but sometime during the afternoon, she stopped feeling sorry for him. All her life, she pitied her defective son for the unfair deal God had given him. But today, she saw a human being at peace with himself and the world. And Graceland realized that her pity was misplaced.

Thomas was complete, more complete than most human beings on this earth. He felt good, content, worthwhile. Probing further into her reveries, Graceland wondered if she had ever felt that good. When she kissed him good-bye, she did it with a sense of relief. She could finally give up the blame, the anguish, the regrets she carried throughout the years for her son. He didn't want her pity. He didn't need it. In his own way, he had found a kind of fulfillment. At least, he belonged somewhere.

Graceland stepped onto the bus, anxious to get home, eager to see her handcrafted shrine, and desperate to get some rest, some sleep, some peace.

FutureDick spent the rest of the day meeting with the Robomaids' engineers again. There were five of them, and they had each been part of this new DomesticApe project. Good upstanding citizens, eager to please their boss, eager to earn their wages, eager to protect the company they mistook for family, eager to put competition out of business by building a better product. And there was nothing illegal about desire. Rather than confront the ethics of creating a robot in the shape of an ape, just to ease a fellow businessman out of the market, they focused on one goal: *Can we do it?*

FutureDick frequently considered if the need to succeed at all costs might be man's downfall. Could last century's scientists build the atom bomb? That was the question. Not, *do* we need the nuclear dictatorship? But, *can* we construct it? FutureDick wondered when man would allow, or if man was ever capable of allowing, ethics into his need to be challenged. Somehow, as one reached for *faster, bigger, better, more,* the dream overtook the morality and left man the most accomplished animal, but also the saddest as well.

Thus the five Robomaids' engineers had no regrets about their new imitation ape entering the service sector. The only glimmer of remorse that FutureDick could detect was the loss of inventory that occurred during the theft. The robbery delayed their project completion. Therefore the profits to be earned were likewise postponed. The carrot at the end of the stick still dangled, glistening, inviting, waiting. But the architects of corporate corpulence offered no new information about the elusive case.

And FutureDick concluded that they were unaware of AceArrow's covert strategy. Would they have wavered in their mission if they knew they were unwitting partners in a death spree? FutureDick would never find out the answer and couldn't begin to discover if the promise of money might have diluted the virtue that all five men felt sure they owned.

The marketing director, Ms. Togazi, furnished little additional information. FutureDick did learn about the media blitz scheduled for next week and about their slick telemarketing campaign. However, FutureDick hoped Togazi's forecasting was off. She was as pompous as hell and reminded him of his high school geometry teacher, who, in his own nasty manner, thought he always had the right answers. Togazi, convinced she was supplying the nation with the next best thing to Hershey bars, had no qualms at all about destroying any business that stood in her way.

Robomaids looked untouchable, a bit shaggy at the edges, but breathing with dragon-fire anticipation at the business coup they were about to pull off. FutureDick stayed clear of AceArrow. He never did reveal his profession to the CEO and still wanted him to think he was a potential investor. There was no telling when they would face each other again, and FutureDick decided to remain out of AceArrow's grasp, at least for the time being.

When Francie opened her eyes, they reminded her that she was still in the hospital room, still waiting, still hoping. The wilting flowers illumined by the filtered sunlight affirmed the harsh awareness that she was cut off from the healthy, alone, insulated, and dependent on the good graces of a white-suited, sometimes caring, sometimes not, medical staff.

Then she caught sight of FD's note staring at her. Francie read it, reread it, read it again, and went somewhere deep inside herself. She continually wondered if she believed in a God. She still didn't know, but she offered thanks to something out there, some force, some benevolence, some strength that pulled her child back.

Francie never wanted anything more in her life than for Josh to recover. The ferocity of her desire frightened even her and increased her respect for the mother of her species. She would go to the edge for her children and probably jump into the chasm if it meant saving her child's life.

Yet Francie didn't think she was unique. She knew most mothers would react with the same blinding devotion if their child's life were on the line. Nature had genetically programmed the female to protect her babies. A mother was the giver of life. She had been naturally mandated to save the race, not destroy it. Consequently, she would give up her life if it meant her progeny's survival. How else could humankind continue? The young must go forward—that's all the human animal could depend on—for the offspring to possibly do a better job than their parents, or their grandparents, or their primitive ancestors.

Francie had lived each night in her dreams, devising new ways to crawl into Josh's brain and pull him out of his stupor. But what she hadn't counted on was the part of Josh that was also the part of her: the willfulness, the determination, the stubbornness to survive. She knew every cell in her body owned a piece of perseverance, not to give up if there's still a bit of fight left. But she never knew how much of herself her children had inherited. She saw moments of tenacity in their eyes, but this was the first time their individual intention was put to the test, the ultimate test: life or death.

Francie instinctively knew she would fight to survive with fury. She'd find one last gulp of air in the rushing waters. But would her children persist with the same gusto? Did they love life as much as she? And as Francie pictured Josh's struggle to challenge his internal pestilence, she realized she had given birth to a warrior, four warriors, for her girls would fight just as fearlessly as their brother. Glutted with the bliss that burgeons when your heart rises renewed from the ashes, she closed her eyes in silent appreciation at her son's rebirth. He had come back.

Without waiting for the nurse, she crept out of bed, put on her robe and seated herself in the wheelchair outside the door. Then she scooted to Josh's room, practically screaming at the elevator panel which took 120 infinite seconds to open. When she appeared at his doorway, he was sitting up in bed, eating, eating like the food was going to be snatched away any moment. Francie didn't say anything. She wanted to watch him, savor the simple act of his swallowing food, as if that were the most accomplished activity he could do. And she loved the relish with which he was devouring his meal.

But Josh looked away for a second and caught his mother

sitting at the door. For an instant, it looked like he was going to jump from the bed. So Francie put her arm out and shouted, "Wait, don't move! I'm coming!"

Then she scuttled the chair to the side of the bed, climbed over the rail, and sat there holding him. She wanted to make sure he wouldn't dissolve, wouldn't melt back into the collapsed heap she remembered from last week. If she held him, no evil could touch him again. But inside, Francie knew they were lucky this time. She was here. Josh was here.

She could soothe his wounds, perhaps fuse some strength into his immature body. But there might be a next time, and a next time, and a time after that when Francie wouldn't be there to offer the safety of her hug, the refuge of her embrace. For Francie understood every mother's agony: each child has to go into the world and find out how to experience that tortuous of all adventures alone. And each mother has to hope that her child remains victorious in the dark alleys of life.

Francie sat and held her boy, soaking up the memory of this moment, exploding with exuberance at his vitality. But Josh started to squirm and whispered, "Hey Mom, I'm starving. If I finish this, maybe I can get some more."

Francie quickly turned away, laughing. She didn't want Josh to see the tears slipping from her eyes. He wouldn't understand yet that ultimate joy also brings a kind of despair, a certain knowledge that all we love is still transient. And Francie called for the nurse to bring more food.

TWENTY-NINE

When Graceland finally arrived home, she was exhausted. During the bus ride, she started to feel tired, so very tired. In fact, she had to take a cab home, something she would never do. Usually she walked, sometimes she took a public bus, but today, she couldn't seem to move. Her body balked, as if hit without warning by a virus that sucked the juice from her flagging bones. Lifting her feet had become an effort, getting in and out of the cab seemed almost an impossibility, and walking to her front door was like a two mile trek. Graceland nearly collapsed on the couch, but she held on to the wall and eased her body toward the kitchen.

She wanted a cup of tea. There would be time enough to sleep. And as she slid along the wall, she passed by Frank's room and stopped in the doorway, where she stood transfixed. There he was, on the walls, on the bed, in the air. He was still here. She knew it. She could feel him. She could breathe him. Any moment she expected him to say, "Hi Mom, what's new?"

Then noisily slicing the silence, she heard his voice, his child questions, his teenage sarcasm, his adult sympathy. The sounds of many years flooded her brain like a rhapsody, and its main theme kept repeating, "I'm here, Mom. I'm here."

She stood in the aperture, immune to the chill of night and oblivious of hunger, caught in a time-lapse of then and now. Whatever hidden vigor she hoarded inside her straining muscles kept her standing for hours, simply staring, thinking, crying. And when Graceland finally blinked into reality, she was shocked to find the top of her blouse damp, overlooking the possibility that her unacknowledged tears had escaped before they had her permission.

Slowly, at a turtle's pace, she shuffled into the kitchen, where she boiled water. She just wasn't feeling too well, a little light headed. But she knew that was probably from not eating. How could she eat? Hunger was the last thing on her mind. She needed to concentrate on paying tribute to a warrior, her warrior, her son.

As she was lifting the kettle to pour, a sharp pain shot down the length of her left arm. She clumsily dropped the pot onto the burner and had to steady herself against the stove. Graceland, having difficulty breathing, her heart palpitating harder, waited a few minutes till she was composed enough to pour the boiling water again. Carefully, with extreme deliberation, she grabbed the kettle off the burner and staggered to the table, where she braced herself against the chair. Graceland, get a grip on yourself, for God's sake. You're just pouring water into a cup.

Trembling, she tried to lift the cup to her mouth, but the pain increased, and she quickly put it back down. She couldn't get the thin porcelain container up to her lips. All she could do was let her left arm hang limply by her side and stare glassy-eyed at a cup of tea waiting to be swallowed. In a moment, she'd stand up and get some aspirin, but right now, she was so tired, so very tired. She went to lift the cup up again, and this time she made it to her mouth, which was opening to receive the dark brown scalding liquid.

But Graceland never felt the steaming brew touch her tongue, nor did she feel the blisters when the boiling water dropped down the front of her blouse onto her chest. All that Graceland felt was the unendurable pain hurtling through the veins of her left arm into her heart.

Your heart and your head vie for status your entire life, but sometimes, your passion points the way before your brain has had a chance to distribute all the facts. He couldn't explain how, but he had this gut-wrenching presentiment that AceArrow was guilty, guilty of mass murder, guilty of annihilating faithful creatures who had tacitly been promised protection.

Although TreadHard had not been at the actual scenes of the killings, the newspapers, the television, and BrickWell simultaneously contributed vivid accounts to his knowledge of the grisly murders. Graphically, these bloody images flitted behind his eyes, feeding his determination to do something. Had he been there, perhaps the emotional concussion of witnessing the brutality would have depleted his resolve. Sometimes when we participate personally in trauma, we're left drained, ready to walk away and say, "The hell with it!"

But not TreadHard. Distance triggered his tenacity. Allies, his senses clearly forged together, showing, shouting, shoving him to retaliate. The imagined DoRight wails blended with the undeserved pain of their innocence and fueled his decision to act. To act now. And after plunging into the midnight of his mind, the preconscious realm, where instincts originate when maxims fail, TreadHard knew what he had to do.

Now, 24 hours later, he was humming. As he pressed the accelerator of his beige Toyota pickup, he burst into "When the Saints Go Marching In." Why that particular tune played through his mind, he didn't know. He just realized he felt light. Goddamn! He felt better than he had in days, in weeks. He felt alive, and TreadHard wanted to voraciously suckle that vibrant feeling of life, of energy pulsing through his veins. Vitality was too precious, and much of our lives, we ignore it—thinking there's always more where that came from. Nothing like a little cancer to correct your assessment.

Well, AceArrow, you bastard. You were good for something. I haven't felt this chipper in a long time. And he pressed his speed to eighty, as he forgot time, forgot pain, forgot all the age-old rules engraved upon his consciousness long ago. It was the eve of his dominion now, and Robomaids had become the destination of his *High Noon.*

Who was left? What hadn't he thought of? Where do you go to solve a crime that is partially solved already? Goddamn that AceArrow! He had the machinery, he had the motive, and he had the supercilious air about him that blatantly spoke the silent words: "Fuck you, world. I'm the one who counts!"

Of course, FutureDick couldn't prove the CEO's culpability. That was the rub. But he felt it. He felt it the first day he visited Robomaids, and he trusted his feelings. They rarely, if ever, deceived him. But what could he do? How the hell could he implicate the blustering bastard? Sure, he could tail AceArrow for the next week, the next month. Who knows? It could take years before the guy slipped up, and he'd probably outlast them all.

No, AceArrow wouldn't reveal a thing. He was too slick. He effectively covered his trail and operated outside his office as well as outside his home. Where in this hellish haystack could FutureDick find that crucial clue? Unlike the renown stalker, Javert, FutureDick held his man at arm's length. The CEO was close enough to make his nose twitch. Yet he came up empty-handed on evidence. The only possible link was lying in the morgue, his flesh riddled with holes of the righteous, unresponsive to FutureDick's inquiries.

But Tully was all FutureDick had left. His apartment was useless. Nothing, absolutely nothing, connected him to AceArrow. The guy lived like a monk. Like some aberration flown in from the twelfth century. What sort of man was Tully?

What made him tick? What made him crawl away from people and devote his life to mechanical men, particularly mechanical men that killed?

The single person who might know was Tully's mom, and she had been strangely uncommunicative when TigerTail questioned her. Perhaps FutureDick could charm her. Any fact she would offer about Tully was more than he had now.

Driving up to Graceland's neighborhood revealed a typical California late-century tract of beige-brown stuccoed ranch-style houses, trees shooting out of adolescence and finally able to shade their environs, a bicycle or two lying on the lawn, and mailboxes in need of a fresh paint job. No luxury here. Just three bedroom, two bath protection against the elements.

FutureDick, trying to devise some word or sentence that would create instant intimacy with Graceland Tully, ran stock phrases through his brain. Nothing worked. Nothing sounded quite as authentic as he'd like. Perhaps a big smile and a "Hi!" might work as well as an "Excuse me, ma'am. I'd like to ask you some questions."

But FutureDick did what he usually did: wait for the moment and act extemporaneously. Nothing canned, nothing rehearsed. He just had to capture the right mood, the right image he wanted to project to Tully's mother.

He rang the bell and waited. He rang again. He knocked. Still no answer. He rapped on the window, although the living room appeared empty. From the window, he could see light coming from two areas: through the living room to what looked like it might be the kitchen and, probably, a bedroom off the hallway.

FutureDick knocked again. Silence. Instead of skulking around the back and possibly provoking some vigilant neighbor, he decided to pick the door lock. It was quicker. With his master key created by SpyMasters, Inc., he didn't have to ruin another credit card by jamming it into the side of the door. Two quick turns and he was inside.

The living room sat mute, its upholstered sentinels watching for intruders, its smell musty from disuse. FutureDick made his way to the lighted room off the hallway. He considered himself a steady kind of person, rooted in the belief that responses must be spontaneous, yet practical. Although emotions lurked at the margin of his decisions, he usually let his pragmatism guide his reason and keep him composed. FutureDick, dispassionate, experienced, felt prepared for the unexpected.

Consequently, when his eyes happened upon Frank's bedroom, he was more surprised at his own visceral reaction to the raw madness than he was at the bizarre appeal to keep Tully living. His vision, startled by Graceland's handiwork, sent a jab to his stomach that, for a brief moment, made him lurch toward the bathroom. But the queasiness passed, and all that remained was the taste of bile backed-up into the rear of his throat. He breathed deeply as his eyes wildly scanned the covered walls. These partitions became a telling tomb, replete with pictures, papers, letters, clothes, and shoes imposed on the plaster in a frenetic, haphazard arrangement, suggesting the artist had a plane to catch and decided to paint her masterpiece before the last call for boarding. The fury of the homemade wallpaper yielded to the empty military shroud placed across the bed.

Now all that remained were the bits and pieces of a personal history treasured by a mother. Funny, no matter what evil an adult child crafts, his mother only sees the baby she held in her arms. As FutureDick's eyes strained to find some item that would offer help, he glimpsed at the two letters lying on the bed, waiting to be read.

Two hours later, he blinked, shaking himself alert. He had been held captive by the venomously true fairy tale that described Tully's involvement in the DoRight mutilations. Starting with Tully's first meeting AceArrow, helping steal the robotic parts, setting up shop in FineWine's garage, and mapping out the trail of carnage, the revealing chronicle detailed AceArrow's master plan.

Tully exposed everything, how AceArrow deliberately communicated through public telephones, used cash for each transaction, made Tully memorize all phone numbers, addresses, names, and burn any paper with notes on it. How AceArrow had read about BrickWell's research and seemed to know the scientist better than he knew himself. How elated AceArrow was when he uncovered the section describing the DoRight's euphoric response to vanilla. That discovery enabled him to concoct a mild tranquilizer without having to worry about a delivery system, measured doses or potency. "If those dumb fucks love vanilla that way, I'll saturate the air with so much of the stuff, they'd wish they were born without noses!" quoted Tully.

Most interesting was the paragraph describing a Mr. FineWine, a software genius who liked to live in his garage with his computer, having forgotten that humans also inhabit the world. Computers and robots. He and AceArrow got along famously. It was FineWine who developed the kill program etched in the robots' memory banks. It was FineWine who pieced the monsters together and created an android army dedicated to destruction.

Tully told his story tirelessly, even the final murder of Francie's household. That killing was not originally planned. But once the newspapers carried the story of the talking DoRight, AceArrow panicked. He wanted nothing left to chance. With regularity, Tully repeated how careful, how methodical AceArrow was. The CEO checked and rechecked every step. He intended to scare the public by killing a few servile DoRights, but he also wanted to go after humans to drive his message into the heart of every potential DoRight owner. In fact, he recited his poem incessantly—just for laughs.

There once were three DoRights,
and they all smelled like shit.
Now the DoRights are gone,
'cause our robots won't quit!

Although AceArrow's humor was hollow, Tully emphasized in his confession that the executive hoped to change public loyalty and open a new market. Once AceArrow fully confused consumers by substantially scaring the hell out of them, he could thrust his DomesticApes onto the scene and offer them at bargain prices. AceArrow had no doubt about consumer malleability. He expected the customers to switch immediately. Killing humans was not a fundamental part of his basic blueprint, but as he told Tully, "We must be flexible. We must be sensitive to the requirements of the situation. And we must stop the bitch from talking to the police. You know, Tully, success is built on adaptability."

The man had a way with words. For $120,000, why should Tully disagree? He loved his work. All he wanted was to carry out AceArrow's commands and get paid, perhaps even institute some of his own strategy. A soldier's duty was to get the job done—correctly. But just in case his commander reneged, he left this document. Just in case AceArrow failed to deliver, he'd make sure the CEO was exposed. Nobody fucks over Frank Tully. Even in his demise, his mother had explicit instructions to deliver this information to the police.

FutureDick read the confession through and then read it again. He wanted each detail to crawl into his bones and reside there. He wanted to live AceArrow's crime anew. Thank you, Mrs. Tully, for not heeding your son's instructions. He clearly told you to destroy this document if AceArrow delivered the money. And you didn't follow his directions. I wonder why? Knowing AceArrow's painstaking attention to detail, FutureDick had no doubts that Tully's mother had been paid. There was the other letter instructing her on what to do with the cash, and you could tell that letter had been read, had been touched, had been handled, had been read repeatedly, so as not to make any mistakes.

But FutureDick possessed an analytic mind, and he knew there was always some instant, some decision, some faulty move or swing that changed the course of a plan, that accounted for failure. Whenever he lost a racquetball game, he could pinpoint the moment in the match when he made the wrong choice. Usually, it was somewhere between the eleventh and fourteenth point. There were no mistakes allowed as you approached the fifteenth tally, the winner's goal. A wrong decision at this juncture gave your opponent the advantage and surely lost you the game.

When you're both barreling toward the finish line, the mental game becomes more important than the physical contest. Your wrong split second judgment at this crucial time seems to drain the smallest fraction of your determination. But that's the only entry your opponent needs. Somehow, FutureDick thought, the other player soaks in what you've surrendered, and at the end, a rival barely requires a scrap of leverage, a sliver of an edge. Then it's all over. You've lost.

FutureDick couldn't help thinking that AceArrow lost when he decided to go after humans. Up till that point, he had it made. No clues. No tracks. Nothing for the police or FutureDick to go on. Just dead DoRights. But AceArrow called it wrong. Not greed, not even power, but possibly over-planning. AceArrow went for the wrong shot—he went for Francie. Humans were unessential to his search and destroy formula, and his revised plan cost him his army, his captain, and his anonymity.

But FutureDick had to admit that another variable entered into AceArrow's exposure. We might be able to control ourselves, our actions, our thoughts, if we're determined enough, rigid enough, but there's no way we can completely control others. We can never get into another person's brain. Yet in that grey matter resides a wealth of resources, individual potential that each human being can tap into. How could AceArrow ever know what Tully was explicitly thinking? How could the CEO predict that Tully would cover his ass? And how could Mr. Mastermind know what Tully's mother would do when confronted with her son's death? We can only know ourselves. That was AceArrow's undoing. The minute our reach extends beyond our own actions, it's bound to fall off somewhere, like a robotic arm that can't stretch any further.

FutureDick had his man. He held the testimony in his hands. But his heart didn't celebrate the victory. He hadn't actually achieved the winning fifteenth point of the game. Knowing how AceArrow's mind carefully schemed, FutureDick realized that the CEO could escape retribution. A good lawyer, a plea bargain, the right money, any number of elements would keep AceArrow a free man.

Who really cared about the death of some chimps? People were harmed, not murdered, so what was the charge? Cruelty to animals? Let the Humane Society handle it. AceArrow would be indicted, but would he be punished?

As FutureDick pondered the possibility of conviction, he walked through the house to the other dimly lighted room. Hypnotized by the torrent of free-flowing facts, he forgot that someone else inhabited this house. Since it had been blaringly quiet for hours, he assumed he was the only one there.

So when he neared the doorway, the drooped figure of an elderly woman jarred him into readiness. For a moment he stood quietly, peeking into the noiseless kitchen, looking for harm. There she sat, chin resting on her chest, legs sprawled, arms limp, a brown stain down the front of her blouse and a broken cup by her chair. A tea bag, china fragments, and a pool of water testified to her last breath.

A dead mother, a dead son, and a host of dead chimpanzees, all because one corporate president wanted a share of the market. A child lying in a coma for a week, a mother terrorized over her son's life, families mourning the death of their human-like pets, and three men hired to protect the peace wiped out in two minutes, purely for a company's falling profits.

FutureDick thought about Francie, about Josh, about the blood dripping down the walls, glistening off the dead DoRight torsos, Emma's agony, death, slaughter, carnage, butchery. And every foul picture that entered his mind blended into AceArrow's face. The more crisply his brain created pictures of massacre and mutilation, the more intensely AceArrow's sneer spun through his consciousness.

That's when he realized he wanted something other than an apprehension. FutureDick wanted revenge, reprisal, an eye for an eye. Somewhere in the course of the investigation, he had invested too much of himself in solving this crime. Perhaps his objectivity became hampered by his humanity. Or perhaps, this time, the silver Mercedes couldn't make its getaway.

It would be so easy to get to AceArrow's office before TigerTail, even easier to confront the CEO and kill him. Simply walk in, point the gun, shoot, and then leave. Better yet, wait by his car, walk up behind him as he grabs the handle and drive the bullets into the base of his skull. All over in moments, and the proud owner of Robomaids wouldn't know who snuffed out his life.

For a second, FutureDick relished the fantasy of a newspaper headline blaring in capital letters: **CORPORATE HEAD AMBUSHED IN PARKING LOT.** So tempting, he could taste the tantalizing flavor of vengeance. And he played with the possibility of murder. No, not exactly murder. Justice. Plain old cowboy-style justice.

But his appetite for dispensing punishment slowly diminished as he thought about Francie, Josh, a family, a future, a life, and he recognized he was still bound by some type of social contract he signed long ago. He never knew when he obligated himself to uphold the law, but somewhere along the way, he had pledged himself to live an ethical life, to support the rules of a civilized society. Although the primeval thirst for retribution pounded relentlessly in his brain, he walked to the phone to call TigerTail.

THIRTY

The plan should work. It had to. Otherwise, he'd not only humiliate his own family, he'd scandalize TriCubed as well. But TreadHard remained optimistic. He had scaled too many cliffs, skied too many mountains, to not trust the strength and speed of his own body.

Besides, he had spent a lifetime defying the fates. His death would be no different. Challenge stimulated him. When he took the dare, he walked the edge, and that kind of adrenaline rush ameliorated the routine of the day to day. Of course, the thrill brought with it a certain addiction, the lust for bigger, for greater, for more intensity than the one before.

But TreadHard was a moderate man, and he had learned to dole out his satisfactions. Although now, near the end, he wanted it all. Temperance be damned. Self-restraint was solely for those still able to count on future trust in months, years, millenniums. He only had the *now,* and he was determined to drain it dry.

When TreadHard pulled into Robomaids' parking lot, he drove around the perimeter of the asphalt till he found what he thought must be AceArrow's car, the charcoal Cadillac with the ACE-A on the license plate. Then he parked where he could watch it. He wanted to pull up alongside the vehicle, but that space was already occupied. Still, AceArrow had parked closest to the building and farthest away from where the security guard would take up his post. In fact, TreadHard was certain the guard could barely see AceArrow's car across the long lot.

With no identification, no credit cards, just lots of cash and a fake driver's license, TreadHard, the patient man, smiled. One side of his truck read *Brilliantine Painters—Any Job is Our Job*. It was three in the afternoon, and the security guard hadn't arrived yet.

The next two hours passed quickly as TreadHard nurtured his sensory anticipation. Over the past few months, he learned to relish excitement. It meant he was alive, which meant the cancer was at least contained. His immune system still cared enough to stave off the crafty invader.

Around five, the cars filled up with drivers, and the lot became almost barren. A few autos remained. TreadHard jumped at the opportunity to back in his truck next to AceArrow's Caddy. Dressed in white overalls and cap, he jumped out, grabbed a brush and can of white paint, and began going over the bold, white lines of the parking lot.

When the guard came on duty at 5:30, he heard the sounds of rock music blaring indistinctly from the rear of the lot. There in the middle of the emptiness was a fellow painting the parking lines. Briefly glancing at the laborer, the watchman busied himself with the paperback mystery he was reading. Friday nights were usually quiet, since no one had been working late on the weekends for awhile except Mr. AceArrow. He was always here. Might as well move his bedroom into his office. The guard was sure the CEO spent more time at Robomaids than he ever did at home. 5:45—all was A-Okay.

AceArrow was nearly there. The ads started next week, and the slogan he went with was catchy. He'd have people hearing the jingle in their sleep: *"If you want your home in tiptop shape, better buy yourself a DomesticApe!"*

He knew it would work. Short, precise bits of knowledge, just like the primary readers in elementary school. The brain wants its information quickly, succinctly, and simply. Get the message to the mind as fast as you can, and let the mind taste it, tickle it, and then decimate it into usable pieces of data.

He didn't underestimate the brain's ability. He clearly knew when it came to selling anyone anything, you had to massage that intellectual organ with ordinary, or as he sometimes called it—uncomplex—input, repeated like a pulsating chorus. The brain was an instrument of habit. It responded to the familiar, and AceArrow planned to make DomesticApes as chummy as possible. When he finished with his media blitz, he'd have families whistling the rhyme in unison whenever they heard it come over the sound waves into their lives.

AceArrow hired a slew of telemarketers to dispense information and close the sale over the phone. He increased his staff of customer service reps to handle the more curious customers, the ones who wanted to see the operation firsthand. Just a few orders, only five hundred, would give him the needed impetus to turn things around. Five hundred orders, paid on delivery, would show his stock holders he had found the magic formula for pulling the company out of the doldrums.

Of course, he knew well it wasn't magic. It was long hours and strategic planning. And it was secrecy. Tully wasn't around to squeal and FineWine wouldn't talk. He enjoyed the work, the money, the anticipation of another project, and the fear of prison. The man was pure scientist. Give him a problem and let him find the solution. How the solution was implemented didn't concern him. His was the world of reason. If there's a question, there must be an answer.

It was Friday afternoon, and AceArrow couldn't think of anything else to do till Monday, the day TV and newspapers smothered the minds of potential customers with the benefits of owning a loveable, serviceable DomesticApe. To AceArrow, his mechanical beasts were loveable. How could you not adore something that existed just to please you? That was real loyalty. That was love. Could his customers understand that living things were too unpredictable? You couldn't always count on them, way too many imperfections, and you usually had to bribe them, coerce them, or at least pay attention to them to gain their obedience.

AceArrow knew if he could meet with each buyer, he would close the sale. He understood the guts of his product, and by the time he finished singing its praises, he'd have the SmithBodies and the JohnsSons ordering one for themselves, one for their daughters, and one for their in-laws. But AceArrow also knew he had to employ others to do the sales pitch, even though he'd be able to outsell anyone who walked into the marketing department. He was the overseer. He knew the forest and the trees of the business. It was his baby.

He hated to relinquish the sales responsibility to a staff of people who worked strictly for pay. They didn't know his androids the way he did. They didn't feel the respect and admiration for the complex web of parts holding his mechanical men together. They didn't understand the spirituality of these cybernauts. These robots were more than machines. They were more than man. They were the closest approximation to God he had ever seen: they were perfection.

As the CEO walked to his car, earlier than usual, his mind was already tackling a new problem: how could he become a one-man sales force? Certainly he could devise a video, a presentation, a way he could expound DomesticApe virtues to the country. He could get into churches, universities, supermarkets, downtowns at lunchtime, freeways at rush hours, buses, trains, planes, bars, restaurants, gas stations, theaters, hospitals—wherever a consumer existed. It was doable with the right transmission vehicle.

Lost in longing, as he considered the *how* of infiltrating the buyer's attention, AceArrow failed to notice the shadow slide up behind him. During the instant his daydream was broken by that momentary awareness announcing someone was near, his knees buckled. It happened so quickly, the scream never left his lips. TreadHard had crept up behind, kicked AceArrow in back of his knees, and slapped a piece of tape over the CEO's mouth as he went down.

Immediately, TreadHard crawled on top of the large man and grasped his wrists, maneuvering handcuffs on at the same time. AceArrow's legs now remained the problem, as he tried to kick TreadHard off of him. But the more agile athlete was able to slide some rope under AceArrow's body and swiftly wrap the rope around the man's legs as if he were preparing a mummy for burial.

TreadHard knew that speed would make the difference in rendering AceArrow helpless, just as speed was his confederate on the tennis court. Don't give your opponents time to think, calculate, or move. You interrupt their reaction. You act before they do. Then they have to reconsider, reexamine their alternatives. But in those lost seconds you've scored your point, and your adversary is in a mini-time warp, caught between what he should have done and what he's got to do next.

And that's what TreadHard did, with meteoric precision, as he prepared his human bundle for transport. He rolled AceArrow onto the back of his pickup, covered him with a tarp, and slowly pulled out of the parking lot, one more vendor leaving the building. With his radio blasting, any sound at all from his concealed antagonist was muffled.

Now, ten hours of driving were ahead of him. He grabbed a sandwich out of his backpack and opened a bottle of Calistoga. He was on his way, exhilarated that his plan was executed perfectly. Although AceArrow was bigger, he was out of shape: too much sitting, too much eating, just too much disuse. In fact, TreadHard felt that particular lightness that comes when you finally decide to act and know what you're doing is what you have to do. It felt right. It felt wonderful!

TreadHard had wrestled a lifetime with the concept of right and wrong. The older he grew, the more he saw the individual abused, trampled by an inefficient criminal justice system, a multi-layered ineffectual government bureaucracy, and a business community that somehow neglected the needs of their people. At times, he felt that we had not evolved much beyond castle and serfs, only the lords of the manor now wore pin stripe shirts with speckled yellow ties and employed an army of knights, who were promised BMW's and condos in the Caribbean.

Somewhere between the ratification of the Bill of Rights in 1791 and the creation of the Global Business Pact of 1999, the nation lost sight of the individual. What counted were corporate profits, stock value, the market share, bonuses, fringe benefits, the bottom line. But ethics, compassion, trust were archaic terms used in nineteenth century novels.

In a world where rights were not revered or protected, TreadHard knew that he had to choose. He had to design his own moral code. He had to act, and in so doing, take responsibility for his actions. He also knew the risk of living with such freedom, the risk of being condemned by a society that sought safety in anonymity rather than security in protection of certain inalienable rights, his right, the mother's right, the child's right to live without the fear of personal violation.

AceArrow had overstepped the boundaries of a civilized community. He played king, assuming he could give and take life, animal or human. Both were crucially equal in TreadHard's mind. Tyrannically, AceArrow had spread his tentacles into the wrong place when he went after the DoRights and their families.

What is justice? Or what is mercy? TreadHard could come up with no general rule except the axiom that those who hurt others should be punished. And those who kill should be punished properly. It wasn't a matter of revenge or retaliation. It was a matter of individual responsibility. AceArrow knew when he crafted his master plan for destruction of the DoRights that he took a risk. The power, the profit, and the challenge inspired the CEO to act in a way that harmed others. He had to stand accountable for his action, for his choice, since he abandoned any concern for humanity when he placed the dollar ahead of life.

What AceArrow wanted had became more important than Francie Franks, her son, and the many DoRights he butchered. Didn't AceArrow's decision ultimately come to one conclusion? Response. Someone, somewhere, was going to be affected by the violence of AceArrow's choice, and how would that someone respond? TreadHard knew how. He had figured it all out, and now he was on his way to Mexico to give AceArrow the time of his life or, perhaps, the remaining time he had left of his life.

Although Josh had to remain in the hospital for another week, Francie was discharged Friday morning. She lingered at his bedside, fluctuating between the desire to finally return home and be with the girls, who she missed tremendously, or stay another minute with Josh. She feared if she walked out of the room, some fiend, some medical twist of fate, might suck him back into oblivion. One more touch, one more kiss, one more gaze and Francie left, promising Josh books, phone numbers, and real food.

Reba was in the waiting room, anxious to whisk Francie away from the infirmary's grasp. She heard too many stories where patients went in for minor surgery but never came out. Complications, they were called. Reba called it conspiracy. They needed to provide living models for their gobs of medical students. "Who was the big *They* behind this infamous scheme?" Francie would ask. But Reba invariably answered, "You know, Francie. The powers that be."

Francie never knew if it was Reba's ex-husband's abandonment or her father dying when she was a child, and it probably was a combination of many unreliable or uncertain experiences, but Reba trusted very few people. She had no use for large institutions, which included corporations, colleges, hospitals, airlines, and government agencies. She just took it as a given that chaos would crop up somewhere in the communication chain, the minute information and services passed through the hands of more than two people.

Of course, SeaBank General fell into Reba's definition of unwieldy organizations, and she stood guard all week long, a sentry ready to beat back the advancing medical invaders. Reba was convinced if something could go wrong, it would, and she continually discussed the quality of service with the nurses, and once with the doctor, much to Francie's chagrin as well as her pleasure. Francie thought Reba was being a bit too cautious. Despite the injuries, she overlooked the fact that Francie never had surgery, just bruises. However, Francie loved her friend's concern, attention, and most of all, her zealous approach to human care. Why didn't everyone care about others that way?

Still, Reba squelched her misgivings about wanting to stay in this huge place one minute longer than she had to and asked Francie to give her a few minutes with Josh. Without a second's hesitancy, Francie smiled and said, "Go. He'll be delighted." Reba was one of Josh's favorite people, a friend, a second mother, a human being he definitely trusted and also loved. She could brighten his sterile hospital room infinitely more than the cards and flowers.

Francie sat in the lobby, and she thought about Josh folded up against the wall that terrible night. She thought about the unrelenting metal monster who nearly killed her, and she thought about FD. When he swam into her brain, the terror of all the other memories faded, only to be replaced with a vast surge of warmth and well-being. He was her connection to the greater quintessence, her completion—her missing link.

She pummeled her way through life, able to go it alone, strong enough to manage home, family, work, and self. Existing on a belief that the moment was all she owned, Francie was efficient, capable, a so-called superwoman because she had to be.

Who else would do it? These were her children, this was her body, this was her life. She'd better take care of it. She didn't get another go-around.

But deep inside, she persistently felt something was missing, a puzzle piece to her identity, a contact—a constant—a something that would fill in the emptiness. And she knew FD was that particular ingredient, that special human being who made her feel whole, made her understand the meaning of oneness. So her heart mouthed the words that her lips lightly whispered, "Where are you right now, FD? I'm waiting. I feel your presence in my brain. I see your face behind my eyes. And I'm waiting, my darling, waiting to start again."

THIRTY-ONE

"TigerTail, we got him! By the balls, man, by the balls!"

"Calm down, FutureDick. You sound as if you've solved the crime of the century!"

"It may well be. If we get AceArrow, we may be able to wage a whole new war against cruelty to animals. You never saw that talking chimp. I did, man. It was pathetic. The guy should be left to rot in the Mojave as far as I'm concerned."

And before TigerTail could respond, his mind shifted to FearLess, such an unnecessary death. But then again, when is death ever decreed a necessity? FearLess, a husband, a father, a man.

"Okay, FutureDick," he said quietly, "what have you got?"

Twenty minutes later, TigerTail knew about Graceland Tully, her make-believe mausoleum, and the full confession from her son.

"Hey, FutureDick, I'm out of here. But you'll have to hang loose. I can't leave till tomorrow morning. I'm giving testimony at eight a.m., and then I'll catch a police jet."

"Aw, shit, TigerTail! I'm aching to arrest the son of a bitch. I can taste it. But I'm sure he's not going anywhere. He's got a company to run. Call me at the RaMada as soon as you land. We'll go to Tully's mom's house first, where I'll show you the confession, and then Robomaids. I promise I'll wear my best smile while you pull out your handcuffs."

"You're on, buddy. Say, FutureDick, good work! No matter how much we suspected the guy, we had no evidence. And who knows what might have happened to Tully's letter in a week or two if no one went in there to inspect his mother's home."

"I don't know, TigerTail. On one hand, I'm elated. But on the other, I'm afraid he'll walk. That's my biggest fear—to see AceArrow free. See you tomorrow."

Telling BrickWell the news brought a kind of closure to the case for FutureDick. After all these years, he still worried about solving each crime. His track record proved otherwise. But he hated to report back to a client, "Sorry, I can't help you anymore." For FutureDick, this was failure. A lost trail. A clueless problem. It didn't happen often, but once in a while, there were those unsolvable instances, crimes that neither he nor the police were able to explain.

The few times solutions to the mystery remained concealed, FutureDick took off for a week and went backpacking in the Sierras. It was his quiet way of working through the complexity of criminology and giving himself permission to be human. People don't always find the answers. Maybe brighter people solve more problems, but everyone loses a game once in a while. Don't they? FutureDick was never a hundred percent certain, so he'd climb his mountains, trying to figure out how to go easier on himself.

But this wasn't one of those bad times. This was victory. This was the conclusion to the endless killing. And BrickWell thanked him profusely. "This will be the first night I can finally fall asleep not worried about being called because of another massacre."

"Let's hope the guy gets the book thrown at him or, at least, that his cellmate is a DoRight admirer."

"What I do hope, FutureDick, is that this sets a precedent for human behavior toward apes. If AceArrow is given the death sentence, man will never relegate chimps to a lesser category again. After all, they hurt just like we do."

"Adam, execution is too good for the bastard. Too easy. Goddamn it! This is the one case where I seemed to have lost any sense of objectivity."

"I know, FutureDick. I know. Easy to do when you really know a DoRight personally. The good stands out so clearly against the bad. I hope the jury sees it that way, too."

Late that evening, FutureDick called Francie, but her answering machine picked up the call. Even so, he enjoyed hearing her voice come through the phone, and he left the message, "I miss you, sweetheart. I really do."

The next morning testified to the truism that the sun can shine while everything around you crumbles. It's those expectations. The minute you set them up for success, inevitably, they become the prelude to disaster. By the time FutureDick and TigerTail left Graceland Tully's, it was 11:30. When they arrived at Robomaids, there was one car in the parking lot: ACE-A.

Beaming, the two men walked up to the building but found the doors locked. By 12:30, they had the security guard opening every locked door in the company. Room after room, floor after floor, Robomaids remained eerily silent, waiting for some pronouncement of its guilt. But no representative jumped forth and said, "I did it! I'm to blame!" Instead, the building stood gagged, muzzled by its outlaw CEO, who, all of a sudden, had become a fugitive.

Dismally, lapsed smiles now transfigured into grimaces, FutureDick and TigerTail drove out to AceArrow's house. By the time they made arrangements with the security company to gain access to the premises, it was 4:30. But the house was empty, at least void of any living things. There was a robot, lots of electronic equipment, and two messages on the Record-a-Call from the night before. The place seemed untouched, beds made, kitchen spotless, no moist toothbrush, no tossed coffee grounds, nothing to suggest a human had inhabited these premises this morning. Saturday's paper squatted close to the front door, forgotten, beginning to bleach from the hot sun. And FutureDick implored some unknown influence not to let AceArrow escape while TigerTail called the station.

After issuing an innocuous all-points bulletin, TigerTail settled down to strategy. They didn't even know what kind of vehicle AceArrow would be driving, where he might have headed, or even how he was getting there.

"I say we start doing the usual, FutureDick. Check the airports, buses, trains, rental companies. We got a shitload of digging ahead of us. Let's just get started. He's somewhere, man. He's somewhere."

"I guess you're right, TigerTail, but twiddling with the touchtone right now will drive me crazy. Let's get over to FineWine's. At least, he's a material witness as well as an accomplice."

"Okay, FutureDick. Let me call the San Ramon station to help us find the travel data. They should be able to do something."

"Can you believe that bastard? We've had him in front of our eyes for weeks, and now when we can finally take him in, vamoose! Vanished! Into thin air!"

"Hold tight, guy. We'll get him." And then TigerTail added, "Unless someone's gotten him first!"

The day was lighting up once again as TreadHard pulled off the road just before he hit Ensenada. If one wasn't familiar with this rugged country, you'd pass by the weather-beaten sign, almost faded beyond legibility. But TreadHard made out the familiar family name of his longtime friend, Guiterrez. Nineteen years ago, TreadHard met Antonio Guiterrez at the

Tecate Half Marathon. They both finished at the same time and still argued about whose toe went over the line first.

Many beers later, they found out only geographic miles separated them, for their attitudes, philosophies, values were quite similar. Antonio had taught world history at the University of Mexico, but left academia when his father died. He preferred to live once more on the family's ranch near the ocean, among his books, his horses, and his cherished hobby: pit bulls.

Guiterrez had gained a statesman's reputation that went beyond Baja as the best breeder in Mexico. His dogs were the sturdiest, the strongest, the most ferocious canines around, and Antonio Guiterrez was a respected name among his countrymen. He never asked questions of his buyers. He didn't care who they were or why they wanted his animals. And because of his complacency with customers that contrasted with his passion for his pups, Antonio enjoyed a thriving business that exceeded even Mexico's borders.

Whether used for fighting, for protection, or for pets, pit bulls were regarded as lethal weapons, and the more vicious they were, the more precious they became as a commodity. Since the dog had a built-in instinct for holding on tight, no matter what, they were revered as guard dogs by those who needed to be protected.

Years ago, with admiration as well as awe in his voice, Antonio explained the dog's history to Bruce. In the early thirteenth century until it was outlawed in 1835, bull baiting was a sport popular in England. The people would gather in a village square or around a ring while musicians played and refreshments were served. There, they would watch several dogs set loose on a bull. The attacks of the gnarling dogs enraged the poor bull, who tried to shake them loose and gore them. However, the bulldog, especially bred for the sport, would violently attack and hold on tenaciously.

Its jaws were broad, massive, square, and the under jaw would project considerably in front of the upper and turn up.

The dog's neck, short, very thick and strong, matched his broad, well-muscled forelegs. He was the perfect fighting machine, built to dig into his enemy mercilessly. The pit bull didn't wrench the limb from his opponent: it was his opponent, in seeking freedom at all costs, who tore himself away from his limb, his finger, his face, his nose.

Bruce never questioned Antonio's zeal for his dogs. Friends never question friends. They just accept one another totally, allowing each to own his peculiar desires, habits, attitudes, loves. And Bruce and Antonio were friends, good friends. At least once a year, they met up with each other, for they were the brothers neither one of them ever had. Confident, they trusted each other implicitly. No questions asked.

When TreadHard drove onto the estate and parked, he looked around at the luxurious tranquility posed by the rambling hills and smell of the ocean. Whenever he thought of a man-made paradise, Bruce conjured up images of Antonio's ranch.

The hills and valleys seemed to go on forever, an optical illusion suggesting this was all there was to the planet. If you walked to the horizon, you would drop off into nothingness, into space, into humanless. But as long as you stayed among the manzanitas and ribbonwoods or walked into the patches of black oak and cedar, you felt convinced of your existence, your centeredness as well as your insignificance.

Around him, he saw bougainvillaea and azalca, reminding him how intense Nature truly was—intimating that some world interior decorator provided vivid flowers for the eye to feast upon, but tempered the visual orgy with a background of treeless mesas awash in tall grasses, lest the viewer satiate his senses. Wherever the eye gazed, there was beauty, natural beauty, part of the bounty man had inherited but quite willfully destroyed in the twentieth century.

When Antonio opened the door, they hugged each other, eager to share their fellowship, their brotherhood, which had to be gulped in spurts of measured time. They had a whole year to catch up on, and Bruce knew that sometime in the middle of the night, he would be heading north again. But he excused himself, saying he wanted to check on the dogs. Give him a few moments, and he'll be right back. Antonio gave him the briefest of looks and said, "My friend, take your time. We have all night to talk."

TreadHard walked out, leaped into his pickup, and drove the quarter of a mile to the pen. It was a fortress encircled with ten foot walls of wood and steel reinforcements, entered through a door with one glass peep hole. The view, broken up by a three foot dirt moat, extended to another window built into a six foot high wooden fence set in concrete to prevent the dogs from digging under it. Inside this stronghold the animals resided, eighteen short, powerfully-built, smooth-coated combative dogs with fierce expressions.

A pit bull's skin fits snugly. Only around the neck and chest do you see a few folds in the skin. An adversary would have to be exceptionally large to grasp the nimble animal in its jaws. Perhaps a lion could do it, but a bear would be humiliated by a large pack of fighting pit bulls. Bruce remembered Antonio's favorite fighting story about the pit bull's nemesis, the African monkey. That was the one opponent the dog didn't continually win against because of the monkey's agility, as well as its ability to grasp a weapon. The primate was deadly.

Antonio, well versed in historical trivia, would talk about the famous Jacco Maccacco, a monkey who conquered some of the strongest, most savage dogs in eighteenth century England. Only weighing twelve pounds, he was a virtual one-beast army. After gaining his celebrated reputation by killing fifteen dogs in fifteen straight fights, Jacco was matched against a twenty pound pit bull named Puss. Many people favored the dog to win. He was bigger, stronger, and, so they thought, meaner.

Before the fight, the owner of the dog permitted the monkey to use a twelve-inch stick in the match. Although the dog fiercely flung himself at the little monkey, Jacco, with the grace of a ballet dancer, sprang at least three feet in the air and fell upon the dog, sinking his teeth in the back of the dog's neck. Riding Puss like a horse, Jacco seized an ear with his paw to prevent the shocked animal from turning to bite. With the stick, he proceeded to violently pound the dog's head. In a matter of minutes, Jacco had fractured the skull of the outwitted dog, who was drummed into unconsciousness.

But pit bulls rarely lost when it came to unsuspecting human adversaries. Trained for guard duty, they were naturally aggressive and dangerous. They could even climb trees, as they used their strapping forelegs like arms and scrambled up the rough-barked trunks. Strong in body and spirit, the dog wants to fight, and he fights to damage, which many times means death to the intruder. Perhaps the dog remembers a blood lust from times past, since it can be driven crazy when the smell of blood reaches its highly sensitive olfactory nerve endings.

Antonio sidled into a sermon when he talked about selectively breeding his dogs for gameness, the dog's willingness to fight to the death. He recognized a spirituality in his dogs that allowed him to see these animals with respect and admiration. Although, Bruce wondered, whose death was Antonio eulogizing? Certainly the pit bull wasn't usually the one gasping its last breath.

With sharp carnivorous teeth built for cutting, holding, tearing, slicing, and crushing, TreadHard cringed at his ghastly mental picture of what was left of the animal's opponent. He would watch a large, raw steak tossed into the pen be torn into chunks, then quickly sliced by the dog's sharp molars, and pieces that would choke a human, swallowed with ease by this uncompromising beast.

And, although Antonio praised it as the most intelligent of all dogs because it learned quickly and never forgot what it was taught, Bruce recognized another sort of splendor. He saw the beauty of tenacity, the beauty of commitment, determination, resolve—the willpower that Bruce understood too well. Sometimes he felt he could penetrate the dogs' thoughts and silently communicate with those quiet, brave beasts, who carried on a life of their own inside their cautious compound.

As he peered through the glass, TreadHard beheld these magnificent animals. Some paced slowly around the pen, others sat and watched, while a couple looked as if they were sleeping. You could never tell with these dogs, for they seemed to be on red alert 24 hours a day, even with their eyes closed. What inevitably caught TreadHard's attention were their wide, invincible jaws. Imposing, like steel vises, built to hold the earth from spinning into orbit or to clamp upon an interloper till he bled to death.

One of the saddest stories TreadHard heard was the tragedy of a child who crawled into the neighbor's yard. There sat the pit bull, vigilant, patient, ruthless, and when the baby crept close enough, the canine went for the child's face and actually bit off her nose. TreadHard always shuddered when he imagined the child's agony, for he knew when one of these dogs bite, its longer underjaw locks with the upper jaw, and any part held in its grip is gone, lost, and most likely, lifeless.

TreadHard suspected a person could escape one of these tenacious beasts, perhaps two, but there collected in a beautiful portrait were eighteen magnificent pit bulls, obligated to carry out their biological imperative. They were waiting, watching, and perhaps wishing.

Not precisely sure how he was going to do it, TreadHard was able to roll AceArrow off the truck. When he ripped the tape off the CEO's mouth, the man looked awful: grey, pleading, wrinkled. TreadHard ignored the offers of money, of partnership, of fame, and rolled AceArrow inside the first door. There was very little working space in the three foot inner compartment, but he had to untie AceArrow's hands and legs and get out in order to open up the other door. That second door was latched by a pulley mechanism and was raised and lowered electronically from outside the pen.

TreadHard bent close to AceArrow's face and grabbed his cheeks with one hand, "I'm not going to hurt you. That would be too easy. I just want you to feel what it's like to go up against the force of your own robots. I've got a surprise for you. Another kind of animal. Dogs! Mere dogs. But these canines are strength in motion, just like your metalmen. Certainly, you can appreciate their magnificence, their single-mindedness, for this is what your dreams were based on."

AceArrow strained to turn his face, making gasping sounds, his breathing labored, loud, throaty, but TreadHard held tight, becoming a pit bull himself, wrenching the man's frightened gaze back to his own eyes. Pupils pleading, saliva spraying, AceArrow's word gushed out, verbal vomit squirting through TreadHard's grip. "They were only apes, you asshole. Fucking chimpanzees! They meant nothing. Listen to me! I can give you anything. I've got it all. You son of a bitch, listen to me!"

But TreadHard was listening. And he heard exactly what he wanted to hear. His ears confiscated the stunted confession that AceArrow had made a pact with the devil and participated in the DoRight destruction. "No, AceArrow, you listen to me and listen hard! The only thing you can give me is the opportunity to place you in the same threatening position as the DoRights. That's all I want, you bastard. I want you to squirm." Before AceArrow could answer, TreadHard added, "Isn't it appropriate you experience the same outrage you perpetrated on the world?"

AceArrow tried to speak, but TreadHard gripped the man's cheeks in a pinched position, and words blended with cries hammered through in a trembling, shrill tone. If one listened closely, you'd hear the sound of fear getting the better of reason.

Then abruptly, the agile yet aging athlete rolled AceArrow on his belly and crawled astride the CEO's back. He carefully unraveled the shackle-like restraints from the man's legs.

TreadHard knew he had to execute the next piece of strategy with precision because once he uncuffed AceArrow, he'd have very little time to break free.

Pretend it's the pinnacle, man. Pretend this last effort gets you to the peak. Pretend it's you or him, since in reality, that's how it is: you or him.

Obstinately, TreadHard bore his body weight down and put his lips to AceArrow's ears where he whispered, "I want you to taste your own torment and think about every DoRight that was torn apart."

Although AceArrow was squirming, TreadHard's body kept the terrified man pinned down. When he pulled the key to the handcuffs from his pocket, TreadHard took a deep breath. Then he slid the key into its lock, digging his elbow deeper into AceArrow's wrist. Now, TreadHard, now. He turned the key as fast as he could and unlocked one side—and that's when he hesitated—that crucial hesitation which determines the outcome of the game.

TreadHard hadn't decided whether to leave the bracelet on one wrist or unlock the second cuff. It didn't matter. In that pause, that moment when an option flew across TreadHard's brain, AceArrow swung his wrist over and grabbed his assailant by the forearm. TreadHard was stunned, not so much by the other man's strength, but by his sudden attempt to finally fight.

Up till now, AceArrow seemed passive, compliant, and TreadHard wasn't prepared for the instant surge of energy that ignited AceArrow's entire body. The man abruptly came alive and was ready to change places with TreadHard immediately. He fiercely knocked the lighter man off of him and swung his arm around violently, letting the swinging metal bracelet slash the side of TreadHard's eye.

Blood leaked across his temple as TreadHard's head went down. But that rapid reflex action diffused AceArrow's next punch, which impacted with air—not TreadHard's face. Missing his target, the frantic CEO was thrown off balance when he plunged his explosive blow into emptiness. And as AceArrow stumbled, TreadHard, with whatever fury he had in reserve, brought his knee up and kicked the bigger man in the small of his back, directly aiming for the kidneys.

In his vehement strike went the visions of blood, of death, of AceArrow's vile scheme, flashes which sporadically blinked through TreadHard's mind like a silent movie that wouldn't come to the end of its reel. With that incisive thrust went the unspoken knowledge that he was preserving his self, his being, his consciousness, for this contest was a life or death struggle, only his life was on the line, not some obscure hero from a forgotten novel he had read long ago. Yet here he was, part of that age-old aggression, convinced he was acting rationally, justified in his appeal to some transcendent virtue, but too keenly aware that he might also be fulfilling his own biological imperative.

As AceArrow went down, convulsively, trying urgently to catch his breath, TreadHard instantly headed for the open door. In a last ditch effort, AceArrow managed to roll over and grab TreadHard's ankle. But by then, TreadHard had gained momentum, and he was able to swing his other leg around and kick AceArrow in the face, spraying gravel into the wretched man's eyes. AceArrow screamed and grabbed his head. He brought his knees to his chest and writhed in pain.

But TreadHard never saw this piteous remnant of a man because he was jumping out the door and securing the latch. And TreadHard never heard the shrieks as he pressed the button to raise the inner gate. He refused to look, just as he refused to judge himself. He would be measured soon enough by a higher critic. Instead, he closed his heart to the demoniacal moans, blocking any last minute remorse for the dying man. The sparse, soulful requiem he released went unheard into the early morning mist. "You were garbage, AceArrow. Just plain garbage.

After explaining to Antonio what he had done and why he had done it, he asked forgiveness from his fellow confidante.

"No forgiveness, Bruce. There's nothing to forgive. I don't

fork out absolution, only friendship. I've known you too long, my good man."

"Antonio, I'm so tired, tired of the pain, the hate, the evil. Something just seemed terribly wrong, and no one was correcting it."

"You know, Bruce, what I value most: a smooth glass of wine, an old friend, and good talk. Let's toast to our brotherhood!"

Antonio walked over to clink the glass of his longtime friend, and he whispered, "I'm going to miss you, Bruce, very, very much. I know you'll put up a strong fight, but I also know you'll decide when to let go."

After TreadHard rested, after they ate, after they talked, both men tackled the messy business of extricating the body from the pen. While Antonio distracted his dogs and fed them, Bruce rolled the now tranquil but ripped and bloodied corpse onto a tarp, securing both ends with rope. Next, he rolled it out into the three foot enclosure while Antonio secured the pen. Both men carried the limp, lead-like body to the pickup and plopped it into the rear.

With the cumbersome task completed and never mentioned again, they returned to the house for more conversation, warm comradery, and the joy that comes from being accepted unconditionally. There were no *should's* on behavior. That was their gift to each other, the prize of a lifetime: who they were, what they were, how they were was approval enough. And each man spent some silent moments by the defunct fire, basking in the glory of their treasure—a true friendship.

Sometime around three in the morning, Bruce put his arm around Antonio, and they walked to the door, not knowing if they'd meet again. But the anguish of the menacing future wasn't dark enough to disarm the invincible bond of admiration the nineteen years had created.

As Antonio hugged Bruce, he softly said, "Be careful, my friend. My heart goes with you."

"Be well, my brother—I will miss you most of all."

THIRTY-TWO

Instead of flying back to SeaBank, FutureDick and TigerTail stayed in San Ramon. Finding out nothing but the details of robot-crafting from FineWine, they returned to AceArrow's office to look for clues to his disappearance. Everything seemed in order, ready for a Monday morning workday. No monies had been withdrawn from his bank account within the last 48 hours. But that didn't mean much in the age of credit cards. They combed his car, went back to his house, questioned Friday night's security guard, and came up acquainted with no more than they knew earlier that morning. The guard never saw AceArrow leave the premises. He swore to it.

Exhausted, hoping to get some sleep before returning to SeaBank, they checked into a motel at 4 a.m. Thinking they might have overlooked something, they were going to question every Robomaids' employee next. Maybe AceArrow partied with some of them during the weekend. Unlikely! Yet no more farfetched than the CEO going into the building and never coming out! They even thought of using bloodhounds to search the area around the company. AceArrow may have played God, but nobody vanishes into pure air.

They also intended to call the Bay Area helicopter lines, all nine of them. If he was airlifted from the roof, he could have made it to the airport. But wouldn't someone have heard that distinctive spluttering sound? Some employee? The guard? No taxi had come to Robomaids on Friday, that they knew. How the hell else do you leave a building? Walk? But where or why would AceArrow walk? The company was located on the outskirts of the city. Improbable. And definitely impractical.

At 7:30, only three hours after they collapsed into bed, the shrill of the phone thundered through their dreams. Both FutureDick and TigerTail snapped awake, startled, physically jarred by the wrenching away from a sound sleep. When TigerTail hung up the receiver, he turned to FutureDick. "Let's go, guy. They think they've got our man in San Diego. Some jogger found a dead body while he was running in the canyon, and the ID on the corpse says AceArrow."

FutureDick couldn't check his grin. Now he really knew the work was getting to him. Since when did he consider murder funny? For some reason, in AceArrow's case, he found it more than amusing. He found it downright satisfying.

"Hey wait, man," TigerTail added. "If this is our guy, the corpse is pretty well torn up. That's what they said. Like half a face, seems the body's been chewed or gnawed. Yet the wallet and credit cards were intact. Can you beat that, buddy? It's like some sort of ghoulish poetic justice! But, Christ, I'll tell you, I'm not looking forward to identifying the body so early in the morning! Even coffee looks bleak right now."

"Sorry for chuckling, TigerTail. Somehow, I'm having a hell of a time finding pity for the son of a bitch."

But three hours later, when FutureDick gazed at AceArrow's half-eaten countenance, he realized that death still had the ability to astonish him for a brief moment. Yet this time his shock was one of relief, of gratitude, of, how should he dare to think it, delight. Perhaps he had been a private investigator too long, and human life was losing its sanctity. But that was a cliche he used so he could sound like the prototype detective he gleaned from *film noir*.

This bloody, partially rotted, partially guzzled, gutted, inert body in front of his eyes screamed silently, "I once breathed. I once dreamed. I once had a choice to do good or bad, and I made my choice." FutureDick clung to his self-composed psalm as it repeated its refrain in his deafened ears. He had to grab onto something. He had seen too much death and needed a shred of belief that provided reason to the rage we call existence. Life would never lose its sanctity, for life was precious. That's all we had: moments to make ourselves. And when something or someone thwarted that grand scheme, they had to be removed.

Congenital knowledge, inherent in our human legacy. Respect the rights of the living, and harmony persists. Violate those rights, and you give up any entitlement to societal protection. You now operate in the realm of speculation. Perhaps justice, perhaps rehabilitation, perhaps a second chance—if you're lucky. But it's simply a wager. Once you step over the line of decency, you become a focus in a free-for-all: anyone's target.

AceArrow had crossed the boundary. He lost his respect for the living, and his evil infuriated some quiet but worthy opponent. Although FutureDick knew he, himself, still adhered to man-made laws, still believed in a rudimentary system of civilized justice, and—as much as he wanted to bring AceArrow to his knees—he still had to operate according to legality, not emotion or secret desires of retribution.

But FutureDick also sensed he was capable of vigilante justice if what he loved was ever threatened. He had lost once, and nothing was going to take his love, his Francie, away from him. She was the missing part, the piece of him that needed to be filled in. She was his completion. And he unhesitatingly understood he would fight to the death, his death, or any other death, if what made him whole were attacked. This was not brutal. This was reality. We were genetically scripted to protect what we love, and, in so doing, we would always walk gingerly among the canons of man-made rules.

As he stared at AceArrow, FutureDick realized he hated the messiness, the taint of depravity that envelops evil. He loathed the blood, the stench, the decay, the impetuousness of decomposition. Still, more than anything, he despised the expression of absolute terror on what was left of the dead man's face. But he cheered the irony. The CEO had ultimately masterminded his own demise. Maybe, he should have loved humans instead of machines. Granted, machines make practical life easier, but humans enrich your soul. They touch the inner place that brings hope to your vision, joy to your thoughts, and poetry to your heart.

Reverberating through his razor-sharp senses, FutureDick gloried in the song that soundlessly brushed his spirit. Loudly, but clearly, the melody chanted, "I'm coming back, my love, to you, to Josh, to life. I'm coming home, Francie. And I'm ready, so ready, to start again."

EPILOGUE

When BrickWell attended Bruce TreadHard's funeral nine months later, he was singled out after the ceremony and given a letter by a gentleman who introduced himself as TreadHard's lawyer. Although the paper is almost transparent in some places, crumbling because of constant handling, BrickWell continues to read it to this day.

Dear Adam,

I have always tried to live a decent life and, above all, remain fair when dealing with the next person. My faith in humanity stayed firm because I constantly met good people wherever I went. Although my successes certainly outnumbered my losses, working with you on the DoRight project was one of the paramount episodes of my existence. I stood at the brink of evolution and watched it turn toward God.

But the desecration of those beautiful creatures was more than I could witness. It was my first confrontation with pure evil, and I couldn't let it go unpunished. I killed AceArrow—not with my own hands. I constructed events so he would find no exit, no escape. I wanted him to surrender to the same kind of vulnerability as our courageous chimps. And I walked away when he cried out for help.

Please forgive me, Adam. AceArrow was a malignancy far worse than the cancer that consumed my frail body. Yet no one seemed to be able to scrape his scourge from our lives. I had to wipe out the pestilence called AceArrow. And I accept full responsibility for my action.

Thank you for the wonder you brought to my life.

Your friend,

Bruce